PRAISE FOR
WAKING THE MERROW

"A prickly and memorable protagonist fights to protect her family from wily merfolk in this promising debut contemporary fantasy."
— *PUBLISHERS WEEKLY*

"You know what's great about Rigney's horror-ific (that's horror-filled and terrific), hysterical debut novel? Besides the bloodthirsty merfolk, our antihero protagonist is an overweight, drunk, subpar mother, who also happens to be a funeral director. I can't even describe the premise of this book without getting giddy, because how many times does a plot involve both vicious mermaids and Rhode Island colonists?"
— *Nicole Hill, Barnes & Noble Book Blog*

"Rigney has struck gold with her first novel. It's humorous — hysterical at times — descriptive and has a nice flow to it."
— *Bobby Forrand, Motif Magazine*

"*WAKING THE MERROW* is a horrifying, addictive, and intriguing twist on the mermaid legend, and takes the reader on a bone-chilling ride through colonial and current times in Rhode Island. This is a fabulous debut novel by Heather Rigney.
Read it if you dare."
— *Penny Watson, Bestselling Author of APPLES SHOULD BE RED*

"In the essence of Stephen King and Clive Barker who are Ms. Rigney's inspiration she manages to thrill and scare with the best of them ... I was hooked from the very first page and while I was scared at times I also couldn't wait to turn the page and find out what happened next. Written as a historical thriller the book does not disappoint at all."
— *John Brownstone, reviewer, MasqueradeCrew.com*

"This book contains several of my favorite things: monster lit, the ocean, a choice of monster that's not like every other book or movie out there, mythology, Gaelic/Celtic stuff, and New England."
— *Bella, Boombabyreviews.com*

"WOW... I mean, seriously WOW. I could not put this book down ... I usually try and find something critical to say about the writing or the story itself, but I can honestly say there is not a single negative thing I can offer about Waking the Merrow. It's an absolutely brilliant novel and I can't wait for the next book by this truly amazing author."

—*Suzy Turner, author of THE RAVEN SAGA*

"*WAKING THE MERROW* by Heather Rigney is a thrilling debut! Razor-sharp wit, sparkling prose, and a quirky, hard-luck anti-heroine make this fun, frightening, and completely unique twist on mermaid lore. A must-read."

—*Carolyn Crane, author of THE DISILLUSIONISTS*

"I absolutely loved *WAKING THE MERROW* ... Heather's writing is very descriptive. Her female heroine, Evie, is someone I could be friends with. I laughed so hard at some of her quips my husband asked if I was all right. I am looking forward to more in this series."

—*JKROWYN, book reviewer for BittenByBooks.com*

"*WAKING THE MERROW* is a delightfully dark fantasy that stirs in colonial history and some eerily fun mythology. Heather Rigney is doing what she's meant to do, and her story will have you laughing all along the way even as the scariest of creatures stalk this plot. I cannot recommend this sassy, dark, intelligent book enough. It's not every day you find yourself rooting for a cantankerous heroine with a hangover, but I think Evie McFagan can and will win you over."

—*Emm Cole, author of MERMINIA*

"Heather Rigney is a wonderfully expressive writer who manages to address an incredibly cliche subject and leave said chiches in her wake. The world she paints with words would not be beautiful if not for her striking and highly original prose but she truly creates a setting that is both dark yet colourful and exciting. If you're a fan of Dean Koontz then steer your amazon trolley this way because you're in for a lot of evil snickering and plenty of dramatic tension backed up with creative articulation. Honestly it was just so good- it's revived my love of reading after a pretty serious book hangover."

—*S.K. Munt, author of THE FAIRYTAIL SAGA*

HUNTING
THE
MERROW

BOOK 2

Hunting the Merrow

Book 2: The Merrow Trilogy

Heather Rigney

For my family, friends,
chosen family, and fans.

It is a joy to say that I have fans.
Thank you all for your love, support,
and the occasional donut.

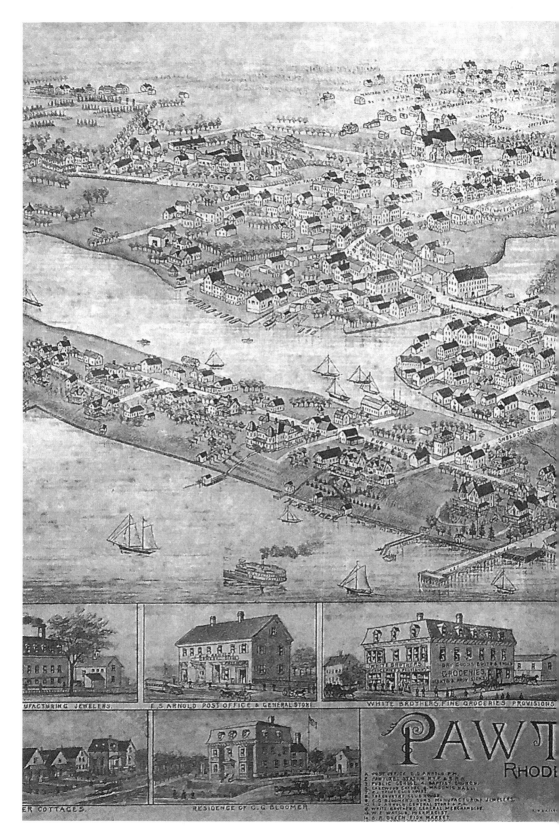

MANUFACTURING JEWELERS. E.S. ARNOLD POST OFFICE & GENERAL STORE. WHITE BROTHERS, FINE GROCERIES PROVISIONS.

ER COTTAGES. RESIDENCE OF C. C. BLOOMER.

PAWT
RHODE

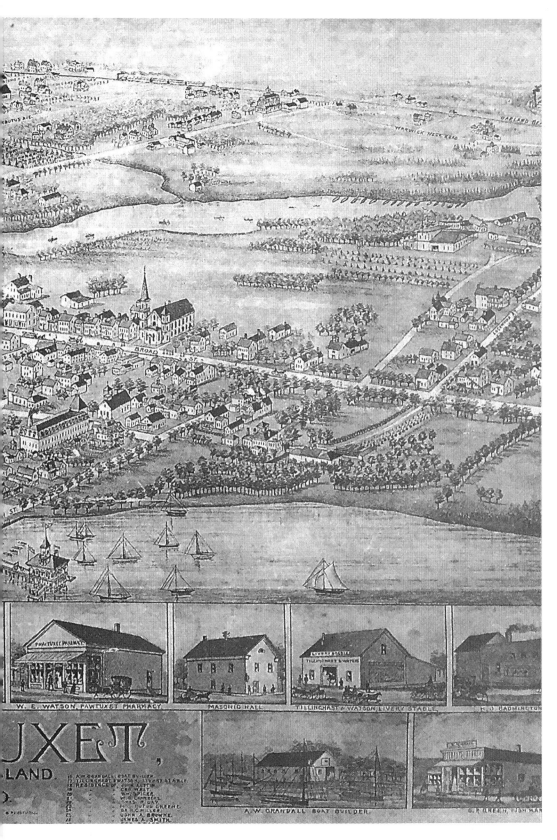

BROAD ST.

W. E. WATSON, PAWTUXET PHARMACY.   MASONIC HALL   TILLINGHAST & WATSON LIVERY STABLE   W. O. BADMINGTON

UXET,
LAND.

A. W. CRANDALL, BOAT BUILDER.   G. F. GREEN, FISH MARKET

1

Evie

The scorching train platform was overflowing with assholes. Most of them hipster assholes—the ones who wear embarrassingly tight pants, stupid old-man shoes, and slouchy hats that look as if they have been run over by a logging truck. The logger had likely pulled over, climbed out of the cab, and said, Hey, I'm not using this beard. You seem like the creative type who brews coffee for a living and owns an obscure breed of dog. I'm thinking of shaving. Do you want my beard? To which the annoying hipster replied, I own a purebred Irish wolfhound and work at Starfuck-You-Very-Much, and yes, I would love your beard—as long the product you've used to keep it supple is certified organic.

The flow of people would not stop. It was becoming

claustrophobic. A woman whose fat ass stretched out her patterned pants, which resembled a Southwestern throw blanket, talked loudly on her phone. She slammed into me as she shifted her oversized bag that looked suspiciously like a dead cat.

"Don't shove me, bitch," I muttered. The blinding heat, the unbearable pounding in my temples, the overabundance of hipsters had pushed me beyond reasonable thought.

"I'm sorry," said the Southwestern cat-killer beside me, the woman I was now imagining as a heap of goo on the floor. "Did you say something?"

I simply stared at her, making sure I held her gaze just long enough to make her marginally uncomfortable. She looked away first, continuing her inane conversation.

"I know, right? I was shocked when I graduated and there was no demand for a bio-philosophy major. I mean, I double-minored in education and web design. I thought I covered my bases."

I rolled my eyes and tried to bend my elbow. The sea of bodies was oppressive, limiting my movement and my ability to find a goddamn diet bar in my bag. That and an aspirin. I had nothing to wash it down with, but I didn't care. I would dry-swallow it. Hell, I would dry-swallow a pumpkin filled with nails if it would stop the pounding in my head.

The air changed. A whoosh of stale stench and an even hotter breeze, much hotter than the already hot-enough-to-melt-your-tits-off wind whizzing by my overheated head, swooped in from the train tunnel. The screech of brakes echoed off the stone walls, and the giant purple commuter rail train roared to a stop.

"Providence!" yelled someone official-sounding over a scratchy loudspeaker. The doors squealed open, releasing even more assholes onto the platform where I stood, helpless, drowning in a sea of sweaty, Boston-bound idiots. We pushed past one another, reversing the flow of commuters, those disembarking, those boarding, those embarking on a journey to save the neck of an ungrateful, long-lost brother.

That would be me. Evie McFagan, sister of said ungrateful, long-lost brother known as Richard Musäus. Go ahead and laugh at my maiden name. For your information, it sounds like moosehouse, and why don't you try growing up as a size extra large with a last name that refers to one of the most non-dainty animals in North America? Then talk to me, after a hellish adolescence, about how "well-adjusted" you feel.

Yeah. Think on that, Freud fans.

Elbowing my way onto the narrow train, I found a seat on the upper level of a double-decker car. A twenty-something boy in a tweed jacket was about to sit next to me but changed his mind at the last moment.

By the way, who the hell wears tweed in a heat wave? Stupid hipsters. That's who.

I watched a young mother with a stroller struggle into the car. She moved backwards, dragging the black contraption that held a passed-out toddler. Both mother and child had curly auburn hair plastered to the sides of their red, overheated faces. She paused to catch her breath and turned her head, looking in my direction. Our eyes met and I saw the fatigue, the weariness, the why-is-this-shit-so-hard? look in her eyes. I stood and hurried down the aisle towards her, then helped her wrangle the stroller into a seat near the front of the car. Her child never woke while we banged the much-abused-looking stroller into the narrow space.

"Thank you," she whispered and flopped down, instantly closing her eyes.

Hell, I don't miss those days.

I returned to my own seat and nestled in. Staring out the dirty window covered in scratchy-looking graffiti with the lovely addition of something unsavory smeared all over it, I could feel the sweat trickling into my cleavage, collecting in all the places where skin met skin. There wasn't much to see in the tunnel, except for dark, stone walls. The air conditioning was either broken or just completely incapable of keeping up with the heat.

After what felt like an eternity, the engine roared to life and, with a lurch, pulled forward. We exploded out of the tunnel as the train gained speed. Rain greeted us with a sudden shower that would probably only add to the humidity and not clear it. The drops slashed at the windows, smearing my view of the scenery beyond the milky glass.

I closed my eyes and allowed my mind to drift through the events of the previous few days. What a shit show. I sighed and pulled out my cell phone. No messages. The lock screen featured my two favorite people in the whole world. There they were, my darling husband, Paddy, and my beautiful baby girl, Savannah, now four and no longer a baby, though she would forever remain one in my heart. I wondered if I was still married and if I would see either of them ever again.

What had I done? I'm so stupid. I really am.

"But he's my brother," I had whined. It was hard to explain why I cared. I barely understood it myself.

"If you leave now, love," said Paddy, his clear, piercing eyes sending a message straight to my soul, "you will not be welcome here when you return."

"What the hell, Paddy? That's a bit extreme, don't you think?" I squeaked, trying to be brave, trying to hold my ground. I'm a big girl who can make big girl decisions, I told myself.

"I'm not going through another epic ordeal. Not ever again. And how dare you even entertain the thought of wanting to put us in harm's way?"

"You can deny the facts all you want, mister, but the truth is ... the bitch is back. Your stupid, aqua family dropped the bloody ball and let Miss Terror of the Sea go. Now she's here, and she will kill my brother. Doesn't that mean anything to you?"

Paddy sat down on the bed. It was late. After receiving the email from my brother, I had plugged Savannah in, handing her a tablet and headphones, pointing to the couch. She had shrugged and gladly plopped down. The four of us—me, Paddy, his aunt Catherine, and our friend and Catherine's new paramour, Tony—had all sat down at Catherine's kitchen table and examined the email from my brother.

Recently, my business has sent me to Boston. I'm not far from you, and I believe enough time has passed. I had been waiting for the right time, the right way to contact you, but circumstances never felt right. But all that has changed. All because of one special individual. Under the urgings of this new friend (well, actually, we are more than friends. Our relationship has moved to the next level and I could not be happier), I have felt the confidence to contact you. It really is such a small world. My friend says she knows you and has urged me to rekindle our relationship, dear sister. Her name is … Nomia.

The three of them agreed that I should ignore the email.

I was not in favor. An argument of epic proportion ensued, followed by me storming out and heading home. After I poured myself a nice tall drink, I sat on the couch and clinked the ice back and forth in the glass. What did I know? Well, Richard was in Boston. And so was Nomia. Richard was blind to the fishy nature of his new girlfriend, who was most likely using my brother as bait.

This left me with two options. One, go rescue my brother, because I am so good at being a hero. I reached up and rubbed the scar on my shoulder, remembering exactly how it felt to be impaled. Yes, being a hero rocks.

That left the second option. Ignore the whole situation. Don't take the bait. Let my brother die and risk the possibility that the man-eating bitch will make quick work of him and then come after us. It had been months since we had heard from Ronan. It took time to contact him. I didn't have time. Richard, that dick, didn't have time either. I pulled out my phone and read the email again. It had been sent that morning, which meant he was probably still alive. Probably.

I got up, set my glass on the coffee table, and headed for the attic. When I returned to our bedroom, suitcase in hand, Paddy was there waiting for me.

"Where's Savannah?" I asked.

"She's staying with Aunt Catherine tonight."

"I see," I said.

"No, love," he answered. "You don't. You don't see. 'Cause if you did, you wouldn't have that suitcase in your hands."

I just didn't know how to make him understand. I couldn't tell him the things I had kept from him. I had told him the basics but left a lot out. It wasn't fun for me to discuss my shitty family. When I'd met Paddy, the orphan thing had been a bonding connection. Our isolation in the world, once revealed, was like a crappy present we gave to one another, something Paddy and I could share and compare, then screw around together to forget. When your pain is reflected in someone else, it becomes a narcissistic attraction. Quite messed up if you think about it.

At the time, he didn't need to know about my brother. I didn't even know about my brother. I hadn't heard from him in years. Richard was three years older than I was. While I was still in high school, he was starting college. Once he left home, he left home. That was that.

I had never desired to discuss the way I had been raised, the relationship my brother and I had forged out of need. Yes, we had been given everything we needed as children. We wanted for nothing—nothing like food, shelter, or college money. But things such as emotional attention, love, kindness—those were radically missing. In essence, we had raised ourselves. Our parents had been selfish and ignored us. They had never bothered to get to know us. I never wanted to discuss what Richard and I shared—our bond of emotional neglect.

Once Mom and Dad died, Richard was all I had left. He was the last link to my roots, my last tie to my grandparents, also dead, in Tarrytown, New York. Some of the happiest moments of my childhood were spent at their home, and I had shared those times with Richard. It was during those visits that we had fostered our connection—weekends in Tarrytown and all those summers spent with Oma and Opa, playing in the woods surrounding their country home way up in the Catskills, far away from civilization and even farther away from my parents. We spent endless hours walking in the woods, Richard and I, building forts, making paths with old rakes, paths that curved in circles around trees so old, we could barely see their tops. I spent time in the kitchen with Oma, and Richard out in the woods with Opa, doing whatever it was they did out there.

When I realized during my drunken college haze that years, not just months and days, had passed since I had heard from my older brother, I was angry. Abandoned yet again. I wrote him off. He was dead to me, too.

Paddy discovered he had a brother-in-law when Savannah

was born. Classy, I know, but you have to understand, when starting a relationship, women are all like, Tell me about your family. What was it like for you? Reveal your inner pain to me. Blah, blah, blah. Paddy wasn't like that. I'm not, nor have I ever been, like that. Paddy never asked if I had any siblings, and I never told him—until I was forced into it.

Savannah was born on a Tuesday. On the first Saturday of her life, a bouquet of flowers arrived addressed to her. It was the craziest thing. She hadn't even lived in the house for a full week, and the kid was getting flowers and mail. That blew my mind. Anyway, the outside of the card read, For my niece, Savannah.

Paddy had flipped out. It was a total Lucy/Ricardo moment with me, the dumb one, doing all the 'splaining.

Why hadn't I told Paddy about Richard? I don't know. I guess I had wanted to keep that part of me to myself. Forever.

And now I was on a train, leaving one family for another. Why? Good fucking question.

Numb from the greenery rushing by my chalky window, I stared out at the suburban worlds of Mansfield, Sharon, and Canton as they tore past my swollen, tired face. Along with all the other travelers whose clothes clung to their sweaty backs, I was spewed out onto the sticky, foul-smelling platform in Back Bay. Richard's email had a signature at the bottom that included a phone number. Thanks to the wonders of Google, I'd been able to track down what I thought was a home address in Boston.

Pulling my wheeled carry-on behind me, I made my way up the obnoxiously long escalator and then out into city. The heat smacked me in the face. It was similar to being smothered with a wool blanket—so humid I couldn't breathe. Nothing smells worse than a city during a heat wave. Boston is especially bad. Being a harbor city, it has the added benefit of low tide. Things that are meant to be beneath the sea now lay exposed, allowed to decay in the summer sun and release their noxious gases into air otherwise perfumed with street garbage and car fumes.

Besides the smell, it's a scenic city. Old—I mean, really fucking old—shit—mingles with the new. Take, for example, the Hancock buildings. Yes, there are two. One small and squat, like a happy, old, fat teapot, and right next to it stands its young offspring. The brilliant blue monolith towers above its parent, dominating the Boston skyline. To me, that's Boston. The new attempting to dwarf the old, to outshine it, while we, the tourists, marvel at the resulting warring dichotomy that somehow works.

I navigated down the city streets, passing Asian women in their wide-brimmed hats, college students in their flimsy clothes, young mothers in Converse sneakers pushing retro-looking prams. I passed vendors hawking hot dogs, the foul smell of sauerkraut burning my nose hairs as I inhaled. Others offered t-shirts emblazoned with phrases like Green Monstah and Yankees Suck. Using the navigation on my phone—a left here, a right there—I moved slowly until I finally arrived at the brownstone row home matching the address I had found on the web.

My stomach squelched with acid, and although the heat had not subsided, my hands felt cold and clammy. This was it. The number matched. I walked up the marble stairs to the landing and looked at the names scrawled next to the buzzer buttons. Apt 1-Fisher, Apt 2-Atwood, Apt 3-Leary, and at the top, Apt 4-Musäus.

I steeled myself and pressed the button. Nothing happened. Now what? In my haste to get to my brother, it had not occurred to me to think past this very moment. I cursed under my breath at my stupidity. I should just go. I should reverse this whole asinine journey and get back to the people who mattered. I should ...

The door opened. A man held the door for me. Not my brother. Just a man I didn't know. He smiled and said, "Hot enough for ya?"

I nodded and walked into the lobby, mumbling my thanks as I stepped past him.

"Have a good one," he called over his shoulder and headed down the steps as the door clicked shut behind him.

I was in.

There was no elevator. Of course there wasn't. It was nine hundred degrees outside. I was, as always, grossly out of shape, and I was carrying luggage up four flights of stairs. Why would there be a goddamn elevator? As I huffed and puffed my way up the steps, I constructed a plan. I would wait outside his door until he got home. When he arrived, I would ambush him and make him understand that his new girlfriend had no intention of dating him, but instead planned to tear him apart, literally. And then she would do the same to me. If he had any sense at all, he would end the relationship, and, and ... I would figure out the rest when I saw him.

I turned and faced the last flight of stairs. Richard's apartment was at the top of the building on its own landing. The blood was pounding in my temples, and I could feel the burning heat in my flushed cheeks. God, I needed to sit down. Almost there.

I walked to the door and knocked. As my knuckles hit the wooden door, it swung open slightly.

Through the cracked door, I called, "Richard?" I was sure to use a soft voice, not wanting to startle him, or her. "Anyone home?"

I waited for a response, but none came. Taking a deep breath, I considered my options. I could wander in and see what I could see, or go home—just turn right around, close the door behind me, close the door on my past, and leave my older brother to his fate.

Guess which choice I made? If you went with option number one, you win an oversized t-shirt with Evie makes bad choices for my entertainment emblazoned across the front. Wear it with pride. It looks good on you.

The room temperature was a good ten degrees cooler than the stairwell. I relished the relief as a cool wave of air from the air conditioner made its way to face. I let out my breath in one long, relaxing groan. Then I entered Richard's apartment. A large leather sectional couch faced me, its back against an exposed brick wall. To my right three long windows lined up in a row. The windows did not have curtains, and I could see the neighboring building close by. The branches of trees that must have grown up from a courtyard, far below, obscured my view into the other apartments across the way.

I was in the living/dining room. To my left, I saw bar stools, indicating a breakfast bar. I stepped in farther and turned to close the door behind me. That's when I saw her. I gasped, somehow managing not to scream, and grabbed my chest.

In unison, the intruder grabbed her chest. There was a mirror behind the door.

"Goddamn it," I cursed under my breath. I looked at my own reflection and realized how rumpled and tired I looked, how exhausted and stressed I really was. Did I look like a woman about to confront a homicidal maniac? No. I looked like shit. As usual.

Glancing around the room again, I noted how sparsely decorated it was. It had the feel of a real estate showing. Everything looked staged, arranged just so, as if it had all been recently bought at a discount home store. There was even a fake potted amaryllis next to the leather couch, but it was covered in dust.

I took a few more steps, making my way towards the kitchen area on the left. That looked staged, too, with a bowl of plastic lemons on the counter. Something crunched as I stepped from the living area into the small passageway leading to the bedrooms, I assumed. Looking down, I saw broken glass everywhere.

I figured it was from smashed wineglasses. I could make out the stem of one glass and, possibly, part of the goblet of another. The floor was dark and sticky, and I was hoping it was red wine. Please let it be red wine. It smelled like red wine. But the hallway had two types of stains sprayed across the pale walls. One was a cranberry color; the other was brighter. Things were looking grim.

I peered down the hall and spotted bloody footprints retreating into the far bedroom. I tried not to step on them as I followed their trail. The bedroom was destroyed, and the window was an explosion of broken glass. It was everywhere, sparkling in the daylight, sending tiny prisms onto the walls. An elegant black-and-white photograph of a tree—the trunk enormous, thick, and imposing—hung at a disquieting angle, perilously close to crashing to the floor. The closet appeared to have blown up. Clothes were everywhere. Ties, shoes, men's underwear, and a few lacy lady things were scattered all around, the bulk of them in front of the walk-in closet. A bulb hung from the ceiling, swaying gently in the breeze from the open window, where hot air floated in, caressing my face as it passed.

Richard, what happened here? Where are you?

There was a bloody handprint next to the open window. The fingerprints were slender and long, not outlines of the thick, strong fingers of my brother. They had to belong to that bitch, Nomia. I would bet my life on it. Fury raced through my body, making me shudder at the memory of the upheaval she had created in my life. I hated her more now than ever.

Something in the closet shifted. I spun, ready to beat the living daylights out of anything that dared jump out at me. My foot landed with a loud crunch. Something made of glass crackled beneath my foot, but my focus was on the closet.

A sweater tumbled out. And I let out my breath in a long whoosh.

Just a stupid sweater. Relax, Evie.

It must have been knocked loose when the place was ransacked. I tried to shake it off, rotating my head in a circle and stretching my neck. That's when I saw the photo on the floor.

I leaned down and picked up the shattered picture frame, gently shaking off the broken glass. My brother stared up at me. His eyes more wrinkled, his skin more leathery from his years outdoors, doing whatever he does, but still him. My brother.

And her.

What the hell was she doing all snuggly with my brother in a goddamn photo?

Look. At. That. Bitch.

All of a sudden I felt like a squirrel was trying to gnaw its way out of my gut. I mean, I knew she was involved. But this. This. This photo. The proof of her existence on this continent. With my brother.

I felt the anger boil my face even hotter than it already was in the wretched, blistering heat. I shook my head, trying to create a breeze to cool me down. It didn't work. I was seething.

This is what I knew. Richard and Nomia were not here, but they were a thing. There had been a struggle. Nomia had been involved. And Nomia had been searching for something.

Why else would there be crap strewn all over the place? What was she looking for?

Well, if I knew anything, anything at all, and if my brother was trying to keep something hidden, I knew exactly where he would hide it. There's something to be said for growing up with another person. You know their dirty little secrets.

I went back down the hall into the bathroom and switched on the light. It was a standard small apartment bathroom in an old building. There was a clawfoot tub against the wall facing the door and a sink on the right, with a toilet sandwiched between the tub and sink. Everything was white. The tile, the shower curtain, the towels. And it was a mess. The bathroom had been equally ransacked. The contents of the medicine cabinet were now in the sink. Shaving gear, prescription bottles, toothpaste, Q-tips. It all swam in the white bowl. The door to the medicine cabinet above hung wide open, revealing emptiness. I wasn't interested in the medicine cabinet.

I stood in front of the toilet and lifted the lid off the tank.

Bingo.

Some things never change. My brother had always kept a stash of porn in a ziplock bag, safe inside the back of the toilet. And sure enough, peering at me from inside the back of the tank, I spied, not porn, but something else, something smaller.

I reached into the cool water and drew out the bag. It had been folded many times, concealing the contents within. Shaking off the water, I opened the bag and pulled out what looked like a skeleton key. An ordinary red tassel hung from the ornate hole on the end, but the other end was strange. There was something different about it. It didn't have the typical teeth-like appendages with which to turn lock tumblers. This looked like a computer chip. I held it up to the light as the realization dawned on me. It was a flash drive.

I heard a noise in the living room and quickly shoved the key into my back pocket. I looked around for a weapon, but all

I could find was a plunger. It would have to do.

I grabbed the wooden stick and held the ridiculous rubber bulb high in the air. Creeping back into the glass-filled hall, I moved as quietly as I could, listening for any additional sound from the living room. A new layer of sweat coated my already soaked body as fear filled my every cell.

I really was not built for this shit.

The shuffle of footsteps echoed in the mostly empty room as I drew closer. Almost there. There was no way I was going to drop out the window like Nomia had most likely done. She was way more agile than I was. It was fight. Flight was not an option.

I took a deep breath, let out my loudest battle cry, and flew— plunger held high—into the living room and ...

I scared the living shit out of a small, elderly woman in a classy red suit. She screamed back and clutched her heart.

"My dear God!" yelled the red-clad old lady.

"I am so sorry! Here, sit down. You are not who I thought you were," I wheezed, exhausted from my battle cry.

"Who on earth did you think I was?"

"Um," I stammered. "Would you like to sit down?"

"No," she said. "I would not. Where is Richard, and what are you doing here? Did you make this mess? Is that blood?"

"Whoa, too many questions. I am Evie McFagan, well Evie Musäus McFagan, actually. Richard is my brother. Pleased to meet you." Here is where I offered my hand, which was received with a curt look of disgust.

I withdrew my hand.

"Do you have any identification, before I call the police, Ms. McFagan? The neighbors had complained about loud noises, and I came to investigate. Richard is an excellent tenant. I find it hard to believe that you are his sister." There was a sniff and an upturned nose following this statement. I kid you not. The old bag turned up her nose at me. It was my childhood all over again.

With my own sigh of disgust, I pulled out my wallet and was about to hand her my license when I suddenly thought better of it. I dashed past her, grabbing my roller luggage on the way, and fled down the stairs.

I did not need to explain any of this shit to the police, and that was where the story was headed. She would need to call the police. Hell, I would call the police if I were her. The place was wrecked. There were bloody prints everywhere. It looked as if theft was involved, possibly murder. And a goddamn mermaid.

I was not about to explain a goddamn mermaid. I booked it down the stairs and out onto the street, regretting that I had given the landlady or super or whoever the hell she was my name.

I had found out as much as I could. Richard and Nomia were not in that apartment. Something had happened. Most likely, Nomia had killed my brother.

Oh my God. My brother was dead!

I stopped on the street, and a woman with a stroller slammed into me from behind. "Watch it, lady! What the hell are you doing?"

I didn't even answer. I just stood there, in the heat, with my stupid luggage. I was alone in the world now. Completely alone.

But wait a second.

Where was Richard's body? It's not like she could eat him all by herself. And that would have left an even bigger mess. What was the likelihood of her dragging him out on her own? I knew she had superhuman strength, but Richard is a pretty big guy. The neighbors had complained about the noises. Surely they would have also complained about a crazy woman dragging a six-foot man down the hall or past their windows in the courtyard. Right?

He couldn't be dead. Could he? Or was she dead?

I had come to Boston to warn my brother. I had failed. Something had already gone down, and I knew less than I did when I had arrived.

Now what?

I needed to get the hell out of Boston. So I headed back the way I had come as quickly as I could.

Once I arrived at the Back Bay station, I grabbed a Diet Coke and parked it on a stone bench next to a wino. I felt that I was in good company.

Pulling out my phone, I saw that I still did not have any messages. Damn you, Paddy.

I pulled up my favorites and pushed his fat face in my contact list. The phone rang. And rang. And rang. Finally, it went to his voice mail.

You have reached Patrick McFagan. I am unable to get your call right now, but do leave a message. Unless, of course, you are Evelyn. Then don't leave a message and do not come home. Thank you, and have a glorious day.

Cheeky bastard.

Where the hell was I supposed to go now? I sat there with my soda and stared up at the giant ceiling. Pigeons swirled around the glass dome, swooping down to pick up stray bits of bagel dropped by passing travelers.

I could hear the whir of the subway somewhere to my left, down below the escalator that flashed stair after stair.

Think, Evie. What should I do? Think!

Should I just go home? Should I call someone else? Who? I have no friends. Wait. There was one … but, no. I couldn't call Rachael. She hated me. I scrolled through my contacts and found her name. But I didn't have the courage to hit send. I just sat there, staring at the phone, wondering what to do. Then it rang.

I pushed the accept call button and said, "Hello?"

"Hello. This. Is. Not. a. Service call. Your. Home could. Be at. Risk for …"

I started sobbing into the phone. The wino perked up and stared at me, then handed me a ratty napkin.

"Thank you," I blubbered and kept crying, loudly.

The robot voice kept yammering away in stunted sentences, and all I could do was cry. Then, out of anger, frustration, the need to vent, I started to talk to the robot.

"Yes," I sobbed. "Hi there. I think my brother's dead, and my husband, Paddy, just kicked me out, and they only had Diet Coke in the machine, and I think I just caught some disease from this nice man in rags!"

"If you. Act. Now. You can secure. Your home …"

"But I'm in Boston," I wailed. Then sniffed loudly. The man next to me made a face of disgust. "You know what? I'm a grown woman. I can just take the train back to Providence and go home. Screw Paddy."

"This offer. Will not. Be around for …"

"Thank you, robot." I hit the end call button and immediately felt calmer. I needed time to process all that had just transpired. Plus, I had bought a round-trip ticket. Who was I to waste a round-trip ticket?

The wino was staring at me.

"You okay?" he asked.

I smiled at him. Here was a man without a pot to piss in, and he was asking me if I was okay. I almost started crying again because of the sheer kindness of his words.

"Are you hungry?" I asked.

"Starving."

"Come on. There's a Dunkin' over there calling our names. Let me get you a coffee and a donut."

"I would love an egg sandwich, and I take my coffee black."

"Done."

Two hours later, I was on my way back to Providence. During my wait for the train, I had passed the time with my new friend, Larry, the homeless guy. The distraction was just what I needed.

As the world south of Boston melted away, I thought about my situation.

How on earth do I always find myself in these predicaments?

I swear, I am Calamity Evie. If something is going to go wrong, it's going to happen to me. It had been happening my whole life. Maybe I cause it, maybe I don't, but it constantly feels like the universe is trying to set my toes on fire.

As things stood, my brother was missing. Nomia, the bitch from the watery depths of hell, was back in my life, and Paddy no longer wanted me in his. My husband had banned me from seeing my baby girl, and I'd just had coffee with a homeless guy named Larry. Wow. I could really fuck up my life in five easy steps.

I needed to find my brother. Once I found him and made him realize how dangerous things were ... what was I thinking? Of course he knew how dangerous things were. He was missing, for Christ's sake. His house had broken glass and blood in it.

"Richard," I said to the milky window of the train. "Where are you?"

After a stinky cab ride back to my house, I found a note from Paddy taped to the liquor cabinet door. The irony of the placement was not lost on me. It read:

> *Dear Evelyn,*
>
> *If you are reading this, then you are home after I have asked you not to come home. Fortunately, we have not had any clients lined up, so I took the liberty of closing the funeral parlor for a few days.*

God, I could hear the snooty lilt in my head.

> *Savannah and I have gone elsewhere. That is all you need know. I suggest you get your*

things and do the same until I am ready to
speak with you about your priorities, i.e.,
this family.

Signed,
Your irate husband

I thought about setting the note on fire, but then thought better of it. Instead, I opened the liquor cabinet and found my friend Bourbon.

Bourbon doesn't judge me, unlike some people I know. I poured myself a tall glass and relished every sip as the nerves in my neck popped one by one, like strings breaking on a violin.

I kicked off my shoes and headed up the stairs, glass in hand. I found myself in my daughter's room.

We had painted it pink the previous summer. Aunt Catherine had a student whose mom did murals. We had hired her to paint flowers and butterflies on one wall of Savannah's room.

Her bed was neatly made, and I could see that her favorite stuffed hippo, Hippy (children are just so original when it comes to naming their stuffies), and his best friend, Zorky the rat, were missing. So was the quilt Aunt Catherine had made for her when she was born.

That meant Savannah and Paddy had vacated for the evening—if not longer. For real. There was no way Savannah would sleep without those three items.

I inhaled sharply through my nostrils and took a long swig, cherishing the smoky flavor. Then I shook my head.

I'm such a fuck-up.

I walked down the hall to the master bedroom and saw that Paddy had taken his overnight kit from the top of his wardrobe. Further proof that I was all alone.

I flopped down on the bed and nursed my drink. When I emptied the glass, I trudged downstairs and got the bottle.

Wash, rinse, repeat.

The world eventually faded away with the daylight.

I woke up around eight the next morning—surprisingly early for me—and cursed the lack of shades in our bedroom. Everything was too bright. My head, too heavy. My mouth, too fuzzy.

I padded down the stairs and considered my options. I could not stay here alone. I was too self-destructive. I was in desperate need of a friend. No, she was not a great friend. Most likely, she would enable me to drink more, but at the very least, I would be supervised. And that was better than my current situation.

Rachael Bass.

I scrolled through my contacts, found her name, and hit send.

"Evie," Her voice was smooth and confident. As always. "It's been a long time, you saucy hag."

"Hello, Rachael. I ..." I couldn't finish. For the second time in two days, I started sobbing into my phone.

"Evie! Evie? Are you there? What's wrong?" All the sugar and sultriness disappeared from her voice.

"Yes," I sobbed. "I'm here. I think my brother's dead, and Paddy sort of kicked me out, and I have a raging drinking problem, and I ... I ... I don't want to be alone! I need a place to stay!"

"Dear Lord. Where are you? Let me come and get you."

"I'm home," I mumbled.

"Stay there. I'll come and get you."

"Uh, okay. Are you sure it's okay for me to come to your house?"

There was a long pause. Then Rachael said, "It's been a long time, but when it comes to friends, I mate for life. Get your shit together. I'm coming, Evelyn."

She hung up. I took a deep breath and blew it out through puffed cheeks. The pain in my head snapped me into action. I gathered up my things, changed my clothes, and stepped into the bathroom. I grabbed an aspirin and a glass of water and headed out the door.

I sat in the driveway on my roller bag and waited for salvation.

Musäus Farm
Berne, New York
June 24, 1991
10:48 AM

Evie

I snapped my gum and heard something important crack in my inner ear. Oma, my grandmother, had her back to me. She stiffened her shoulders at the stove, then turned away from the delicious cinnamon buns she had just iced.

"*Dat's* how a lady acts?" she asked in her harsh German accent.

"Yup," I replied, sticking my tongue into the wad of gum in my mouth. I had just pressed it into a thin, slick pancake. Holding the disc of goo against my teeth, I sucked in—hard.

Snap!

"Spit it out," said Oma, holding her hand under my chin.

I obliged and spat the gum into her palm. It sat there, all pink and wet. We scrunched up our noses at it.

"Dis-gusting," she muttered as she threw the gum in the

trashcan under the sink. "Why you act like this, Evelyn?"

It was a great question for Evie, age fifteen. I could file it in the forever-expanding *Evie Sucks at Life* drawer, under the subheading *Unanswerable Questions* or, better yet, *More Things I Don't Give a Shit About.*

But instead, I gave her the same response I gave my parents, my brother, my teachers, and anyone else who noticed me long enough to, in turn, inevitably judge me: I stared blankly, then blinked a few times.

Oma, however, wasn't as easily put off as the others. She didn't just sigh an agitated, over-exaggerated sigh, roll her eyes, or storm off the way the others did, which was the reaction I always hoped to illicit with my blankness. Oh no, not Oma. She pressed on and on and on and on in her thick, broken English.

"You are beautiful girl. You are smart girl. You think you fooling everyone. You not fooling Oma. Oma sees you. Oma believes in you. You will do great things one day. This," she poked her gnarled finger hard into the table, "you mark this down."

I really wanted to believe her. But the proof was in my pudding ass. I was a nobody, a nothing, an ugly, overweight (I hate saying fat, I really do, but it does apply here), good-for-nothing loser. And I really truly, truly didn't give a shit about anything.

Well, except Oma.

"Why the hell do you care, Oma?" I would shout.

Oh, that would get her schnitzel all crispy. Beneath her over-sprayed, tinted blonde hair, I could watch the steam escape her ears. Her careful tendrils, as if she had just stepped out of a

1960s soap opera, quivered with exasperation as she relentlessly berated me. On a side note, I have no idea how she found the time to achieve that coif, nor do I understand how she kept it looking so perfect all week long. I think she wrapped her head in toilet paper before she went to bed. Maybe that had something to do with it.

"You," she would snarl, "You do not question me. You come up here, year after year with your brother, and I undo all the ... the ... *Scheiße*. What is this word? *Bullshit!* I undo all the bullshit your parents do, or do not do. I build you back up, and always you return broken. Why is this? Why you not returning better? *Why?*"

Except her pleas of *why* would always sound like *vie*, and this would set me off. I would start giggling and shouting, *"Vie! Vie, Fräulein? Sprichst du kein Deutsch? Schnell! Schnell! Mein Strudel ist fertig!"*

This would result in her chasing me around the kitchen with a dishtowel, snapping it at me. "I've got you strudel, *Fräulein!* Right here!" *Snap!* "Und here!" *Snap!*

Except this particular time, my grandfather walked in through the back door, slamming the screen behind him. Heinrich Octavius Musäus. My Opa. Killjoy in green jeans.

Like the air from a tire with a nail jammed in it, all the joy in the kitchen leaked right out through the screen and into the yard. Neither Oma nor I breathed. We froze in the mirth that, as we stood there looking at him, looking at each other, evaporated into the ether like mist off a lake.

He scowled at both of us, the disgust and disappointment

palpable on his weathered face. Beneath his white beard—marred only by the nicotine stains around his mouth and nose—a pipe, empty of tobacco out of respect for his wife's kitchen, clicked against yellow teeth. The decayed state of his incisors reminded me of rotten wood, brittle and fragile, yet resilient in the damp elements that seeped into their existence.

He tore into my existence.

"*Isst du schon wieder? Damit verbringst du deine Zeit? Unnützes Mädchen!*"

I knew enough German by this point to pick up the sentiment—he was not happy that I was eating (again) instead of making myself useful. But I would in no way sass him. He terrified me. I never had the courage to say anything to him, let alone defend myself.

I hung my head and stared at the crumbs on the floor. Feeling my unease, Oma moved between the two of us, blocking Opa from my view, blocking me from Opa.

She murmured something sweet in their native tongue while I longed for the distraction of my brother, the shelter of my brother. Opa, like everyone else except Oma, thought the sun rose and set on Richard. The two of them were as thick as thieves. As soon as my brother was old enough to hold an axe, they began to spend all their time together, alone in the woods. That day when Opa had put the axe in Richard's hands had marked the end of our forest explorations as children.

But now, Richard was nineteen and away at college. This was my first summer at the farm without him. I never realized how much he had served as a buffer between me and my grandfather. I knew Opa didn't care for me, but with Richard gone, Opa was downright hostile. Even Oma couldn't contain his wrath.

"Was soll aus dir nur warden? Nichts! Du bist auch nicht besser als deine Mutter. Ihr Blut ruinierte unser Erbgut und hier, hier ist der Beweis, er sitzt in meiner Küche und isst mir die Haare vom Kopf."

I tried to wrap my head around his words. Something about my mom ruining the family. And something about me eating too much hair (or maybe I got that wrong), and something about my worth. Or the lack thereof. He was right. I *was* nothing. To this day, there are so many moments where I still think those words, *You are nothing.*

Some sentiments are written on the soul in an ink that never washes away. When you are too young to understand that the ink is poison and the words are meaningless, these ill-appointed beliefs spread their venom into the subconscious. It is there, beneath the surface, that they fester and infect your dreams and your self-perception. It takes a brave, clear-minded person to slowly, over time—and with a lot of help from a good therapist—suck out the poison and spit it someplace where it won't hurt anyone else.

Then again, some people take that venom and spit it back at anyone who crosses their path.

"Why can't you be more like your brother? Strong, brave, useful? You should have been born a boy. Then I could have done something with your soft, doughy ass. I would have made a mountain out of you ... could have made a mountain ..." He said in English, making his point abundantly clear.

"*Heinrich!* Enough! Go. You are not needed here." Oma turned him, placing her small hands on his large shoulders, and gently coaxed him towards the back door. She shooed him out into the warm summer day as if he were a child.

I watched him from the safety of Oma's table. I saw him look at the sky, then slink away. He disappeared into the forest like a villain from a fairy tale.

I could almost see the shadow of my brother, following close behind. But Richard was gone, and I was all that was left. A sad reminder of all that was not. I looked at my grandmother, forcing myself to hold in my tears. They hung in my eyes, like thick sour milk, threatening to pour down my face. I would not give him the satisfaction.

Instead, I thought of a large tree. A strong, thick tree with a trunk the size of one of those ridiculous SUVs that were popping up all over the roads. I willed that tree into existence. I willed it to grow to its full height, right there in the forest with my grandfather. Then I willed it to smash Heinrich's tall, mean-spirited body into a thousand bloody pieces. In my mind's eye, I saw his old leather boots sticking out from beneath the trunk of that enormous tree.

The notion was ridiculous, but I thought about it anyway. Because if a tree did fall, you bet your sweet ass I would smile.

Standing behind me, my grandmother ran her small, gentle fingers through my hair. I let my shoulders fall. The sobs came rapidly. I let my breath, held tight during my grandfather's tirade, release itself from my strained lungs. It flowed into the room, mixing with the anguish in my ragged voice. The dam in my eyes gave way, and the tears fell.

But Oma shushed it all away. She held my head to her chest. Between my hiccups of defeat and uselessness, I breathed in Oma. She smelled of flour, of green tomatoes, of talcum powder laced with violets, and of hairspray. She rocked me until my cries subsided into sniffles.

"We make a pie now, no?"

I laughed, then I cried some more. A pie was not what I needed, and yet it was exactly what I wanted.

I've heard some women don't eat when they're sad, depressed, or even stressed. I have no idea how those bitches comfort themselves without the power of pie, or any other food. Food is my frenemy. It is there when I need it, and it is there when I don't. It doesn't judge me. It doesn't yell at me. In all its purity and wonder, food nourishes and makes me feel there is a reason to go on. Sometimes, that's enough.

"Okay," I said in a small voice. "Let's make a pie."

"Good."

She held me close and kissed the top of my head, then sang her pie song. *"Gonna make pie. Gonna make a pie. Gonna make a pie with my heart in the middle ..."*

We cleared the table and gathered what we needed for our baking project. We decided on blueberry. When it came out of the oven, scenting the overly hot room with the intoxicating smell of baked sugar and the unique tart scent of blueberries, it encircled my heart with a warm embrace.

Later in the afternoon, after my sadness had subsided, we

heard the sharp crack of a shotgun somewhere deep in the surrounding woods. Neither of us said a word, neither of us caught
the other's eye. We just ignored the sound and continued to eat
our pie in the vast silence that followed.

That evening, Oma and I made fried chicken. We ate
together, exchanging only a few words. Most of our conversa-
tions went unfinished, our words trailing off into the haze of
the evening. Opa had not returned. Before we went upstairs to
bed, we left a plate on the kitchen table piled high with warm,
golden pieces of chicken covered with a crisp linen napkin.

Early the next morning, when I came down the stairs, my
hair a mess and sleep still sticking to the corners of my eyes, I
saw that Opa had returned. He sat at the table shoving greasy
pieces of chicken past his white beard. He still had on the same
clothes he had worn the day before. Evidence of his own lack
of sleep draped all over his leathery brown face.

I hadn't cared if he returned or not, but looking at Oma, I
could see that Opa's nocturnal absence had left dark smudges
beneath her eyes as well. She must have kept an all-night vigil.
She looked exhausted, but it had not stopped her from making
a full breakfast. Her warm smile shot across the room, soothing
my jangled nerves as I stared at Opa.

I found the strength to move and sat down at the table, cautiously shooting Opa glances, trying to judge his mood, but I
could not gauge it. He ignored me. Indicating to Oma that he
needed more milk in his glass, he turned his head, and the angle
from which I saw him changed. My jaw dropped. A huge claw
mark ran across the sharp line of my grandfather's jaw. Three

long scratches tore down into his neck, ripping his beard, revealing raw pink skin beneath.

I sat there, staring at him, still afraid of his wrath, and although I desperately wanted to know how he had acquired such a wound, I didn't dare say a word.

His clothes were dirty and bloody, and I could see from the way he was sitting—one foot jutting out beside his chair, the other tucked beneath the wooden table—that one of his shoes had been partially torn to bits.

How does someone lose part of a shoe like that?

I turned and stared at Oma. She gave no indication that she had seen the state of her husband's clothes and body. She just smiled at me, fatigue dulling her normal cheerfulness, looking like an old, once brightly colored, worn-out dishrag. Meanwhile, Opa just kept shoveling chicken into his clawed-up face. For whatever reason, he paused and looked at me over his fork, the malice still present. The moment passed, and he went back to eating. I thought my presence had gone undetected. I had been wrong.

With his mouth full, he said—in English, to my astonishment—"Go outside and get my knife, girl. I left it on the chopping block."

I couldn't move. He never asked me to do anything, and he had just asked me to touch his knife? I glanced at Oma. Her sleep-swollen eyes stared back at me, wide and wildly frightened. His knife never left his person. I learned at a very young age that his knife was not something to be discussed, let alone touched. And he had just asked *me* to go fetch it?

Something was definitely wrong.

A warm summer breeze merrily swept through the kitchen door, stirring pots on the pot rack, gently teasing the hanging herbs, releasing their wonderful scents into the already wonderful-smelling kitchen. All this made the request, the clawed-up grandfather, the zombie grandmother seem all the more ludicrous. A nervous smile crept across my face, and I bit the inside of my cheek to quell the oncoming maniacal giggle that threatened to unleash itself. I turned to Oma for help, but she kept her face turned to the stove.

"Go on!" he shouted.

I flinched, then stood and darted out the door, relieved to be away from him. The grass, still wet from the morning dew, squished between my bare toes, and the ground below felt warm. The early summer sun had begun to roar in the bluest of blue skies overhead.

I moved around to the back of the house, close to the woodshed and the chicken coop, to where Opa kept the chopping block. Low, cautious clucking gurgled from the caged chickens as my footsteps alerted the little beasts of my approach. Just for the record, chickens are disgusting. They're noisy and they smell. They smell bad, really bad.

I held my breath as I approached their disgusting lair. Once the stench of chicken shit gets in your nose, it stays there all day long. I was so focused on not letting the smell infiltrate my senses that I almost tripped over the large tarp covering something big and log-shaped. My bare foot struck something warm and soft beneath the harsh, blue plastic, which crackled as my foot hit it.

That's when it happened. I puked all over the place.

Purplish-blue vomit sprayed all over the side of the coop, the tarp, the grass, the chickens, everywhere. The pie, mixed with the fried chicken from the night before, evacuated my body at breakneck speed, and it wouldn't stop. I stumbled backwards, the puke still rocketing from somewhere deep and vile within me.

I fell to my knees, bent over, my hands landing in the wet grass, wet with dew, wet with the stuff that was supposed to be inside me. I crouched there, like a dog. My hair fell in my face, but I didn't care. I kept dry heaving into the green grass, hoping to God that this wretched activity would just stop—for Christ's sake.

It took a while. There was a lot of spitting and gagging. My body felt horrible, achy, and strained from the use of muscles I didn't even know I had. My head pounded, a steady drumbeat in my temples, and I desperately wanted to go to sleep, right there, next to whatever was under that tarp and those God-awful chickens. Somehow I summoned the strength to stand. I wiped my face on the sleeve of my ruined nightgown and looked around.

The knife shone like Excalibur, sticking up from the chopping block, about ten feet from where I stood. I just needed to grab it and get back to the kitchen.

You can do it, Evie.

I tried to take a deep breath, but the nausea remained, thick and menacing. I looked down at the tarp. At the edge, where the plastic met the grass, a stain spread, thick like raspberry jam.

That's not jam.

The understanding that a dead something lay inches from my feet slammed into my already ailing head. With my stomach in knots, I bent down and reached for the edge of the tarp. My fingers had barely grazed the plastic when I saw the wisps of hair sticking out from the top of the bundle. It did not look like animal hair. It looked ...

I dry heaved again. Nothing came out. There was nothing left to come. I needed to get away from there. I sprinted past the heap and pulled the knife from the block. I darted around the other side of the shed and coop, steering clear of whatever awful dead thing was waiting for me on the other side.

My God. What had Opa done?

Fear, sharp and ice-cold, punched me in the chest. My brain spun. Questions popped up like angry critters in a whack-a-mole game. I just kept slamming them back down and repeated a mantra I had created on the spot: *I do not need this shit. I do not need this shit. I do not need this shit.*

As each question popped up, I answered it with my new motto.

Q: Did he kill someone?   *A: I do not need this shit.*

Q: Why did he send me out to the shed?

A: I do not need this shit.

Q: Do I call the police?   *A: I do not need this shit.*

Q: Is he going to kill me?   *A: I do not need this shit.*

I came around the side of the house and stopped. I needed to control my breathing. Be calm. Deal with this. I had Oma and myself to take care of. I needed to put our safety first.

I glanced down at myself. I was a mess. Puke stained the front of my nightgown, and I was holding a bloody knife.

Holy shit.

In my hand lay the ornate hilt. Blood oozed all over my hand. I hadn't even noticed it when I had grabbed the blade from the old stump.

I closed my eyes and wished to God that Richard would magically show up. There's a saying about wishing in one hand. Well, my hand was full of the other part of that saying and so I, alone, had to deal with the situation—without Richard—still sleepy, barefoot, covered in my own vomit, holding a bloody knife.

Q: And whose blood is it?   *A: I do not need this shit.*

I took a deep breath and let it out slowly. I tipped up my chin and pushed the door open with my non-knife-wielding hand, then slammed the weapon down on the table in front of my grandfather.

"Evelyn! You reek of vomit." My grandmother rushed over to me, a dishrag at the ready, like I was still a small child. But I was no longer a child. Not anymore.

You do not go out to the woodshed, step over a body, vomit, retrieve the murder weapon, and still say that you are, indeed, a child. I knew, in that moment, that my childhood had officially ended. My childhood lay under that blue tarp with whatever else lurked beneath it.

Oh my dear God.

I opened my hands in front of her, my hand covered in blood, to stop her fussing. I looked down at my palms. I looked at my grandmother, then back down. Her eyes followed mine.

"Let me clean you up ..." she mumbled, not missing a beat, not acknowledging the horror of my hand, the horror of who sat in her kitchen and shared her bed.

I heard the sharp squeal of Opa's chair, straining against the wooden floor as he pushed it back to stand.

He started laughing. A deep, baritone laugh. My whole body shook, and I felt my grandmother's frail hands now grip my wrists, attempting to still the shudders that racked my insanely spent and dehydrated body.

I turned, slowly. He raised a napkin to his face and wiped away a bit of chicken and some of the blood from those mysterious scratches along his face. The wounds must have cracked when he laughed. He threw the cloth down on the table and grabbed the knife.

Turning towards us, he gave me the once-over.

I searched his face for the usual disappointment, and, oh believe me, it was there, along with something else. A faint hint of amusement, a glimmer of a notion, you might say, mixed with, perhaps, surprise.

I trained the wrong one.

He said the words in German, then shook his head as he headed out the door, slamming the screen behind him.

I fell apart, sobbing, crumbling into my grandmother's warm embrace. All the whack-a-mole questions in my head came blubbering out, in a nonsensical stream of half-words.

She didn't answer or even acknowledge the fear or the confusion as it poured out of me—much like the vomit had—in a gush of raw, violent energy. She just rocked me and sang the pie song.

In time, she cleaned me up and forced me to drink several glasses of water teeming with bright green sprigs of mint, then put me to bed. I spent the rest of the day there, exhausted, moving in and out of a fitful sleep. When I awoke, the sun had descended over the wide expanse of trees. I went to the window and looked down at the coop and woodshed.

The bundle had been removed.

All that remained was the faint outline of what looked like a large person, as if a great giant of a human had lain down in the grass, in the cool shade of the coop, to rest and then bled out all over the place.

I shuddered, in spite of the nearly ninety-degree heat, which to me felt like twenty. I grabbed my own shoulders and shivered, staring at the strange indentation in the stained grass below. I stayed there at the window for a long time, then went back to bed. This time, I didn't dream at all.

The next morning, when I went down the stairs, my grandfather was gone. Oma told me that he had gone on another bear-hunting trip and would not be back for a long time.

Bear hunting.

That was no bear. I knew it, Oma knew it, but she never mentioned what had happened, and I never brought it up. Not then, not ever again. I filed it away, buried it deep, then heaped all the good kitchen memories with Oma right on top of it until it became a dream.

Just a bad dream I had one summer when I was fifteen.

But I can tell you this: *I never ate blueberry pie ever again.*

3

Nomia

The brilliant blue sky spread above me. I sat alone, perched on a smooth gray rock while the sea ebbed and swelled, ignoring my small insignificant existence. A ripple of clouds stretched along the horizon, as if fingers, long gone, had raked lines in the purest of white sands. Gulls cried out to one another, nagging and screeching, reminding each other of their sins. Needy, unpleasant scavengers of the dead, they have always steered clear of me. I sneered at them, annoyed by their putrid existence.

Below me, water splashed against the rock jetty, misting me with a fine spray of brine. I licked my lips. The salt on my tongue soothed my jangled nerves, reminding me of the first time I had tasted it, the first time I had experienced the ocean.

You may think my story began in the sea. You would be mistaken. My life has always been a series of crooked paths, ever veering towards the unexpected, the difficult, the path ill-chosen. A wise woman had foretold this, and this same Greek woman had given me my name.

Nomia. The name had belonged to a nymph, beloved by the people of the woman's homeland deep in the Nomian Mountains. That woman was long gone, vanished, taking my mother with her as they embarked on their own path, their own journey. Their final destination is still a mystery. A mystery I hoped to solve some day, but not that day. On that day as I sat by the sea, I faced another fork in my own road.

Crossroads provide an excellent time for reflection, to look fore, to look aft. In my fifteenth year, I experienced the vast ocean for the first time. We had arrived at the top of a high cliff overlooking the sea, my crossroads. The cool air moved little beneath a dark and angry sky. As of that moment, the morning sun had been unable to burn away the cloudy film hovering above the flat surface of the inky-black waters.

My view had been unobstructed, and the sea went on without end. All that water, forever stretching towards the horizon and beyond, overwhelmed my senses. I had never felt so small or so insignificant. There before me lay an entire new world, completely foreign to me, and my mother had called it my new home. Havet. That word, so similar to the English word for haven. But the ocean never evolved into my haven, had never delivered solace, not like it had for my sisters.

Licking my lips again as I sat on the rock, I tasted the salt once more. I thought of my sisters, of our blessed life just before it all went to hell, so very long ago. The brine always reminded me of them and of better days. They had been my haven, not the sea.

I can still picture them, all of them, on that morning when I saw the sea for the very first time. They had gathered around me, touching my arms, my hair, my face. Creating a ritual for me. I was so frightened, yet so excited. They had told me about the sea, about the change my body would undergo once it embraced its origins. I had never been in the salted sea. I had only experienced the change in fresh water. How different could it be? Hearing is one thing, but experience another.

Each of them, so elegant, so graceful, had come before me, placing a kiss on my brow. On that grayest of gray mornings, each of my sisters shed her clothes. They were spectral visions of white, their bodies glowing against the ashen sky as, one by one, they took flight and dove off the cliff.

When the first one disappeared over the edge, I had run to the lip of the land, desperate to see where she had gone. The rocks below looked menacing, the maw of an angry beast eager to gobble me up. I had recoiled. How could my beautiful sisters survive such a thing?

But as each one dove, joy had burst forth from them, like a palpable explosion. It had filled the air, as tangible and ethereal as fog. Gleeful cries descended with each one, down, down, down, as each hit the surface with a subtle splash. They all cleared the rocks, their bodies, like birds, flying far out into the air, then arcing in graceful curves, far beyond the danger below me.

One after the other they left the cliff, until I was left alone—or so I thought. I stood at the precipice, wondering if I would shatter into a thousand pieces once my own body, so dark, so different from my sisters', hit the jagged rocks far below.

I heard movement behind me and turned to see my mother, my beautiful mother, who was neither my mother nor beautiful, had moved closer behind me. She had placed her strong hands on my shoulders and whispered in my ear.

This is your moment. You will not fail. I am here. I will always be here, my night daughter.

Her words of encouragement, affirmation, and ongoing support had filled my heart with strength and love, and with that fuel inside me, I leaped and flew away from my former self. The adrenaline from the fall filled me with an intoxicating fire, a fire that I still chase like an addict. The wind blasted through my hair, the skin on my lips, my eyelids as the rocks beneath me flew towards my face. I screamed in glee and in horror as I plummeted past the jagged points. It had been an illusion from above. I did not burst into a thousand shards. As I hit the water, my body opened, like a flower, like an infant being born. I felt the twinge of my nerves and muscles responding to the new liquid. I felt the change take over, felt it rip my body apart, then put it back together, newer, stronger, adapted to the new environment.

I opened my eyes, and in the dim green light of the sea, I could see my sisters, their hair floating around them like clouds of milkweed blowing in the wind, smiling at me, their lips pulled taut over vicious teeth.

I smiled back.

Nix swam to me. This I remember. My closest sister, my caretaker, took my hand, which felt so different from mine, so much more suited to the turbulent water of the sea, and together we swam. I swam in the skin I was intended to own. The power of my body propelled me through the cold, murky depths. But Nix pulled away, turning to smile at me, her face and body language eager for me to follow, to keep up. I struggled to stay with her, to not lose her, or any of them, as they swam through kelp forests, chased seals, and twirled with schools of fish, fantastically pushing the limits of their bodies.

Limits. So many limits.

My abilities paled beside those of my sisters. As we raced through the waves, I felt an unfamiliar fear rise in my chest, gripping me, holding me back. I could not keep up. I watched, for the first time in my short life, as my sisters faded away, disappearing from my view as I struggled to move my body with the same ease as they did.

After what felt like an eternity, they noticed my absence and returned. Confusion and concern crawled across their beautiful faces. But I had no answers. In the woods, I had always been in the lead, laughing over my shoulder as they ran behind me, calling my name, calling for me to slow down. And so it had been in the rivers and lakes, but in the deep, salt water, I was—to everyone's horror, including my own—slow.

When we returned to the beach, they tried to comfort me, reasoning that my inexperience with seawater made me sluggish. It was something that would build over time, they said. My endurance would increase the more I was exposed to the place where I belonged, they said.

But it never did. I never caught up to them. My prowess in the saltwater did not improve. I was different. Always different. Always a league behind.

They whispered about me when they thought I could not hear them. They said things like half-breed or, even crueler, nytteløs, the Danish word for useless. They whispered about my father. My father. I knew nothing about him. I had asked once and was told little. He had been a good man but had died long before I was born.

Was he like us? I had asked. The answer, yes and no. But never more than that. As for my mother, my birth mother, I knew even less. Was she like us? The answer, oh yes, very much so. She had been kind, distant, quiet, but strong and powerful. She had needed to go on a journey, for my sake. That was all I was told. I had come to believe it was all I needed.

I had a family of sisters and a mother. They surrounded me, cared for me. Why question my origins?

On my rock in the Elizabeth Islands, I looked out over the water, the crashing waves, the whitecaps stretching far to the horizon. It had been centuries since I had sat on this very rock and wondered how my life would take shape in this wild new land. I was so different then, so stupid. I took everything for granted. Youth is wasted on the young, they say. When you have lived as long as one of us, this phrase has even greater meaning.

I wish I could do it all again. I would do it right the second time around. If only I could. So much time, and almost all of it wasted on folly, on selfish vanity, on myself. How long had I lived beneath this canopy covering our miracle of a planet? How many times had I surfaced, gazed upwards to marvel at the billowy vapors that danced and twirled in the atmosphere, and thought about another person besides myself? After that first year on the Long Land, now known as Cape Cod, it hadn't happened too often.

It needed to stop. I had been selfish for too long. My soul, spread thin from years of existence, felt as though it could disappear like clouds dispersing into the vista of the bluest day.

Did I even have a soul?

Once, I had been compassionate, empathetic. But those human notions, reflective of my more mammalian DNA, had blinked on, then off—green then red. Like lights leading me home, to disaster. Red, right, return. I had ignored their call, and instead had responded to my selfish desires, discarding the needs of those I had loved. And every time, my choices had led to tragedy. It had been years, decades—centuries, even— since I had shed a tear for another living soul. The numbness of my emotional state had grown exponentially as the years had passed, a nod to my more reptilian side, I suppose. The part of me that was undeniably not human—the part of me that did not feel, that only strove to survive—dominated over all other thoughts or moral concerns, the mechanics of my existence. Survival of the fittest.

I have stared into the eyes of fish on more than one occasion. They reflect nothing. Emote nothing. They exist, and that is all. My own tumultuous existence? No different from that of a leviathan. Cold, calculating, violent. It was the shroud I chose to wear to veil me from the rest of the world. I wore it valiantly, denying that I could feel human emotions, denying that I could feel at all.

I once saw a human child thrust forth into the world, covered in primordial fluids, the visceral compost of its mother's womb. The infant did not look to its creator with love and adoration. This strange, tiny creature did not even seem to be aware of anything, least of all its mother. Its eyes were deep voids. There was no love, no compassion, no empathy. It was purely instinctual, in need of fundamentals, which it was incapable of acquiring on its own.

No different from a reptile.

I wondered, how can this new being have a soul? Maybe, like its eyesight, it had not been realized. Perhaps the soul lies dormant, waiting for the right moment, waiting for the world to reveal its divine purpose.

As for me, I often wondered if my soul had developed at all or if I was created without one. Much like the anomaly that is me, an anomaly amongst my own species. Perhaps being born soulless is another part of being a half-breed. Or if unbeknownst to me I was born with a soul, could it have disappeared? Washed away over time, like the thin, fingerlike clouds above me?

I picked up a shell dropped by one of those awful flying gulls and spun it into the sea. I watched it skip over the surface, then disappear, a small white spot sinking into the dark black water.

I heard movement behind me and turned to see her, my sister Nix. The scar on her face was even more beautiful than the first time I had noticed it as a child. I had asked her about it, just once, when I was very small. It was the first time she spoke about the bad men. She told me as much as my young mind could handle. She told me how they had hurt her and taken the lives of our sisters. Their names were not ones I had known nor would ever have the privilege of knowing. Then she would say no more. Her face had grown as cold as stone and her eyes had narrowed while her shoulders flew back. Not wanting to upset her, I hadn't asked again.

I shuddered. I have seen the things men do to women. The things they do to the women they fear. I shudder at the thought of what really happened to her, of how the scar on her face had appeared, and even worse is contemplating the origins of the one on her inner thigh.

This woman, my brave sister, came over and sat down beside me on the rocks. Her feet, as always, were bare. Her hair had been gathered into a knot. I smiled at her, but her face remained emotionless.

"What?" she barked at me.

I jumped a bit. She had spoken, and she had used English.

"What were you smiling at?" she asked.

I needed to tread carefully. This was the most she had said to me since we had left Boston.

"With your hair like that, you remind me of the young college students, the ones we saw in Woods Hole."

She did not answer, but instead turned her head, interested in something, probably nothing, far to her right. The sea lapped against the rock, filling the silence between us. I kept my gaze on the back of her neck, longing for her to turn and look at me, to acknowledge my presence. But I did not expect her to do so, to grant me what I desired. I deserved nothing.

The sea sprayed the two of us. The gulls swooped, lashing out at one another, and then she reached up and touched the top of her gathered hair, patting it softly. She let her hand fall to grab a pebble, tossing it into the water.

It was enough. I smiled, knowing that she had considered my words, perhaps even construed them to be a compliment. Since arriving on the island, she had been forced to be among people again, no longer allowed to ignore the human side of herself. No longer allowed to reside, without interruption, beneath the sea.

It had been a long time. She barely understood anything. The world had moved on without her since she and my sisters had decided to abandon the world of men. Technology, industry, commerce, social interactions. All these things were foreign to her. It was as if she were newly reborn and seeing the world for the first time.

She needed me. I knew this drove her mad. She and my sisters had always needed me. I helped them sustain their dirty habits. Here on the island, in our new isolation far from Narragansett Bay, far from our family, I felt as if I had been given amnesty, an opportunity to begin again, to wipe the slate clean. For the first time in centuries, I felt the urge to take care of someone, out of love and not obligation. It had been a shock to us both. My sister. I raised my hand to touch her shoulder, but thought better of it. Instead I, too, grabbed a stone and threw it into the sea.

"How much longer will we stay here?" she asked.

"Not long," I answered. "I'm seeing him again. Next week-end. I think it's working."

She shook her head, then scoffed in disbelief.

"What?" I asked.

"You're falling for him. That was not the plan," she said without looking at me. She kept her eyes on the sea.

"No. I'm not," I said defensively in English, then switched to Danish, The plan is still the plan.

"We shall see," she said, then stood and walked back across the rock jetty towards the trees.

I stayed behind, stewing. The plan is still the plan. I turned and looked at my sister, watching her disappear into the woods. She knew nothing. She was only angry, as always.

When the Irish had abandoned us in Boston, we had returned to Bull Island to find the ones who had befriended us, centuries before, when we had first crossed the great Atlantic. It was a good place to begin my penance. To right the first wrong in my endless list of sins. To find Abbona. And, if we ever did find Abbona, then perhaps Nix would forgive me. Perhaps.

Will I ever reach the end of my list of sins?

A gull swooped down and dropped an oyster. It landed on the hard surface near the place where I sat and shattered into white fragments, the slimy beige interior oozing over the rock. I could smell the pungency of the poor destroyed creature. I stood and stretched, then kicked the remains of the bivalve into the water. The gull screeched at me in frustration. I hoped it choked on a pebble.

The day had begun, and I needed to get back into town before midday when he checked his email. I needed to confirm my plans. We had nothing on the island. No electricity, no running water, nothing, but that suited us just fine. We had lived with less for longer periods of time. I had hoped my sister would accompany me today, as she sometimes did, but based on her most recent interaction, I doubted it would happen.

I had enjoyed the few times she had chosen to join me, even if she had sulked for most of the journey. I loved to see the world through her eyes, as if she were my child and I her mother, showing her the ways of the world as I should have done with my own child.

My own child. My Pearl.

A horrible mother ... Where is she now? I asked myself. Hopefully with David someplace far, far away. Someplace safe. I was a monster. I am a monster. They deserve better. I am not fit to raise a child, I thought. But maybe, maybe if I could right the wrongs, maybe I could learn to be a better mother. I could seek them out. Right the wrongs.

Right the wrongs. My new mantra. Wipe the slate. Clean up my act. Start fresh. One step at a time.

I walked the way Nix had gone, back to the hut we had built together, but she wasn't there. Off to continue her search for Abbona. She needed her space. I understood. I set about the task of gathering what I needed for the boat ride back to Woods Hole. I stuffed the latest stolen wallet and a black hoodie into a bag, then made my way down to the hidden dock at the center of the island.

One year had passed since we had arrived in that cold spring. The summer had been beautiful, but the winter had been harsh, cold, and unforgiving. So had my sister. As soon as our shelter had been situated, she had started a radial search for Abbona. She left early each morning, before dawn. Searching the waters and the far-off islands, leaving me to my thoughts, my plans. And each evening she had returned, defeated. Day after day, she had continued, even after the blaze of the leaves had fallen from the trees, and the snow had come in great billowing drifts. It had slowed her down, but not much.

We had been deposited in Boston. With our newfound freedom, we had crossed the harbor and headed for Hull. With my limited abilities, the going had been slow, and we had needed a water craft to continue. Making our way onto land under the cover of darkness, we had no trouble finding an empty summer cottage and acquiring clothing and supplies not likely to be missed by people who truly had so much. Once we had what we needed, we made our way back down to the water to find a marina.

I had acquired a boat before. Our kind is especially good at adapting. It's what we do, what we have always done. You can accomplish almost anything if you look and act as if you belong wherever you are.

I selected a small but efficient craft, one that would allow us to travel back and forth, to weather a harsh winter if needed, and, most importantly, to establish contact with our target. We had stopped to refuel once along the way and had decided to spend the night moored just off the coast of Plymouth. Our goal was to traverse the Cape Cod Canal early the next morning. That first night, bedding down to sleep in the vessel, listening to the water lap softly against the hull, I almost thought the stars—so much clearer and present at sea, away from the lights of Providence Harbor—would fall from the cavernous sky and set our little boat aflame. I had glanced over at my fair Nix, but her eyes had been closed, either asleep or feigning it.

The next day, we rode through the canal, under two magnificent bridges, watching the men who came early in the morning to fish from the bike bath that ran alongside us. I could feel the years sliding off my back like water. Nix, the wind setting her long, white hair aloft as she gazed out at the familiar landscape, said little. It had all changed so much, but I could see her looking for a glimpse of what had been. She had been so happy here, once.

Until I had ruined it all.

If she needed to speak to me, she would not meet my eye. Instead, she kept her gaze averted even as she spoke. A concerted effort to strike out at me, yet again, for the wrongs I had committed against her. I accepted my punishment, and in my acceptance, felt a great weight lift from my shoulders. Instead of raging against her anger in response, I answered her with kindness and understanding. Something she desperately deserved. It was new for me, and it gave me hope that things would get better.

As we approached Onset, I taught Nix how to steer the boat, allowing her to guide us southward. A fast learner, she picked it up easily. Our destination? The Elizabeth Islands, off the southwest coast of Cape Cod.

The islands are privately owned now. Before the turn of the nineteenth century, a prominent family had bought the islands for their own personal use. At some point, the islands became a land trust and are now publicly accessible. Choosing this as our new home presented a risk of discovery. It tested the limits of our ability to hide. It took some strategic maneuvering of the boat to go undetected over time. We would move it systematically, so as not to draw suspicion from the locals. But once the summer tourists left, no one really came by.

Nix was the one who had found the place that suited our needs, Bull Island. The heavily wooded island was home to an abandoned structure and a public access dock. There was also an inlet that curved into the interior of the island. At high tide, we could guide our boat inland and moor it in the shallow waters. It had been a fortunate find. The cove prevented the heavier ocean waves from pummeling our little craft.

We set to work right away. Within a few weeks, we had made a modest attempt at creating a domicile worth calling a home. We scoured the neighboring islands, going as far north as Bourne, in search of raw materials to make our home habitable. The heavy manual labor had felt good, soothing my mind, allowing me to process all that had occurred back in Rhode Island.

Our mother was dead.

Nix and I never spoke about it, but as we had put together a framework for our new existence, I could feel the weight of our mutual mourning gathering around us like storm clouds.

Our mother. Our cruel, distant mother.

For centuries, she had dominated the landscape of our lives, dictating our every move, ruling over us with an iron fist. There were a few times, here and there, when she would disappear, then return, even more domineering than ever, irritated that we had not grown up enough to replace her in her absence. It had always been a sticking point between my sisters and me that I was the one she favored. But what they failed to acknowledge, or even notice, was that I was the one who took the brunt of everything. Being out of the spotlight, in my opinion, would not have been such a bad thing. So many of the bad decisions I made in my life were in an effort to get the hell away from her and the rest of my family. Blood is the same thickness as seawater. I never had a chance …

Once Nix and I had set up our island, I took her to the mainland in search of a means of communication. We headed for the Woods Hole Oceanographic Institute, blending in with the young co-ed biologists, lurking in common areas, smiling at the right people. Acquiring information, money, food. It had been a long time since Nix had gone hunting with me. It was a good distraction for us both.

After a few trips to Woods Hole, I found what I needed. The library. Open to the public Monday through Friday from eight to five. Once I got my hands on a computer with Internet, I found the one we sought and set up an online dating account.

Modern dating is surreal. People are so easily manipulated by a skilled predator. With the power of the World Wide Web, I've found that, with little effort, I can access any information about any individual—an address, photos, choice of music, restaurants, movies. All of this information gathered in just a few hours while sitting at a desk, pushing some buttons.

I used the information to create the perfect bait. Someone my intended target could not resist. I pushed another button. Waited. Then the trap snapped closed.

My talents have been honed over the centuries. I adapt. I learn. I hunt. These have always been the keys to my survival, to the survival of my family.

The hunt for Richard had been no different.

Evie

"You look like dog shit."

I shut the car door as I slid into the passenger seat of a pumpkin-orange VW Beetle convertible. The black top was down, giving the car the look of a decapitated jack-o-lantern.

Ladies and gentlemen, meet my estranged best friend and our accountant, Rachael.

She sat in the driver's seat, her slightly wrinkled cleavage up front and present in her low v-neck shirt, harboring a long chain that disappeared somewhere in her boob crack. The shirt was stretched beyond the proper limits of any cotton knit garment, and the words *Bitches Get Shit Done* blazed across her ample chest. Her kinky auburn hair was disheveled, as if she had just rolled out of bed. She may or may not have slept in said bed, depending on whether or not she had entertained a transient occupant.

Rachael, in painted-on yoga pants, planted a hand on her hip and looked at me over her bejeweled sunglasses. Her hand, ending in clawlike red nails, gripped the steering wheel like a talon. She said nothing, then pushed her sunglasses back up her nose and checked her mirror. Bracelets adorned with multiple stupid charms jingled as she shifted the car into reverse.

"I've had the worst fucking decade and I need a goddamn drink," I said in a huff.

She flipped her long hair back over her shoulders and said, "You smell like you've already had a drink—or twenty."

"Please, bitch," I said. "Don't throw shade at me. I know I've been a shitty friend. The thing is, I have no one to talk to. You're my only hope, Obi Rach Kenobi."

Her lips, dry and flaked with the remnants of red lipstick, cracked into a wry smile.

"You're no princess," she said. "And your dad's not blowing up your home planet, but I do love you." She shifted into second gear and the car glided forward, turning onto Park Avenue.

I wanted to cry. The relief of acceptance, of love offered, was overwhelming. My already puffy eyes were clouded with tears. I wiped my cheeks on the back of my arm.

"Evelyn Musäus McFagan! Are you crying?"

"Fuck you," I said.

We drove the rest of the way in silence. The sun speckled its way through the trees, now green and full with new leaves, and the warm wind felt good on my swollen face.

Within eight minutes we were at her house, and I dragged my little rolling suitcase through her front door and into her living room.

"Go make me a drink," I said as soon as she was inside.

"Don't you sass me in my own house, heifer."

"You're right. That was rude." I smiled at her. "Go make me a drink ..." I paused. "Bitch."

"I will cut you, Evie," she said, as she walked into her kitchen. "I swear I will."

I heard the fridge open and the grinding of ice in the freezer. "I will cut you so bad, people will look at you." *Clink*. Ice hit glass, followed by the *glug glug* of liquid being poured. "And scream, *Dear God!*" Here she used a high-pitched voice. "*Hide your children! That thing will eat your babies!*"

She padded back into the living room and handed me a highball glass filled to the top with bourbon. Two happy little ice cubes twinkled up at me in the amber liquid.

"I missed you," I said and tapped my glass against hers. "*Prosit.*"

"*Prosit,*" she said in response, then tipped the glass back. The drink was gone in two swallows. She shuddered, then whooped, "Good morning! That's better!"

Flopping down on the couch, she kicked off her sequined flip-flops and lit a cigarette. "So what, exactly, is going on?"

"Can I just sip my drink?"

She stuck out her lips, forming a duck face, and said, "Sure. Take your time." Then she blew a smoke ring at the ceiling.

I settled into her leather couch and looked around. Not

much had changed. The walls were still scarlet red. Elvis on black velvet still crooned above the couch, and the fringed lamp still sat on the end table. I breathed in the smell of dead cowhide, nicotine, and stale perfume—or was it cologne? It was frightening and comforting at the same time. Ah, yes. The smell of my bad behavior, fueled by a friend without limits. The smell of how out of control I could allow myself to become.

I was about to open my mouth and lay it all out when a young man walked past the doorway in very tight Calvin Klein underwear. I swung my head to the side, leaning over the arm of the chair, almost spilling my drink, trying to get a good look at the young butt that had just passed by.

I glanced at Rachael, toned legs crossed, painted toenails bobbing up and down, drink in one hand, cigarette in the other, and the biggest stupidest grin on her face. That look said, *You saw that, right? Uh huh.* That *was just in* my *bed.*

"There's orange juice in the fridge, babe," she called to the kitchen, then winked at me. "I buttered that little baguette."

"Hmmmm," was all I could eek out before I hid my face in my drink. She still had it.

For as long as I had known her, Rachael had been able to bag a man, or a boy half her age, with both finesse and consistency. She was the definition of a cougar, an older woman on the prowl, but she owned it. She saw it as her hobby. As she had said in the past, a man screws a woman half his age and he's a hero. A woman does it and she's a slut. So be it. I'll be that slut, and I'll be happy, she proudly stated.

And for as long as I had known her, she had always been *happy*. No skeletons in her closet, no unrequited daddy love she needed to recreate. Nor did she pine for the family she had never created. She did not have an empty hole in her heart that she filled with men, booze, and cigarettes. She was simply *happy*. It was why I loved her, wanted to hang out with her, wanted to be somewhat like her. The downside? She used to get me in a lot of trouble. Her bohemian idealism often took us to somewhat unsafe places.

But while Rachael always maintained control (she knew her limits) I did not. Thus the flaw in our friendship

"Hey, babe?" came the voice of Mr. Calvin Klein. "Where's your cereal?"

"Oh honey," she cooed. "I don't keep that shit in the house. I'll make you a fresh green drink."

"That's all right. I need to get back to the dorm anyway." His voice grew louder as he approached the living room. "Oh, hey," he said when he saw me. "I didn't hear you come in. I'm Steven."

Then the polite young man, still in just his underwear, offered me his strong hand in greeting. I moved my highball glass to my left hand and shook his enormous mitt.

"Charmed," I said, managing a meek smile.

"Nice to meet you," he smiled back. "I'm off. Gotta go pack. My parents are picking me up around five."

Rachael stood and placed her arms around Steven, one of her hands finding its way to his ass. "Let me help you find your clothes."

She guided him, by his butt, back down the hall to her bedroom. I heard squealing and laughter as the bedroom slider
opened and closed.

Rachael returned, her hair even more tousled. She adjusted
her shirt, flopped back down on the couch, and picked up her
still-lit cigarette. She took a drag, then picked something out of
her teeth with her dagger-like nails.

"He's a senior in the culinary program. Pastry."

"I see," I said.

"Went to France last semester." She took a long drag.

"Uh huh."

"He learned all about croissants, tarts, macaroons, and older
women." She moved her lips to the side, a coquettish smirk on
her face, then exhaled.

"He's very polite."

"In some ways." She breathed out more smoke, still towards
the ceiling, then commanded, "Spill it."

"Spill what?"

"Where have you been? Why are you here now? Why are
you on the outs with Paddy? I wish he didn't hate me. I didn't
make you drink *that* much."

"I think it was the wig that put him over the edge."

"I didn't make you wear that."

She was referring to one of the last times we had hung out, a
few years before Savannah was born. She was dating some British guy who tended bar in South County, the unofficial name
of Southern Rhode Island, but not too south—that would be
Westerly. Whatever, it's a Rhode Island thing. *Rhode Island.*

For such a small state that is *not* an island, there sure are a lot of regional issues.

Anyhoo, this bartender boyfriend was throwing a party with one of his housemates, who I think he had dated but hadn't gotten over. I observed a bit more than I wanted to that night, but that's not the point of this sidebar. The theme of the party was *Tarts and Vicars*. Naturally, we raided Rachael's closet and wore her sluttiest clothing. Wanting to mix it up, I tried on this adorable brunette pageboy wig. I thought I had it going on, all Uma Thurmanrific.

We had a great time. I, of course, had *too* great of a time. Unable to drive back to the Village, as was our plan because Rach was going to stay with her man, I had called Paddy. Or maybe Rach called him. I don't remember. Someone called Paddy, and I passed out. When my knight in a shining Volvo arrived, he walked into the remains of the party and asked around, "Has anyone seen my wife? She's got blonde hair."

Well, it all rolled downhill from there. It was not the first time I had worn a wig and gotten in trouble when I was with Rachael. The next morning, while I nursed a mother of a hangover, Paddy had declared Rachael a bad influence. I had to reevaluate my priorities. I also needed to dry out a bit. Rachael declared Paddy too domineering. Our friendship declined, and when I got pregnant, she disappeared altogether. At the time, I was pissed.

But I get it now. Her life path did not have room for children. That was her choice. It was not mine. I chose to reproduce. Well, circumstances sort of forced the reproduction issue. It had not been our original plan.

When Paddy and I first met, we had agreed that our child-hoods had not been all that wonderful, so what was the point? Why bring kids into the world only to disappoint them? Well, the universe has a way of fucking with you. It likes you to think you have everything all figured out, that you have everything exactly where you want it to be, and then the universe comes along like some giant, meddlesome toddler, and chucks your crap all over the place, leaving you with a *WTF* look on your face. Finding out I was pregnant had been kind of like that.

Yeah, me a parent. I totally rock at that—not. Hey, lately I'm not the one causing all the problems. *Paddy* chose to leave *me*. If I had been in charge, I would be with my family right now, not with Rachael. Not that I don't enjoy being with Rachael. I sipped my drink and looked at my friend.

"Paddy doesn't *dislike* you."

She crossed her arms and stared at me.

"Well, he doesn't *hate* you."

"Whatever," she said, uncrossing her arms and taking another drag of her cigarette. "Why are you here? With lug-gage?"

"Where do I start?" I said and closed my eyes. I had no idea how much I should tell her. It all sounded completely ludicrous.

Mermaids. My life according to mermaids.

For Christ's sake. How the hell do you explain *mermaids*? I heard it in my head and cringed. Better to stick with a loose version of the truth. Better to leave the whole aquatic man-eater aspect alone. So instead, I told her about my brother. I told her that he was dating a woman who had attacked me a few years before.

"She's a complete lunatic! I mean, I met her at the playground a few times, and she was totally whacked. And then I was out at night, walking around the Village, and the bitch tried to drown me! Can you believe that?"

"Wait. *What?*" Rach knitted her brow and leaned forward. "That's insane! Wait a second. Were you …"

"Was I *what?*"

"How do I say this delicately? Where you, uh, drinking *excessively* again?"

I inhaled deeply, relishing the secondhand smoke. This was a turning point. Do I admit that I was—correction, *am*—a total lush to save face?

"Yes," I said and hung my head down. Best to just let it ride. "I had been on a bender."

"I see," she said and leaned back. "So, uh, did you …"

"Did I *what?*"

"Did you,"—she paused a moment, thinking about her word choice—"*provoke* this woman?"

"No!" I yelled, a little too forcefully. "She was a total lunatic! Still is a total lunatic. Paddy and I had to get a restraining order against her. She's not supposed to be anywhere near me or my family."

Not a total lie. The Irish Society of Merrow, or whatever the hell you call them, did, sort of, put a restraint on Nomia. How that bitch escaped her restraints was a story I desperately wanted to hear.

"So why *are* you here? I don't get it. I feel like you're not telling me something."

"Paddy made me choose. Savannah and my husband. Or my brother, Richard."

"And you chose Richard, *because* ..."

I jumped up. I needed a drink refill.

"I really don't know," I mumbled.

"Make me one, too!" commanded Rachael, shaking her empty glass at me.

I walked back to the couch and took the glass from her.

"Let's get a nice buzz going, then head out," she said and smiled up at me.

"Oh, Rach, I don't want to go anywhere beyond your back patio. Do we have to?"

"*Seriously?* Do you not know what day it is?"

I stared at her. Then blinked a few times.

"Wow. You are so out of it. It's Gaspee Days."

Shit. I *was* out of it. My eyes grew wide as I remembered. The 5k road race down the Parkway, followed by the parade. Then, all the parties all over the neighborhood. It was the beginning of June, and in Pawtuxet Village that only meant one thing—*Gaspee Days*. The entire Village was in full-tilt party mode. Everyone on the parade route was gearing up for an entire day of drunken revelry.

"I was wondering why you didn't take the Parkway to get here..."

"'Cause the street's shut down, duh." She looked at me like I was an idiot, then smiled. "I'm headed to Hazel and Shep's house for the day and *you* are coming with. Wig optional."

I groaned. "Hazel and Shep's? *Really?*"

They lived on the Parkway and were infamous in the Village for two reasons. One, their Gaspee parties were always epic. The night before the parade, as other parade watchers meticulously put out lawn chairs to mark their spots on the route, Shep and his guy friends set up the *lawn bar*. One of them had built the three-tap bar out of pallet wood, or homegrown bamboo, or some other obnoxiously sustainable form of lumber. It was completely operational and even had a foot rail around the front. It was the envy of every man in the Village.

Hazel and Shep's second claim to fame involved their extra-curricular marriage policy. They're swingers. Personally, I am both intrigued and repulsed by their arrangement. Intrigued because *how often do you get to meet swingers?* Probably more often than you think, but that's beside the point. I had heard there were a lot of other swingers in the Village, but I don't know who they are. I'm not even sure I *want* to know who they are. Some images cannot be erased from the mind, and going about my daily business in the Village and then having to wipe out any unwanted thoughts of shared partners is not something I really want to get into the habit of doing.

I don't shun what they do, and I've tried not to be judgmental, but the thought of swapping personal junk around town just skeeves me out. I'm a one partner, one set of parts kind of gal.

"Oh, don't be such a prude," said Rachael. "I'm not asking you to go and open your legs for the neighbors. We're just going to have a few drinks, talk to some interesting people, and cheer on local Girl Scouts and militia geeks. It'll be fun! You look as if it's been a while since you had any fun."

Really hard to argue with that reasoning.

"Now, go and change into something that shows off those curves of yours while I finish my deviled eggs."

I sighed heavily, threw back the rest of my bourbon, then pulled my suitcase down the hall to the guest room.

Rachael kept the room for her mother, who occasionally visited from New York. Her mom was a piece of work. Very judgmental, very loud, very rude. I loved her. The room was painted midnight blue with giant collage photos everywhere. The snow-white bed called my name seductively. I threw myself backwards onto the down comforter and stared at the stars painted on the ceiling. I had never noticed them before—not that I spent a whole lot of time on my back in Rachael's guest room. That was her job.

I heartily LOL'd.

"Ow!" My laughter was cut short as something dug into my lower back. I reached around behind me and pulled out the key-shaped USB drive I had found at my brother's place. I toyed with the ornate red tassel and wondered what could be on it. What could be so important that Richard would hide it in his toilet tank?

"Hey, Rach?"

"Yeah?" she called from the kitchen.

"Do you have a laptop I could borrow?"

I heard her coming down the hall. "What do you need, doll?"

"I stole this from my brother and I want to see what's on it."

I held up the flash drive for her to see.

"Is that a USB drive? It's cute, but it could be chock-full of viruses or something. My laptop is my life. All my clients' information is on there."

"Don't you back it up?"

"Yes, but I don't know where *that* thing has been." She made a face at the USB drive as if it were granny panties.

I gave her my saddest puppy-dog eyes. "Puh-lease, please, please?"

"Ev, I don't know. Can we discuss this later? Maybe after the party?"

"I don't even know if I want to go to the party," I said, putting on my best pouty look.

"Look," she said. "You go to the party with me, and I'll let you stick your brother's thingy in my port."

I burst out laughing.

"Okay. Deal."

5

Caratocos, elder scholar

irthing is relegated to the shallows, away from the hazards of deep water. Yet the size of our small population, (*Homo aquaticus*, in direct correlation to our cousin *Homo sapiens*), is directly attributed to the dangers of our breeding process. A birth, in any particular tribe or pod, is a miraculous, rare occasion and a terrifying experience. The female body is in flux. In most observed cases, in terms of birthing, the mother's ability, or perhaps will, to change her outward, physical form becomes secondary to the body's inner clock.

The process by which we receive oxygen within our gills is present in utero, as observed in a medical procedure performed circa 1643. In this particular case, the offspring had been saved by direct removal from the mother's body. Through the most unusual, irregular circumstances, the mother had been unable (or perhaps unwilling) to transform into a physical state suitable for vaginal birth. The result of her decision, or lack thereof, forced the midwives to make a decision for the mother. It is still unknown why the female made such a fatal choice. However, the information gained by opening the abdominal cavity of the female after the incident proved to be invaluable to my research.

It was most fortunate that I had been informed of the imminent birth and allowed to assist the midwives in their delivery procedure. The child was in an aquatic state, encapsulated in amniotic fluid, the tail fully visible while the gill flaps in the throat region flexed in preparation for saltwater immersion. An umbilical cord was present. It is assumed that nutrients and oxygen are transferred to the child through this, much like they are in *Homo sapiens.*

I did not have the tools to fully investigate the absorption of oxygen. It is understood that the *Homo aquaticus* derives oxygen through the use of gills. Water passes over the gills, which cull oxygen present in the water and then deliver it throughout the body via the circulatory system. Tiny blood vessels found in the gills are easily viewed when the gill flap is lifted. It is possible that the mother absorbs water transdermally, further processing the oxygen via the circulatory system and then passing on the oxygen-rich liquid to the fetus by way of the umbilical cord, along with any and all gill-derived oxygen taken in during submersion.

Multiple births are one of the rarest of occasions amongst our kind. One such case stands out among all others. The circumstances of the event proved to be the substance of legend. The more prophetic individuals of my tribe claimed to have foreseen the arrival of *The Two.*

As a person of science, I found their prophecies both tedious and dangerous in terms of influencing the more weak-minded members of our group. In any case, it was decreed that The Two would be born on a seventh day, under the first quarter moon, during a neap tide in the spring.

This is a most agreeable time for any birth, multiple or single. The position of the moon in relation to the sun would create a gravitational pull that would allow for a lower high tide. Therefore, the risk of tumultuous waters in the shallows would be greatly reduced.

This information furthers my belief that prophecies, usually based in known facts, are frequently used for purposes of manipulation.

In any case, these particular twins were born to a male and a female of great respect and standing within our tribe. Their arrival had been greatly anticipated, along with the belief that these two would one day join our tribe to the nearby land-dwellers, furthering the bonds between our two peoples.

In that respect, the prophecy was half true. It could not have been known that one of *The Two* would choose to leave the tribe forever, in search of greater fortune somewhere inland on the great continent.

In any case, their birth, albeit a complex one, was miraculously free of complications and was celebrated on both land and in the sea. It is good to note that this had been a time when the land-dwellers were still somewhat respectful and knowledgeable of our ways. A time before the Great Reaping, when many of our species were wiped out by the arrival of invaders.

The elders, who rarely left their homes any longer, too old, too preoccupied with their studies, came to witness the miraculous arrival of two small souls. One male and one female. Both fair-haired, both in excellent health. The girl, *Clíodhna*, and her brother, *Ciabhán*. Two of the most fabled individuals of our tribe.

There are still songs about these two, even in present day. However, their story has been grossly reconfigured over time. In the last recorded document that I discovered, the two were not twins at all but were, instead, lovers.

In those pages, it is written that Clíodhna was a land-dwelling deity, a queen amongst the fae folk, while her brother was said to have been a mortal man who fell in love with this queen. The pair eloped to the sea, where she fell asleep on the shore, while her lover went into the woods in search of game. Her sleep was so deep that the young girl did not notice the incoming tide and so was swept out to sea, where she drowned. This legend states that her cry can still be heard amongst the rocks and caves, a high keening when a storm is at hand.

But these legends are only stories, a far cry from the reality of *The Two*, Clíodhna and Ciabhán. The pair grew into strong, competent adults, both respected and revered among their companions. Ciabhán did indeed marry a land-dwelling girl, and their descendants live on to this very day. A pact was made between our people and theirs—that we should bury their dead with our own beneath the waves.

As for Clíodhna, sadly, one could only ponder the fate of the fair-haired girl. She left us forever, never to be seen again.

Clíodhna

The forest had been quiet for days. No sign of travelers, malignant or otherwise. As she navigated farther into the dark wood, the trees had grown denser, more gnarled and twisted, blocking out much of the sun and leaving the undergrowth sparse and pale. The wildlife, cautious and inquisitive, had all but disappeared.

When Clíodhna had first entered the wood, the small, tiny creatures—so different from the ones she had known on the mainland of her home—had delighted her whenever they chose to reveal themselves. They brought comfort to her self-imposed solitude.

The independence, the knowledge that she was reliant upon herself for everything—nourishment, shelter, even social interactions—grew gradually more familiar. Solitude, to her, had felt at first like an ill-fitting coat. Not quite the right size, but good enough to keep the elements at bay. Now she felt herself growing into it.

She was heading to where the sun began its daily journey— east. She set her course each day by the rising sun, shedding the skin of her former life with every rotation of the earth.

Though the forest was dense, she had chosen a route that kept her close to a wide river. The nearness of the water comforted her, allowing her the opportunity to occasionally travel in the cool, running waters, enjoying her alternate form. Keeping her clothing tightly wrapped in waterproof seal fur, Clíodhna threw the bundle ahead of her, allowing the current to carry it along.

Every time she entered the water and allowed herself to transform, her thoughts ran back to her family, her people far away to the west, in the waters of Ireland. Clíodhna would note the hours of the day as they passed and mark her time against the monotonous, rigid schedule she had once kept.

The survival tasks of her tribe, carefully constructed over the centuries to ensure the success of her people, had been one of the main reasons for her departure. The bulk of the work had always fallen on the females, while the males enjoyed a different sort of existence, under the pretenses of saving their strength for when the need for protection arose. Her brother had never understood her unhappiness. He had not experienced their world the same way she had. He had not seen her life as a repetitive, endless circle, but instead, he thought her perspective and viewpoint had been corrupted. How could she not enjoy being a creature of the sea? Their life was unique, blessed, and holy. How did she not see this?

She had not seen it, because she had been busy scaling fish, tending fires, washing clothes, and cooking, just a few of the many dull tasks she was required to perform, all weighing like a heavy burden upon her small shoulders. To her, it had been a repugnant existence.

And once her brother had made his final decision to marry that land-dweller, her heart had broken into a thousand, tiny shards. She had attempted to gather the pieces and repair herself, but it had proved useless. Her heart would never be whole again, it would never heal.

So she left. Without permission, without a trace. She had simply packed her clothes into a sealskin and headed for the great beyond. She dove into the familiar waters for the last time and swam south and then towards the vast mainland stretching far to the east. Her final goal had been to reach the Eastern Sea. She was strong, capable, and resourceful. She had eventually reached the mainland and set off over the land, questing to find the great ocean to the east.

In the forest, the river current grew stronger. Heavy rains over the previous few days had swelled the waterline so that the river overflowed the banks. Large branches and debris flowed past, occasionally smashing into rocks. White, frothy waters roared in her ears, and Clíodhna found that she could not conceal her smile. She felt more alive than she ever had in her entire life.

Tossing her bundle ahead of her, allowing it to travel of its own accord, Clíodhna dove into the current and listened to the dull, endless howl of the river. She saw fish, so different from the ones she had left behind in the Northern Sea. These were more reminiscent of the forest, their color palette reflective of their surroundings. Brilliant mossy greens, deep russet oranges, and darker tones, as rich and velvety as the soil on which she had walked. Clíodhna watched as they struggled to swim against the current, avoiding her, the large predator in their midst. They passed by her, journeying upriver. Sometimes she saw a river otter or another midsized creature, their sleek bodies undulating in the greenish waters.

Surfacing, she threw her head back and took a deep breath, narrowly avoiding a sizable boulder mid-river. As she looked ahead, she spied the first structure she had seen in nearly a full moon cycle.

A large building sat nestled against a hillside, spanning the entire breadth of the river. An immense wooden frame spun in the current. A waterwheel. The mighty wooden wheel turned, pulling the current into the paddles, up and over, carrying it to deposit on the other side. It had been a long time since she had seen a mill.

Beyond the wheel, the edge of the river seemed to disappear over a precipice, as if she had discovered the edge of the world. She could hear falls. The speed of the churning waterwheel and the mist rising in the distance told her that the drop was considerable. She would need to gather her clothes and get out of the river. *Where were her clothes?* She watched in horror as the bundle bobbed over the lip of the falls and disappeared.

The sun had begun its daily descent, and the light rapidly bled from the sky. Cursing under her breath, Clíodhna made her way to the river's edge, careful to keep her head well below the water. The structure meant land-dwellers. She eyed the building from beneath the surface and swam towards the nearest bank. Constantly looking around her, cautious of the storm's debris, Clíodhna propelled herself forward, then suddenly stopped.

Something large moved off to her right. She turned and worked her body to hold her position in the current. Large rocks loomed off to her right. Something was moving among them. The pale-green murk obscured her vision. She caught movement again, just beyond the limits of her peripheral vision. Familiar, a swift, serpentine, undulating motion. Then it was gone.

An icy shiver went up Clíodhna's spine. Something felt wrong. Steeling herself, she flexed her claws, then moved towards the immense boulders. She ran her tongue over her sharp teeth, then opened and closed her jaw, loosening the tight muscles within.

The setting sun made the waters ever darker, forcing her eyes to adjust to the fading light. Another flash of movement, this time off to her left. She snapped her head around. But it was only a log, spinning in the swift current, bobbing and crashing towards the falls. Keeping her focus on the place where she had seen the rippling motion, she moved towards the boulders, closing the distance between herself and the riverbank.

From beneath the surface, she could make out the shadow of the giant wheel, moving endlessly in an infinite circle. Large pylons supported the structure above, ending deep in the sandy bottom, securing themselves amid piles of granite. She peered up through the wheel and could see the mill. The gaps in the treads flashed in front of her line of vision. One second she could see the wheel's support beams, the steepness of the bank. The next, she saw only bars of wood. The turning created a staggered, flashing view of what was beyond the wheel, creating a mesmerizing effect. Clíodhna felt calm as she watched the ceaseless spinning—riverbank, wood, riverbank, wood, a dark figure, riverbank, wood. *A dark figure?* She cocked her head to the side.

As quickly as she saw it, the shadow of whatever else lurked in the water disappeared, absorbed into the fading light. Perhaps a log, perhaps not.

Unnerved, Clíodhna drifted. She felt the need to surface, but suddenly the strong pull of the wheel sucked her towards it. Panic ignited in her cold chest. She struggled. The immense, churning, wooden structure pulled at her, threatening to crush her between wood and stone. A cry tore loose from her throat as she pushed harder to distance herself from the turning apparatus, but as much as she tried, she couldn't escape the wheel.

Her gills fluttered rapidly as she struggled, desperately searching the waters for anything that might help her escape. She started to loose her forward momentum. While her overly large eyes widened, she futilely clawed the water, grasping for nonexistent purchase.

The roar of the wheel thrummed in Clíodhna's head, competing with the rapid pounding of her heart. She slipped closer and closer, the mechanism eager to devour her.

As the first splinter of wood struck her pale fin, she felt a

tight grip on her arm, pulling her from destruction. She struggled to see through the gloom of the turbulent waters. Silt and
debris churned, spinning past her face, tearing small lines in
her skin as they flew past. *Friend or foe?* Her will to escape the
wheel outweighed her fear of whatever grasped her arm.

She reached out, wildly grasping with her other hand to feel
what held her. To her surprise, Clíodhna discovered the familiar
feeling of another hand on her arm. She grabbed the owner of
the mysterious hand firmly on the wrist, strengthening their
bond, and prayed that the person's strength could save them
both.

In an eternity of seconds, she broke the surface of the water
and narrowed her eyes. In the dim light, she saw a man, who
was not just a man, treading water beside her.

Like those of a frog, two bulbous eyes with irises the color of
river silt nestled themselves on either side of a massive skull, an
enormous brow stretching across it. Not even both of Clíodhna's
hands could span the distance between his mud-colored eyes.
Thick hair sprouted above each bulging eye, giving the man a
menacing disposition. Beneath his ears, she could see gill slits,
the telltale sign of another water dweller. The dark hair on his
head fell in stringy locks framing his square face, while his facial
hair was patchy and interrupted by ragged, crooked scars that
crisscrossed his face like an old road map. The jagged lines ran
across his cheeks, over his wide, flat nose, and zigzagged across
his broad chin. His mouth drew most of her attention. Like a
frog's, it stretched from ear to ear, creating the widest mouth
she had ever seen. Large fleshy lips curled over themselves, only

partially obscured by the stray curly hairs sprouting from his massive, tangled beard.

His features and chiseled face, harshly weathered by both sun and wind, stared at Clíodhna. He cocked his head to the side, then grinned.

The hideous smile sent Clíodhna backwards, away from her malformed savior. Something in his eyes had set her off. *The window to the soul*, her mother had once said. These windows were dark, cloudy, ominous. Every fiber in her being screamed for her to get away. She recoiled instinctively.

His face changed suddenly in response to her reaction as a vicious snarl flashed across his floppy lips. His hands, webbed like hers, the same hands that had just saved her, reached out, grabbing her arm and tearing into her hair. She screamed as she felt the strands rip from her scalp.

They went under. The wheel roared, the water churned, Clíodhna screamed in spite of the uselessness of her cries. There was no one to help her, no family, no kin to hear her distress and rush to her aid. She had done this to herself, balked in the face of the unknown. She had been foolish to believe herself invincible. And now her folly would be her undoing.

Reaching out, Clíodhna tore into the muscular flesh of his arm, dragging her own claws deep into the sinew of his fore-arm. But he did not let go. His grip tightened, tearing into her skin and muscle. The blood swirled around the pair as they descended. Curious fish, drawn to the movement and strong scent of blood, flickered at a safe distance, circling just out of reach, like crows awaiting carrion.

She braced herself, fearing that he would throw her into the wheel and allow the great mechanism to shred her to pieces, but he did not. With incredible strength, he resisted the pull and dove below it, Clíodhna in tow.

In horror, she glanced up and into the belly of the giant wooden structure, steadily moving, endlessly spinning. For the second time, she found herself drawn to the peaceful turning. The wheel seemed to call to her with a soothing, comforting voice that, in other circumstances, would have held her captivated like a small child. Now the harshness of her reality snapped her away from the alluring call. As it turned, she felt her innocence fleeing, being torn from her, lost in the spin.

Near the steepness of the bank, she saw something that turned her heart to stone. There, chained to the embankment, an iron cage swayed in the strong current, tethered by a heavy chain. It was not empty.

A pale, bloated corpse of a woman floated in the current. Dark locks of hair flowed away from the lifeless scalp, downstream towards the falls. They headed straight for her.

Clíodhna looked at her captor in horror. In defiance, she spun her body towards him and bit down hard on his thick wrist. He cried out and let go. Clíodhna broke free, but the strong current grabbed her and sucked her towards the wheel.

She didn't care. The dead woman in the cage nodded in approval as the wheel took her. A huge wooden slat smashed into her back, knocking her into a bent position, wrapping her around the wood, her head almost touching her backside. The sharp angle stunned her for a moment, preventing her from crying out. As she regained her senses, she reached up and grabbed the next slat before it smashed her in the face. Spinning around, she saw the man propel himself towards her. Her fingers connected with the wood and she used it to her advantage. The wheel took her and she ascended. The male, the cage, the corpse, all rapidly disappeared from view. As she surfaced, she considered letting go but thought better of it and grasped the side of the wheel with her other arm. Her lower extremities dangled below her as she rode upwards.

The forest with its serpentine river dividing it in half like a gaping wound opened up before her. Elegant in the dim gloaming, trees allowed their leaves to reach out and grab the last remaining light of the day, holding it in their vibrant greenness. The small stone mill adjacent to the river glowed a brilliant orange, bathed in the retreating golden light. It appeared peaceful and inviting. The whole world around her seemed to beckon Clíodhna, whispering to her, coaxing her to join the night.

The wheel continued turning, bringing her to the other side. She saw the falls. Frothy, white waters screamed and tore at the jagged, violent rocks that lined the drop-off. Clíodhna's eyes grew wider. Whipping her head from left to right, she searched for a solution. There, along the lip of the falls, two large boulders, both the size of swollen haystacks, held a thick tree trunk from plummeting over the edge. A variety of debris piled up behind it, creating a ragged nest of sticks and storm carnage.

Pulling herself upwards as the wooden wheel thrust her forward into the empty air, she spun around and willed her legs into existence. The change came slowly, and she feared she would not make it in time. Her newly formed feet came to rest on the slat below, and she bent forward, diving toward the twin rocks.

Her body sliced through the air, and she hit her mark. As she slammed into the river wreckage, sticks and branches tore into her skin, leaving long, crimson gashes along her pale body. The crack of the wood heralded her impact, startling birds, recently roosted for the night, into flight. They screeched and fled for the heavens.

The water stung her wounds, and she gasped. She squinted in the low light, searching the river's edge, looking for a good place to climb out of the river. She spied a sandy bank, worn away by the current, a viable exit point.

Clíodhna winced at the pain that spread deep across her back. Her muscles cried out, fatigued from the stress of the events and the strain of her struggle. She was so close to escape. Rest would come later. She calmed her mind, focused on her nerves, her muscles, her skin, willing the change to come.

It did not come.

She tried again, breathing the night air deep into her lungs, concentrating on what needed to be done. *Nothing.* She would have to swim with her legs. Panic settled into her chest, but she willed it away, forcing her heart to stop fluttering. Gritting her teeth, Clíodhna pushed off from the decaying tree trunk and took a deep breath. She dove down into the darkness, trying once again to force the change. It continued to resist her call.

She surfaced. Using her arms and kicking her long legs, she moved along the surface of the water. A long mournful cry came from somewhere along the riverbank, a dove called to its lost partner. Insects orchestrated their bodily instruments, filling the evening with song. Transfixed by the night music, she never heard her pursuer surface. Never heard him appear behind her.

The blow came to her head. A blinding white pain, bursting brilliant displays behind her now closed eyes. It was excruciating, consuming her awareness. She drifted into the night sky, far above her prone body. Held in a dark embrace, entwined with a most violent man, Clíodhna floated in the river, her fair hair fanning out around the strange pair. From somewhere in the night sky, she felt his hot, rancid breath on the back of her long neck. Then his strong arms encircled her body even more tightly as he dove down into the river.

The Merrow Codex
Species Archive
#12 - Vodník

Caratocos, elder scholar

*Encountered by Jonas, Seafarer, circa 1400 AD,
on an overland trip to the far Eastern Sea. All
following information herewith transcribed was
accounted to me, Caratocos, upon Jonas's return
to our waters.*

Believing himself to be in the Bohemian region of the Great Continent, close to the Germanic tribal lands, Jonas came in contact with a strange, aquatic creature prevalent in the northern Slavic regions. It was called a *Vodník* or *Vodenjak*. He had been traveling by river through great forests when he first encountered the creature sitting on the bank, staring out across the swift-moving waters. Male, muscular, and hulking, the creature had long, unkempt hair that fell around large bulging eyes, while its wide, gaping mouth sat beneath an odd, flat nose. The greenish scaled skin, like kelp, was similar to our own. It had a tail that seemed longer, more serpentine than ours, curling and uncurling in the rushing river.

While it sat, pushing lips laden with excessive skin in and out, Jonas silently moved out of the water and hid himself in the trees, eager to observe such an odd specimen. The creature did not move. It sat still, seemingly waiting for the sky to grow dark and the day to come to an end. Jonas had nearly abandoned his post to search for appropriate shelter for the night when he heard a shout from the opposite bank.

Across the way, two men stood. One was in a state of enragement for he was bound at both wrist and thigh, making his movements stunted and haphazard. His captor stood by his side with his hand firmly grasped around the bound man's arm.

Who were these strange fellows? Jonas did not know, but he feared discovery and so kept himself hidden. The creature on Jonas's bank, however, seemed very excited by the arrival of such a pair and began to splash the water. It jubilantly revealed and gnashed its great teeth, now released from the confines of its overly fleshy lips.

The captive man heard the splashing across the river and recoiled at the sight of the horrible creature. The bound man fell to his knees, pleading with his captor to be freed. The captor paid little attention to the pleading man and instead pushed the unfortunate soul into the river—without removing the binds.

The man fell like a stone, sinking down beneath the current, then surfaced, his head bobbing up and down in the rushing waters.

The creature dove in towards the man and disappeared. He resurfaced an arm's length from the drowning captive who wailed, fruitlessly, for salvation.

At this point in his telling, Jonas grew distraught. It took him some time to collect himself before he could continue the story of the bound man. With a heavy heart filled with despair, Jonas finally concluded his tale. The man in the river, rest his soul, became fodder for the wide-mouthed creature, who happily tore the man apart, eating every bit of him as if he were at his last meal. Once the captor had disappeared into the forest on the other side of the river and the satiated creature had swum away in the current, Jonas sent a message to our own gods—a prayer on behalf of the fallen man's soul.

However, this horrific scene did not mark the end of Jonas's interactions with the creature known as the Vodník or Vodenjak. Fate had more in store for Jonas.

Several months later, while traveling as a land-dweller in a colder climate north of the awful scene on the river, Jonas entered a tavern in search of warmth and food. Having learned the rudimentary basics of the local language, Jonas struck up a conversation with the tavern keeper who inquired about Jonas's lodgings for the evening. Jonas stated that he would be taking shelter not far from the tavern, along the banks of a well-known, nearby river. The tavern keeper would not hear of it and bade Jonas to stay in the stables for the evening. Jonas had protested, not wanting to sleep so close to people he did not know.

The persistent tavern keeper insisted, his arms flailing, his face growing redder and redder. Jonas, unfamiliar with some of the more subtle colloquialisms, found himself at loss when it came to the translation and meaning of the owner's protests. The tavern keeper pressed on, trying to make Jonas understand that a malevolent beast known as a Vodník swam in the river, eager to devour any lost soul it might encounter in its travels.

Realization dawned on Jonas. *Could this be the same creature he had encountered a few months prior? Yet he was so far from that location ...*

He asked the tavern keeper if this Vodník traveled long distances—perhaps an odd question to ask. The tavern keeper did not know but further insisted that Jonas spend the night, which, reluctantly, he did.

No ill events presented themselves to our dear Seafarer that night under the tavern keeper's care. Jonas rose in the morning to lend a hand with the chores and even stayed on a few extra days to help with the building of casks. Then Jonas said his farewells to the tavern keeper and his family and continued to the river. He kept to the banks, always keeping the river on his right side, frequently climbing the tall trees along the shore, searching for the fabled and feared creature.

After two days, Jonas found him. This particular specimen of Vodník appeared much larger than the one he had encountered to the south. Nearly the size of a horse, the creature's enormous head sat like a great boulder upon thick, broad shoulders. Its immense tail, thick and long, coiled alongside the great beast like a serpent. Just like its cousin to the south, this northern giant had greenish skin and eyes that bulged like those of an oversized fish.

It sat perched on a rock near the riverbank, its massive head staring dumbly down, while it slowly and repeatedly unfurled and recoiled its impressive tail. Jonas took one look at the thing and decided to leave it well enough alone.

Vodník, he thought to himself, *should be avoided at all costs.*

Having seen what the other, much smaller beast had done to that poor captive, Jonas crept silently back into the forest and determined to return to the waters of home, far away from such violent creatures.

Once he had finished telling me his tale, Jonas expressed a desire to put aside his seafaring ways. I do not believe that he has left the waters of home since then.

Dolský Mill
Confluence of the
Elbe and Kamenice rivers
Bohemia
Late Summer 1607

Clíodhna

She inhaled the smell of hay, mildew, and oil. A haze of light, like a kaleidoscope of colors, flickered beyond her lids. Clíodhna did not want to open her eyes. If she didn't open them, it didn't exist. This reality, this moment of her long life—one that, until now, had been filled with joy and wonder—would not be truth, if she just kept her eyes shut.

The passage of time felt foreign to her. Behind closed lids, she observed the light changing from dark to light and back again, while the noises of her surroundings flitted in and out of her ears. The early evening music of the birds and the insects accompanied the rising darkness, always framed by the roar of the wheel, spinning nearby. She could hear the large slats endlessly slapping the water, pushing through the surface, only to return and repeat the task on the other side.

A warm breeze flowed over Clíodhna's bare skin and she shivered, then turned her head to the side. Her eyes still closed, a single tear ran down her cold cheek. Her initial wounds had healed, dressed by her captor, but his kindness had ended there. Coarse fibers scratched and tore into her skin at her wrists and ankles, now worn raw from useless struggling. But the pain between her legs was the worst. The beast-man with the greenish skin and disgusting, wide mouth had inflicted horrors on her prone, restrained body. She had heard of this act, had known that it could happen, but never believed that she would fall prey to another. Not her. She was merrow, born strong and proud, a carrier of ancient blood that coursed through a species known for its strength and vitality. Among her kin, these acts were normally confined to the rituals of courtship, of procreation by two individuals dedicated to the honor of continuing the bloodline. Here they had been inflicted upon her without her permission or consent. In the beginning, each and every time he climbed on top of her to satisfy his urges, regardless of her protests and screams, he stoked a fire in her being, adding coal after coal to the furnace of her rage. But over time, as the days shifted to night and back to day again, the fire had dwindled into a smolder that threatened to expire, much like Clíodhna.

At first, she had attempted to transform, to will the flesh of her legs into one, hoping against hope that the force of her transformation would rip through the heavy binds that held her prisoner. But her ability to change had completely left her.

She concentrated over and over again, to no avail. The hell of her situation spiraled before her in an infinite chain of violent events, and so she chose to surrender, to allow death to come for her. She chose to never again open her eyes.

Perhaps sensing the change, the loss of fight in his imprisoned plaything, her captor attempted to feed her, forcing a wooden spoon overflowing with some sort of foul-smelling stew between her lips, but the act—*was it kindness? mercy?*—only reminded her of the forceful act inflicted on the rest of her body. She refused his nourishment. Once, her eyes still closed, she spit the food into his face. Her act of defiance was answered with a hard slap across the face. And so the days passed away. Her will to live expired with each turning of day into night. She drifted. Halfway between her hellish reality and halfway between memories, long gone.

They, the stories of her past, came to her like smoke from a cooking fire, swirling through her self-imposed darkness, imploring her to escape, and then becoming more tangible, more urgent like the call of a loved one to come home. Her mind conjured sensory details, and their richness both comforted and cradled her broken body and soul.

She saw the rocky shore of her birth, its crags and sharp edges a danger to most, but not to her, not to her kind. The smell of the surf, a deep, acrid smell, steeped in the thick brine of the mother sea. Brilliant, lush greens and blues and the frothiest of frothy whites, all in flux, all forever moving, ebbing, and returning. She recalled the exhilaration of finishing her daily tasks, the knowledge that she was free from her routine, free to explore the coast, to join her darling brother, the other half of her cleaved soul.

Running from the small stone cottage, her mother calling to her, some sort of a warning, the mothering warning, easily ignored by all carefree offspring. She shed her clothing, not caring where her shift landed. She would find it later, it was not important now. The ocean called to her, sang to her, and she heeded the call. At the water's edge, the surf pounded the sand over and over again, then pulled away, like a shy lover. Her body tingled, almost burned, as her skin, her muscles, all of her being responded to the song of the sea.

Clíodhna shivered, holding off the change until she reached the safety of hip-deep waters. Then she dove. Her body rippled like the deep blue surface, her skin unfolding like an exotic flower to expose the beauty of her true form. Her eyes widened, her pupils enlarging to adapt to the darkness. Pulling in water through the gills in her neck, she felt the rush of oxygen as she transferred her intake. The indescribable joy of the change was something she repeatedly wished she could share with her land-dwelling cousins. She felt pity for them, pity that they would never experience this part of their shared world.

Seeking the kelp beds, she often searched for seals and other marine life, greeting them cautiously, not wanting to offend a protective mother guarding her new offspring. The seals spun in their folly, chasing one another, nipping at the slower-moving, older members of their family.

Gliding through the water, she trained her ears and used her sense of smell to detect her twin. She heard him off to the north, where she knew he would be. Clíodhna surfaced and scanned the horizon. In the distance, she saw him break through.

Ciabhán.

Her twin shook his head and beads of water flew in all directions, catching the light, sending prisms of color across the cloudless blue sky. He thrust his arm, holding a spear laden with fish, high over his dark head. He spun one way, then the other, and she saw a look of irritation, then amusement appear on his angular face. A seal poked its snout up alongside her brother, snapping at his catch. In response, Ciabhán placed the flat of his palm on the young pup's nose, gently pushing him down.

She smiled to herself, a warm secret smile that she reserved for him, and him alone. No one else brought her as much joy as he did. She knew the way she felt for her brother upset her mother, but she didn't care. He was hers and would always be hers. Clíodhna felt no need to seek the comfort of another.

From across the expanse of water that separated her soul from his, her brother, who had once held her in their mother's womb, looked up at her, and they caught one another's gaze. But alarm filled her twin's eyes. He raised both his arms and waved them frantically, shouting something she could not understand.

Clíodhna squinted, trying to decipher his words. She struggled to hear him, to understand his warning. Fear entered her heart and drove her back to the foul bed where her body, no longer hers alone, now lay in the darkness waiting for the monster to leave her. The North Atlantic disappeared, her beloved faded back into her memory.

She wept openly at her loss, cursing herself for leaving the comfort and safety of her home. Clíodhna now understood the warnings of the elders. Their warnings had come to fruition. This was her new life, and it was not a life worth living. In time, fatigue arrived and claimed her for his sullen bride, smothering her consciousness with the relief of a fitful sleep.

Time moved. A slow and steady climb towards an unknown destination, and during that journey, something changed. Somewhere in the depths of her soul, in the place she had carved out to escape her life, to await death, she felt a change in her existence. It was a strange feeling, a feeling that somehow she was no longer alone.

A life force, foreign to her, took control, and she felt her body strengthen. Her senses heightened. The foulness of her captor's smell grew ever more intolerable. The nearness of him forced her to dry heave and convulse.

Then one day she smelled something else, something warm and pleasant, a scent of food that gave her hope in a way she could not explain. She sniffed the air, still not opening her eyes, and breathed in the wonders of this new scent. Something stirred in her abdomen. Was it a hunger, or was it something else? Day after day the scent returned, wafting into her nose. She found herself aching for it, looking forward to it. Something was happening to her. Something different.

She was with child.

The idea filled her with horror, and yet, she could not deny it, she felt hope and excitement. This child was hers, fed by her body, despite its foul origins. Her captor may have been the catalyst for this new life, but she and she alone was the creator from here forward.

The knowledge forced Clíodhna to open her eyes. And for the first time in a long time, she opened her mouth and screamed, allowing her voice to echo off the walls of her prison. Her eyes, blurred from underuse, had trouble focusing. She was in a room with walls of stone and no windows. Light streamed in from a narrow opening—*a door?*—off to her right. When she turned towards it, the world seemed too bright, too disorienting. She heard footsteps on the stairs, growing louder and louder until the light-filled rectangle dimmed—*him*.

Even more disgusting than she remembered, the sight of his face, with his overly large lips and knotted, unkempt hair, filled her with complete revulsion, but she kept her emotions inside, not wanting to give away any more of herself than she already had. The two stared at one another. Captor and captive.

She made a decision in that moment. She thought of her child, imagined the tiny face that would not look anything like this creature, but would look like her, would look up at her mother with love and only love. With this thought, she looked at the man, and Clíodhna attempted to soften her gaze.

The large creature returned her expression. A crooked, broken venture at what might be considered a smile crawled across his scarred and ragged face. He sat down beside her on the bed, and she fought all of her impulses to recoil from his presence. Instead, she opened her mouth like a tiny fish in search of sustenance. She stuck out her chin, and opened her mouth again and again, hoping to relay her need for food to this foul man.

Cocking his head from side to side, he looked at her with curiosity but not understanding. Clíodhna continued with her hunger pantomime until realization spread over him, his eyes brightened, and the horrible thing fled the room. She heard him crash down the stairs and then the rustling noises of him moving about. The banging on the stairs heralded his return to where she lay, bound, naked, and exposed.

He sat back down beside her on the bed and placed something soft in her mouth. The moment it passed her lips, she recognized the smell, the same smell of hope and life. *Bread.* She ate eagerly, swallowing, nearly choking on the large chunks of dark warmth that the man anxiously provided as if she were a tiny bird still in the nest.

In this way, he fed her and then stroked her hair as if she were a dog. When the light in the doorway faded away to nothing, he left her alone in the darkness of the night. With food in her belly, Clíodhna gazed up for the first time at the wooden ceiling above her and listened to the night birds as they called to one another somewhere beyond the confines of her room.

Morning came, and the man returned with something brown and familiar in his giant gnarled hands. He had found her seal-skin bundle. With a tenderness she had not yet seen from this strange, foul creature, the man unbound her wrists, then her legs, and helped her to her feet. She stumbled and collapsed into his arms. The smell of him was nearly unbearable, but Clíodhna understood her tenuous situation. Her actions would either destroy her, or hopefully, with luck, prolong her life for yet another day. She kept her face still, devoid of emotions. The man propped her up, but seeing that she was unable to stand on her own, sat her back down on the bed. Then the man did something astonishing. He dressed her.

When he finished, he rebound her ankles and wrists, this time leaving Clíodhna in a sitting position on the bed.

The joy of wearing her own garments, of smelling her own smell and the faint scent of her own people, brought her tremendous joy. The man looked at her and saw the happiness in her face. His ugly features softened, and he reached out to touch the hem of her collar. A tender gesture. Clíodhna did her best to keep her heart rate steady, her face placid like the waters on a windless day. If she was to get away, she did not want to incite his wrath. Instead, she attempted to reach out to his face, but could not, the restraints on her arms limited her movement, her gesture falling short of its mark.

A cloud crossed his face, as if a great sadness filled him. He dropped his large hand from her neck and placed it on her wrist. She attempted to implore him with her eyes, looking at his face, then down at her bound wrists.

Abruptly, the man stood. He gritted his teeth, grinding them, creating a most wretched scratching. She thought for certain that he would set himself on her again, and the horrors of the past few months would begin anew. But he did not. The man howled an awful, bubbling cry. Then he left the room.

She heard a door slam somewhere on a level below her, and then the world grew quiet. Uncertain as to what she should do—*Would he return? Should she try to leave?*—she waited. She had no answers.

He did not return for three days. Accustomed to her prison, she felt gratitude for a full belly and the clothes on her back, but when he did not come back after the second day, she grew frantic. On the morning of the third day, she tried again, thrashing with all her might, to pull free of the large ropes that cut into her tender flesh. The pressure in her bladder and bowels grew unbearable, and she soiled her clothes. She cried out, hoping that perhaps he could hear her and would come to her aid. Nothing. She heard the wind, the rushing of the river, and nothing else. In anger, she screamed, all of her frustrations pouring out of her in a shrill cry. Exhausted from her exertion, she hung her head. That's when she noticed the knife on the floor, the tip of the blade sticking out from under the bed.

The light was fading from the day, but a single ray of sunlight shone through the open doorway catching the blade just so as it reflected a duplicate image of itself on the stone wall beside her.

Stretching out her leg, she could almost get her foot near the knife. Clíodhna tried again. The rope cut deeply into her ankle, but she pushed through it, ignoring the blood as it ran down her foot. Using what little strength she had left, she extended her leg one more time. She gritted her teeth and strained as she stretched. A crack filled the air as the rope broke free of the bed and her foot slammed down on the blade.

She whooped in delight at her success. Using her toes, she slid the knife closer to her. After several attempts, she managed to use her toes to grab the wooden handle, pulling it up onto the bed beside her where she could grab it with one hand.

He had left enough play in the restraints to allow her arms more freedom of motion. This was her chance, but as she brought the blade up to cut the ropes that bound her wrists, she heard the door open and slam downstairs. He had returned.

Panic coursed through her veins, and she slid the knife between her breasts, hiding it in the confines of her bodice. There was nothing she could do about the loose rope by her ankle. So she let it be, settled in, and attempted to calm her racing heart. She waited again for him to appear.

The stairs shook with the pounding of his great weight. He burst into the room, a line of dead quail and fish held aloft, a strange hideous grin on his wide face. His expression changed as he took in her soiled clothes and the ripped restraint on her leg. It was the look of a child realizing that his pet needed care, care he had forgotten to give.

Dropping his bounty on the floor, the man bent down and loosened her restraints. He spent the next hour cleaning and washing her body with great care. After that, he never disappeared again.

One day he left her legs unbound for the entire day, rebinding them before nightfall. The next day, he unbound her arms. The following week, he removed her restraints altogether. To Clíodhna's surprise, he led her down the stairs, taking great care with her severely atrophied muscles as she descended the narrow wooden staircase. He guided her, like a child, into a room where the mighty wheel turned a giant stone, grinding wheat into flour. He placed her on a sack on the floor, where she spent the day, watching him work. His size and strength allowed him to perform the work of two, possibly three, men. Often he would complete a task and look to her, giving a nod in her direction, adoration shining in his beady eyes. She would nod back, a coy smile on her lips, her heart a cold, cold stone.

Her legs were not strong, and her range of motion was limited. It bothered her to be unable to walk very far without becoming winded, but she endured it and took the nourishment he gave her. Living alone, she surmised, he had developed the ability to cook with skill. As the days passed and her strength grew, he made her stews comprised of quail, fish, and other meats she could not identify, which she devoured like an animal. He laughed as she held the simple wooden bowl to him, begging for more.

The stew was often accompanied by the aromatic bread she had grown to crave. Noticing her love of the bread, one day he gave her honey, smiling shyly as he left it next to a small, round boule. Graciously, she accepted the gift, nodding in approval at the sweet delicacy laid before her. They had no way of talking to one another, their languages being so completely dissimilar. Most communications took place through hand gestures, including a lot of pointing.

He no longer attempted to mate with her. The relief was immeasurable. She assumed he felt secure in his belief that she would not attempt to leave. Therefore, his need to dominate her was no longer necessary. Perhaps he thought of her as his wife now. She could adopt this role. This was something she could pretend, something she could use to her advantage.

One day, she sat idly on the stone floor observing the

strange man at his work. Leaning back, she stretched her arms over her head and felt a strange movement in her abdomen. It startled her, and she cried out. The man turned, alarmed, and stared at Clíodhna. Understanding what it was, she smiled and reached out to the man, guiding his hand to her swelling stomach.

He knelt down on the stone floor beside her with his greenish hair, his clothes, his face all dusted with pale powder. The man's hand stayed on her belly for a long time. He held his breath. A few moments passed and the quickening came anew, a small pulse against his hand. Clíodhna felt it and her eyes rose from her lap to the man's face. His wide mouth grew into a gruesome smile, his bulbous eyes lit from within. He nodded to her, and she nodded back.

The days passed, the winter passed. Her body changed, and as the life grew within her, so did something else. The beastly man had grown more gentle, more careful in the way he treated her. He brought her gifts—a woven blanket and a new dress, though the origin of such a dress filled her with a sort of dread as she remembered the corpse in the cage beneath the wheel. Nonetheless, kindness warmed his demeanor, and Clíodhna wondered if this new existence, this new life could work for her. Clíodhna looked at her captor with new eyes, and something cold in her heart warmed just the slightest bit.

Could she grow to love the grotesque creature who had imprisoned her, violated her, made her with child? Could she overlook these things if the now was infinitely more secure than the days of the past? Most of her being fought against these small, nagging notions, but as the child grew, her resolve to leave diminished. Could this be her destiny? To stay with this man?

She thought of the child within her. She thought of the knife, hidden beneath her bed. She needed more time. How could she survive in the woods on her own, with child? How would she give birth alone? Perhaps the decision would be made clear once her child came into the world.

Longing to go outdoors, to walk along the river and experience the change from winter to spring, Clíodhna looked longingly out the small window at the top of the stairs. Her captor had yet to allow her to leave the mill. Whenever she ventured near the door, he gently guided her back to the interior, shaking his head, a strange smile on his frog-like face.

Often, as if she were a child easily distracted, he would provide her with something to amuse her attentions. Sometimes it was a strange trinket he had fashioned from bits of wood and reed. Once it was a necklace made of metal and pale blue stones.

He sensed her continued boredom and brought her other, more practical things to amuse her. He brought her his clothing to be mended, which at first offended her. However, this had been part of her duties at home, and so she had taken up the task. Another time, to her delight, he placed a fishing net near her feet. She spent many days deftly improving the neglected tool and was rewarded with fish stew the evening following the completion of her work.

But the outside world still called to her, and she kept a

watchful eye for an opportunity to go out alone. Now that she was no longer bound, the man rarely left the building except to hunt and gather food. One day, soon after the sun had set, she heard a voice from beyond the river. Someone shouting, a drunken sort of singing. The man looked at her and she at him. In all the time that she had been in the man's presence, she had never heard nor seen another living soul.

Clíodhna stood up from her chair and moved towards the window. The man stood abruptly, and anger, a fury that she had not seen since their earlier times together, tore over the man's face like a storm racing across the horizon. He pushed her back down into her chair and scanned the room, his eyes frantic. Clíodhna felt fear return to her heart but did nothing to resist the man as he bound her to the chair.

Grabbing a knife from the table, the man extinguished the candles and crept out the door, leaving Clíodhna alone, bound to her chair in the dark. In his haste, the man had not tied the ropes tightly enough, and Clíodhna had little trouble slipping free. The ropes slid from her wrists and coiled in a heap on the floor at her feet. Moving easily in the dark, she, too, went out into the night.

The chill of the evening greeted her, making the hair on the back of her neck stand up. Her skin rippled with tiny bumps. She had been used to the coolness of the stone building, but it was far cooler outside. Early spring insects, just waking from their long naps, buzzed and orchestrated songs, finding one another in the darkness. She paused and listened.

At first, she heard nothing, only the insects. Then she heard a faint noise, a splashing, close to the river's edge. Clíodhna moved, barefooted, as always, across the new, dew-laden grass, and made her way down to the water.

The full moon had risen quickly, shining down like a great, luminous pearl. Its pale light bathed all that it touched. The river's surface danced in the moonlight, a thousand points of light flowing towards the great wheel and then on to the falls beyond, farther than Clíodhna had ever been.

The splashing continued, farther upriver, drawing her curiosity like a moth to a flame. As she drew closer, she heard a low moan, followed by a violent scraping and grinding. Beneath a small grove of trees, she saw movement. Clíodhna ducked behind a large boulder near the riverbank and crawled to the top to gain a better vantage point.

The scene before her drained all the blood from her face, and she almost lost her grip and slid down the great rock. The activity below burned into her consciousness, scarring her and forever changing her view of the man—her captor. She had once believed him to be a monster. Then she thought otherwise. What lay before her, his true nature on display, confirmed all that she had first believed. She could never stay with this man, could never raise a child with him. He was evil incarnate, and he needed to be destroyed.

Another moan came from the grisly scene below. A man, the one whose drunken voice had previously filled the evening with song, lay drenched and dying before her while the beast of a man fed on his shoulder, tearing away large chunks of flesh with his wide, cavernous maw.

Clíodhna closed her eyes and felt bile rise to the back of her throat. Moving as quietly as she could, she crept back down the rock and returned to the mill.

As she wound the ropes around her ankles and wrists, her mind grew calm and her plan became clear.

She would destroy him, or she and their child would die trying.

Evie

"Hey, Rachael! Come over here. Let me look at you. Take it all in."

Hazel Johnson grabbed both of Rachael's hands in her own and held them up in the air, giving her a slow once-over. When she was done with her inspection, she grabbed Rachael's waist and kissed her full on the lips. I watched in horror.

"Oh," she said, glancing over Rachael's shoulder. "Hello, Evie." Her tone was flat—like her ass.

Okay, that's not entirely true. Her ass is not flat. It's very toned. I only say this because Hazel is hot and she knows it. She always has this sophisticated, bohemian-chic thing going on, like she just stepped out of the pages of one of those catalogs named after a university department, like *Archaeology* or *Ichthyology*.

Hazel's thick, full hair, always neatly secured in a high pony-tail, swings when she walks—in time with her perfect ass. Her voice is like a lounge singer's, all coos and purrs, like audible honey. *Then there are her shoes.* Always gorgeous. Always expensive. The shoes are reason enough for me to hate the bitch. She must have one hell of a closet. I have never seen her wear the same shoes twice. Not that I notice her shoes. Every single time I see her.

Because I don't.

The other half of Hazel's perfection, Shep Johnson, moseyed over. He's the kind of guy who does that—*moseys.* He's all swag when he walks. Also very toned, Shep has a way of carrying himself so that he appears taller than his true height—think certain Scientology actor with a Napoleon complex. His posture is perfect, another contribution to the crazy, charismatic glamour he throws around. And, *just for the record*, what a stupid name. I mean, is that his *real* name? It sounds like a name for either a preschool teacher or a porn star, or both, which is equally disturbing—just like him. Shep is the type of person who can put his arm around you, tell you that you're the worst person in the world, and somehow, you feel grateful to him for letting you know. He just flashes those perfect white teeth and the world melts away.

Oh, and did I mention he has a man-bun? That might be his kryptonite. Then again, I've noticed young chicks dig guys with man-buns. Oh, and scruff. He's a card-carrying member of the around-the-clock-shadow club. It's sexy.

If I had noticed. Which I had not. Mostly.

He looked happy to see me, which I knew was bullshit. It was just part of his charm. A way of letting everyone know that he's ... *a good guy*.

"Evelyn," his voice warm and soft in my ears. *If you like that sort of thing.* "How's Paddy?" *He knows Paddy?*

"He's peachy keen!" *Peachy keen? Who says peachy keen?*

"Great, great. There's sangria at the bar. Go help yourself." Then he winked.

Really? Does everyone equate me with alcohol?

Here's the thing about the Gaspee parade. It's an excuse to get shit-faced by noon. Everyone knows that's what the day is all about. The parade is a byproduct of the drunken annual summer kick-off. In truth, the parade commemorates the anniversary of the burning of the HMS *Gaspee* and is held a couple of weeks after Memorial Day. Perhaps you've heard of *the spark that started the American Revolution?* If not, don't worry. It's not like history's all that important. *(I'm winking here.)* But for those who care, sometime back in the late 1700s, a bunch of pissed-off locals shot a British captain in the groin—then burned his ship.

I guess the guy was a real asshole. And so we Americans, here in Pawtuxet Village, vigorously celebrate our notorious act of sedition by getting drunk on someone's lawn as high school marching bands and tiny-car-driving, fez-wearing old men roll on by.

Whoohoo! 'Merica! Fuck, yeah!

Heading over to the bar, I grabbed a red cup and peered into a vat filled with slices of citrus fruit elegantly floating in greenish liquid. A sign read, *Spicy Jalapeño Mango Sangria.* Interesting. I shrugged and grabbed the ladle. Stirring the beverage, I fondly remembered all the frat parties I had attended in college. Mystery punch had been served at so many of those events. Nothing good exists at the bottom of a red Solo cup. Nothing.

As I was ladling, a tall woman, around my age and wearing a backpack, came over to the bar.

"Hey," I murmured while taking my first sip. *Gah!* It was so spicy it burned my tongue and the back of my mouth. I stared down into the cup while tears ran down my face. Then I drank deeply.

"Have we met before?" said the tall backpack wearer. "I'm Roxy."

I took another gulp of sangria, winced, and coughed out a response. "I don't think so."

"Do you and Hazel ... know each other well?"

I didn't like the pause after *Hazel.*

"Um," I stammered, "I don't know Hazel all that well. I came with Rachael Bass."

"Oh!" she said, all singsongy. I didn't like the sound of that either.

"Rachael and I have been friends a long time," I said as quickly as I could, realizing I was not helping.

"Oh, I get it." Then she winked at me.

What's with all the winking? Was that code for something? Oh God. It was code for something. I wasn't interested in the code, or the winking.

"So ..." My mind raced, desperately searching for anything unrelated to sex. "Are you here alone?"

Roxy grasped her straw with two dainty, black-lacquered fingernails, then sucked hard. Her cheeks puckered, making her cheekbones even more pronounced. She looked over her straw at me and replied slowly, "No. Why do you ask?"

I am, and always will be, a royal troglodyte. *Are you here alone?* Brilliant question. Why don't I just go to a sketchy bar on the wrong side of the tracks and ask if anyone would like to meet me out back to ... you know, trade recipes?

"Um, just making conversation. Oh look, Girl Scouts!" I pointed to the street and waved at the wholesome young girls carrying American flags and a banner advertising their troop number in brightly colored felt. They waved back.

"I came with my husband. He's here somewhere." She looked around, still holding her straw seductively—too seductively. Roxy scanned the crowd with her eyes but did not seem to find what she was looking for. Her gaze returned to me. She frowned.

"Will you excuse me?" she asked and walked away, not awaiting my answer, not needing my permission to excuse her presence.

I found a lawn chair with an excellent street view and settled in. One sangria, two sangria, green sangria, blue sangria. The day flowed on as the parade participants filed past. People came and went, hopping from party to party along the parade route. Many wore running clothes, race numbers still pinned to their shirts. Evidence that they had participated in the annual pre-parade race. Some were drunk. Most were well on their way. *I was well on my way.*

Rachael checked in on me a few times, asking if I was all right. It was a lame attempt at appearing polite. She didn't really care about my well-being, as I'm sure she was on the lookout for her next conquest. I wondered if she and Hazel had ever … I didn't want to finish that thought.

I needed a burger, so I grabbed the arms of my lawn chair and attempted to stand up. *Goddamn it.* Drunk again. My head swam and my tongue felt heavy. I sighed at my idiocy. *The first sign of conflict in my life and what do I do? Go right back to my shitty habits.*

A water cooler with a little spigot near the bottom sat on the edge of the bar. I filled my Solo cup with water, downed it, and repeated. Each time, the water in my red cup grew a little less green from the residual sangria. My head cleared a bit, and I could feel all my cells soaking up the much-needed non-alcohol-based liquid. I breathed in deeply and smelled charred meat. Following that smell led my drunk ass to the grill stationed near the street. Billowing clouds of smoke and the sizzle of cooking fat filled the air. Lucky me. Shep stood manning the grill.

"What can I get for you, Evie? Are you interested in my meat?" He asked with a big, toothy grin. Part of me felt flattered. The other part wanted to throw up in my mouth. Actually, I think I did.

I managed a lame smile. "I just need something to eat. I think I had too much to drink."

"*You?* Too much to drink?" He shook his head, then flipped a burger, smashing it down with the flat side of his spatula. The meat hissed.

I kept my smile in place and chose not to engage. I didn't have the energy. Instead, I grabbed a plate and held it out. Shep dumped a burger on my plate.

"Enjoy!" Then he winked again.

I tilted my head to the side and said in my best fake Southern accent, "I sure will! Thank you, good sir."

I walked away, not looking back, and returned to my chair. The parade, believe it or not, continued on. A bunch of bagpipers, sweating in the early afternoon heat, strolled up the Parkway. Their shrill pipes heralded their approach. I devoured the burger, grateful to have something, anything, in my stomach as I watched the sweaty tartans pass on by.

The sangria fog made it difficult to focus, but I suddenly felt nauseous and, for whatever reason, couldn't shake the notion that someone was staring at me. *Was it the heat? The drink? The stress of the previous few days?* I just wanted to lie down. I looked around for Rachael. I needed to leave, but I couldn't see her. *Had she gone up the street to another party?*

I looked up and down the road. Diagonally across Narragansett Parkway, a vacant lot sat, unwanted by all who saw it—like a blemish on a first date. The house that had originally occupied the space had burned down years before and no one had rebuilt it. Arson and insurance fraud, they said. Who knows. Now the eyesore of a foundation sat neglected, surrounded by weeds, trash, and, sadly, beautiful homes.

Through my drunken haze, I noticed a person staring at me, someone crouched in the rubble of the abandoned lot. I casually looked behind me, thinking there must have been someone behind me attracting this creepy attention. No one stood behind me. I again glanced around me. *Nobody.* Everyone was on the other side of the yard, closer to the bar. I sat alone. I put my plate down on an empty lawn chair, stood up, and walked towards the street. The person did not move. Whoever it was remained in a crouch.

A marching band replaced the bagpipers in the parade lineup. Loud, shiny brass instruments and dark-colored polyester uniforms covered with rope and epaulettes. Brightly colored flags held by girls in what looked like excessively fringed cheerleading outfits flew into the air. One second I could see the figure in the empty lot, the next I could not, my view obscured by fluttering fabric.

I couldn't cross the street. The steady stream of the marching band members was too thick, too obstructive. Instead, I walked down the sidewalk in the direction of the vacant lot, trying to get a better view. My vision cleared. The person stood. Then she pointed at me.

Nomia.

Her hair was loose, and it hung wildly around her shoulders. She looked dirty and thinner than when I had last seen her. A flimsy, once white, tank dress hung on her emaciated form. I stood there, staring at her. She stared back, her bony finger outstretched while loud trumpets blared, filling the space between us. She was mouthing something, but I couldn't make it out.

I felt the coldness of fear crawl up my ankles, giving me goose bumps the whole way up my legs. The blood rushed from my face to my feet and I felt the familiar nausea increase by tenfold. The bile rose in my throat. I had wanted to find her, but she found me. There she stood. Right there, across the street from me. Only twenty feet separating us.

The drummers snapped their sticks against the snares as their feet slapped the pavement in time with their manufactured cadence.

Evie. They are gone …

I could hear her. I closed my eyes and willed her voice out of my mind.

Evie. I am weak.

I squeezed my eyes tightly shut. My hands flew to my ears as I screamed, "Get out! Get out of my head!"

Evie …

"No!" I screamed. "No! No! No! Get out!"

I heard nothing. I opened my eyes. A giant float glided past. A huge flatbed truck piled high with hay bales and young children in Little League uniforms stared down at me—the crazy, screaming lady. Their mouths hung open, and one woman grabbed a pointing child, holding him to her side while shooting me a warning glare. Sweat formed at my hairline, and I could barely breathe. The truck rumbled past, clearing my view.

She had disappeared.

I looked along the parade route and could see her running up the crowded sidewalk towards the Village. I glanced back at Hazel's house. No one had even noticed that I had left or that I had a just made a scene. In a flash, I thought about just letting her go, letting it all go, but then I thought of Richard. Nomia might be my only way of finding him, so I started running towards the Village. Within seconds, I was out of breath. I can't run for shit. But my side of the street was not as congested as Nomia's. I could see her shoving people out of the way as she moved through the crowd.

I caught up to the marching band. I could still see her dark head bobbing up and down in the sea of parade watchers. I saw her cross over the bridge, the very same bridge where I had first encountered her aquatic ass a few years past. Winded, I continued my pursuit. We ran through the business district, the main area of the Village along Broad Street in Cranston. She kept running, past the bars, past the bank, past the post office. And I followed.

My head pounded. I couldn't breathe, and the crowd grew thicker and thicker on my side of the street. But I made sure not to lose sight of her. She cut across the parade route and turned down Sheldon Street, where she had once lived with her husband, David, and her daughter, Pearl, now long gone from the Village. I reached the corner and turned. The street started out flat, then descended quickly as it sloped down towards Pawtuxet Cove. I had turned the corner just as she disappeared down the hill. I realized where she was headed—*the Point*, a long peninsula that ran parallel to Broad Street in the Village. It was lined with beautiful, historic homes, and almost every one had a guaranteed view of the water. The Point was where the wealthier Villagers lived.

Sheldon Street ran west to east, ending at Fort Avenue, which ran north to south. Fort was one of two main streets on the Point; the other was Seaview. As I began my descent down towards Pawtuxet Cove, Nomia turned south on Fort.

An interesting tidbit—Aunt Catherine lives on Sheldon. As I approached her small cottage overlooking the Cove, I could see that her car was not in the driveway. Unsurprisingly, she was not at home. She hates Gaspee Days.

I paused, bent over, and put my hands on my knees, scowling at the perfection of Aunt Catherine's stupid abundance of irises. Thankfully, the nausea had subsided, but I still couldn't catch my breath. I wheezed in and out like a boiling tea kettle. My chest felt incredibly tight, and a slick of sweat covered my entire body.

Should I call out to her? Should I keep following? I no longer heard her voice in my head. I needed to find out what had happened to Richard. I needed to know what that bitch planned to do next. So against all better judgment, I continued to follow her towards the sea. History repeating itself. Except this time, I had the benefit of daylight. Daylight was good. Scary murders don't happen in daylight. *Right?* That sounded comforting. I was going with that.

When I reached Fort, she was already gone, having turned onto Seaview. *Goddamn it!* That bitch was in shape! Wheezing and panting I wogged (walk jogged) after her. I made it around the sharp corner on Seaview and saw her head bobbing along towards the end of the Point. A huge house squatted like an ornate giant behind large iron gates at the very end of the peninsula. I was halfway down the street when I saw her push the button on a call box next to the gated driveway. A second later, the iron bars swung in and then gently closed behind her as she disappeared up the sidewalk towards the house.

I had a flashback to the first time I had seen her in her aquatic form, from the bridge in the Village. She had come out of the water, naked, in November, and had disappeared onto this very peninsula. *Could this be where she had gone that night?*

I had no idea who lived at the end of the Point. There were rumors that one of the residents was a well-known maker of adult movies, but I could never get anyone to confirm that rumor. I also heard that another Point resident had made a fortune from wind chimes. Yes, you read that right. *Fucking wind chimes!* You're kicking yourself right now. *Why didn't I think of that?*

I hear you.

I stood there, halfway down Seaview Avenue, pondering my next move. She clearly wanted me to follow her. *Or did she?* She hadn't waited at the gate but had gone in without me.

I tried to calm myself, to listen for her creepy voice in my head, but something in my gut told me to return to the party. Maybe all I really needed to know for now was where I could find her. Maybe running up to some strange house, one that had its own fortress of a security system to keep out idiots like me, was not the greatest of ideas. *See?* I can be taught.

I turned around and slowly headed back towards the Village, still catching my breath and plotting my next move. When I arrived at Shep and Hazel's, Rachael could barely put two words together. She leaned against some young thing who looked barely old enough to drive and draped her arms around his strong-looking neck. *Good Lord.*

"Hey, Evie! Where the hell ...?" She paused here and I waited for the barf as she swallowed heavily and put a hand to her throat. False alarm. Turned out to be a belch. "… did you go? Come have a drink with me and, uh …" She turned her head to look at her newest victim, but she was swaying too much and had trouble focusing on his face. "What's your name, darling?"

"Rick, ma'am."

"Did you just *ma'am* me?" she slurred.

Nothing good came after the slurring. I looked around. All the partygoers had played musical partners in my absence. None of the original pairs remained. Shit was getting real. Too real. I took this as my cue to leave. I did not want to get in on any *swappy swappy*. I had a man. I could barely handle that one relationship. Hell, I couldn't even do right by him. Why would I want to add another partner to the mix? Why make one *more* person miserable? And, besides, I had a lot of thinking to do. *I missed Paddy.*

Oh shit! *Paddy.* I needed to warn Paddy!

"Rach, I'm tired. I'm going to walk back to your house, can you give me the keys?"

"Huh? Oh! You're leaving?" she whined.

"Yes. I'm all done now."

She made an exaggerated frown face, then dug down the front of her pants for the house keys. I groaned with disgust.

"Here, honey. There's SnoCaps in the cabinet—if you need them." She winked at me, and something in my heart went soft. She always remembered my love for SnoCaps.

I made a heart with my fingers and she undraped her arms from Rick's neck, returning the gesture, and then blew a sloppy kiss at me.

"I'll be off, then," I said and winked at Rachael. "Nice meeting you, Rick."

"Um, have a good evening, ma'am."

"Yeah, yeah," I said, waving over my shoulder. I really didn't mind the *ma'am*. That felt normal. Not much else in my life could be labeled *normal*.

The day was transitioning from light towards darkness. The sky took on a gorgeous shade of pink, reminding me of all the things the world had to offer in terms of beauty. As I gazed up to where the sky turned velvet, my mind wandered back to my family. I needed to let them know that they were in danger. *Again*. Oh God. What if Paddy had taken Savannah to Prudence Island? His family was used to thinking of Prudence as a safe haven, but things hadn't worked out so well for me when I sought shelter there. Maybe my husband would be smarter *this* time.

Paddy needed to know that Nomia had come back. She was here in the Village and not in Ireland for whatever reason. His stupid family had dropped the ball. They had promised us safety. They had promised that they would take her ass out—or kill her sister, Nox, Nuk Nuk, or whatever the frig she was called—if Nomia acted up. So what the hell was she doing on the Point?

Paddy had been right. Although couldn't one argue that she would have shown up on our doorstep even if I *hadn't* gone to Boston, defying Paddy's wishes? So who was right? Who was wrong? Probably me. I'm such an asshole. Feeling the stress settle in my shoulders, I shrugged and took out my cell phone. I tried to call him again, but I got the same berating message. I rolled my eyes and waited for the beep.

"Hey," I said, trying to inject false cheer into my voice. "It's me, but you probably knew that, and that's why I'm talking to your voice mail and not you. So hey, voice mail. Could you let Paddy and Savannah know that I am thinking of them, and that I love them, and I'm back in the Village? I don't know where Richard is, and I just saw Nomia on the Point. So yeah. That bitch came back and I'm 99.9999 percent positive it was not my fault. Don't know where you are, but wherever you're staying, I hope it's far, far away from Rhode Island! Miss you! Happy Gaspee Days!"

I punched the red button to end the call and shoved the phone back into my pocket. I sighed heavily. Mostly just to hear my own frustration. Mostly to keep the crazy at bay. I could feel it coming. The part where I lose my shit because I am so stressed. *Think of something positive, Evie. Get it together. Think of Paddy and Savannah.* Were they looking at the same night sky? Were they thinking of me, as I thought of them? Probably not. They probably hated me right now. Or at least Paddy did. I hope he didn't tell Savannah all that much.

"Christ!" I screamed up at the stars.

How had I landed myself back in this same situation? Paddy was right. I had stirred the pot and look what happened. Just when I thought I had put all this shit behind me, here I was. Again. But was it my fault? It's always my fault, so yeah. The answer is probably a resounding—*yes.*

I felt helpless. Completely useless and helpless. I could do nothing to fix the situation, so I walked up the hill to Rachael's house and hoped that there was something decent on her DVR. Preferably not pornographic. I needed to check out for a while.

Clear my head. I also needed to clean house, as in, *get rid of Nomia for good.* And I needed to find Richard. I considered my options as I walked.

Tomorrow—'cause I sure as shit was not heading over there alone and in the dark—I could march right up to the gate and demand to speak with Nomia. The gate would open, and I would say ... *what, exactly?*

Rachael would need to go with me. That crazy ho could talk her way out of anything. *An enraged wife?* No problem. *An infuriated guy who had just caught Rachael two-timing with his girlfriend?* No problem. *A homicidal mermaid?* Really, what's the difference? Then I had a brilliant idea. An earth-shattering, amazing idea. I could just leave a note at the gate! I could leave a written request for an audience with Queen Aquabitch. It would read:

> *Dear Queen Aquabitch,*
>
> ~~*So, what's up? How are you?*~~ *I know you saw me the other day, and I know you saw me seeing you. What the hell do you want from me? And where the fuck's my brother?*
>
> *Warmest regards towards your imminent demise,*
>
> *Evie*
>
> *The bitch you almost killed.*
> *(Except, I kicked your ass.)*

Oh, sure. That was totally the right thing to do. Let me just whip out my fuzzy pink pen and Happy Bunny stationery and get right on that. Walking up to Rachael's front porch, I burst out laughing. I could clearly see my note in my head, and then I could see it in Nomia's hands. Sometimes I crack myself up. Thank God for that. The laughing felt good. I remembered feeling good. I wished this whole merfucking mess would just go away so I could get back to feeling good.

Then just like that, the good feeling was gone. There on the porch sat an envelope with my name on it. I looked up and down the empty street. The streetlight winked on, then off, then back on again, filling the pavement with a pool of stark gray. I heard a dog bark in the distance, then someone yell at it, then nothing. Crickets chirped, and I thought I could hear the faint chime of a channel marker, way out in the bay. I held my breath and ripped open the envelope. A message on a single sheet of white paper nestled inside. I took it out slowly, then read:

> *E-*
>
> *If you want to find your brother, meet me at The Elephant Room.*
>
> *Tomorrow at 10 a.m.*
>
> *Come alone.*
>
> *-N*

No, the irony had not been lost on me. Her handwriting—her handwriting was *perfect!* A little old-fashioned looking, like

Old-World longhand, but I mean, *really?* Did she have to be gorgeous, able to transform into an underwater creature, *and* have perfect handwriting? Did she have *any* flaws? I mean, beside the whole homicidal one. *But really?*

She wanted to meet. My palms started sweating, and I almost hyperventilated. I fumbled for the keys in my pocket and let myself in. After making some microwave popcorn and dousing it with SnoCaps, I sat down on the sofa with a tall, ice-filled glass of bourbon and thought about all the events of the previous twenty-four hours.

Here's what I knew: Richard was either dead or missing, although something told me he lived. I just knew this. I had a key-shaped USB drive but no way of accessing it without Rachael. Yes, I had tried before making popcorn. Her laptop was password protected. Dead end. And then there was Nomia. She had made contact with me, through my head. I shivered at this. I will never, ever, ever get used to that bitch being in my head. *WTF? Why? How?* That shit was cray-cray weird. *What had she said?* So much had happened in such a short amount of time. I needed to calm down and concentrate. She had said something about being weak. Something about someone being gone. *Who was gone?*

Damn. Nomia seemed frightened. Nomia was one of the spookiest things on this planet, and *she* was *scared?* What could possibly scare the shit out of the boogey man, boogey woman, boogey merwoman? And why come to me? If something was scary enough to scare her, what made her think *I* could do anything about it?

I stress-ate my popcorn and thought about the meeting in the morning. She had chosen a very public place. The Elephant Room, a crêperie in the Village. Who the hell would believe that a crêpe place, owned by an adorable Mexican family, would make it in the Village? As if *that* makes any sense. But let me tell you, you have not lived until you've had a *Crêpe Relleno* made with love. They even served booze! So you know I loved the place. And tomorrow I would be meeting my archnemesis for booze and crêpes. *Shit was messed up.*

I barely slept that night. I think Rachael rolled in with Steve, or someone or several someones, soon after midnight. I heard things I wish I could unhear. I had more of an education than I needed at the time, but it distracted me from my terrifying meeting in the morning. I was up at dawn, sitting on the front porch swing, huddled with a cup of coffee. Rachael had one of those automatic coffeemakers. It went off at five in the morning. Scared the shit out of me. I had been up, staring out the kitchen window, when the damn thing started up. Once my heartbeat returned to normal, and I realized what had just happened, I gratefully poured myself a steaming cup of joe.

I gently glided back and forth, watching the scarlet sunrise. I remembered the old sailor's saying, *Red sky at night, sailor's delight. Red sky in the morning, sailor's warning.* I felt the warning and I shivered. The screen door creaked open, and Rach stumbled out in a sweatshirt and men's boxer shorts.

"Those are not your underwear," I said, keeping my eyes on the dawn sky.

"Nope," she said and shoved me over, a cup of coffee in her

own hands. "What's up?"

I handed her the envelope. She read it once, then put her mug down. It clicked against the makeshift outdoor coffee table littered with cigarettes and Victoria's Secret catalogs. Then she read the note again.

"What is this?"

"It's from her. The woman we have the restraining order against."

"*What?* Does this bitch have a name?"

"Nomia. Her name is Nomia. As in, No-mia."

"Okay. Why is Nomia leaving notes for you on *my* porch?"

"That really is the million-dollar question, isn't it?" I sipped my coffee and looked around. Aside from a sleek-looking tom-cat, probably taking his walk of shame home, the street was deserted. "She came to the party yesterday. That's why I took off for a while. I chased her. She's staying at that big, gated house at the end of the Point."

"Huh," said Rachael.

"Huh, what?"

"That's John's house. He's divorced. His wife lives in Boca or something. He's always got some young thing on his arm down at the bar or on his boat. Total sugar daddy."

"Well, that would be a good place for Nomia to shack up."

"But I thought she was with your brother?"

"I went to Boston, and everything was a mess. There were pictures of the two of them, but the place was wrecked, and Richard wasn't there. I saw a lot of blood." I had to stop talking. I choked up and tears filled my eyes. Rachael put her arm around me. It felt good. "I don't know where he is. At first, I thought Nomia had something to do with it, but now ..." I shook my head. "Now I'm not so sure. I think she's scared."

"Shit, Evie! Why didn't you tell me your brother was in trouble yesterday? You don't think he's dead, do you?"

"No. I don't know. Don't yell at me!"

"Sorry. Sorry. But what do you think is going on? Why was your brother's place a mess? Why is she back down here, cozying up to John?"

"That's what I need to find out."

"Well, I'm going with you."

"No, you're not. I don't want to drag you into this."

"Look," she said, turning to face me. "You showed up on my doorstep with all your baggage, both in *and* out of the stupid-ass rolling cart of yours. You already dragged me into this. Besides, this is a great opportunity for me to go all incognito." She looked at me with a crazy grin on her face.

I knew that grin. Oh no. "Oh no," I said. "What are you thinking?"

"I've been sneaking around with this married guy in Providence, or at least, I think he's married. Anyway, we wear disguises and meet up. It's very hot."

"What are you getting at?"

"I'll go to the E Room with you—in disguise! If shit gets crazy, I'll be there! I've got your back, sister!"

"Rach, I don't know about this," I said. I appreciated the offer, but I had caused enough damage in the lives of people I loved. I didn't want to bring anyone else into the Evie Cluster

Fuck.

"Well, it's a free country. I already know what time you're going, and *where* you are going. Nothing can stop me from just showing up, in disguise."

"No," I said, "I guess there is nothing stopping you."

"Damn straight, bitch," she said and sipped her coffee. "Damn straight."

Dolský Mill
Confluence of the
Elbe and Kamenice rivers
Bohemia
Late Spring 1608

Clíodhna

Ash, as light and elegant as new-fallen snow, swirled and disappeared into the night sky. It fell on Clíodhna's dark hair and came to rest on her shoulders. With her brow set in firm determination, she brushed away the smoky debris, then clasped her hands together, allowing them to come to rest on her large, swollen belly.

The stars, brilliant in the velvet sky, quivered and danced in the glittering blanket of darkness. For whatever reason, the night sky always seemed lower than the overwhelmingly bright blueness of day. The moon above hung like an enlarged egg, full and round in the sky, echoing the fully developed shape of Clíodhna's belly far below. She noticed a wide, hazy ring around the moon announcing the imminent arrival of snow.

An unexpected surprise this late in spring.

Her face, turning serene in the amber light, observed the flames as they licked the reeds of the thatched roof. She narrowed her eyes and scanned the outer walls of the mill, which had been her prison for the previous year. Nothing moved except the hungry flames as they licked the structure clean from the inside out. A loud crack burst from the structure and Clíodhna winced, startled by the suddenness of the explosion. A beam or some other sturdy wooden support groaned and crashed down. Its demise echoed across the clearing, which separated the flame-engulfed mill from the dark forest.

She turned away, the fire instantly warming her back, and walked towards the trees. The heat grew less intense the farther she walked. Once she could no longer feel the blaze, Clíodhna broke out into a run, retreating towards the safety of the darkened wood. Not once did she turn around. She left and never looked back.

As she ran, Clíodhna buried the savagery of her actions deep within herself. She imagined a deep chest lined with a cloth the color of the night sky above. Then she envisioned herself pushing all that had just transpired, starting with her ill-fated arrival at the wretched mill, down, down, down into the depths of the chest.

One whole moon cycle before Clíodhna stood in the clearing, watching all that she had known for the past year burn to the ground, she had given birth to something other than the child within. She had given birth to a plan.

Many hours after the horrors at the water's edge, where

she had witnessed the death and dismemberment of a human being, her captor, now and forever labeled a monster in Clíodhna's mind, had returned. He seemed agitated, restless, unaware of his stolen bride. While he paced, wiping away the blood and other unmentionable substances from his face, his chest, his hands, Clíodhna, still bound to her chair, had worked out the intricacies of a plan, a plan to free herself from her waking nightmare forever.

Clíodhna spent the next month convincing herself that this man could not help his true nature, that his duality—his gentleness combined with his violent nature—proved his inability to recognize right from wrong. And so on the next full moon, Clíodhna had given herself over, for the last time, to the side of the man that had been a kind and loving person. In the moonlight, staring out the doorway to where a beam of moonlight beckoned her, Clíodhna listened for the telltale sounds of the man's sleep, brought on after he had been satiated by her last act of kindness. As he snored in his slumber, Clíodhna slipped from the bed and crept downstairs to gather the supplies she had hidden over the previous weeks.

Climbing the stairs once more, she kept her breathing easy and reminded herself, over and over and over again, that *this* was the only answer. The only solution to so many problems. She called to memory the events of her initial kidnapping, of how the man, no, *the monster*, had taken away her freedom and had made her his slave. She moved with purpose, acting on behalf of herself, on behalf of the woman beneath the great wheel, whoever she had been, and finally, on behalf of the fallen man, the one whom the monster had ingested.

Before she began her work, she looked around the room one last time. Then Clíodhna carefully placed two chairs on either side of the mattress, tipping their backs against the bed frame. With shaking fingers, she tied one end of the rope to the first chair, then carefully wound the heavy, hempen strands through the open backs of the chairs, around the sleeping man, around the bed itself, all while placing the full weight of the binds on the chair seats and not on the man, allowing him to continue his last peaceful slumber.

Gathering the last end of the rope, she moved out the door to the nearby stairwell and passed the thick cord around the banister. Then using all her strength, she pulled the rope, tightening the bind and securing the beast to the bed. As fast as her fingers could manage, Clíodhna tied off the rope with a complex taut-line hitch, calling upon her knowledge of knot-work buried deep within the chasms of her mind.

The man came to full consciousness and roared at Clíodhna. He thrashed about, further tightening the ropes, sealing his own fate. The man's already bulbous eyes grew even wider with confusion, rage, and fury, but Clíodhna was undeterred. She verified the man's confinement, calling upon the memory of the man by the river, the way his eyes had grown dim as this thing before her had gnawed on his bones. She held this image in the forefront of her mind. She reminded herself of the freedom, her maiden journey, aborted by this wretched beast. Her life forever changed, forever burdened by his presence through the child she now held in her womb.

With these thoughts foremost in her mind, Clíodhna descended to the first floor and fetched as many oil lamps as she could gather before returning upstairs. She placed them on the floor and went outside to gather kindling. The full weight of her plan slammed down on the man. Understanding transformed his face into a mask of fear. His screams turned into pleading, the mewling of a hurt animal, but Clíodhna pressed on with her task. She packed the bed with bits of dry material and other flammable substances. She ignored the man, ignored his desperation in the same way he had ignored hers on this very same bed. She returned again, filling the room with blankets, hay, leaves, anything she could find, creating a nest of death. When she had finished, she poured oil over the man's body, soaking the bed linens and the mattress, saturating all that she had brought into the room with the thick, pungent oil. She doused the walls, the beams, the floor, ensuring that nothing would escape the all-encompassing blaze.

Standing in the doorway, she looked at the man one last time. This abomination of a man, who now had tears rolling down his cheeks. His large frog-like eyes stared at her, his face filled with sadness. She felt pity, but not enough.

Clíodhna struck the tinder box and watched as the hungry little flame jumped from her pale finger and found a feast of sustenance. The fire rapidly spread across the room, eating all it encountered, growing from a tiny little being into a raging, ravenous creature. The man's screams filled the space where, many months before, her own screams had gone unanswered, unheeded, ignored. The circle was now complete.

As his bulging eyes met her own hardened gaze, she slammed the door on him forever and barricaded the exit, secure in the belief that she had done a great deed. She had rid the world of a depraved monster.

This last memory found its way into the chest within her mind. Clíodhna buried it beneath all the brutality she had suffered in her early months in the mill. Then she smashed down the lid, closing it, locking it, and finally lighting the chest on fire as well.

Leaving the mill and its horrors behind, Clíodhna fled into the forest, which swallowed her whole. She embraced the shadowy tranquility of the trees. The absence of light within the woods did not frighten her. What more could be done to a person? Her life had been altered forever, her body violated, her will broken. But yet, she still existed and would continue to exist, for the sake of the child within.

Clíodhna wrestled with returning to the Irish sea, but the shame of what had transpired crushed the thought before it materialized. She would not go back to Ireland—not now, not ever. She would not return to the water, would not allow her aquatic side to be released. Instead, she would raise her unborn on land. There would be no need for the child to ever know its origins.

Clíodhna ran until she could run no farther. The rage that had driven her grisly exodus slowly ebbed away, leaving her exhausted beyond reason. The significant weight of the life she now carried, combined with an array of new, spreading aches from her intense exertion, announced their presence, and her body screamed for rest. However, in spite of these unpleasant impositions, she had not felt this alive, this strong, or this aware of the world around her since she had first left Ireland.

Her body howled for sleep. The need could no longer be ignored. Scanning the woods, Clíodhna spotted a pile of rocks nestled against a hillside, illuminated by the moon. Climbing the rocky embankment, she broke and gathered low-hanging pine boughs that fell over the incline. Tucking them under her arms as she went, she made her way towards the large boulders. A cleft in the enormous rocks, left by a glacier thousands of years before her time, made a small cave, large enough for her to pile the boughs and bed down for the night with some degree of security. Sleep came without any trouble, and for that, she gave thanks to the old gods.

During her slumber, a snowstorm swept across the forest, blanketing the woods with a thick cover of new-fallen snow, bleaching the color from all that her eyes could see. Clíodhna pulled her legs up to her swollen abdomen and hugged the child to herself. *Freedom.* She allowed the air to release from her lungs. She exhaled with confidence, safe in the knowledge that her captor had perished.

Looking out from the hillside in the early morning light, she saw a clearing in the distance. She listened but heard nothing. The absence of sound, the whole of her world muted by the falling snow. *How far had she come in the night? Far enough? Where should she go?* The answers would come in time, or not at all. None of it mattered any longer. She needed to travel, but for now, she needed more rest. Clíodhna smiled and closed her eyes. The snow continued to fall.

Her body awoke before her mind. She needed to relieve herself. Climbing out of the shelter, she yawned, stretched, and did an internal scan of her body, gently sending messages to the tiny swimmer within. A small twitch sent her waking fear away. The child lived. Hunger filled her mind. She would need to find food for them both, and soon.

With the clothes on her back and little else, Clíodhna set off into the world, comforted by her recent liberation. She could go where she pleased. Along with her freedom, the day belonged to her.

The snow continued to fall as she walked through the forest, delighting Clíodhna, who smiled at the wonder around her. Snow, a rarity in her homeland, brought her joy. She marveled at the way it accumulated on the ground, once so small in the air, then becoming a mass that touched everything, all beneath a colorless sky.

How could something so small become so significant?

Rubbing her belly, she felt the life within return her gesture. A small limb—*a hand? a foot? an elbow?*—glided across the thin membrane that separated their touch.

Something so small *had* become significant.

She shuddered at the thought of the child's arrival. It would have to come out eventually. *But how? How could something as big as a basket find its way out of her body?*

Best not to focus on such things. Nature had a way of moving on, of surviving. Clíodhna felt certain that the arrival of her child would happen regardless of her ability to prepare or not.

As for today, she only needed to find food.

She walked all day, the growing hunger gnawing away at her consciousness. She needed to eat something. The river had eluded her. If she could find it, it could provide fish, but she hadn't found it. Her sense of direction had been scrambled in the night, the blanket of snow camouflaging all that she encountered. Twice she found her own deep footprints in the snow and realized that she had traveled in a wide circle. Panic set in, and she constantly scanned the trees and the snow, searching for signs of small creatures. But in the deep snow, none were to be found. Clíodhna pressed onward.

Coming over a rise, she spotted a small stone dwelling below, nestled alone in a snow-covered clearing. With a high roof at one end and many colorful windows along the side, the sturdy structure seemed as ancient as the forest itself. Spying the wooden cross atop the tall end of the building, she recognized it as a house of worship. Relief washed over her. She could find shelter there.

Clíodhna recalled from her childhood in Ireland stories regarding the hospitality of these people. If she remembered correctly, the holy person, and or the caretaker, might grant charity to wanderers. If indeed a truly kind and benevolent individual resided inside, he might take in a woman in need, without question. Perhaps this dwelling held such a good, kind soul. Someone who might take pity on Clíodhna in her maternal condition and would, perhaps, provide her with food and even shelter for the evening. With hope in her heart, she made her way down the hill to the entrance.

The enormous and ornately carved door of the building towered above Clíodhna's upturned face. Swirling roses and thorns intertwined, winding their way across the expansive surface. Lifting her pale fist to the massive slab of wood, Clíodhna knocked, then waited. No one came. No one answered. She leaned her head against the door and listened. *Silence.* Looking out at the darkening forest, she saw no one. She turned her attention back to the door and pushed. Hard. To her surprise, the immense barrier gave way. Ancient iron hinges squealed like frightened hogs. Her own stomach, hidden somewhere behind the habitation of the tiny, internal passenger, growled in response. Her hand flew to her abdomen, as if she could contain the loud noise. She failed to do so. In defiance of her touch, her empty belly released another, more urgent groan.

If anyone had been inside, her loud arrival might have alerted the occupants to her presence. But no one came to greet her, either in kindness or in hostility. Clíodhna stepped inside, then pushed the enormous closed door behind her. The chapel held a damp, moldy scent that oozed from the stone walls and clung to the bare, wooden pews.

Moving into the interior, Clíodhna approached the simple altar at the far end of the chapel, opposite the immense entrance. She moved with caution, all senses on high alert. The eerie and all-consuming silence overwhelmed her ears. To return indoors after experiencing the freedom of the natural world unnerved the young mother-to-be.

As the quiet crept into Clíodhna's head, she spun back and forth, watching the door behind her, searching the shadows of each pew she passed, looking for a crouching individual with bulbous eyes. Her hand flew to her mouth, and she bit down on her ragged fingernails, hoping that her stomach would keep quiet as she made a sweep of the building. As the distance between her and the altar decreased, the floor creaked like an old, arthritic woman. Each step brought forth a squeak and a pop as the ancient planks groaned beneath her weight. Clíodhna winced at each intense disruption to the overpowering silence. But no one came.

After what felt like an eternity, she arrived at the altar. The wide, flat surface yielded nothing, no clues, no indication of occupation. Only a heavy layer of dust remained. As the sun fell below the tree-line and the daylight dimmed, a single shaft of sunlight illuminated a mostly red and blue stained-glass window above the ornate front door. The light cast an image of an enormous, blue-clad woman across the pews and center aisle. Her large, plain face, serene and hopeful, stared up at the ceiling from the simple wooden floor. A crown lay across her delicate forehead, while a golden orb encircled both her head and the crown. In her arms, she held a small infant, wrapped in a bundle, another golden circle hovering over its tiny head.

Clíodhna smiled at the other mother. Perhaps, whoever she was, this queen could find it in her heart to watch over both Clíodhna and her unborn. This woman in blue looked as if she could provide both hope and a watchful eye. A mother to all in need.

Clíodhna needed a mother—right now. Feeling as if she had the Blue Mother's blessing, Clíodhna continued on with her search and headed towards the posterior section of the build-ing. Behind the altar, she spied a door. Perhaps it had been the former keeper's private quarters. There might be stores of food, laid aside for the keeper's return. Clíodhna vowed that if she did find anything consumable, she would replace all that she took. With her breath held in her chest, she cautiously opened the door and found herself in a small interior room. She let the air out of her lungs. The room lay empty.

Cabinets lined one wall, and a small bed rested against the other. Moving to the cabinets, Clíodhna, now secure in the belief that she was alone in the structure, eagerly pulled all the doors open, one by one, in search of anything she could eat. Luck, or the Blue Mother, had smiled upon her. In the last cab-inet, she found tightly sealed crockery which held a few small dried fishes.

Eagerly, she devoured each one. Her saliva helped bring a bit of softness to the heavily salted, dehydrated fish. She ate as quickly as she could and then lay down on the hard bed, falling into a deep, dreamless sleep.

The night passed, and she still slept. Day broke, and she slept. Night fell again, and Clíodhna continued her slumber. Her extensive exhaustion, combined with the safety of the chapel, created a protective bubble around her weary body. When she awoke after the second day, Clíodhna felt a direct connection between her newfound fortune and the benevolence of the Blue Mother, her new savior.

With her belly full, her mind and body at rest, Clíodhna made her way out into the main room of the chapel and sat cross-legged in the center aisle. She stared upwards, gazing at the great stained-glass window. There, high above Clíodhna, the Blue Mother held court. Still peaceful, still full of grace, her small infant still snuggled securely in his mother's arms.

The crown captured Clíodhna's attention. Simple in construction, neither overly ornate nor laden with excessive jewels, it was just a gentle reminder to all who beheld this elegant woman—this was the queen of all mothers. *The Blue Mother Queen.* Clíodhna rubbed her own future infant, secure in her womb, and spoke, in her mind, to the lovely lady of the window.

Blue Mother Queen, please find it in your heart to keep watch over me from now on. Guide my unborn safely into the world. And if I do not survive the birth, please watch over my child ...

No answer came from the window, but Clíodhna experienced a strange, soothing comfort all the same. She had never understood why the land-dwellers had spent so much time in places such as this, but sitting here beneath such an understanding, kind deity, Clíodhna felt a kinship to her land cousins and their devotion to a woman such as this one.

Clíodhna wondered if the Blue Mother Queen required a sacrifice or an offering. Feeling both strong and rested enough to venture outdoors once more, the mother-to-be stood with some difficulty and walked towards the giant wooden door. The sun greeted her as she left the chapel, bleak, but still evident. The giant, pale celestial body, still so far away at this time of year, peeked through the trees and smiled down on Clíodhna, beautiful in her fertile state. A warmth spread through her body, and she endeavored to hold onto the moment for as long as she could. Sighing, Clíodhna entered the forest in search of something appropriate for a queen.

She never made it beyond the trees. The bolt from the crossbow hit her in the back, near her right shoulder, knocking her to the ground. Her last thought was of the Blue Mother Queen's face, serenely looking down on Clíodhna as her crimson blood flowed freely, staining the newly fallen snow.

11

The Merrow Codex
Archive #32 - Wasserschutz

Caratocos, elder scholar

As previously stated in Archive #3, the threats to our kind are numerous, but none so much as the *Wasserschutz*. Their origins stem from what is known as the Eastern European region of the Main Continent.

Information initially gathered during the first Jacobite conflict in Scotland circa 1715, north of our home waters, was collected from several *Keepers*. The conflict also involved a massive purge, the likes of which had not been seen since the Great Reaping during the Roman occupation of Britannia, sometime in the fifth century AD.

The raids and the outright slaughtering of our kind during the Jacobite rebellions were performed by a group who called themselves Wasserschutz, a Germanic term loosely translated as *water protectors*. These individuals took the guise of Hessians—mercenaries sent to aid King George II and his English soldiers in the suppression of a Catholic uprising. Specifically, they opposed those who sought to restore the Catholic-oriented House of Stuart to the throne of Great Britain.

The Wasserschutz used the opportunity to seek out our kind and systemically defile and decimate each and every *Homo aquaticus* they encountered, all in the name of their god, Jesus Christ. There is confusion regarding this religious rationale, based on what we have learned of the god, Jesus. Our sources revealed him to be a kind, benevolent man who, like our people, had been persecuted by the Romans.

The cruelty of the mass expulsion of our people seemed particularly brutal in the treatment of the females. Several Keepers in that region had observed evidence of defilement, both before and after death, afflicted on the local tribe of Selkie. It is believed that their acts of aggression came from a place of misunderstanding regarding the nature of our peoples.

This outrageous act of near genocide at the hands of the Wasserschutz is why our kind has retreated farther and farther away from our land-dwelling cousins.

The Wasserschutz, well-trained hunters, large in size and demeanor, excellent marksmen and riders, a nearly unstoppable force. Some among them have a sort of unique tracking skill that allows them to specifically seek and target our kind. They are a primarily male society; no females have been recorded as part of this particular group of warriors, which might explain the lack of empathy regarding the feminine sex. One particular observation was sent forth by the Keeper Magnus, who resided in the northern part of Scotland, close to the Orkney and Shetland Islands.

Magnus stated that he had been on his way south to Aberdeen to check in with a Seafarer named Conor. The pair met regularly, in the spring of each year, to swap news and pass along any relevant information. When Magnus arrived at their usual meeting place, Conor was nowhere to be found. It had not initially alarmed Magnus. Conor, not well-known for being where he should be when he should be, had kept Magnus waiting in the past.

A popular fellow with the local females, Conor frequently sought out the company of the fairer sex on the occasions when he visited dry land. Naturally, Magnus assumed that Conor had entertained himself farther to the south on his way to their meeting.

Magnus settled in and watched the sea, certain his dear friend would appear to him among the waves at any moment, a large smile on his handsome face, a clever tale on his tongue. But Conor did not arrive that day nor three days after that. Thinking that his friend had found a particularly delicious diversion and would not be coming, Magnus headed home by way of the coast.

Not more than a few hours into his journey, Magnus encountered Conor in quite a state, bleeding extensively from his shoulder. He took his friend to shore and made camp along the beach, tending to Conor's wounds. After his basic needs had been met and comfort of sorts had been provided for him, Conor found his words. He told Magnus that he had traveled from the north and had hoped to intercept his good friend, Magnus, to warn him before he, too, came south.

At this point, Conor suddenly became quite frightened, scratching at his wounds and insisting that their campfire be extinguished. But Magnus had refused and searched among his things for a draught to calm his injured companion. Once the drink had been imbibed by both merrow, Conor grew more still, more sullen. Magnus had needed to urge the tale out of him.

Finally, in a stream of words that fell from his lips like rain from the sky, Conor explained that he had seen terrible things along the northeastern shore of John O'Groats, close to Duncansby Stacks. While passing close to the shore, he had heard screams and surfaced to discover the source of the commotion. Two riders, he said, wearing all black with tall metal helmets, had just ridden down a girl, an ordinary girl, or so Conor had thought as he watched in terror from the safety of the sea.

The riders laughed, circled their mounts, and then rode back to where the young woman lay, barely moving, on the shore. The pair then dismounted and dragged their victim into the sea. The girl, broken, bleeding, and screaming had called out for mercy, but the men had laughed at her, dragging her writhing body deeper and deeper into the water, shouting as they went.

There was little Conor could do but watch the events unfold. The men stripped the girl of her clothes and then held her under the water. When they pulled her body from the surf, Conor saw the transformation begin as the girl screamed in agony. It was at that moment that Conor knew—the men's victim was a Selkie, those who can turn into seals.

As her body began to contort with the change, the men grew quiet, their faces transfixed on her lower half. Conor winced, knowing the awful feeling of the change when accompanied by even the slightest of injuries. He could not begin to imagine the unbelievable pain she withstood, knowing full well that her body was already badly broken. Within moments, the girl had transformed into her second form, albeit still broken and bleeding.

The men, wearing their ridiculous helmets atop their wretched heads, then skinned the girl alive while she screamed and screamed and screamed. She screamed until she could scream no more. When the ghastly deed had come to an end, the despicable men left her corpse to float on the waves. Seagulls screeched from above, fighting over the unexpected bounty left for their enjoyment.

The men took her pelt to their horses on the shore, and from satchels hanging alongside their saddles, they pulled forth many other skins to which they compared their newest acquisition. The sickness in Conor was so great that he cried out, unable to contain his revulsion of the vile evidence—the slaughter of so many Selkie folk.

But it had been an awful thing for him to give notice of his presence and position. The men turned and saw him. They shouted and taunted him, attempting to entice the young merrow to the shore. Conor had been about to dive back under the waves, but the luck of his people had left him on that fateful day. Unknown to Conor, high up on the cliffs above them all, a third rider had taken aim with his crossbow and sent a bolt through Conor's shoulder.

Conor dove down, blood streaming out behind him. He did

not stop. He headed north, in search of Magnus, his friend. By the time he felt safe enough to surface, he realized that Magnus would have already started his journey south towards Aberdeen. Bandaging himself as best he could, Conor had made slow progress to find his dear friend and warn him of a potential senseless, barbaric attack.

After the telling of the tale, the gravity of the events crushed Conor's soul, and he wept openly for the loss of so many Selkie people. Magnus had listened solemnly. He then gave his companion the last of his drink, promising to keep watch through the rest of the night.

The pair of merrow waited several days until Conor's strength had returned enough to travel. Then the two made their way north to warn more of the Selkies they knew who resided along the coast farther to the north, among the Orkney Islands.

Unfortunately, the pair arrived too late to notify many of the danger. Burned villages greeted them along the coast, while skinned corpses littered the waves and vast flocks of scavengers swooped down to pull apart the poor ravaged souls. Many of the outlying islands, the places inhabited by those people they sought to protect, had also been attacked.

The wake of destruction was clearly marked with sights no creature should ever see. Magnus and Conor warned those they could find, and once they felt that they could no longer continue, they turned south to our waters. They brought the warning to us, here in Ireland.

As of this writing, we, the merrow of Ireland, have not yet

experienced the wrath of those that call themselves Wasserschutz. Perhaps they know not of us. Perhaps they have not
come far enough south.

We hope they never do.

12

The Middle Rhine Valley
Late Spring 1608

Clíodhna

The pain in her shoulder cried out, breaking the silence of Clíodhna's unconsciousness, tearing her from the surf, ripping her from her brother's embrace. She fought to stay in his arms, but the fire in her shoulder burned with the heat of a thousand suns.

She opened her eyes but saw nothing. Disoriented and confused, she needed a moment to replace the pieces of lost time. Suddenly, her head cleared and everything flew back into place, slamming Clíodhna into the now. Her hands twitched, eager to feel her abdomen, to ensure the safety of her unborn, but she could not move her arms or her legs.

In a cruel twist of fate, Clíodhna found herself bound once more. Angry tears formed at the corners of her eyes, but she kept silent. She could not, would not cry out.

Why? Why had she left the mundane waters of home? Why did this heartless world endlessly seek her out as a target of abuse?

Why, when she thought herself so strong, so invincible, had the world endeavored to keep her down, to oppress her? To teach her that she, a female alone in the world, was hardly better off than a young fawn, alone in a forest teeming with wolves?

The bitterness of her situation flooded her veins, forcing hot tears to stream across her feverish face. Her anger distracted her from her pain, her bound wrists and ankles, and from her unknown whereabouts. She needed to use this anger, channel it. There was still fight left within her bones. Clíodhna took a deep breath, held it, then listened. Her body swayed and bounced in time with—*what? Could she be in a carriage? Where was she headed?* She heard the creak of grinding, wooden wheels. She was on the move.

Clíodhna tried to ignore the ache in her shoulder and her lower back. She focused, allowing her surroundings to inform her of her situation. She could hear more than one carriage, perhaps three or more. They moved in unison, bouncing along the same rock-strewn road.

Breathing in sharply, she realized that she was not alone in her confinement. Two or maybe three other scents filled the air around her. All female. She recognized the familiar feminine scent of women who had not bathed in a long time. One in particular held a scent so intimately familiar, redolent of the sharp, salty scent of the sea. But the wind shifted and the scent faded away, leaving behind the pungent odor of horses—a sweaty, earthy blend with the added sweetness of hay.

Clíodhna detected the oiled wood of the carriage and something else—an animal unknown to her. For her to notice its existence in addition to the horses, it must have been sizable. The beast gave off a deep musk, rich like the forest floor, but she could not identify it or determine its location.

A breeze passed over her cheeks, cooling the wet tears on her face. *A window? Somewhere above her?* When she focused her hearing towards the direction of the breeze, she heard men's voices—gruff, gritty tones that faintly rumbled and echoed somewhere behind her own carriage. She could not place their dialect, but found their speech reminded her of the beast in the mill. The words fell with guttural, curt syllables, spoken with firmness and authority.

The voices faded in and out, then passed close by, disappearing ahead of Clíodhna. She identified the click of hooves as the horses carrying the men traveled past her slower, heavier carriage. She hated the riders and hoped their beasts of burden would throw them and trample their riders.

Time crawled, and Clíodhna waited. The stiff position of her body brought intense discomfort while her shoulder screamed for attention, but there was little she could do except lie still and suffer. She drifted, passing between consciousness and unconsciousness, between the now and the past.

She saw her brother, the beast from the mill, the luminous face of the serene Blue Mother Queen. All of them spoke to her in their own way. Sometimes she understood what they said, their faces urgent and full of concern, but mostly she did not. She felt frustration change the course of the dream, putting her in further peril. A cool hand reached out in the darkness and touched her shoulder, soothing the fire in her wound. The pain subsided. Clíodhna smiled up at the Blue Mother, who hovered over her.

Thank you, Mother.

Sleep now, my child.

Clíodhna drifted into a deeper sleep. Her unconsciousness floated above the pain, above her bound body, above all that had transpired, all the tragic events leading up to the present. She sought out the rhythms of the ocean's tides, allowing the thrust and pull of the waves to carry her, support her, as the healing water rinsed clean both her wound and her soul.

When she awoke, she could see. Dawn had arrived. Brilliant rays of light illuminated her wooden prison. Deep, umber-colored wood surrounded her, interrupted by the window through which the breeze and the men's voices had flowed in the night. Three thick iron bars filled the portal, allowing little more than voices or air to pass through. Turning her head, Clíodhna stared into the face of a woman. Clíodhna recoiled, startled by the close proximity of another being.

The woman's eyes were large and dark, much narrower than Clíodhna's, which were similar to a fish's overly round iris. Her skin and hair shone a deep russet brown that reminded Clíodhna of warm, rose-toned clay. Her face seemed to glow in the early morning light. She had a subtle beauty, an exotic allure that seemed to come from deep within the woman's soul. Tendrils of the woman's hair, which matched her eyes—dark, like a seal's pelt—coiled down from an intricately patterned scarf wound tightly around the top of her head. A deep scar of pink, tender, new tissue tore across the woman's brow, now furrowed with concern, her attention flickering between Clíodhna's eyes and the wound on her shoulder. Looking down, Clíodhna saw that her wound had been dressed. A pale bandage, seeping with yellow ooze, covered her shoulder. The sharp pain had almost disappeared, replaced with a deep, dull ache.

The woman spoke to her in a hushed voice, but Clíodhna did not understand the language and shook her head in frustration. The woman's face fell. A chance at communication lost to them both.

Had this dark woman dressed her wounds?

Judging by the concern in her eyes, Clíodhna thought perhaps she had. Clíodhna closed her own eyes and concentrated once again on her surroundings. She still detected the same mysterious smell that had eluded her in the night, only now the odor intermingled with two other scents in addition to the one that drifted from this new, dark woman beside her.

Again, one of the scents held saltiness, a bitterness, reminding Clíodhna of home. But then the smell dissipated, gone like so many other things she had lost. This awareness of others around her, other women in her same position, piqued her curiosity, but she did not have the ability to move, to turn her head and see her traveling companions.

Clíodhna made a concentrated effort to discern the other strange odors of the women nearby. One held an earthy, woodland fragrance, with strong, feral undertones—too visceral, too animalistic. It set Clíodhna on edge, an olfactory warning, *stay back*. All these individuals, whoever they were, did not move, did not make their presence known to Clíodhna, so she assumed that they, like her, lay bound and flat on their backs, waiting to face their new fate.

With little else to do, Clíodhna closed her eyes again and listened, trying to ignore the needle-like strands of hay poking and scratching the most inconvenient places on her body. She heard horses and men, some riding, some walking, their footsteps crunching along the road. Hooves clicked and clacked on the gravel, but then she heard something else. Low at first, a baritone rumble that grew louder, developing into a growl so fierce, it made the hair on the back of Clíodhna's neck stand on end.

The carriages, including Clíodhna's own, stopped moving, and shouts erupted from the men outside. A high-pitched howl burst from within Clíodhna's own carriage, piercing her ears as she lay unable to cover them. The cry came from the owner of the alarming smell. The mournful, fear-filled keening sucked the breath from Clíodhna's lungs. Deep within her womb, the swimming infant lashed out, eliciting a moan from Clíodhna. The owner of the agitated voice howled louder and louder, echoing the increasing bellows and growls that came from somewhere farther ahead in their caravan. A man screamed, a ghastly death shriek that pierced through the howls. Then the noise stopped, cut short, followed by a sharp crack and a high-pitched whine from the rumbling animal.

Silence, brief but ominous, descended on the caravan. The frantic woman in Clíodhna's carriage sobbed, then repeated over and over again, *Sergei! Sergei! Sergei!* She did this until the woman on the other side of Clíodhna barked a curt command.

In response, the other woman grew quiet, her sobs turning into a low, muffled cry, interrupted intermittently by a whispered *Sergei.*

Shouts rang out, and the carriages moved forward again. The men's voices were no longer audible. The entire atmosphere surrounding their caravan had changed. Clíodhna could feel it in the air. The wheels turned, the horses plodded along, and the men trudged on as time carried them all. Soon the caravan slowed. Shouts echoed around the carriages, and the steady pace of the creaky wheels came to a gentle stop. Horses whinnied and snorted, scraping their hooves along the earth, eager to be allowed to graze. In the distance, doors opened and slammed shut. Heavy objects fell to the ground with loud thuds, and not far away, Clíodhna heard hay being distributed for the horses, a gentle shush followed by eager neighs and loud, wet inhales.

The hinges of her own carriage groaned as a door she could not see opened. The air in the carriage changed as the coolness of the oncoming night flooded into the small interior. Breathing in the cleaner air, Clíodhna scanned her body and felt the sharp pressure of the child within suddenly pressing against her bladder. The color drained from her face as she realized her desperate need to relieve herself. She hoped her captors would have some shred of pity for her condition.

A male voice yelled into the carriage, a biting urgency ringing through his sharp words, their meaning lost to Clíodhna. Try as she might, Clíodhna could not bring herself to a sitting position. The angle of her large belly and the tight binds on her arms prevented her from moving at all. She lay still, paralyzed like a worm.

The dark woman beside her sat up with ease, her arms unbound, which struck Clíodhna as odd. Looking down at Clíodhna, the woman smiled and said something, which Clíodhna did not understand. She responded with a blank stare. The woman sighed, then reached over and grasped Clíodhna by her shoulders, pulling the pregnant woman into a sitting position. Gasping at the pain from her injury, but grateful for the assistance, Clíodhna took a moment to compose herself and then managed another weak smile. Looking around for the first time, she took in her surroundings.

Burlap blanketed the hay covering the bottom of the carriage interior. It was a sad attempt at comfort for the four female prisoners. Directly across from Clíodhna sat the tallest, palest woman she had ever seen. Her hair, her body, her eyes—all completely absent of pigment. White locks, the color of fresh snow, fell over her shoulders, stark against the dark gown that hung on her lanky frame. The woman reminded Clíodhna of a lengthy, slender piece of driftwood. Her willow-like limbs, elegant and long, did not look capable of supporting any weight at all.

This pale creature, so elegant, so strange, held the familiar ocean scent. Clíodhna tried to catch her eyes. *Are you like me?* But the lithe woman would not return her gaze. She stared at a space somewhere beyond the open door. She maintained a regal air, evident in the tilt of her head, as if she were better than all of them, better than her captors, better than her fellow captives.

A large man, with a long, dark coat and a face like beaten leather, reached into the carriage and grabbed the elegant woman by her pallid hair, jerking her out into the fading sunlight. She screamed, a high-pitched wail, baring sharp teeth like Clíodhna's. This caught Clíodhna's attention. She looked closer at the woman, at her white neck, stretched at a most awkward angle by the cruel man. And there they were. The gill slits. A kindred spirit.

Clíodhna called out to her, speaking in her native Gaelic. But the woman, her hands bound like Clíodhna's, did not answer. She only shrieked on and on. She disappeared into the oncoming night, out of Clíodhna's sight, dragged against her will out of the carriage, her keening growing more and more distant.

That left three. Clíodhna, the dark woman, and the third. She was the one who had a connection to the silenced beast, Sergei. This woman—no longer agitated, only sullen—surprised Clíodhna. Small and tiny, like a little bird, she was a stark comparison to the now absent white merrow. This birdlike beauty had dark hair wound in intricate braids around her delicate head. Similar in color to the wood of the carriage, slightly dark and warm, reminiscent of the forest, the diminutive woman's skin looked unwashed. She wore a long flowing skirt that held more colors than Clíodhna had ever seen in her entire life. Never had she seen such brilliant fabric, embedded with sparkling bits of stone that reflected the light from the open carriage door.

The forest girl, for she was very young, scowled at Clíodhna with green eyes, furthering Clíodhna's belief that this woman belonged to the woods. Her dark furrowed brow seemed to pierce

Clíodhna's soul. This young thing sat farther back in the carriage, and so Clíodhna had the misfortune of leaving next. She made no protest, hoping that her docile behavior would yield her better treatment for both her child and herself. It did not.

The cloaked man initially grabbed Clíodhna's arm to pull her out of the confined space. But his gentleness rapidly evaporated as he then seized Clíodhna by her neck, crushing her windpipe. Involuntary tears rolled from her eyes as she gasped for air. When she cleared the doorway, the man slammed her onto her feet, then reached down into his boot and produced a long blade. The steel glinted in the fading light, and Clíodhna waited for the coolness of the metal to open her skin.

The man moved behind her and pressed himself against Clíodhna's back. She could smell his foul skin, the leather of his coat, and his rank breath. He lingered there, against her, a little too long. Clíodhna waited for the blade, but instead the man leaned over and cut the ropes between her legs, then kicked her forward.

She stumbled but did not fall, walking onward, continuing in the direction she had been pushed. She did not look back. Clíodhna took a few short steps, the blood slowly returning to her legs, then felt the man behind her once more. He grabbed her by the hair and dragged her to a small cooking fire close to a group of trees near the roadside.

There he unceremoniously deposited her on the ground next to the white merrow. Clíodhna tried again to meet her eyes, but the pale woman would not reciprocate the look, keeping her cold stare on the distant trees. Clíodhna followed her gaze but saw nothing but a dense forest as far as the eye could see. The firelight illuminated the fair woman's breathtaking face. Her bone structure, a perfect symmetry of nature, held eyes as pale as ice. Clíodhna could not help but stare at her.

A thud startled Clíodhna from her inspection of the cold, colorless merrow. The dark woman, the one who had dressed Clíodhna's wounds, was dropped to the ground beside Clíodhna. Turning to face the new woman, Clíodhna's jaw dropped. The woman had no legs.

At first glance, the upper part of the woman's body appeared perfectly normal, but as Clíodhna examined her more closely, she noticed strong, overly developed muscles in the woman's arms. Her shoulders appeared higher than normal, rising like a shrug toward her ears. The half-woman did not need restraints. Clíodhna assumed the men held little stock in the likelihood that this particular captive would run.

The half-woman's firm arms hung loosely against her wide torso. Clíodhna stared in amazement as she then used her hands to walk over to the fire. Balancing on one arm, the small woman threw a piece of kindling into the growing blaze with the other.

The child within shifted and Clíodhna moaned from the unbearable strain on her bladder. She crossed and uncrossed her legs, while deeply inhaling, the color in her face draining away with each passing moment. The half-woman turned from the fire and stared at Clíodhna, observing her discomfort. Then she yelled to one of the men standing nearby.

A short, round kettle of a man ambled over. His face bore scars around his mouth, and his hair peeked out at odd angles from below his floppy hat. The kettle man glowered at all the women, then spit on the ground between Clíodhna and the pale merrow beside her. He leaned back, his bowlegs curving into an awkward arch, then rolled his shoulders. Moving his long coat away from his body, the plump little man revealed a hatchet and a sharp, imposing blade tucked into his strained belt. Shifting his weight from side to side, he hooked his thumbs into his belt then spat again.

The half-woman addressed the man. Her voice seemed stern, yet pleading. Several times, she nodded her head towards Clíodhna as her voice rose in urgency. The man seemed to understand after a short interchange took place between the pair, which ended with the man jerking Clíodhna to her feet and shoving her towards the woods. He barked at the half-woman, who nodded in response. She leaned on her left hand while pointing with her right, indicating that they should go into the forest. Clíodhna moved forward, and the half-woman followed. So did the man.

Clíodhna, beyond caring who was around while she made water, let them all watch her attempt to relieve herself. The fluid pressed urgently against her innards and Clíodhna gasped. With bound arms, she attempted to squat down but could not. She almost fell over. When she attempted the feat a second time, Clíodhna felt the woman's hand bracing her back, holding her in place to ease the imbalance of Clíodhna's inability to use her arms and her thick, swollen belly. Turning to look at the half-woman, Clíodhna offered a small smile of gratitude, then stood. The woman nodded in return.

Relief spread across Clíodhna's face and body. She had the intuition and generosity of the strange woman beside her to thank for her body's release. Clíodhna felt an immediate kinship with this new friend, and so she looked at her and spoke her own name, carefully sounding out each syllable, while nodding her chin down to her chest.

"*Klee-oh-na,*" she said, repeating her name three times.

At first, the woman did not understand. She cocked her head to the side, squinting her strong brow. On the third pronunciation of Clíodhna's name, the woman's face changed, her thick eyebrows rose in understanding, and a grin smoothed away some of the woman's harsh features.

"Ah!" she exclaimed, then pointed to Clíodhna. "*Klee-oh-na!*"

Clíodhna nodded vigorously, then smiled in return. It was the half-woman's turn. She pointed to herself and said, "*Arr-ah-too-sah.*"

It took her a few tries to wrap her mouth around the syllables, but Clíodhna managed to master Arethusa's name. Their moment was cut short by the stout guard, who kicked Clíodhna to the ground while shouting angrily at the two women. Arethusa scurried to Clíodhna's side. As she helped the pregnant woman right herself, she slipped her dark, calloused hand around Clíodhna's swollen abdomen and looked into the face of the soon-to-be mother. Then she whispered a word, just one word, loud enough so that only Clíodhna could hear. The word fell from Arethusa's lips, sinking like a stone cast into the sea.

Nomia.

13

Evie

I walked through the door a few minutes early. It was the day after the Gaspee parade and foot race, so most people were home, nursing their hangovers, waking up on their lawns, wondering why their mouths tasted like low tide, before remembering that they had drunk themselves into oblivion, with the start of the parties at nine the previous morning. Therefore, The Elephant Room was mostly deserted. I had only been in a few times. I found their cocktails too amazing. I do bad things after I leave places where the cocktails are *too amazing*.

The restaurant had two areas. The bottom section held tables and chairs nestled next to floor-to-ceiling glass doors, which looked out on Broad Street. In the cooler winter months, the doors stayed closed, but on this beautiful morning, they all stood wide open. A nice breeze flowed through to the second section on the upper level, accessible by way of a long ramp.

The upper section created an easy conversational environment with sturdy love seats and lounge chairs, scattered coffee-house style. One woman with blue hair appeared to be a permanent fixture there, furiously typing away on a beat-up laptop with a Star Wars decal emblazoned across the front.

Deep, melodic trance music wafted down from the speakers in the ceiling. The new agey sounds flowed over the lazy fans. The place sort of reminded me of an opium den. With crêpes. And martinis.

Planning my strategy, I opted to sit in the section with the tables and chairs, where there were no other customers. That way, should shit hit the proverbial fan, I could make an easy escape right out the big open doors. Besides, the front area had a more formal feel. Things were weird enough. I didn't need to be all cozy on a love seat with the woman who had tried to kill me.

I sat down at a table, close to an open door, and a slender, dark-haired server approached.

"Good morning," she said in a sultry voice. "I'm Melanie, and I'll be taking care of you today."

"Hello, Melanie. I'm Evie. I'll be your customer," I replied. "Can I have a mimosa? And can you pour it like you hate the owner?"

She laughed a deep, genuine laugh and said, "I don't hate him—*today*. But I'll see what I can do." She smiled at me before asking, "Are you meeting anyone or dining alone? No judgment."

"None taken," I said. "I am meeting someone. It's not a happy meeting, so if I look terrified, and my glass is empty, can I slip you a twenty right now to make sure my glass stays full?"

"I don't have a problem with that," she said. "And you can keep the twenty. It's my job to make sure you're happy."

"Then we're going to get along swimmingly, Ms. Melanie."

She nodded and headed up the ramp, returning a few minutes later with a tall purplish drink.

"*Purple?*" I pointed at the glass.

"Yes," she said. "There are blueberries and *plenty* of the other good stuff."

"Oh," I said, skeptical, and took a sip. "Not bad." It was surprisingly delicious. "This will service my needs just fine." Another winning laugh, then she was gone, back up the ramp to the service counter.

The vantage point where I sat revealed the latent trash from yesterday's festivities. On my walk into the Village from Rachael's house, I had noticed that the city of Warwick, the south side of the Village, had done a bang-up job of cleaning overnight. I even noticed the tracks of a street sweeper, leaving the gutters of Warwick sparkling clean in the morning light.

When I'd crossed over the bridge into the city where I live (and pay ridiculous taxes), I noticed the soda cans, the crumpled paper napkins and coffee cups, the shredded white bits of paper from those obnoxious firecrackers that kids just love to throw at the ground. *Snap!* Burned paper goes everywhere. *Nice job, Cranston*, I thought bitterly.

As I sat there, internally grimacing at the trash, I noticed a woman walking up the street towards the Village from the Warwick side. Beneath a wide-brimmed sun hat, the woman's hair, long and white-blonde and secured in a braid, swung as she walked. Her hips and chest were noticeable in her pale-yellow, hippy-style sundress. The fabric contrasted nicely with her long tan legs. My coffee and charcuterie shop buddies up the street might call her *fetching*.

If you were wondering about my old men friends—Joe, Angelo, Giovanni, and Tony—they refused to come into The Elephant Room. When it first opened, they went in to check out the new scene but were horrified to discover that The E Room did not have olive and cheese plates. There were other things *inherently wrong* with the new place, but wanting to support the new guy, they had drafted a list of demands and presented them to the new owner. If he met them, they would become regulars. I looked around—no old men, no self-service coffee dispensers. I'm guessing their demands remained unmet.

Back to the fetching woman. She walked right in the door and looked straight at me, tipping down her sunglasses. I frowned.

"Rachael," I said, shaking my head.

"I'm sorry," she said in a weird English accent that did not sound English at all. "Do I know you?"

I sighed deeply and tried to suppress the smirk attempting to bubble its way onto my face. "No," I said. "My mistake. I thought you were someone else."

"No bother," she replied in the same bad accent. "I'll leave you to it then. I'm off to enjoy a morning cocktail on the landing.

Cheerio." Off she went, up the ramp, her fake braid swinging over her curvy ass.

I looked back out the window, and there she was. *Nomia.* She stood in front of the gas station across the street, staring at me. I heard her voice in my head. *You came. I didn't think you would.* I couldn't breathe. The nausea kicked in like it always did, and I realized that I really, really hated it when she was around. I found her mind-emails incredibly intrusive. In truth, it freaked me the hell out. I didn't know what to do, so I waved at her. She didn't wave back.

Nervously, I glanced up at the bar separating the top level from the bottom. The English blonde not-Rachael sat there, looking down at me. She nodded ever so slightly. Turning back to the street, I no longer saw Nomia. I looked back at Rachael. Her brow was scrunched up, as if the sun were in her eyes. I swung my head back to the street, but my view was blocked. Nomia stood directly in front of me.

"May I sit down?"

I wanted to vomit and couldn't find my words, so I nodded, and she sat across from me. She looked awful. Her eyes, so beautiful in my memory, had sunken deep into the sockets of her skull. It looked as if she hadn't slept in days. Her hair, once so luminous, hung limp, greasy, and unwashed around her face. Even her skin looked dull and gray. And she was thin. Not that I ever saw her as anything but a skinny bitch, but this was different. All her impressive, toned muscle? Gone, leaving nothing but flesh and bones. The button-down shirt and jeans she wore hung on her like a scarecrow's clothing, all loose and baggy.

"You've looked better," I said.

Hey, if this meeting was all about the two of us putting our cards faceup on the table, why start off with lies? She looked liked shit, so I voiced this observation as tactfully as possible. Apparently, when confronted by a mortal enemy in a social situation, I become polite. *Weird.* She didn't say anything but fumbled with the buttons on her shirt.

"This is awkward," she said.

"No shit."

Melanie showed up, as if on cue, and asked if Nomia would like something to drink. She ordered water and asked for a menu, but I think it was only for show.

"Where's Richard?" I said.

"I don't know."

"Bullshit!" I shouted. Someone somewhere up in the lounge area gasped, and it wasn't Rachael.

"Look," said Nomia. "I'm guessing I know about as much as you do. Did you go to Boston?"

"Yes," I replied.

"Was his place still a mess?"

"I knew it was you! *Where is he?*" I hissed.

"The place was a mess when we got there. Someone had been waiting for us."

"Who is *we? Who* was waiting? *Who?*"

"I'm so tired, Evelyn," she said. "Please, we don't have much time. My sister Nix is in danger, and so is your brother. What do you know?"

"Oh, no," I said, trying to keep the volume of my voice to

a bare minimum. "You don't get to come in here and make demands. Not after what you've done to me, to my family. I thought I was done with you, and now you come in here and demand information from *me?* I don't think so. I've been kicked out of my own house because of you! For all I know, this is a trap and your wretched, crazy-ass family has done something to my husband and child!"

She looked down at her lap, and her stringy hair fell across her face. She mumbled something. Something I couldn't hear.

"*What did you say?*" I snarled.

She looked up, and her eyes met mine. There was a sincerity in them and a deep fatigue, the kind I had seen many times in the grieving faces of those who had lost someone in a long arduous battle against mortality.

"I don't know where it all went so horribly wrong," she said.

The part of me that had counseled so many families, guided them through the darkness of their grief, that humane part of me, the part that is not a giant fuck-up, kicked into gear. The funeral director took over.

I rubbed my face with my hands, trying to wash away all the pain and fear from this horrible, wretched woman. I knew that if I was going to find my brother, I needed to listen to her. So that's what I did.

"Tell me what happened," I said.

Over the next hour, she told me some awful things. She told me that she had intended to destroy me and my entire family, starting with Richard, but something went wrong with the plan. She had fallen in love with my brother.

"*What the fuck is wrong with you?* Don't you have a husband?" I growled.

"Not anymore," she replied. "He's gone. I can't find him or Pearl. Not that I blame him. I was a terrible wife and even worse at motherhood. They're better off without me."

That didn't sit well with me. Here she was telling me that *she* was a shitty mother. Well, sister, I wrote the book on being a shitty mom, but I would *never* give up on Savannah. *Never.* I shook my head in disgust. "I don't get it," I said. "What is *wrong* with you?"

"That's a great question," she answered. Her gaze drifted towards the street. "I've wronged so many, many people. I don't even know where I could start to fix all the wrongs I've tallied up over the years. But I tried to start with Nix—and now, with you, to some extent. I think whoever took Richard also took Nix."

"Whoa. Whoa. Whoa. Back up," I said. "Aren't you supposed to be a thousand leagues under the sea? *In Ireland?*"

"Here's the thing. It doesn't add up. We left Rhode Island and went to Boston to book passage on a ship."

"I'm sorry," I said. "Maybe I don't understand how this whole mermaid thing works, but I was under the impression that you can swim—you know, pretty well. Why the hell do you need a boat to travel across, you know, *water?*"

"I can't swim that well."

"*What?* I'm sorry. I don't think I heard you right. Did you just say *you couldn't swim all that well?*"

She nodded. "We're not all the same, you know."

"No," I said. "I don't know. I don't know shit. All I know is that you have made my life a living hell. You have opened my eyes to a world, your world, that I never knew existed, and let me tell you something, sister, my life would have been a whole lot better if you had left me off your screwed-up submarine. *And what the hell are you talking about? You can't swim?*"

"It's a long story. I don't fully understand it, but that's the way it is. I can't swim long distances or I might drown."

"Holy shit," I said, leaning back. "So you do have flaws, beyond the whole homicidal thing."

"I never wanted to kill anyone," she said. "A lot of the things I've done were not right, but I've had my reasons."

"You had your *reasons?*" I said. "Like someone put a gun to your head and forced you to eat people?"

"Something like that," she said. Then she leaned in and whispered, "You're not free of sins, are you, Evie? Don't tell me you've forgotten about what you did to my *mother.*"

"This is fucked up," I said and rose to my feet. "I can barely swallow any of the shit you're dishing. I don't even know if I have the bandwidth to continue this conversation."

My head was pounding. A monster of a headache threatened to eclipse my entire consciousness. I needed to get the hell out of there.

"Melanie!" I yelled up the ramp.

"I knew this might be a lot for you. We should meet again, but it has to be soon. We are running out of time," she said and reached out for my arm.

I recoiled instantly. The familiar feeling of queasiness I only associated with this bitch rose up inside me like a viper about to strike.

"*Don't fucking touch me,*" I hissed.

"Richard," she said. "He told me about Oma. I'm sorry for your loss."

I just stared at her. I couldn't speak. This was madness. This woman—who had killed my neighbor for sport, who had broken into my home, who had threatened to kill my entire family, and who had then brought a horde of female predators to my summer home—wanted to offer me *her condolences? And what did she know about Oma?* I looked outside, searching the sky for locusts or a hailstorm of frogs. It was the only explanation for what was happening. When I looked back, she was at the door.

"Your friend makes a better redhead," she said and nodded up to Rachael in the upper level. "Blonde is highly overrated." She walked out the door and disappeared around the corner.

On the table in front of me was a note with an address.

> *If you're serious about finding Richard,*
> *meet me on Tuesday, 8:30 PM.*
>
> *Bring your friend.*

I recognized the address. It was the one at the end of Pawtuxet Point.

Melanie appeared beside me.

"You hollered?"

"Um," I stammered, still staring down at the note with her sadistically perfect handwriting.

"Another mimosa?" asked Melanie.

"No," I said. "I think I need to stay sharp. Just the check, please."

Melanie nodded and walked back up the ramp.

"Rach," I raised my voice. "You believe in mermaids?"

"Sure, honey."

"Good," I said, throwing some money down on the table. "Get your ass down here. We need to walk and talk. I have a story to tell."

Nomia

We stood on the dock. The others looked up at us from the harbor waters. I stretched, wet, naked, and tired, but mostly wanting to know why we had stopped. We had traveled north along the coastline from Rhode Island, but I had struggled to keep up. The hearty Irish sea-faring merrow, used to long oceanic journeys, had reached their limit with my lack of abilities. Nix, barely fatigued at all, refused to meet my eyes. She stood with her back as straight as a tree, her chin aloft, oblivious to the cold and her nakedness.

Beneath the ink-black sky, a cold wind blew in from the harbor, ushering in the new day as it announced its arrival. Far away, from the same direction these barbarians had come, I watched the sun slowly claw its way up over the horizon, desperate to make its presence known, as if it sought to say, *You will pay attention to me.* A force such as this celestial body had taught me so much about power, but what had I gained by wielding it? *What had I learned?* I stood on a dock, with my sister, who had once loved me but now hated me with a fire more intense than that of the relentless sun who killed the night each and every morning.

I shuddered even though I wasn't cold and angrily tugged at the leash around my neck. The rope had chaffed a ragged wound in my skin. It burned from the saltwater. I glanced over at my fair sister. Her ragged scar, received from a hunter long before I was born, ran from brow to chin, matching the deep pink tissue along her thigh.

I had always admired her scars and marveled at my sister's strength, her power, her ability to survive. A chasm gaped between us, even though we stood a few feet apart. I might fall down dead if she turned and met my gaze. Feeling a small shred of my brazen, old self, I reached out to her and grazed her arm with my fingers. She flinched, then, without looking at me, spat out these words in our native tongue:

Don't touch me, serpent.

I sighed. The years had gathered the scraps of our damage, of our sibling offenses, and had dressed us with garments made from our ugly carnage. We wore that foul clothing around our hearts, defensively pushing us away from the sisterly love we had once shared.

Seeing her anger, her silent defeat as she stood there—an involuntary captive at the hands of those whom *I* had wronged—chipped at something in my own frozen heart. All at once, I felt every ounce of the pride I had once felt for Nix, all the love, come rushing back to me, melting the ice in my soul.

I vowed to make things right.

I tried to speak to her with my mind, something I had not done in centuries. *Nix, my sister, I will make this right.* I could feel her resisting me, driving me out with her own walls. Gone was the trick of our youth, our secret game of speaking to one another. I would wear her down. After all, it was just the two of us now. The two of us against the Irish, against the world.

I stared at them, these Irish who called themselves *merrow.* Hideous, every single one of them. Like walruses, they bobbed in the water, barking at one another, bickering and shoving. A heated discussion happening among them.

The one they called Murtagh pulled himself up on to the dock and addressed us. "We've watched you swim," he said in English.

I said nothing.

"You're not very good at it."

I kept my silence.

"Why?"

"It's a long story," I sighed.

He seemed to consider this for some time, looking down at his brethren in the water. They seemed unconcerned with Murtagh's affairs. He shrugged, shook his head, then turned back to us.

"We will need to book passage for your crossing."

I nodded.

He nodded in return as he crouched down and shouted to the

men in the water. More arguing. I tried to understand what they were saying, but, not ever having a reason to learn Gaelic, my understanding of the crude language was deplorable. I could only make out a few words, a phrase here and there.

From my eavesdropping, I gathered enough information to understand that my passage was not a cost they were willing to undertake. It would require making contact with land-dwellers, and they were eager to get on with their long journey home. I lost more of the conversation to my lack of understanding, but then I heard a word I did know, associated with a name I had come to loathe. Evie McFagan had a brother. That brother lived nearby. *Interesting.*

Murtagh finished his discussion with his brothers, then stood and addressed us.

"Lean forward."

He had pulled a blade from behind his back. I stared at him, unmoving. Nix saw the knife and moved forward with unnatural speed, a menacing look on her face, surprising all of us. I hadn't thought she cared.

Murtagh held up his hands in defense and shook his head. "No, no, no," he said. "We're done here. You can go. If you return south to Narragansett Bay, we will know. We will find you, and we will kill you. The journey ahead is yours now. Make smart decisions. Go forward from here. Start a new life."

He leaned forward and grabbed my neck, slicing the rope. After he did so, he backed away quickly, then offered the knife to Nix, handle facing towards her. She eyed him up and down, then hesitantly took the blade and cut the rope from her own neck. When she had finished, I watched as she weighed the blade in her hand, turning the hilt over and over, examining the weapon.

In rough English and with a heavy accent, she said, "Good knife." Then she flipped it in the air, catching the sharp edge in her palm, offering the handle to Murtagh. He took it and nodded. Then he was gone.

We both peered over the edge of the wooden dock into the filthy waters of Boston Harbor. Nothing but a few pieces of listing garbage ebbed and flowed in the gentle current.

And that was how we found ourselves. Naked and alone, without family, without a home, stuck in a city we had avoided for centuries, wondering what to do next. *Without a family. Without a mother.* Our mother, Kolga, was dead, and that bitch who had ruined everything had taken her away from us.

Still avoiding each other, we turned and looked at the enormous skyscrapers lining the harbor. I stared up at one of the buildings closest to where we stood, an overwhelming archway with a glittering gold dome on top. As the stark sun struck the amber surface of the dome, it sent brilliant shafts of light into a thousand directions at once.

A plan formed in my mind. A good plan. One that would take a few years to fester and swell into a fantastic plan. A plan to beat all plans. I let the intricacies of the plot weave themselves into a recognizable framework. In my mind, the dots connected, and the plan took shape. Boston was out of the question—for the moment. We needed to heed Murtagh's advice. We needed to move on. The Bay, our home for so very long, was out of the question. But there was another answer.

In our native tongue, I spoke to my sister, "We will go to the Island of the Five, near The Long Land. We will return and try to find the Seawomen. There we will heal as we mourn our mother. In time, when all is forgotten, we will come back to this city and seek the one she calls *Richard*—the one she calls *brother*. Then when the timing is right, we will avenge."

Nix looked at me, and for the first time in many, many centuries, she smiled.

15

The Merrow Codex
Species Archive #14 - Bestla

Caratocos, elder scholar

*B*estla, The Mother, or *Kolga* was first encountered by the Seafarer Murtagh in his early journeys to the north, the home of the fair people living beneath the snow-covered cliffs. Some say she is eternal, that she lived before time began. Perceived as a giant, a fierce warrior, and the mother to many, her origins are unknown, her species still unclassified.

She lives beneath the waves. That much we know, but her offspring, from the accounts we have received, seem varied and numerous with some records pointing towards thirty-four children. Some live on land and some beneath the seas. Her male offspring tend to favor dry ground, while the females take to the waters. Nothing is known about the mates she chooses. No recorded history has ever revealed the patriarchal origins of her multitude of children.

The land-dwellers speak of her as if she were a goddess among men—a great and terrible goddess, Bestla, capable of bringing on storms and other travesties. Other accounts, usually from womenfolk, describe her as a protector of mothers. With her own many offspring, it is not surprising that she would carry an awareness and a degree of care regarding those who bring life into the world, thereby keeping a watchful eye and protective hand over those who need protection the most.

Kolga, as she is known by her many daughters, is taller than most male merrow by nearly half. Her pigmentation, by all accounts, has been reported as nonexistent. Paler than the native land-dwellers of the north region, her lack of pigment could be partially attributed to her reported nocturnal nature, coming out only at night to watch over her many children, both biological and adopted.

When Murtagh had arrived in the land of the northern snows, he had gone into one of the busier seaport villages in search of information, as is the way of the Seafarers. While warming himself at a tavern one evening, Murtagh heard mention of The Mother. Curious, he pressed for more information as he sat by the fireside, enjoying the stew and mead so prevalent in that region. The locals spoke of The Mother in hushed voices as if she were nearby, waiting to descend upon any naysayers within earshot.

Leaning in close to those who spoke, Murtagh learned that no one had heard from her since the death of her son, many, many years past. They spoke of her son—a great terror, one who had done something so terrible that no one left their homes at night. After his demise, the local people had rejoiced, but The Mother had disappeared, retreating into the deep waters beneath the fjords. Time had passed, and she did not return. They thought she had died of grief.

News of a water species piqued Murtagh's interest. Reaching into his traveling cloak, he produced a few gold coins in hopes of urging the locals to spin the tale further, to tell more of this most intriguing character. With great reluctance and the aid of a few generously filled tankards, the locals unraveled a story, a most terrible story, one ending in tragedy for all involved. This is what they said.

It all started on a moonless night, when their great king had been torn limb from limb by a horrible monster known as The Son. News of such a grievous assault spread like wildfire across all the neighboring kingdoms. Something had to be done. The Son would need to be executed and their great king avenged. This beast they called The Son had been terrorizing the countryside, stealing sheep and other livestock, cutting holes in fish traps and nets, and peering into the windows of the good county folk. Never before that assault had the monster done more than these petty crimes in their region.

Murtagh inquired as to The Son's origins. This abomination of nature belonged to *The White Mother, she who lived beneath the ice.* He had a name so terrible that all who heard it would tear at their hair and scream at the atrocities afflicted on their once great realm. Even when pressed, they still would not speak his name. Therefore, in this account, he is referred to as The Son.

This domain, the same realm where Murtagh now sat listening to this incredible tale, embodied not one, but three kingdoms. Unity and amicability among the three kingdoms did not always exist, but after hearing of the loss of their fellow king, the surviving two kings convened in the Great Hall, a sacred structure shared by all three kingdoms. They demanded vengeance.

Who among them was strong enough to go against The Son who lived deep within the mountains? Who indeed?

As fate would have it, a ship carrying thirteen great warriors had made port in the sound that same morning, as if the gods themselves had intervened and sailed these adventurers straight into the kingdom's harbor. The leader stood taller than any man in the land. Anyone who looked upon him knew that he had the strength and courage of a hero, a powerful hero. He carried a broadsword on his hip the likes of which had never been seen anywhere in the land. Children flocked around him, begging to touch the steel. The impressive man laughed and threw coins to the young, tousling their blond locks.

The two kings knew that the gods had answered their cry for revenge, and so they bade the newcomers to meet them in the Great Hall. Beneath the mighty beams and ancient timbers, an impressive trove of gold and treasures lay at the feet of the kings—an offering of payment for the head of The Son. Being adventurers, the warriors reveled in the notion of a worthy opponent—a fierce kingslayer.

The two sides struck a deal and the band of warriors organized themselves in the Great Hall. For a fortnight they lit roaring fires, flew their battle flags, and beat their thunderous war drums, announcing their intentions of malice against the horrible creature. But The Son did not return.

Another fourteen nights passed, and still they heard nothing. Their talk wandered towards future adventures yet to be discovered, somewhere, anywhere beyond this cold, dark land. They murmured to themselves. They decided to leave on the morrow. All agreed. The Son must have moved on, they told themselves. The sight of their collective strength had been enough to drive the beast back, deep into the mountains, where he would remain and no man dared to venture.

So the men relaxed and amused themselves with acts of hedonism, celebrating their last night with their hearty northern friends. They lit the enormous fires outside the Hall. They feasted with the local people, and beautiful, tall, exotic women were brought in for entertainment. New rhythms on the war drums could be heard across the kingdoms, a wild cadence of merriment, a welcome change from the angry thunder of the previous month. The villagers joined the warriors as they raised their cups in celebration of life, of triumph, of having won a victory without fighting a battle.

Multiple children came into the world nine months hence. Most were born without fathers. Once the moon had hidden behind her veil of clouds that night, the fires died down, the men grew tired of their carnal distractions, and the Great Hall fell quiet. That was when The Son returned.

While the men slept and dreamt of happier times, *He whose name one does not speak* took to the rafters, unnoticed by the drunken, slumbering men far below. The monster's incredible size and bulk did not encumber his movements. Like a lithe, limber child in the trees of youth, the beast hooked his arms around the great timbers and, with silent speed and elegance, he swung from beam to beam, descending on his slumbering victims without a sound. They say the first man who fell never cried out, for the horrible beast tore his head from his body and threw it into the fireplace, where the man's face, still peaceful in his permanent slumber, sat with his eyes closed forever.

The Son struck again and again from above, plucking man after man from where he slept, some from the bare bosoms of women who, for reasons known only to The Son, were left untouched. The men received no such amnesty. He tore them apart, like a sullen child pulls the petals from a flower, carelessly casting the pieces aside. Now bathed in blood, the remaining men and women, roused from their slumber, awoke others with their screams of terror. Many died before anyone knew was happening.

When the head warrior from across the sea awoke, he grabbed his powerful broadsword and stood at the ready. The remaining adventurers followed suit, eyeing their leader with weary, blood-shot eyes. The Son, incited by the blood that surrounded him, went into a frenzy and never saw the steel that struck him.

On that moonless night, the strong warrior, the Hero they would herald through song in all the Great Halls of the north for many years to come, had put an end to the harvesting of men. With one great swipe of his broadsword, he parted arm from body. A howl filled the Great Hall, the ghastly cry ringing through the villages of all three kingdoms, echoing off the fjords and across the wide sound. Then The Son, cradling the stump where his arm had once been, disappeared into the darkness.

The carnage had been great that night, and many a loss was suffered, but the Hero had not finished the job. The beast still lived! Therefore, the Hero could not collect his bounty. This detail mattered little to the warrior. Armed with the knowledge that he faced a worthy opponent, one who had taken down five of his own men and twenty others, he vowed to destroy the creature if it was the last thing he ever did. The villagers hung the terrible, bodiless arm above the entrance of the Great Hall, a warning, should the body ever return, that his demise would soon follow.

Far away in the steep mountains, the place where The Son called home, the beast had returned to his domain, his body bloodied, his gait different with a lost limb. But he did not return to emptiness or solitude. What the Hero and the men of the three kingdoms did not know was that The Son did not live alone. He had many brothers, and when they saw what had happened to their strongest brother, they swore revenge.

It seems, the locals said to Murtagh, who listened with great intensity, that there are two sides to every story. Both do not always see the light of day. Sometimes, when a great and powerful character in a story speaks, he is the only one heard. It takes a wise man to ask, Why did this happen? What is the other side? Murtagh smiled at those who told the tale, for he knew that they were wise to recognize this. And so he asked, *What is the other side?* And they told him.

The king had not gone to his grave at the whim of The Son's madness or boredom. The Son had acted on behalf of his family, his mother's family, Kolga's family. The king had defiled one of Kolga's daughters, one of The Son's sisters. And so The Son's violence had not been senseless. It had been an act of revenge. His latest attack on the warriors of the Great Hall had been an offensive one, a means of disabling his newest opponent. So, when he, the avenger, had returned to his own kin missing a limb, his brothers vowed that they would not let such a thing go unanswered.

The next night, they lit their own fires, setting the tops of the mountains ablaze. And they beat their drums, striking fear into all who heard the terrifying sound. Most in the kingdoms had no idea that so many of Kolga's offspring lived near to them and had done so for a very long time.

The Hero and his surviving band of adventurers heard the drums from the mountains and saw the blazing fires, yet this act of aggression did not frighten them. They were ready and willing to finish what they had started, ready to avenge their fallen brothers and friends. Armed and angry, they struck out through the forest when the last rays of the sun disappeared over the vast sea.

The band of adventurers was skilled in battle. The brothers, strong in their own right, were not strong enough to resist them, and so they fell one by one at the hands and swords of the men who had come from the sea.

Once more, The Son, unable to protect his family, watched, helpless as the foreigners cut down his brothers, like wheat in a field. When they had mowed a path of fallen brothers, they found The Son, still bleeding and near death himself, cradling the stump of his missing arm and waiting for his own end. The Hero looked at The Son, and The Son returned the great warrior's gaze. The two mighty men spoke to one another—but no words passed either one's lips. Their exchange ended in mutual nods, an acknowledgement of each other's prowess.

The Hero swung his great steel and brought it across the The Son's neck, and the terrifying creature fell down dead. Knowing that a courageous flame had just expired, the Hero took the fallen creature's body and cast it into the sea, as was the custom far away in his own country—a respectful way of sending the soul to the next life.

In the depths of the sea, Kolga knew what had happened. She broke the surface of the water near the body of her fallen child, her hair as white as the foam that surrounded her. She had loved him dearly, and her scream could be heard echoing across the fjords and into all across the north.

No one saw her after that. Not for many, many years. For decades to come, the story of The Son found its seat in front of the hearths of all three kingdoms on many a cold, dark night. Children shuddered at the mention of The Mother's name, hiding their faces in their furs. They kept away from the caves at the bottom of the fjords where they knew Kolga slept in her grief, crying out occasionally and sending sprays of seawater against the jagged rocks.

Time passed, and then one day, a girl appeared in the market. She was tall, taller than the tallest man, and she was fair, fairer than the snows that fell all winter long. A more beautiful girl than any who had lived in any of the three kingdoms. The elder generation saw her and spoke in hushed tones. The crones saw her and tore at their hair, for they remembered the tales of the great white Mother. Could this be Kolga? Reborn in another form? No one knew.

The girl walked among the people on market day, her long white hair moving freely behind her as she strolled past the fish stalls, bits of bone and shell woven in several tiny braids that swung gently in the warm breeze of the endless summer day. She spoke to no one. She just stared the offerings in each of the stalls as if she were seeing the world for the very first time.

The people in every home spoke of her that evening, and quite a few of the men hoped they would see her again. Many seasons passed before anyone did, and the villagers had almost forgotten about the white beauty. But then, on another treasured summer day, the kind of day one remembers in the depths of winter, the beauty returned to the market. This time, she came with three sisters, each one a shade or two slightly less lovely than she was, but nonetheless, each a striking beauty in her own right.

They moved among the people, examining the sellers and their wares. They passed the men, who stood with their mouths agape, and then they disappeared. Again that night, while the sun still shone as it did at that time of the year, the villagers spoke of the gaggle of white beauties who had moved among them that morning in the market.

Who were these women? Where had they come from?

The crones knew who they were. They tore out what hair they had left as they clucked their tongues. A bad omen, they cried.

News traveled, as it always did, to the kings of the three kingdoms. One king had a wife, whom he loved and cherished, and so he waved this silly banter away with his jeweled hand. The second king listened with great interest, until he saw the look on his sour queen's face, ending the discussion for good. The third king had no queen. He, an eager young man and motivated, listened to the tale of the four white sisters with great interest.

If these striking women truly were the daughters of Kolga, the young king imagined how glorious it would be to have such bride, a bride of great physical prowess who would bear him many strong and powerful sons—sons who could grow up to claim the other two kingdoms for him, creating a dynasty. The dream grew like a fire in his mind, a blaze that burned away every other thought in his crowned head. He would not rest until the most beautiful of these women sat beside him in his own hall.

He sent out word. Whoever found the white sisters should bring them to his hall and in exchange be granted a fertile tract of land. This decree sent many eager men into the wilds, hungry with the thought of land and the idea of capturing such a thing of beauty.

Much to the dismay of the more productive, level-headed people of the villages, very little was accomplished during the following few weeks. Fish were not procured from the sea in the usual quantities, fields were left untended, and the livestock was poorly managed. Every man with a desire to quickly better himself sought the white women of the market.

When Kolga, who had not forgotten—or forgiven—the grievous act done to her offspring, heard of the king's decree, she gathered her daughters to her and told them the tale of their long-lost brothers, for these daughters had been born many, many years after the fall of their great brother. The oldest and wisest of the sisters, Íss, named so because her eyes were the clear gray color of ice, expressed a desire to leave the cold lands to seek a life elsewhere. The youngest daughter, Nix, did not agree. Strong and skilled with many a weapon, having been trained by the strongest of her living brothers, Nix believed that they should stay and fight for their independence.

But Kolga could not bear the loss of another child. Her wounds had not healed from the death of her Son and so many of his brothers, and so she gathered her daughters and took to the sea, heading south away from the land of the midnight sun. A shepherd boy, who had been tending his flock in the green fields at the most westerly point of the realm, watched as the women, thirteen in all, turned into fish and swam out into the deep waters. No one believed him, but they were enchanted by the idea of these women turning into fish, and so the story was passed from person to person, village to village, until it reached the ears of the ambitious king.

He did not give up but continued his search for the white women, long after the eager village men, previously so eager to better themselves, had abandoned their dreams and returned to their ordinary lives. So obsessed was this ambitious king that, as the story goes, he can still be seen on long summer nights, when the sun refuses to set, wandering along the westernmost cliff, searching the waves for the white women who became fish and swam away.

Murtagh thanked the men and women in the tavern for their impressive tale and mulled it over that night after he returned to his shelter near the beach. Certain that he had found others like himself, he determined to seek them out on his own. The next day he, too, traveled south, always asking in the taverns and marketplaces for stories of beautiful, white women—women who could become fish.

In most places, people openly laughed at Murtagh, thinking him daft, but every now and then, he would hear of a band of women, the mother of which was the most terrible of them all—a great she-beast of a woman who could rip a man's limb clear from his body. It was then that he knew he was on the right track. But the trail of the tales of men's limbs disappeared the closer he traveled to the southern part of Gaul, until everyone who heard his tale smiled with the wonderment of the telling but had nothing further to add.

Murtagh realized that he was close to home and so had returned to our waters with nothing but these tales to tell.

In recent years, the Seafarer Ronan has sent word of Kolga and her daughters. They live in Narragansett Bay, a sizable inlet in the region called New England, on the North American continent. Ronan had reported witnessing several violent events inflicted by these females in that area, many involving the barbaric act of human consumption.

As of this writing, a group of our own warriors has been sent to Narragansett Bay regarding an incident, or incidents, in which Kolga may have acted against our own descendants residing in those waters. These particular descendants may be of Ciabhán's lineage.

Bohemian Forest
Winter 1605

The scant, remaining light leaked away, swallowed whole by the encroaching ebony sky, while cold, ethereal powder fell. White. The earth, the trees, the entire world. All of it, white.

When the rain pummeled the forest, the force of the sky's release would create a deafening cacophony. The elegant snow, in direct contrast to the harsh, unforgiving rain, did the reverse. This particular discharge of the heavens dispelled all of the world's resonance, leaving a void of reverberation, a silence that permeated everything the snow touched, devouring all sound like a starving beast. Birds did not sing, animals did not scurry. Time slowed down, and the lazy snowflakes meandered to the frozen earth.

All along the blanketed forest floor, long, reaching shadows crept across gnarled roots of ancient, snow-covered trees. Their branches, encrusted with a mantle of colorless powder, drooped down towards the earth, resisting the urge to break beneath the burden of winter weight. Like obedient sentinels, the solid trees stood, as they had for a millennium, watching, impassive to the occasional activity at their feet.

She was being followed. The girl ran but could not hear her footfalls in the deep snow. She made no noise as she raised her bare legs, then thrust them back into the drifting powder. Like fresh-ground flour, the snow fell in sweeping cascades from her legs, her hair, her back. She ran swiftly, with purpose. She ran for her life.

Ragged plumes of moisture tore from her chest, the only disturbance in the forest. A beacon for the one who sought to destroy her—to rob her of her blood, her flesh. The girl's breath heaved forth from her lungs, spiraling in front of her as she moved. The warm air mixed with the falling wisps of frozen water intricately knitted itself into delicate flakes, disappearing as quickly as it fell. She headed for the river, but could not hear it. Not a trickle nor a gurgle, not one bubbling indication of the life-giving waters of her other home.

The river was so very far away.

The girl had been collecting what little kindling she could find. Stopping to clear the drifts, she had paused and lifted her head, bewitched by the blackness of the trees, so dark against the blinding white of the relentless snow. She had become transfixed, her gaze frozen. The newness of the white world caught her off guard. In winter, gray dominated the landscape. The sky, the land, even the old, worn and tattered garments she wore reflected the bleakness of winter. But when the snow fell, her world changed. The world was reborn. *White. Everything white.*

The girl shook her head and returned her attention to the task at hand. The thick, pale blanket of snow made the gathering all the more difficult. How long before the sun set? The clouded sky did not reveal the source of light, making it impossible to track the time remaining before complete darkness. She stared upwards, gazing again, hypnotized by the falling sky, when a cry, faint but shrill, maddening like the laughter of someone who had become lost in his own mind, broke her silent meditation. The hair on the back of her neck stiffened. The chill of fear, the first coldness she had felt all day, crawled across her chest and settled in like an unwanted visitor. Sweat formed on her upper lip, and although she wanted to, she could not swallow.

The eerie noise came again and the girl smiled, then shook her head. It was a black grouse, a male, crying out in the distance. Her amusement lasted only a moment. The grouse had been disturbed. Its call was a warning to others hiding nearby. Something big had come. She recognized the fear in the bird's call, the fear that now owned her as well. She spun in the clearing and saw her footprints in the newly fallen snow. She cursed her foolishness, tension tightening the space between her shoulders.

The grouse had gone silent while the forest held its breath. The girl turned her head from side to side, scanning the white landscape, the blackness of the trees. A cloud of tiny frozen particles flew into the air as she threw down her bundle of sticks. The cloud momentarily obscured her vision, and her body trembled as it dispersed, revealing a man astride the largest horse she had ever seen. The pair stood at the edge of the clearing, the man's wide-brimmed hat hiding his brow. His long cloak, dark as a raven's wing, flowed behind him.

The girl knew what the cloak concealed, a wide variety of sharp objects, all designed to tear her apart. The large stallion, as black as the man's cloak, snorted and circled, inflamed by the sight of her.

She knew why they were there, and both man and beast knew what she was. Their eyes met. A low whine escaped the girl's pale mouth. Every muscle in her body screamed the same word ... *run.*

He smiled as she took off. He lived for this part. When these creatures, normally so cold, grew warm from exertion, it made their blood flow more quickly. The man in black waited, observing the way she moved through the forest, allowing her time to feel safe, to feel as if she had made progress in her flight. His horse whinnied. Liver-colored lips snarled, revealing the bit firmly placed between strong, menacing teeth.

Snow collected along the brim of the man's wide hat. It dusted his shoulders and covered the tops of his worn leather riding boots. Reaching inside his cloak with his gloved hand, he felt his blade, warmed by his person. His fingers lingered on the hilt as he watched the girl retreat into the darkness. Once he could no longer see her, he freed the knife from its ornate sheathing. Spitting into the snow, he relieved his mouth of the bile that had brought him to her. She was his now. It was only a matter of running her down.

The man clicked his tongue, then kicked his boot into the beast's flank. But the stallion needed no urging. It had been trained to track and destroy. The large creature, more than eager to complete his mission, charged forward. Snow flew up in a cloud as they took off into the thick forest. He followed her tracks and saw that she was headed in the direction of the river. This brought another smile to his lips. Almost time.

The excitement grew within him, warming the inside of his legs, urging him towards his quarry. The light continued its aggressive exit from the day, but his eyesight, attuned to the darkness, tracked the footprints, their gait ever widening. He continued his pursuit, moving swiftly through the trees, increasing his speed as he heard her cries ringing through the woods.

So many moons ago, his first kill had been on an evening like this one. He'd been a boy of eleven at the time, and both he and his uncle had tracked for days high above the River Rhine. Perhaps the one they hunted thought the high precipice made her untraceable. Man and boy had crept up to her cave before dawn, flushed her out, and pursued her along the cliffs, far above the mighty river. Fighting back the intense pain in his gut, he had kept his concentration at an even keel, watching her, waiting for the right moment.

The thing had looked over the steep edge of the earth, then back at her pursuers. A smile split her face in two, both her large eyes glowing with smug self-satisfaction. The look had stayed there, affixed to her foul face, right up until the moment when the quarrel from his crossbow found purchase in her pale throat. His first time. The memory of her falling backwards, clutching the wooden shaft, staring at him with fear, revulsion, and confusion came flooding back to him as he now closed the distance between himself and his fleeing target.

The great stallion increased his stride as the pungent scent of their prey filled his flaring nostrils. Froth flew from the bit that clacked between enormous white teeth. At the last moment, the pale girl turned and looked into the mouth of the dark horse. She screamed in terror, in defiance, half-turned, facing the beast that sought to trample the life from her veins. In those close, intimate seconds, something transpired between the beast and the girl. Their eyes met. Large, impressive, red-rimmed orbs stared down at the girl with hunger and eagerness, while the girl stared back with fear and confusion. In those few milliseconds, she searched for a reason, an answer to the only question that burned in her mind. *Why?*

The great hooves struck her back, and the question went unanswered. She did not cry out as the crack of her bones echoed off the silent trees. The man in black circled his horse to where she lay, a crumpled mess of gray clothing, hair white as the snow, and blood, so fresh and crimson it took his breath away. The girl shifted her shoulders, the desire to live still remaining within her broken form. Her breath rose into the air, a warm cloud swirling amongst the delicate, descending flakes. The man dismounted, blade in hand, and approached her.

"Mädchen, du warst so nah am Fluss."

She did not answer him. She *had* almost made it to the river, but she could not answer him. A low, guttural moan escaped her lips. The blood flowed out of her, burning a stream into the snow. Somehow, she managed to find a small reserve of energy, just enough to crawl, just enough to will the nails of her hands to change, to grow, to become talons.

The man bent down next to the girl and released a deep, booming laugh. Birds, roosted for the night far above the strange couple, tore into the night sky, screaming as they fled. In response, the dark horse nickered softly, then raised his head over and over, restless, eager for his master's return. The metallic scent unnerved the large animal, flooding its senses with tension.

"Sag mir, wo deine Schwester ist." The man grabbed the girl's colorless locks and yanked her head backwards to face him.

Her large eyes rolled backwards in their impressive sockets, her mouth gaped open, revealing long, sharp teeth within. A gurgle came from her ivory throat, and blood dribbled onto the snow beneath her. She did not answer. She would never betray her sister.

The man in black turned her head back and forth, examining her neck. As he did, the girl gurgled once more, then choked, her body violently bucking against his strong arms. The man did not release her but held her steady. In the last of the light, he sought and then found that which had always fascinated him the most—the long feathery slits, like those of a common pike or trout, visible as he moved the girl's head. They opened and closed, gasping for air, much like her dangerous mouth. Here, too, along the gill lines, tiny trickles of crimson dripped from the slivered openings, leaking down her dingy bodice.

An abomination of nature. He was bound by his calling, his birth, to eradicate her kind from the world. Leaning closer to her face, so beautiful, yet so horribly wrong, he whispered into her ear, just above the bizarre gills.

"Sprichst du nicht mit mir?"

No answer. Only gurgling.

The man put the blade to her beautiful face. He watched her, watched her eyes, looking for a shred of fear. He found only blazing hatred. He smiled down at her as he dragged the steel from her left eyebrow down to her perfect chin. She grunted but did not cry out, refusing to give him the satisfaction of hearing her pain. The new wound oozed, but she remained silent.

The man laid down his steel, placing it carefully in the deepening blanket of snow. He pulled her head back even farther, stretching the limits of her muscles and her injuries, lifting her torso farther away from the ground. The hoof prints were visible on her broken back. Her right thigh, a good portion of it in tatters.

She finally did cry out, a shrill keening that filled the silent clearing, startling the man's horse, which neighed in return. He grinned. Satisfied. As he lifted her farther, her bodice slipped down, revealing her chest. He could see the mounds of her breasts, their ivory skin, full and round. Her rose-colored nipples grew alert in the frigid air. It excited him to see her this way, exposed, available to his whim. She would not be the first creature he had had his way with. She would not be the last.

Reaching around her shoulder, he placed a gloved hand on her breast, cupping the ampleness of her form. He moaned in her ear, enjoying the intimacy of the moment, relishing the sensation of her breast in his hand. His right hand remained in her long, white hair, now matted and covered in her own blood. The girl sobbed, a small wet noise that slipped from her throat against her will. It urged the man on, exciting him further. He considered how much time she had left, and what he could accomplish before she expired.

The hand came from the side, a talon with razor-sharp claws. It tore across the man's face, leaving four long slits, not unlike the gills beneath the girl's ear. Only these were wider, longer, more grisly as they burst and peeled open, like a carelessly ripped-out seam. The man let go of the girl, and she fell back into the bloodstained snow. Unable to turn herself, she lay there and listened to the man's screams.

Through her good eye, and in what little light remained, she caught a flurry of movement. Snow flew into the air in a cloud as a figure of enormous size and stature struck with speed and strength. The girl heard the howls of both man and beast. The ground shook as the dark horse fell, slamming into the frozen earth. She felt it where she lay. The horse screeched a final time, a terrifying noise, high-pitched, the cry of something so frightened, so terrified, that only death could end its misery. The beast knew it. The girl knew it. The blood-curdling cry flew to the heavens and then stopped, replaced by a wet squelch as a spray of warm, sticky blood flew across the clearing and landed on the girl's chest.

A mournful roar, followed by indeterminable speech, most likely curses, came from the man in black. But his mouth must have been damaged. The girl could not understand what he was saying. The words were garbled and wet as if the man yelled through shattered teeth. In time, she didn't hear from him any longer.

The scene around her slowed down as she drifted. Her conscious and unconscious mind took in random, unlinked images, sounds, smells from her surroundings, flooding her with moments she understood and many she did not. A dreamlike existence surrounded her as she floated between this world and the next. Her physical being did not ordinarily feel the cold, did not understand cold, but nonetheless, she felt the warmth of her own blood fleeing her wounds. As the blood of the dead horse cooled on her chest, she felt strong hands lift her broken body, a deep voice whispering in her ear.

Nix, my dear one, we will make you well again.

The metallic smell of blood flooded her senses, overwhelming all other thoughts as Nix was cradled in large, familiar arms. She leaned her head against her savior's chest and listened to the strong, steady heartbeat. It echoed against her ear. *Lub dup, lub dup, lub dup.* Nix managed a small crooked smile. Turning her head, fighting the immense pain, she looked up at the large face looming over her small broken form.

Nix reached up to brush away a long, crimson-stained braid from the blood-smeared, ivory skin.

Mother, you found me.

His family located the crumpled and mangled form of the man in black the next morning. When he had not returned to camp, they had, with effort, tracked both man and beast to the grim scene in the clearing. Snow had covered the gruesome pair, nestled together on the forest floor. Only part of the man's long, dark cloak remained visible above the layer of fresh snow. They brushed the cold powder away from his face, said their prayers, and prepared a large fire for his disposal. The man's face had been nearly unrecognizable. Four long wounds created by strong talons, the size of which they could not imagine, traveled across the fallen man's face, obliterating much of his nose.

The man's uncle sat in the snow regarding his nephew long after the others had set about gathering the necessary provisions to build a funeral pyre. He had been their best hunter. His loss would be great.

The initial examination of the clearing revealed a second set of prints, barely visible under the freshly fallen snow. Enormous prints, bigger than any of their own. What type of man could make footprints of this size? How could a girl, living in the forest alone, waiting for spring, waiting for the ice in the river to subside, have eluded their greatest hunter?

They had underestimated the situation. Missed something. What was the connection between the giant and the girl? Had it taken her? Her body did not lie among the carnage with their fallen brother. What did it want with her? And what a fantastic kill the giant would make! The ultimate hunt. An adventure worthy of song. They could sing that fantastic tale for years to come, teaching the next generation of their great purpose, their incredible bravery. In the firelight, the men's faces glowed with amber light, their pupils widening with dreams of a great behemoth.

As they passed the goatskin, filled with warm liquid courage, they speculated about what the creature might look like. Would he have enormous fangs? Did he have one enormous eye? Did he eat the bones of men? And, most importantly, who would get the prize of his head, *sein Kopf?*

"Ihr." *Her.* The voice came from the shadows, far from the warmth of the fire.

"Ihr Kopf," said the man in black. *Her head.*

His brethren turned in alarm, spinning towards the voice of their departed brother, who had not departed at all.

He continued his garbled speech and said in his native tongue, *I will take her head and mount it on my wall. So help me God, I will.*

17

Clíodhna

The white merrow, pale as the vast northern waters in deep winter, died late in the night.

Earlier that evening, as she had pulled a bone from the cooking fires, she introduced herself to Arethusa as Íss, a word in her language that meant ice. She was the oldest of twelve sisters, some still in this world, some not. Those that lived would come for her, guided by their mother. All this she told Arethusa, the only one who understood her language and who later—much, much, much later—told this to Clíodhna. When Íss had finished speaking with Arethusa, she tipped her chin up sharply and stood. Wielding the bone, still smoking from the fire, she slit the nearest captor's throat. Everything immediately turned to chaos.

The small forest girl had sprung to her feet and run in the direction of the snarling, rocking carriage on the opposite side of the campsite. Clíodhna could smell Sergei, the mysterious beast held captive within. Transfixed by the sight of the tiny girl in action, Clíodhna stood, mouth agape, staring at the events unfolding before her. From somewhere beneath her colorful skirts, the girl pulled a tiny blade. *When had she acquired the knife and why had she not used it until this moment?* These questions went unanswered as Clíodhna watched the young girl decimate three men who attempted to restrain her.

Another man, tasked with the unfortunate job of guarding Sergei, also stared in astonishment as the girl cartwheeled and flipped her way aggressively towards him. With a flourish of brilliantly colored fabric, the blade came from nowhere. It flashed in the firelight, and the man went down. Within moments, the girl had sprung the door open to free the creature within. Clíodhna lost sight of her, but only for a moment. Then what she saw brought a smile of wonder to Clíodhna's lips. The girl screamed out in triumph from atop her mount. Sergei. An enormous brown bear with a great maw and claws as sharp as razors. He stood as tall as a tree on hind legs larger around than Clíodhna's waist. And he roared, announcing his freedom and expressing his anger towards those who had kept him from his partner, this small forest girl.

Arethusa called to Clíodhna, snapping her attention from the bear and his diminutive rider. Turning, Clíodhna saw that Íss had taken Arethusa upon her own back, where she clung to the tall merrow's neck. She motioned to Clíodhna to follow them, and the strange trio of women ran into the dark forest. The taller female, who did not seem in any way impaired by the added burden of Arethusa, moved with grace and speed. They ran through the woods—listening to the cries of the men and the victorious roars of the now liberated Sergei—exhilarated by their own newfound freedom.

In the hours before they all slept, Íss took off into the woods in search of her family, assuring Arethusa that she would return once she had located her sisters and her mother. Clíodhna, grateful for the kindness of the exotic merrow, attempted to give her thanks, but Íss refused to make eye contact with Clíodhna, turning her back on her when she spoke. Íss disappeared into the darkness. Clíodhna awoke to the sound of Íss's screams. Her last act had been to cry out, to awaken and alert the sleeping fugitives so that they could flee once more

It had been the forest girl astride Sergei who later found the fallen merrow. With heavy hearts, the strange pair carried Íss to the clearing where, according to Arethusa, she was to have been reunited with her sisters. How the location had been chosen and how word had made its way to Íss was now gone with the dead merrow. Circumstances and language barriers gave Clíodhna only parts of the story.

Wind breathed through the trees high above their heads, like water in a stream, its steadiness filling the absence of words. Birds sang to one another—their harmony repeating, joyful yet short songs, occasionally interrupted by the curt hammer of a woodpecker at work on a trunk somewhere in the distance.

Beneath the sheltering canopy of green, these women, bonded by the cruelty of men, stared at one another. Clíodhna and the half-woman Arethusa, as well as the girl who only spoke to Sergei gathered around their rescuer. Even in death, her beauty and grace held true, captivating the women who mourned her passing. Their mutual gaze fell on their fallen sister, her hair like milkweed, blowing in the gentle breeze. Her body lay on the forest floor, cushioned by a carpet of green ferns, their leaves like feathers, so new they were almost yellow. Sergei kept his distance. He crossed his great paws in front of him as he lay in the brush, slowly licking the blood from his fur.

The strange group waited. They waited for the dead merrow's family. They waited to tell the news of her passing, of her bravery, of the role she had played in their escape. They also waited to discover their new fate. *Had they traded one devil for another? Would her family destroy them all? Wrongfully blame them for Íss's death and then dispatch them?*

As they stared at one another, holding their vigil, the birds grew still, leaving only the hush of the wind. Sergei stopped his grooming and lifted his massive skull. He sniffed the air and looked to his mistress, whose face had gone taut, anticipating the change of circumstances. A low rumble boiled in his throat, sending chills down Clíodhna's back. She turned and looked at the forest but saw nothing. Only the thick trees, lush in their green prime, swayed in the gentle breeze. She spun around and around, searching for the disturbance, sniffing the air as Sergei had done.

The scent floated on the wind, ownerless, but the presence was real. The scent of the sea, feminine perspiration, and a menacing undertone—the metallic odor of blood. The women shifted, uncomfortable, fearful of the unknown. Their freedom had come at a high cost, and perhaps they did not own it, not yet.

They appeared like mist, all at once, permeating the space in the clearing. The owners of the scent surrounded the refugee women, no longer alone in their sorrow. Female warriors. Ten in all. Each one a replica of the fallen merrow, now at peace in the center of the clearing. Their skin mirrored hers, white as the ice of the northern seas, their hair as pale as new-fallen snow. Subtle variations in height and features—higher cheekbones here, fuller lips there—distinguished one from another. Each bore a genetic connection to the next, like a long chain comprised of strikingly independent links.

Each one wore a flimsy shift of a dress. None of the garments looked as if they had been washed in decades. They wore no shoes, and their hair mostly hung down, falling in intricate braids festooned with ornaments of shell, wood, and bone.

These pale, fierce women flanked the trio, lining the perimeter of the clearing. They had come to collect their beloved daughter and sister, but they had arrived at a funeral.

The largest and eldest among them, so incredibly tall, even taller than Íss, and regal in a way that commanded respect and devotion, moved through the outer ring and dropped to her knees in front of the fallen merrow. She leaned over the younger woman's face and whispered into the dead merrow's ear. Clíodhna could not hear or understand the communication, but the hushed words rang of care and compassion. This must be her mother. When she had finished, the large female brushed the hair away from her daughter's closed eyes and laid a tender kiss on her forehead. She scanned the clearing with her strong brow, then said something sharp and forceful, but she never raised her voice.

The other white merrow moved as one towards their fallen sister. Each one of them took something from her own hair and laid it along Íss's body, kissing her on the forehead as the first had done. Then they returned to their stations around the edge of the clearing.

Clíodhna watched how each one met the large one's eyes after leaving their dead sister. This tall one, the tallest of them all, could only be Íss's mother. The mother of them all. When the last of her daughters paid their respects, the mother moved to her lost child one last time. From the folds of her thin garment, she produced two coins and placed them over the dead girl's closed eyes. After leaving a soft kiss on her daughter's lips, the great mother stood. Her ridged brow furrowed deeply, as if a rib bone had been placed above her colorless eyes. She turned her gaze to Clíodhna and spoke. The words, deep from the great woman's large throat, were directed to Clíodhna but fell to the wind. Clíodhna did not understand.

Arethusa stumbled forward on her palms and looked far up at the great white mother. The two addressed one another. Arethusa gestured to indicate Clíodhna's pregnant condition, and the tall woman appraised her with great intensity, making the hair on the back of Clíodhna's neck stand on end. Instinctively, her hands flew to her abdomen. *What did this great mother want from her?*

Clíodhna didn't know how to join the conversation, but she perceived her options were limited. Having reached some sort of an agreement, Arethusa nodded to Clíodhna and then smiled.

With unease in her heart, Clíodhna turned to the forest girl and Sergei, but the pair had vanished, leaving behind a large depression in the grass and the fading scent of the great beast.

Arethusa reached for Clíodhna's hand and squeezed it. Clíodhna squeezed back. One by one, the pale women left the clearing. The once innocent twin from the Emerald shores and the half-woman trailed behind them, leaving Íss to the wind and the will of the forest.

18

Evie

"I'm shaking," I said, holding out my fingers for Rachael's inspection. My breath came out in irregular puffs, and I had the same old nausea I always did around that horrible woman.

"Evie!" cried Rachael. "I've never seen you so upset. What is going on? She didn't seem *that* bad."

I looked over at Rachael. She was still wearing her wig, which looked absolutely ridiculous.

"Take that wig off, for Christ's sake," I barked. I needed to vent some of the ugly energy coursing through my veins.

"No way!" said Rachael. "My hair looks like shit."

"Suit yourself," I said. "Must be hot as hell."

Rearing its flaming head as it climbed up the sky, the sun had torn the morning apart, setting fire to our little corner of the earth. We walked through the Village, headed for the coolness under the trees along Narragansett Parkway.

"This is going to sound like I've been tripping, but I swear to you, all this shit really happened," I said.

We walked. I talked. She listened. We walked all the way to the neighborhood known as Governor Francis Farms, meandering through the hazy streets of suburbia that eventually gave way to the old beach community near Gaspee Point Beach. We passed tiny homes with sloppy vinyl siding and piles of firewood stacked up for the winter. Formerly beach cottages, the houses were now filled with year-round residents. It was hard to imagine snow while I was sweating my ass off.

As we strolled, I told her as much as I remembered, but I left the Kolga part out. For years, I had tried to bury what I had done. The possibility that I was just like Nomia—savage, a murderer—made me hate myself even more than I already did at times. Some nights I woke up in a cold sweat. I would get up and pace, smoke endlessly, hoping the nicotine would erase the horror of what I had done. No point in telling Rachael any of that. It wouldn't help the situation.

"You did *not* kick her ass, did you? Really?"

"Huh?" I had just finished the part where I tackled Nomia, but my mind had been on Kolga.

"*Nomia*," said Rachael. "*You* kicked *her* ass?"

"Oh," I said. "Um, yeah. I have no idea what came over me. I think it was right around the time that dickhead impaled me with his spear."

"*What?*" cried Rachael. "This is hard to process, Evie. I mean, *mermaids? A mermaid war? Impalement by spear? A tribunal?* I mean, come on. That's kind of lame if you ask me. *A tribunal?* Who does that?"

"Well, I never thought about it like that, but yeah, I guess a tribunal is kind of lame. Oh, and they're not called *mermaids.* They're called *merrow,*" I said. "It's an Irish thing."

"*Merrow?* Whatever. Jesus Christ!" She stopped dead in the street and looked me in the eye. "Really. Like really, *really?* Like, *for real life,* really? This is all happened?"

I stopped walking. Reaching up to my neck, I pulled the collar of my t-shirt down to the front of my shoulder, exposing the silver-dollar-sized, pinkish scar between my collarbone and my heart.

"That's where it entered," I said, then turned around and jerked my shirt down in the back. "And that's where it exited."

I felt Rachael's cool fingers brush against my shoulder blade. "Evie," she said in a hushed tone. "You're not shitting me."

I turned back to face her. "No," I said. "I'm not."

"Holy shit on a shingle," she said, then covered her open mouth with her carefully manicured fingers.

"Yeah," I said. "Holy shit on a shingle."

She dropped her hands and planted them on her toned hips. "I'm in."

"Rach," I said. "You're my friend, but this goes beyond the limits of any normal friendship. This shit is dangerous."

"Honey," she said. "This shit is *exciting!* You know me. I'm always looking for a new high. This is too deliciously dangerous to pass up."

I smiled weakly, then my eyes filled up. For someone who,

for the most part, feels absolutely useless and unlikable, it's amazing to me that anyone would bother to be my friend, let alone put his or her life on the line. Since Paddy had turned me out, I had been feeling absolutely lost. This extended hand—the opportunity to face this ordeal with another person backing me up—was incredible. It was almost as difficult to believe as my mermaid story.

"Thank you," I said. "But it would be completely selfish and unfair to humanity if anything happened to you."

"*Unfair to humanity*," she said, then chuckled. "Yes, if anything happened to me, *man*kind would be robbed off all this." She gestured up and down her body. "*But* that's something I am willing to sacrifice. Evie, I want to help. I think I understand the risks."

I didn't really think she did. Maybe I was being selfish, maybe I was just so tired of doing everything on my own, but that day I gave in to the selfish side.

"All right," I said. "But don't ever say I didn't warn you."

She put her arm around me and smiled.

"Now, tell me more about the naked mermen …"

The Middle Rhine Valley
Early Summer 1608

Clíodhna

Clíodhna wouldn't hold the infant. She couldn't stand the sight of her small, dark head. Couldn't tolerate the mewling, the crying, the incessant crying. The child howled endlessly from hunger. While she had still carried the infant within, she had caressed her abdomen, sending love inside herself. She had sung countless songs, sharing melodies of her youth with the small being inside her. She had imagined wonderful things about motherhood, how it would unfold, like a well-made quilt, each piece delicately sewn to the next, until all the pieces were one, and in the end, she would shake it out and admire her hard work.

That was not what had happened. She had done the hard work, she had sewn together, with her own body, her own flesh and blood, all the pieces of this new life, and yet, when she looked at it—she only saw *him*.

Him. The baby smelled of *him*. Reeked of *him*. So much so that she would feel the vomit rise in the back of her throat until she nearly choked on it. She swallowed it back down, with the taste lingering in her mouth for hours. The child became an *it*, a thing, a foul thing, no longer a child, no longer a *she*. She would not feed it, would not allow the child to be brought to her, even when her breasts—so full of milk, she thought her chest would burst—cried out to her for release from the unbearable tension of liquid stretching her skin to its outer limits. The thought of *it*, the child, *his* child, anywhere near her body made her skin crawl, as if a thousand tiny insects nibbled away at every one of her pores.

The white sisters had fretted, had held the neglected child, cooed to her, sung to her, swaddled and swung her to and fro. They tried to coax Clíodhna to take the child to her breast, but she had refused and instead had curled up inside herself and slept endlessly. Kolga had watched the events unfold, remaining silent, observing the change the birth had brought to Clíodhna. When the new mother refused to feed the infant, she stepped in.

The great mother of them all entered the room of the abandoned farmhouse where they had sought shelter during the birth. Kolga stood over the young mother, where she lay, fading away to nothing. Clíodhna slept in a deep sleep, the kind that comes from the exhaustion of a birth. Kolga then sat beside her, silent, staring down at the foreign girl from a foreign land, and waited for her to awaken.

Sometime near dawn, as the first rays filtered through the stone casement and the birds awoke full of shrill songs, Clíodhna opened her eyes and stared up at the great mother. She had trouble focusing and blinked at the large woman who stared down at her with intent and purpose. Although they could not speak to one another, they communicated with expressions so very different from one another.

Please do not make me become a mother, Clíodhna pleaded.

There is no choice in this matter, Kolga responded, then stood and left the room, returning with the inconsolable child. She knelt down next to the reluctant mother and pointed to Clíodhna's chest, damp, always damp, with the milk she had refused the child.

Clíodhna shook her head.

Kolga reached out and took Clíodhna's garment from her shoulder and placed the young, howling infant against her mother's breast.

Tears streamed down Clíodhna's face. This was not what she wanted, but Kolga had reached the limits of her sympathy. There was a time when life was all that mattered. Survival was all that mattered.

Nix had discovered the house before the child had been born, when Clíodhna could no longer walk, her face a mask of discomfort and pain. The little stone cottage greeted them with a face full of broken teeth and empty eyes. The moldy, damp walls seeped like infected wounds.

They welcomed the shelter, even if it was dank. They all needed to stop. Each and every one of them was carrying her own heavy burden of suffering on their journey back to the safety of the sea and needed to rest from the effort. They had cleaned the meager central room, using branches to sweep out the dust, clearing out the chimney and boiling water in an old but still useful cauldron in the old, stone hearth.

A small room in the back of the house had been designated for Clíodhna. The sisters had gathered soft, leafy boughs to make a comfortable place for her to lie down and ease the burden of her tiny passenger, eager to enter the world. When the dawn came on their second day in the cottage, the baby girl had been born.

Nomia.

Arethusa, who had been so attentive, so wise during the birth, named and swaddled the babe, holding her close upon her arrival. Clíodhna passed all that was left in her body, all that had once belonged to the new life, and then she had fallen into a deep sleep, too exhausted to hold the product of her intense exertion. They had let her rest, and perhaps that had been their first mistake, perhaps that had encouraged the crack to become a chasm between mother and child.

In the days leading up to labor, Clíodhna had grown angry, restless, and disoriented. She spoke with great fire about the fiend who had put life in her. She babbled and pulled at her hair, calling the name, *Ciabhán,* over and over. Her face grew more ashen each day as she told anyone who would listen, whether they understood her or not, that she had *thought* she loved the child within, she had *thought* she could handle what was to come, but now she felt differently. Maybe the child would be better off without her. *Couldn't they take the child from her? Couldn't they release her from her burden?*

The sisters, already deep in their own grief over the loss of their eldest sister, only looked at this new woman with pity and sorrow and shook their heads. She babbled night and day. They could not understand her words, but they understood her sentiment. They knew she did not want what was coming. As they traveled towards the sea, they had avoided Clíodhna and kept to themselves. It was Arethusa who looked after the bewildered mother and listened to her endless rantings about the beast from the river, the one that had cursed her with this burden.

Each evening, when they had all grown too tired to walk and all of the younger women were asleep, Arethusa and Kolga developed a habit of conversing in the evenings. Neither of them required much sleep, and so they would spend their evenings, as the stars spun above them, discussing their lives late into the night. They discovered similarities that transcended their outward appearances. Intelligent survivors, both had lived on the fringe of the world of men, forever fearful for their own safety and for the safety of their children.

Arethusa let on that she, too, had been a mother to many, but her offspring had been taken from her, enslaved, and sent off for the entertainment of others because they had had the misfortune of being born as half-persons like their mother. Kolga understood. The pair carried the same weight, the same guilt of their individual heritages. In this way, night after night by the evening fires, the threads of conversation were woven into a blanket of friendship.

When Clíodhna started to break down, to spiral, losing her composure and sanity, Arethusa had been there to listen. She then told Kolga the tale of Clíodhna's impregnation. The great mother had listened, nodding, as she took in the sad and sordid story. When Arethusa finished, Kolga had been quiet, staring at the fire, lost in her thoughts.

After some time, she had asked for more specific details regarding the nature of this creature that had attacked and held Clíodhna hostage, but Arethusa was at a loss. But she had done her best to remember all that Clíodhna had told her about the strange man. She quietly told Kolga the bits and pieces she knew, careful not to awaken the resting woman who slept fitfully nearby, her armed draped across her swollen abdomen, her brow knitted in frustration and fear as she battled whatever demons lurked within her dreams.

Kolga nodded and stored the information within her. When the time came for her to kneel down and force the young mother to feed her child, she did so with an informed and loving heart. Kolga had lost too many children. She would not witness the loss of another.

Once Clíodhna had reached a point in her recovery where she could travel once more, the strange band of women struck out again in search of the comfort and safety of the sea they had left behind. Arethusa knew she could not follow the women into the sea, but she did not speak of the future. She had learned, long before, that life was best lived in the now. She took care of Nomia and her mother, Clíodhna. She spent her nights swapping tales with her new friend Kolga.

They moved slowly. The needs of the infant required frequent stops, and the band of women, as capable as they may have been, knew well enough to stay off the main roads. The growing question on everyone's mind was what would happen once they reached the sea. Arethusa and the baby would not be able to travel by water, not yet. Something needed to be done.

One morning, as they broke camp, Nix approached her mother and told her about an incident in the night, one that had alarmed the young girl with the scar that ran across her face like an angry bolt of lightning. Nix had been on second watch and had set herself up in the trees. She enjoyed the coolness of the night breeze, the feathery touch of the new leaves brushing her skin as she sat motionless, alert, ready for a fight, should it come. A rustling off in the brush caught her attention, and so she had sat upright, focusing her sharp vision, accustomed to dark places.

In a small clearing, near a large rock, stood Clíodhna. The muscles in Nix's back relaxed. The young mother must be relieving herself or feeling restless from Nomia's nocturnal feedings. She turned her attention away from Clíodhna and silently leaned back into the warmth of the sturdy tree trunk behind her. Nix believed Clíodhna would move on, head back towards the safety of the camp, but she stood there for a long time, swaying. Nix thought it strange, but almost everything about Clíodhna struck Nix as odd.

The young mother continued to oscillate back and forth, her hair hanging down behind her, swinging in time to Clíodhna's gentle movements. Then she raised her arms above her head. Nix saw the baby, held aloft by her mother in the middle of the night, away from the safety of the camp. Clíodhna slammed the child down on the ground and walked away.

No sound came from the bundle. The infant did not move or cry out. Nix bolted from the tree, landing on her feet in a crouch. She ran, without a sound, towards the clearing. Clíodhna was nowhere to be seen. To Nix's astonishment, the child on the ground was alive, eyes wide open and staring up at the star-filled night, perhaps too stunned by her sudden descent to the earth to do anything but lie there, waiting for her mother to retrieve her.

Nix glanced around the clearing, searching for someone, anyone more qualified than she to handle the tiny infant. The two regarded one another, and then Nomia let out a howl. Startled, Nix reached down and picked up the crying infant, holding her to her shoulder as she had seen done by Arethusa and, on occasion, Clíodhna. The child stopped crying, growing quiet, and nuzzled into Nix's neck. Nix's eyes grew wide with alarm. No one touched her, not ever. Not since the day she had received her scars. She would not allow it. Contact with another being was inconceivable, until this moment. Gently, she pulled the child away from her shoulder and stared into the new being's dark brown eyes, so different from her own, which were as light gray as an overcast morning.

The small child reached out to Nix, her tiny fingers wriggling in the moonlight. As a single tear rolled down Nix's cheek, she pulled Nomia closer to her, and the little hand reached towards her pale face, the tiny new skin grazing against the violent scar. Then Nomia grabbed hold of the young woman's long, white hair and did not let go.

In the quiet of that night, alone, together in the darkness, Nix knew that something had changed. It wasn't anything she could put into words, but somewhere, deep inside herself, she knew that her path had taken a sharp turn. She breathed in the newness of the tiny person. She inhaled the sweet smell of moss and the greenness of the trees around her. The night breeze lifted her hair from her back, cooling the damp skin beneath. In that moment, she accepted the change in her life's path, and she turned to walk slowly back to camp in search of Arethusa.

She later told the story to Kolga, keeping the feelings she had experienced to herself, unsure of the proper way to express such things, unsure if she *wanted* to express such things. But her mother, as most mothers do, understood. She saw the change in her daughter, who had suffered immensely, and yet, she had survived and *thrived* after her brutal attack. Kolga saw the softening in Nix's eyes, the subtle curl of her lip—almost a smile, but not quite—as she spoke of the child with specific and detailed observations.

Clíodhna's behavior did not alarm Kolga. She had expected this, but it meant that a course of action would need to be implemented sooner rather than later. Kolga waited until that evening to seek counsel with Arethusa. The pair formed a plan.

The next morning brought rain, which diminished visibility and turned the mood maudlin. The women gathered the few belongings they had, placing their meager provisions and bedding into satchels. Attaching their goods to rain-soaked backs, they set out with eyes averted as sheets of water soaked them to the bone. They traversed muddy pathways, walking through deep puddles that sucked at their legs and held them fast, seeming to never want to let them go.

Onward, south and west, the band traveled to where the winters were warmer and the summers cooler. The second day they came to a village, much larger than the ones they had skirted thus far. They could smell it before they could see it. The rain had subsided, leaving the air heavy, low, and tangible. Steam rose from large boulders along the path, while the stench of excrement, both human and animal, permeated their hair and their damp clothing, climbing into their nostrils and poisoning the air they breathed.

All of the women wore scowls of disgust as they trudged forward. Their collective mood grew as foul as the air. The heat of the day crept in, causing their garments to cling to them and making their packs seem heavier than when they had started out that morning. One of the sisters came forward and announced the need for nourishment, the desire to stop. Kolga looked back at Arethusa, who had been riding on her back in a makeshift sling. The small, dark woman nodded, then tipped her chin toward the ground. Kolga swung Arethusa from her back and lowered her down to the dark earth. The two spoke in hushed voices before coming to an agreement. A solemn look hung on their faces like the foul air.

On the previous morning, before they had ventured out, before the rain had fallen like tears from the sky, Nix had approached Clíodhna and motioned to the small, swaddled but neglected infant lying on the grass by her side. Bleary-eyed from a night of crying after the discovery that she had not rid herself of the child as she had thought, Clíodhna had only stared at Nix with both malice and sadness, then turned away.

Nix had reached down and gathered the child into her arms, retreating into the darkness of the woods. She emerged just before they left with a strange contraption made of wood with newly woven green twigs as lashing. Inside the strange basket, Nomia cooed. Nix, pleased with her handiwork, slung the child on her back and followed the others away from their camp. If Clíodhna noticed, she did not say a word, but she fell limply in line behind the other traveling women.

There, near the outskirts of the odorous village, Nix was called forward. Kolga spoke to her, looking down on her fair, scarred child, who tipped her face up to her mother with reverence and focus. Words transpired between the two. Nix turned her gaze to Clíodhna and stared at her for a long time. Then she took off at a run towards the woods, away from the path leading to the village.

All of the women took note, staring at their younger sister with the strange contraption strapped across her back, her pale body disappearing into the darkness of the trees. All except Clíodhna, who ignored the retreat of her child. She stared listlessly in the opposite direction.

Arethusa watched the young mother, her own face heavy with sadness. On her hands, she propelled herself towards the Irish merrow, then reached up and took the woman's hand in her own.

The troop of white merrow again gathered their things. One by one, they passed Arethusa and touched her shoulder with long, bony fingers. Clíodhna paid no attention to this gesture of farewell. She moved forward when the last of them had passed, seemingly unaware that Arethusa was still holding her hand and not moving in the direction of the other women.

Clíodhna stopped and looked down at the small woman, confusion wrinkling her lovely brow. As the last of the women left the pair, their fair bodies swallowed by the rain-darkened trees, it seemed as if Clíodhna finally understood.

They had been left behind.

Clíodhna fell to her knees and sobbed. A deep, long howl

tore from her chest as she pushed the palms of her hands deep into her eyes and raised her head to the gray sky above.

"I could not be its mother," she screamed to the heavens in her own language.

The pair sat in the woods until Clíodhna could cry no more, until all the sorrow from the previous year of her life had drained from her, leaving an enormous void in her soul. Vacant, but somehow lighter, Clíodhna stood and stared down at Arethusa as if she was noticing her for the first time.

"Where will we go?"

Arethusa smiled. Then she pointed east.

Evie

W hen we returned back to her house, Rachael said, "We need to know everything we can before we meet with Nomia. We need to organize our thoughts, get our shit together."

"Agreed," I said. "I just don't understand the connection to Richard."

"No," said Rachael. "That's not adding up at all. Wait. Before we left for the party at Shep and Hazel's house yesterday, you said something about a USB drive from your brother's place. Where is it?"

"Get your laptop," I said and headed down the hall to my room to find it.

"Where did you find it?" yelled Rachael.

"The toilet," I yelled back and grabbed the key. I headed

back to the kitchen.

"Did you say *toilet*? That's disgusting."

"He used to keep his porn in the toilet tank when we were kids, all wrapped up in a ziplock bag."

"Hold on," said Rachael. She was sitting at her kitchen table, booting up her computer. When she was finished typing in her password, she said, "So, let me get this straight. Your brother used the toilet to hide his porn. You found this out *how*? What were *you* hiding?"

"Beer," I said. "It seemed like a good spot for it. Always a fresh supply of cold water."

"Freakish," she said shaking her head while she clicked shut a few open windows. "But clever."

I shrugged and handed her the USB drive. She plugged it in.

"Get over here," said Rachael. "This is fucked up."

"What?" I asked. "What's fucked up?"

"This stick is an encrypted bootable drive. I'm going to have to restart my laptop." Then she made a noise like an angry cat.

"What's that all about?" I said. "You're freaking me out with your mumbo-jumbo talk and angry cat noises."

"Sorry," said Rachael. "I just hope this doesn't wreck my laptop. This is dangerous. I don't know what's on this drive, but it has its own internal boot system. Which means it can act like a mini-computer, all on its own."

"Hmmmm," I mumbled. "Yes, yes. I see what you mean."

"You do?"

"Fuck no."

She pressed her stained lips together and rolled her eyes at me. The computer made a *bing*, then started back up again. Two symbols appeared. The first was an icon of lipstick with Rachel Bass beneath it. The second was an icon of an elaborate birdcage with the word *Sammlung*.

"This is the point of no return," she said.

"Meaning?"

"If we click on that birdcage, I might never see my files ever again."

"You're a good friend. Click the damn birdcage. Wait. Don't you have a backup system?"

"Yes, I have a backup system, but in theory, this could fry my hard drive. I'll do this because you are my friend and it could help save a life, but if this destroys my computer, you're buying me a new one. Immediately."

"Deal. Click it."

Rachael guided her pointer arrow thingy to the birdcage icon and clicked. The screen went black and two curtains swung in from either side. They hung there on the screen, gently gliding back and forth.

"It's doing something," said Rachael.

"How do you know?"

"Those swinging curtains are an indication of a platform loading. I'd bet my Coach bags on it."

A gilded frame suspended from golden ropes lowered itself down to center screen.

"Very theatrical," muttered Rachael.

The frame had a text box which read, *Password*.

Rachael looked at me.

"Yes?" I said.

"We need a password to go further."

"Oh," I said. "Hmmm."

"It's probably at least twelve characters with either a number or a special character or both. That's the typical standard for a more secure password configuration. It might be three or more words strung together."

"Got it," I said. "Try Rochester Poly Tech 1994, all one word."

She typed in the letters which instantly turned into dots, then hit the enter key on her keyboard.

The screen shook and the box cleared itself.

"Nope," said Rachael. "That's not it."

I squished my lips together as I thought.

"Maybe try that again but put the '1994' first?"

She did. Shaky, shaky. No.

"Okay," I said. "Try *I hate my sister.*"

Rachael stared at me.

"No?" I asked.

"No," she replied.

Think, Evie! If I were Richard, what would be important to me?

Then I got an idea.

"Try *Heinrich Octavius Musäus.* Be sure to use an umlaut on the *a* in *Musäus.*"

"Yeah," said Rachael as she pressed the option key and then the 'u' key. "I remember how to make an umlaut." She hit the 'a' key then said, "It's not my first time at the German rodeo."

"Right," I said.

Rachael hit enter again.

Shaky, shaky. No.

I watched as Rachael typed with unnatural speed. She tried the name with a *1* at the end. Nothing. She tried it with a *1* at the beginning. Nothing. Then she put the *@* symbol at the end.

The little frame floated back up to the top of the screen, and the red curtains parted. A black screen stared back at us until a gilded, elaborate birdcage swung across the display, freezing into place when it arrived at an angle on the right side. The words *Willkommen in der Sammlung* appeared for a moment before fading away.

"What did that say?" asked Rachael.

"It was German," I replied. "*Welcome to the Collection.*"

"What is this?" whispered Rachael.

"I don't know," I said.

Elegant, beautiful, intriguing, but I had no idea what it was or what it had been doing in my brother's toilet. More frames dropped from the top of the screen, this time on the left side. Each one held a single word, *Explore, Eat, Experience, Embrace.*

"Is this a location?" asked Rachael.

"I have no fucking clue. Let's explore, shall we?"

Rachael clicked on the word *Explore.* The screen cleared for a moment.

"You broke it," I said.

Before Rachael could answer, the screen came back to life with a photograph of a coastal building.

"Wait a second," I said.

"Oh, I know that building," said Rachael. "It's on Providence Harbor. The one on the East Providence side, near that Tockwotton retirement home."

"I thought that was a fancy restaurant," I said.

"It is," said Rachael. "I went there on a date after it opened. Lots of local celebrities. Very expensive. Very, very chic."

The photograph sped towards us, or rather, our view zoomed in towards the building over the harbor. It focused on the upper level of the three-story building, mostly glass and steel. The expensive, street-level shops zipped out of view as we seamlessly entered through the glass windows, skimmed across the elegant dining room, and stopped at an elevator near the back wall.

The screen went still.

"Click the elevator," I said.

Rachael looked at me, then turned back to the computer. She hesitated for a moment before guiding her mouse to the elevator doors. *Click.* An audible *ding* sounded from Rachael's laptop speakers, and the doors opened. Another pop-up menu appeared. This one gave us two choices: *continue after entering PIN*, or *return to main menu.*

"Since he used our grandfather's name, try *1912.*"

Rachael typed the numbers in and hit the enter key. The screen went dark, then reappeared. This time, we were facing the inside of the closed elevator doors. With the familiar *swish* of an elevator, the doors parted, and we were in a tunnel made of stone. I felt dizzy as our view zoomed along the stone passageway, stopping in front of one of the most impressive doors I had ever seen. Made of mostly brass, several intricate gears tangled and intertwined all over the front. A prominent wheel, not unlike an ancient ship's steering wheel, sat front and center like a mighty hatch opening. Another pop-up window prompted us once again to either go back or enter the PIN a second time. Without a moment of hesitation, Rachael entered the PIN, and the giant wheel on the front of the door spun.

The door swung open, and the screen went dark. Cages, similar to the one we had seen on the start-up menu, appeared from simulated smoke, like an elaborate magic show. There were five in all. Another gold frame dropped down and swayed in the air, as if it truly floated in front of us.

Experience? it asked.

"Well, we've come this far and nothing really has happened. So we might as well *experience* ..." said Rachael, using an announcer voice when she said the word *experience*.

She clicked away and the frame floated back up. A word appeared on each one of the cages, *Defense, Oddities, Pleasure, Arts, Consume.*

"Where should we go first?" I asked.

She clicked on *Pleasure.*

"Shocking," I said and rolled my eyes.

Several ornate windows, like silhouettes of real windows in a Victorian-style home, appeared. The shades were drawn down and the rooms looked backlit. It was as if we were standing on a sidewalk looking up at a home after dark. I suddenly felt a little icky. After a moment, the silhouette of a very curvy woman appeared in one of the windows. She pulled the shade up and bent over to peek out at us. *Too young.* I hoped she was at least in her twenties. Her curly blonde hair framed an angelic face with full, pouty lips. Clad in lingerie that barely contained her endowments, the girl winked at us, then pulled the shade back down. A button with the option *Buy* appeared below her window.

After the first window lit up, each one presented a new female temptress, each one a little different from the previous. One had a whip, one appeared dressed like a baby, one had insects crawling all over her—and she didn't seem to mind.

"What the hell is this?" I said in disgust.

"I'd like to think of myself as an open-minded person, but whoa—insects. *Insects?*" Rachael swallowed noticeably. If she felt like I did, she had probably just thrown up in her mouth.

After the last window shade lady completed her task, a pop-up screen appeared. It read, *We have something for everyone. If you would like to see more of what we have to offer, please proceed to the next screen to complete the necessary bitcoin payment details.*

"What the hell is *bitcoin?*" I asked.

"If the weird girls offering their wares weren't the first indication, then the bitcoin is a sure sign that this is Dark Web stuff," said Rachael.

"I'm not familiar with Dark Web. Explain."

"If you wanted to buy an illegal endangered leopard coat and have it delivered tomorrow, you would use the Dark Web. If you wanted to buy obscure illegal drugs anonymously and have them show up in your postal mailbox, you would use the Dark Web. If you want to have sex with something you most certainly should not be having sex with, you would use the Dark Web."

"Oooooooh," I said, rolling out the *o*. "I get it. It's like the black market, only online."

"Indeed it is. It's also very useful for downloading movies and television shows when you don't have cable or don't want to pay for cable."

"I'm guessing you don't have cable."

"*Ding, ding, ding!*" Rachael chirped, then winked at me.

"I'm kind of relieved," I said.

"What do you mean?"

"Sticking it to the cable company. That's how you know about this spooky Dark Web business, *right?*"

She shot me a mischievous look. "Go on thinking that, Pollyanna."

"I'm going to pretend this conversation never happened. I'm also going to scrub any thoughts of you and the Dark Web from my mind."

"Whatever lets you sleep at night, doll."

"*What-evs*," I replied. "Go back to the home menu. Can you do that?"

"I think so," she said. "Let's try this …"

Rachael hit the escape key and the screen darkened, then reappeared with the home menu. The four E's returned: *Explore, Eat, Experience, Embrace.*

"Try *Eat* this time," I suggested.

Rachael obliged and the display changed from black to red. What looked like a tall restaurant menu appeared and then opened in front of us. I glanced over the contents that were listed, and a few of the items caught my attention, *ortolan, fugu, Chilean sea bass.* Other items I recognized, but some, like *casu marzu topped with Mellified Man on toast crisps,* left me at a loss. That particular one was an appetizer. Priced at $5,000.

"Five thousand dollars for what and *what* on toast?" I exclaimed.

"What is this is?" asked Rachael.

"Freaky shit. This is *freaky-ass* rich people shit."

I whipped out my phone, because I just had to know, and typed in *Mellified Man.* What I saw horrified me. There were countless pictures of mummified old people in vats of honey. It was my turn to be sick. I showed the screen to Rach.

"I don't want to see any more. I'm shutting this down. I think we get the idea here."

"Agreed."

"Okay," said Rachael. "This is what we know."

It was later that evening, and we were on her back patio, smoking and drinking Long Island iced teas made with some gluten-free vodka she was crazy about. And we were still trying to piece together the Richard and Nomia puzzle.

"Richard was into some weird kinks, and he was trying to keep this a secret. Do you think he knew about Nomia's true nature?"

"I don't know," I said and took a long sip. "This is all so mothertruckin' crazy."

"Agreed," she said and took a long sip of her drink. "Well, need to get organized. What's the plan?"

"Right," I said, not feeling all that clear or organized. "We need to find out if she knew about this *Sammlung* place."

"You might want to ask her how she gets inside your head, while you're at it."

"Yeah! Excellent point! If we are going to have a roundtable discussion about the fucking aqua-paranormal, I want some goddamn answers!"

"Yeah!" yelled Rachael. "I'll drink to that!" We clinked glasses and laughed, but there was an unease to our merriment. It hung over us like a cloud. We could be as flip as we wanted, but the truth was we were scared out of our minds.

I slept most of the next day. Exhaustion took over and put my body on autopilot. I needed the rest. I got out of bed sometime after noon. Rachael had left for the day and stayed out for most of the afternoon. I hardly did anything beyond smoking, drinking, and fretting, wearing a rut in Rachael's postage stamp of a backyard. We got takeout that evening, and said little to one another. Rachael asked if I minded if she went out. I didn't care. I was still so tired, I passed out around nine that evening. The vodka and Tylenol PM helped. *Yeah, I know.* But I *did* wake up the next day, so keep your judgment to yourself.

Tuesday I spent the day coming out of my skin with anxiety. I kept staring at the clock, which moved at a glacial pace. By three in the afternoon, Rachael couldn't stand my pacing any longer and made us a pitcher of margaritas. We spent the late afternoon and early evening catching up and reminiscing. But the conversation felt artificial and forced— a way of making the time pass, while avoiding any real issues like my current situation or our imminent meeting with a very dangerous creature. By seven that evening I could hardly stand it. I was on the porch, pacing, ready to go.

An hour and a half later, the two of us stood at the gate on Seaview Avenue, swaying, but only a little bit.

"You push the button," I said.

"No," said Rachael. "You do it."

"No. You."

The gate swung open, and we looked at one another.

"Here we go," said Rachael, and she strutted right up to the house. I looked around, up the dark, empty street, at the tall bushes lining the driveway. I suddenly felt very sober.

"Wait up, Rachael!" I said and ran after her.

Tall, opaque doors loomed at the end of the sidewalk, framed on either side by large, potted hibiscus plants. An anemic overhead light illuminated the gray slate doorstep. Rachael reached out and rang the doorbell. I held my breath. Footsteps approached the door from the other side. With a click, the door opened, revealing Nomia in a white slip of a dress. She looked even thinner than she had before.

"You came," she said. "Both of you." She looked relieved, which I found odd.

Rachael stuck out her hand. "I'm Rachael Bass, Evie's friend and accountant. So, you're the bitch who tried to kill her."

Nomia looked as if someone had just slapped her. It was kind of refreshing.

"Well," she said. "That's not completely inaccurate. Come in." She moved aside and gestured for us to enter. Her face turned placid, unreadable. I liked it better when she was unnerved.

A massive staircase swept upwards behind her, disappearing into the darkness of the second floor. We entered the home and walked down the short hallway. Behind the staircase, an enormous, sunken living room sprawled out before us. A fireplace, wider than a compact car, shot up from the center. The back side of it flanked the staircase. In front of the hearth was a circle of white leather couches.

Beyond the couches, directly opposite the fireplace, an entire wall of glass looked out on the now dark Narragansett Bay. Boat lights, both red and green, winked through the night as the vessels traversed the dark waters. With the start of summer, the Bay was hopping with nautical traffic. High above, in the glittering night sky, the distant lights of a plane grew brighter as it aimed towards the airport in preparation for landing.

Many times I had passed by this house on leisurely walks, imagining how grand it must be inside. So far, the interior matched the pretension of the ridiculous front gates. I was not disappointed. This house was meant to be gated.

A bottle of wine and three glasses had been set out on a large oval coffee table between the two curved couches. Rachael immediately poured the wine, took a glass, and plopped down on the white couch. Several drops of wine splashed onto the white leather. She just looked at it. I cringed.

"Where's John?" asked Rachael.

Nomia left her glass untouched and sat down across from her. "He's in Boca."

I grabbed a napkin and blotted the couch as I sat down next to Rachael, shooting her a warning look. I picked up my glass of wine. I was so nervous, the goblet almost slipped out of my sweaty hands.

"We have … an arrangement," said Nomia.

"Oh, I bet you do," Rachael snapped back. She grinned knowingly and tipped her glass up at Nomia.

Nomia smiled in return. "I'm sure you, of all people, understand my circumstances. It's Rachael, correct?"

"Yes," said Rachael. "That's my name. What's your game, sister?"

My eyes grew wide as a thought entered my head. "Wait, wait, wait," I said. "You didn't eat John, did you?"

Nomia smirked. "No," she said in a quiet voice. "He's always been very kind to me. I can assure you that he's fine. One of his kids had an event, and he flew down a few days ago. Would you like me to call him? Do you need confirmation?"

"No," I said. "I'm not here to check on John. I'm here to find my brother. Where is he? Why are you being nice to me? Or are you just bullshitting us?"

"I'm not bullshitting you," she said. She toyed with a stray thread on her dress. "Like I said earlier, I just need to make things right. We need to find our siblings, Evie."

"But," I said, "I need some answers first. Where have you been the past three years?"

Over the next hour, she explained it all, laying her cards on the table. She told us about her plan to destroy me through my brother, how she and Nix had hidden out on an island somewhere off the coast of Cape Cod. Then she told me something I am still having a hard time swallowing.

"But then your brother made me see how angry I was, how angry I have been. He helped me to start letting go of the past. To start letting go of the pain I was feeling, the pain I was causing. Your brother is quite amazing, Evie."

I almost threw up. No, really, I did.

"What?" I choked.

"Your brother is a remarkable man. I want you to know that I had nothing to do with his disappearance. We had come back to the apartment after dinner one night, and his place was destroyed. There had been a man in the bedroom waiting for us. He knocked me out, and when I came to, Richard was gone. I was bleeding and scared. I jumped out the window, too afraid to go out the front. I left Boston and went back to the island. My sister was gone, and our home had been turned upside down. Nix is strong, and I could see that she put up a fight, but I found her head scarf and it was covered in blood ..." She stopped and stood, her words dying in her throat.

I watched her back as she turned away from us and, at that moment, I felt something I never thought I would feel for her—*empathy*. Losing a sibling, someone who has traveled through life with you from the very beginning, is a terrifying notion. It's like a mirror view of your own mortality, and it's also like losing a piece of your own soul. We had both lost the same piece. It was the only thing we had in common.

If she was telling the truth.

I thought back to what I had discovered in Boston. The bloody handprint next to the window. The mess in Richard's apartment. But it did not explain why he was missing or why the place had been turned upside down.

"Do you know if they were looking for anything?" I asked.

"No," she said. She held my gaze. She did not look away. She was telling the truth. I believed her.

"Well, I think I know what they were looking for. But I have no idea why they would have taken Richard," I said as I pulled out the USB drive.

21

Transatlantic journey of the
Dutch vessel The Eendract
Translated logbook
January 25, 1624 - Left Amsterdam
March 1624 - Arrived in
New Netherlands

Pieter Thienponthe, First Mate

March 23, 1624

We made land today on a day so gray I had begun to wonder if I would ever see color again. The wind had threaded through and bound itself to the sails, bringing all the salt from the sea with it. The brine saturated everything—our hair, our clothes, the wood on the deck, the thick ropes that coiled like serpents everywhere one turned. The salt found its way into our noses and our dreams, absorbing all the moisture, destroying all the happiness we thought we had stored away.

We had begun to believe that God had forgotten us, an insignificant dot on a vast expanse of nothing, having sailed across

His unforgiving, uncaring ocean—so calm one day, and yet on an angry day, it would raise its massive hands and pound us down with its watery fists. We often feared that our modest craft, which had carried us thus far, would burst into a thousand tiny slivers and we would drift, like a leaf on the breeze, into the depths where leviathans awaited to devour us, splintered ship and all.

We relied on our happy dreams to carry us through. Dreams of maidens and mothers, so fair and beautiful, their voices like the sweetest songbirds. Or perhaps, dreams of our youth, when we jumped into cool lakes on the hottest days of summer. And the water, clean and fresh, not caustic and cloying like the sea surrounding us now, would slip over our skin, as smooth as silk and refreshing as chilled cream, and bring us joy and release from the oppressive heat.

Yet today, the summer heat was as distant as that dream of youth. The cold air snapped and bit our sails, wracking the pulleys, slamming them again and again into the masts.

But we finally saw land.

At first just a small suggestion of darker gray on the horizon, it grew ever wider, ever stronger. My heart expanded with relief, with the knowledge that I would walk on a still surface once more. I would smell and taste and truly know the color green and many others that I had deeply missed on our voyage across the endless blue and gray. I would, finally, step off that godforsaken vessel.

The voyage was arduous, and not all who started our journey disembarked when we finally did make land today. So much has happened. I barely understand any of it. Has it been a dream? Have I really seen what I have seen? Did the events that unfolded, like petals off a dying rose, truly take place? Or did I eat something spoiled? Have I fallen to the sickness of the sea?

Has it all been a dream?

Day 1 – January 25, 1624

At ten and a quarter, we left under Captain Adriaen Jorissen. We chose our watch and deck crews, after which the old man gave all aboard, including passengers—our cargo on said journey—a harangue in the following fashion:

Now then, I, Master of this Ship, come with the intention of trying to make a voyage, not to fool my time away in idleness but to do my best to deliver these good men, women, and children who seek colonization in the New World. Now, you shall all have enough to eat and drink, and as long as you do well by me, and respect the good passengers aboard, I shall endeavor to do the same by you, but when you do not—look out. There are, on such a voyage as this, a great many hard thoughts and feelings, and sometimes we may seem overbearing, but it will be better for you all in the end, for I have been through it all and know just what it is.

These men (he pointed at the mates) are my officers and I intend for them to be officers. I want that you should respect them and obey them the same as you would me and never stand but one call from them. If they give you a job, then do it, and do it as well and as quickly as you can, as to be ready for something else to do.

To ye good people of the Netherlands seeking a new life, keep out of the way, get yourselves back in the hold, or make yourself useful.

After Captain had finished his fine speech, he sent the crew and passengers forward to their duties in their new home aboard ship. As it was, the water was quite rough as we were guided out from The Port of Amsterdam into the open seas. Many passengers, and some of the greener crewmembers, vomited overboard much of what they had eaten in the previous day.

The latter part of the day brought showers. A good thing. The deck needed a rinsing.

Day 2 – January 26, 1624

Already, we have had occasion to speak to the crew regarding one particular passenger. A fairer woman I have not seen in my twenty-seven years on God's green earth. Dark hair, slim figure, and a most curious nature about her. She walks across the decks as if she had been born to it, not the usual stumbling and gasping we have seen with the other new cargo. No, not this woman. And traveling alone.

This last piece of information, combined with her natural beauty, is what has the crew in such a state of ridiculous amorousness. Captain took notice immediately and asked the woman to remain below deck for her own safety and for that of his crew. But twice since, this fair woman has come up and walked along the bow, scanning the waters, searching for something with much intensity.

She brings a sense of excitement to our voyage, but there is part of me that chills when I am near her.

Day 7 – January 31, 1624

This evening after the sun had set for the night, there was a skirmish near the bowsprit. A bit of shouting brought all in earshot from their slumber, or other nightly endeavors, whatever they might be. Upon raising a lantern to the scene, we found that same confounded woman, in garments less modest than necessary for appearing above deck, and one of the new deckhands, Jan Velde, struggling to restrain the young lady.

When pressed for information as to the reason for the disturbance, Jan replied that he thought she had been about to jump from the bow. He had grabbed her just in time.

Most curiously, the woman did not seem to be distraught by her apparent need to rid herself of this world. Rather, she was more upset at Jan for attacking her. She spat many insults at him, at least that seemed the intent of her words, for she spoke in a language unknown to most present.

The incident was brought to the attention of Captain, who was quite angered at being disturbed by such events. He bade us to leave the girl in his quarters, and as of this writing, she has not yet emerged.

I will omit my opinion of such events on behalf of our leader from these here records.

Day 12 – February 5, 1624

It has been five days since the incident on deck, and the *Fair Lady of the Bow*, as some of the crew have begun to call her, has found a new home in Captain's quarters. Any and all whisperings have been quelled by withering looks from Captain. This *Fair Lady* struts along the deck as if she owns it, much to the chagrin of many, but none so much as Jan, whose face could have scraped the siding off our boat when he saw her leave Captain's lodgings this morning. That woman had a look about her like a cat that has just eaten a nestling.

Day 15 – February 8, 1624

A bit more excitement to speak of. It seems there are *White Sea Ghosts* following us. Cooper states that, while on watch, he saw three white women with tails as white as their hair trailing the ship.

After a bit of investigation, we discovered the source of said *White Sea Ghosts* in Cooper's belongings. It seems that he had been keeping wine in one of his barrels for some time. He had been letting it age much longer than usual, the result of which is a much thicker, more potent concoction. I did not partake in the sampling myself but did note a marked difference in those who had.

White Sea Ghosts, indeed.

After tucking him in for the day, it was decided that he be relieved of his watch this evening. Carpenter has agreed to step in.

Day 16 – February 9, 1624

White Sea Ghosts spotted again!

This time by Carpenter. After a futile inspection of his person for evidence of Cooper's special wine, Carpenter swore on the soul of his dear departed mother that he did not drink any of Cooper's concoction. However, he did admit to having stayed up late the night before to play dice with some of the other hands.

We are running low on reliable watchmen.

The Fair Lady of the Bow has made a nest in her namesake. She can be found pacing the deck day and night, when she is not entertaining Captain. She is always searching the horizon. I suppose, like us all, she is eager to see land once more.

Jan has continued to harass her and was reprimanded once again by our esteemed leader. Grumblings among the men have ensued.

Day 23 – February 16, 1624

A grave day. Jan Velde has gone missing and is presumed dead. This is a most suspicious turn of events considering his quarrel with the *Fair Lady of the Bow*. Some suspect her involvement in the disappearance, but how could a woman of her size throw a man as big as Jan from the bow? And if she were as strong as such, how would she do it without anyone noticing?

I find it a truly a ridiculous notion. However, I am staying clear of that woman, nonetheless. My skin crawls each and every time I have the unlucky circumstance to pass her on deck.

In any case, regarding Velde's death, Jan took part in the passing of Cooper's concoction last evening, which has become a nightly event and provides us with a more plausible cause of death. A few of the less pious gentlemen in our cargo have also partaken of the beverage, attempting to prove their manliness but rather showing their stupidity, for they are useless on the morrow.

At sunset, Captain spoke a few words on Jan's behalf once the storm winds and rains that had pounded our decks had died down. Third mate, Neels Houben, is second cousin to Jan on his mother's side and had filled Captain in with a few personal details.

Day 31 – February 24, 1624

Food stores are running down. Attempts to fish have been thwarted by bad weather. Halfway through our journey now. Morale is low.

Day 38 – March 2, 1624

Another deckhand has gone missing. Luc Schoonenburg was on watch last night. He was no longer there in the morning. No one wants to go on watch. Captain refuses to allow double shifts, blaming the lost men on irresponsible leisure-time activities. He gave the entire crew a firm talking-to this morning. This speech culminated in Cooper's cask being thrown overboard, on Captain's orders. The loss of both drink and two men has everyone in a foul mood.

Services for Luc are scheduled on the morrow, at daybreak. It is my hope that if he did go over, he broke his neck in the fall. I shiver at the thought of one lone man treading water in the dark as we receded from his view. God rest his soul.

Day 42 – March 6, 1624

Forgive my poor handwriting as I record the notes of the night just passed. My deplorable penmanship is a direct attribution to the rough seas we are now sustaining as well as the shaking of my hand, and heart, from last night's events.

Let these here records show that I am of sound body and mind. What I witnessed was true, of that much I am sure.

No one wanted to take watch last night. Men came down with all manner of illness and injury to avoid the task. If we were not two-thirds through our journey, we might have entertained the notion of turning back, but such is not an option. Onward—the only clear choice. And so we fell to the drawing of straws for watch.

I, hoping to set an example of bravery for some of the more dim-witted crew, drew first. When my open palm revealed the shorter straw, I laughed out loud. Another foolish gesture, I see now with a fresher view, as I look aft on the evening's events. However, as previously stated, I had a duty to uphold, a standard to set. So when my watch came, I did my duty with my head held high, chest proudly out, and not a shred of fear clinging to my consciousness. These men, I thought at the time of my ignorance, needed to be taught a lesson. I climbed the jib with the deftness of my youth and the motivation of a man possessed.

The moon was full in her nest of stars, shining down upon us, keeping the blanket of water lit with her light. Orion rose, taking aim as he always does, and we kept the first star in his belt, Mintaka, just off the topsail yard, heading towards our destination to the west.

The first few hours passed with little incident. A few good men gathered on deck and told stories. One particular yarn had been circulating about a sailor who had hopped around all day ignorant to the canvas drawing pinned to his backside. It depicted the man as a rabbit, including his badly cut hair and his enormous teeth, which truly resembled the rodent he had just brought to life.

The mood grew darker as one of the men pondered if the *White Sea Ghosts* would make an appearance that evening. I remarked sharply, on behalf of Captain, that no such thing existed. A folly, if ever there had been one, invented by drunken, lazy men. That quickly silenced them, though the stories of merriment soon returned.

In time, the storytellers departed to their racks for some rest, and I found myself alone in my cold—bitter cold—perch, thankful for the silver moonlight above. Hour after hour, I scanned the horizon, taking in the immense blanket of water.

And then I saw them. *My dear God in heaven, what abomination of nature did I witness under your blessed night sky?*

Three at first, then four. Pale as the moon above, all women, all swimming alongside our ship. I rubbed my eyes, for truly I was seeing some sort of an illusion brought on by the late hour and foolish talk of the *White Sea Ghosts*. But no, this was no illusion. They moved closer, towards the portside.

I descended to the deck and ran aft, following their progress, keeping my gaze on the water as I went. And still they came. As I moved along the deck, my head turned, I collided with that awful woman, *The Fair Lady of the Bow*. I tell you, I have never met a woman with such strength. She stood as still as our mast. My being bounced off her person, even though I had been moving at a fast rate. The familiar chill ran up my spine as my eyes, adjusted to the dim light, recognized our esteemed captain's plaything. She addressed me with a low voice, inquiring after my well-being, then pulled me to my feet with the physical prowess of one three times her size. I veritably flew into a standing position with her aid.

And then she was gone, passing me quickly on her way below deck.

I scanned the portside once more and saw, to my dismay, that the creatures in the water were no longer visible. Well, I thought to myself, either I am dreaming or we passed over them when I crashed into that woman. I continued aft, climbing towards the poop deck, hoping to catch a glimpse of whatever I had seen previously. I found nothing. Nothing, except for several ship's lines trailing in the water, floating in our wake. To my knowledge, these heavy lines served no purpose in the water at this hour. I looked about. I was alone. I wondered who had put those lines there.

I grabbed hold of one of the ropes and heaved the line, coiling it on the poop deck beside me. I grabbed hold of the other, tugging mightily, fighting the eager sea. But the sea seemed unusually strong for such a calm night. Something held fast to the other end of the line. I put my back into it and tugged with all my force. I was met with much resistance, and the line slipped from my grasp, sending me, for the second time that evening, onto my back, where I stared at the night sky above me. I got to my feet, furious at this folly but slightly rattled by the thought of what could be on the seaside end of that line. I stood still, scanning our wake, and then—*I saw them again.*

This time there were five. Five heads, womanly heads, trailing in the frothy foam behind us. In the dim moonlight, I swear on the soul of my beloved mother, they stared back at me with eyes like brilliant points of light. Then, to my astonishment, one of them broke the surface of the water and I saw—how do I write this here, without anyone thinking me mad? But it is my duty to report what I saw, and so I shall. There in the pale moonlight, I saw a woman—no, not just a woman—a woman who was both a woman and a fish! Her chest, exposed in the moonlight, was that of true woman. But below her waist ... a tail! With my mouth near my knees, I stared at the sight before me. This could not be real. Could it? I had heard stories of the sirens, mermaids, half-woman, half-fish told by many a seasoned sailor, but I had never believed a single word—until last night.

And not one but five! A veritable pod of women with fish tails, trailing our vessel!

I started shouting. I could not be the only one to witness such a thing. I would be considered mad! I shouted and shouted until Cooper stood beside me, wondering at all the ruckus.

Do you see them? I asked him.

Aye, he answered, nodding solemnly as if he had just seen the devil himself, dancing on the water behind us.

Then they were gone.

As I write this, I wonder if it happened at all ... but Cooper saw it, so I was not alone in my dreaming. Now I am faced with the task of informing Captain that we are either all mad or a group of mermaids is truly trailing our fair ship. I have a long day ahead of me, for I do not think I will sleep much this morning after the events of last night. It is my hope that, if they do exist, these are benevolent creatures and mean us no ill will. I truly hope so.

Day 43 – March 7, 1624

My reputation is at stake. No one believes that Cooper and I saw ... what did we see? I now doubt mine own mind. After a long night in the elements, shivering and staring at the same night sky and water for a long period of time, perhaps I *had* been dreaming. Having Cooper as my only witness does not help my situation, for I fear his credibility is tenuous, at best.

I tried finding that woman, but she was in Captain's cabin all this day. I did, however, discover her name. It seems that she does not have, or perhaps is unwilling to provide, a surname. She goes only by *Nomia*.

Day 45 – March 9, 1624

I have done some investigating on our strange passenger *Nomia*, otherwise known as our *Fair Lady of the Bow*. Not one person seems to have known her prior to boarding our ship. For one who has brought quite a bit of excitement, I would surmise that at least someone would have known of her. A most peculiar state of affairs.

I tried to broach the subject with Captain, but he will not hear ill of that woman, and unfortunately, my tarnished reputation does not garner the same audience it once did with our leader.

My concern for the safety of those aboard grows ever stronger.

Cooper and I have discussed the matter privately, and many of the crew are rallying to keep a closer watch on this woman.

Day 50 – March 14, 1624

The fare is no longer fair. Our bread is now old and wormy. The cook had to shake the cask to the side to get the worms out. Our meat is scantily distributed and most certainly at its end. Many now prefer the mush to all else offered.

That woman, Nomia, has not left Captain's side in many a day.

We are on to her.

Day 56 – March 20, 1624

Land must be close! A bird was spotted off the starboard side this morning. No land in sight, but that bird. That glorious bird!

It can't be much longer now ...

Day 57 – March 21, 1624

Nomia has gone missing. We searched the entire ship and all efforts yielded nothing. *Nothing.* Not even her belongings, though no one seems to remember her having brought a thing aboard. Not a single shred of evidence remains to prove that her person had been with us these past two months.

If it weren't for the distressed look on Captain's face, we'd all be happier believing she never existed at all.

Is it the news of her disappearance or the telltale signs that land is not far from us that is the source of levity and mirth among crew and cargo? It is difficult to say. But the merriment and lightening of step is much agreeable to all who have it.

May she be at peace, wherever the *Fair Lady of the Bow* is now, and may we have no incidents on our return journey to home.

– Pieter Thienponthe, First Mate

22

Evie

We asked Nomia if John had a computer. Of course he did. Nobody has a house on the Point without a goddamn computer. We fired it up and showed her the contents of the USB drive. Nomia clicked on the word *Oddities*. A screen opened with more birdcages, but these were different from the others we had looked at before—larger, more ornate. They reminded me of pictures I had seen of Victorian zoos. The red background contrasted against the cages, silhouetted in black. They swung for a moment or two, and then a rolled-up banner appeared above each cage. Nomia moved the mouse over one of the banners and it slowly unfurled, revealing a canvas carnival poster. Gravity took hold when the cloth hit the bottom of the screen, giving it a little life-like bounce. The poster read, *Glow Girl!*

Nomia kept her mouse hovering over the slightly swinging poster, garish with bright colors and a primitive drawing of a girl whose back was towards us, her chin resting over her shoulder, one eye closed in a knowing wink. She wore a bathing suit, like a pinup model from the '50s. Tiny stars floated in the night sky that surrounded her. Pale blue like a robin's egg, her skin seemed to glow against the night sky while her brilliant red-orange hair was elegantly coifed in a 1940s style victory roll.

An informational word bubble floated over her poster. It read:

> *The Infamous Glow Girl! Come see*
> *Aurora! The mysterious glowing girl!*
> *Her skin is blue like the sea and sky!*
> *You've never seen anything like her!*
> *Not only does she glow in the dark, she*
> *dances with a flaming hula-hoop! A real*
> *crowd-pleaser, Aurora is also available*
> *for private sessions. Book your time with*
> *Aurora now. Let her light brighten your*
> *world ...*

"I'm sorry? What the hell is that?" said Rachael. "I've never heard of such a thing! What a crock of ..."

"Shhhh! There's more," I said.

Nomia rapidly went from cage to cage, allowing the canvas carnival posters to drop, revealing more and more of the *Oddities*. In addition to *The Glow Girl*, there were four others: *The Angel, The Beast Girl, The Twistable Girl,* and last but not least, *The Mermaid.*

The poster featured a girl with the body of a woman and the tail of a fish. Her hair was white. White as snow. White as Nix's.

Nomia's hands flew to her mouth, tears forming in her large eyes.

"*No*," she whispered.

"Click on it," I said.

She didn't move. Her shoulders shook, and tears rolled down her bony cheeks.

"When I first saw you at the parade, you said that *they* were coming for you. Is this what you meant? Are these people who run *Sammlung* the ones you are afraid of?"

"I don't know. But my sister! How could this happen? I knew someone was after us, but I had no idea it meant *this!* And Richard. He must be tied up in all of this somehow, right? He had this USB stick in his apartment. Is he alive? Is he dead? Why did he have this?"

"Too many questions," I said. My heart filled with sadness. *Could Richard really be dead? Am I the last Musäus?* It didn't feel like I was, but then again, what the hell do I know? "Why would they take him and not kill him? You were with Richard probably more than anyone. Do you know if he was involved with these people? Was he working on something for them?"

I'm not really sure what my brother does, to tell the truth. That's a sad fact of life, but he was never all that chummy with me once he hit his teen years. He kept to himself. He could have been a CIA operative or a transvestite opera singer. It's not like he told me shit.

"It's possible," said Nomia. "He was really secretive about

his work. I do remember him mentioning something about going to Rhode Island to meet some people. But at the time, it didn't mean anything. Perhaps it still doesn't mean anything. He told me he was a strategic planner, and I think he said his last client was a wind energy company out of Sweden."

I nodded like all this totally made sense to me. For the record, it did not.

Nomia pushed back her chair, then stood. "We came here, so many years ago, we came to America to avoid the *Wasserschutz*. I need some air," she said and walked in a dreamlike state towards the patio door. It opened without a sound, and she headed out into the night. The darkness swallowed her the moment she slid the door shut behind her.

What was that word, *Wasserschutz?* It meant *water protector* in German. That much I could make out with my primitive German skills. But what the hell did she mean? I stared at the sliding door. Too late to ask her.

"Click on it," said Rachael.

"What? Click on what?"

"The mermaid chick. Her sister. Click on it."

I sat down in Nomia's chair, still warm from her frail body, grabbed hold of the mouse, and clicked. A blue screen appeared. It took a moment, but our eyes adjusted to the new, brighter screen. It shimmered, like light shining through water. *Water.*

"*My God,*" I whispered. "I think this is a live feed of a tank."

I noticed a time stamp down on the bottom corner of the screen. It matched the time on the computer. And a little icon that looked a lot like a compass appeared at the bottom, beneath the tank viewer.

"What does that do?" said Rachael in a hushed tone, her red nail tapping the computer screen and creating a ripple in the gel-based monitor.

I guided my pointer over to the compass, pushed the east arrow on the compass, and held down the mouse button. The screen scrolled to the right in a slow, slightly jerky way. The view revealed more blue, more blue, more blue and then ...

"What's that?" I said.

In the corner of the screen, just beyond the frame of vision, a dark, narrow shadow floated. I pressed down on the right arrow again, but the camera would go no farther.

"That could be anything," said Rachael. She leaned back and folded her arms over her chest.

I turned around to look at her, and when I did, her eyes went wide, intent on the screen behind me. Her mouth opened just a little, and she placed her hands on her knees and leaned forward. Slowly, I turned back to the screen. White hair floated into the camera's view, all but confirming Nomia's worst fear—*Nix*. The unmistakable hair. She had been incarcerated in some sick, underground black market circus. And she was for sale.

Rachael and I sat and watched the hair float in front of the screen for several minutes. I have no idea what Rachael thought, but I felt ill. Sure, she had tried to kill me, but ... *Nix is stuck in that tank like an aquarium fish, available for private sessions?*

"This is wrong," I said, turning to Rachael. She was staring at the screen. My heart thumped against my chest, and I could hear the blood pounding in my ears.

Rachael stood suddenly, put her hands on her hips, and said, "*That's bullshit.* I don't care what it takes, but we're getting her out. We're getting all those bitches out. Women are not for sale—no matter what shape, size, color, or species they are. Period."

I let the air whistle between my teeth. I hadn't even noticed that I had been holding my breath. All of a sudden, I felt lightheaded, dizzy.

"I don't know, Rach," I said. "I mean, how the hell are we going to break into a top-secret fortress unnoticed, waltz around, find Nix, and then bust out all these girls *and* an incarcerated mermaid without anyone noticing us? Or killing us? And what about my brother?"

"He's got to be involved in this somehow. Maybe Nix knows something. Maybe he's there, too. If he's not dead." She looked over at me and bit on the tip of her finger before mumbling, "Sorry."

I sighed. "It's all right. For what it's worth, I don't think he's dead. Continue with your theory."

"It's a sex club, right? We saw that in the *Pleasure* section. Well, we just so happen to know people who know sex clubs."

"*We know people who know sex clubs?* What are you talking about? Not me! I don't even like showering with the lights on. I know very little about the sex industry, but—oh. Wait. You do ..."

Rachael had that stupid smug look on her face she gets when an idea pops into her head. I felt the familiar tingle at the top of my spine. This meant trouble. Nothing good ever happened after that stupid smug face. She pulled out her phone and started texting.

"You're texting Shep and Hazel, aren't you?"

"Right," she said, nodding without looking up from her smartphone. I have never seen anyone text as fast she can. *Click, click, click.* Her fingers were a blaze of speed and sound.

"Done," she announced.

We watched the screen and waited. Nix's hair floated in the water—its owner, just off-screen. The light continued to shimmer. A fake blue ocean for a very real ocean creature. *Poor thing.*

The sound of Rachael's phone, a sort of seventies porn *Chica-bawm Chica-ba-wam,* heralded an incoming message, pulling us from the live cam.

"Yes!" said Rachael. "It's Hazel. She says Shep knows a guy."

"It's Rhode Island," I said. "Everyone *knows a guy.*"

"Yes, but not every Rhode Islander knows these guys or admits that they know these guys."

"So now what?" I asked.

"Shep's going to contact his guy and get back to us. In the meantime, we should fix ourselves a drink and keep an eye on our aquatic friends."

I didn't know what to say. Everything had just hit full-tilt boogie mode. Suddenly, I was friends with Nomia and all fired up about saving one of the creatures who'd tried to kill me, along with a whole bevy of exotic freaky ladies. My brother's status was still woefully unknown to me, while my future included a trip to see a *guy* in the Rhode Island sex industry.

Up was down, down, up. Cats living with dogs. Sushi from gas stations seemed okay. Well, maybe things weren't *that* messed up, but you get the idea. I was starting to understand why Paddy no longer wanted anything to do with me. If you looked at my situation from the outside *(How do I say this without swearing? Fuck it, I can't.)* my situation was *fucked.*

Rachael went over to the slider, held her hands over her eyes, and leaned on the glass, peering out into the darkness.

"You see her?" I called.

"Nope. Too dark."

"Guess she needed some time to process," I said. "I sure do. You know what would help?"

"What?"

"Bourbon. My friend Bourbon always fixes things. Can you see if he's hiding over there in the bar area?"

"You really have issues, Evie," said Rachael, shaking her head, but her tight ass headed over to the bar anyway.

I have issues? Damn straight, I have issues.

A few moments later, I heard ice cubes clinking against crystal behind me.

"Here," said Rachael. "It's whiskey, but it's all John has behind the bar." She took a swig from one of the glasses and then made a *pah!* sound followed by a long wheeze.

"Good stuff," she said, coughing up a lung.

I took a sip out of my glass. The amber liquid was smooth and warm. Just what I needed. I cradled the glass to my chest and looked at the screen. The hair had swished and then had disappeared while Rachael had been over at the bar. Seconds before, I had been left with an empty view.

"You see her?" called Rachael.

"No," I said quietly. "She just sort of disappeared."

Where'd she go?

I moved the camera all around, but found nothing, so I sipped some more. Rachael dragged a chair over beside me, and without her eyes leaving the screen, clinked my glass.

"Cheers," she said.

I didn't answer, just kept on sipping, my eyes on the brilliant blue screen. Five minutes passed, then a hand, a talon, covered in scales, crept in front of the camera, and I heard Rachael gasp.

"This is for real, isn't it, Evelyn?"

"Yes, Rachael," I replied. "It's as real as it gets."

I leaned in closer. So did Rach. The hand folded down all of its fingers except one, the middle one. She held her triumphant hand signal of defiance in front of the camera for a few moments, and then, in a flash of scales, Nix flew up past the camera and disappeared.

Rachael leaned back, then nodded at the screen.

"Good girl," she said. "Good for you."

23

Caratocos, elder scholar

Information recorded via transatlantic transmissions from Ronan, a Keeper along the shores of what is known as Narragansett Bay, Rhode Island. The following account describes early interactions with a small group known as the *Wampanoag Seawomen*.

There are several reports of various *Homo aquaticus* found along the northeastern seaboard, extending from New England to Nova Scotia and New Brunswick. The Passamaquoddy Tribe, who reside along coastal Maine and into New Brunswick, speaks of the *Halfway People*—smaller species of fish-born individuals (see Archive #25).

The Seawomen lived along the coast of what is now Cape Cod, known to the first people as the *Long Land*. The Seawomen were a part of the Wampanoag tribe. Folklore among the Wampanoag described these females as having square eyes, green hair, and webbed fingers—much like ours. The male counterparts to this particular group preferred to live on land, while the females resided primarily in the ocean.

At one time, several different pods of Seawomen could be observed thriving near the following areas: Sandwich, Truro, Martha's Vineyard, and Chatham. The group Ronan encountered resided in the area known as the Elizabeth Islands, close to Martha's Vineyard, but their territory encompassed the areas around Falmouth, Bourne, Onset, Mashpee, Nantucket, and the eastern shores of what is now Rhode Island.

Peaceful, fair, kind, generous. These were the words Ronan used when describing the Seawomen. Their numbers had dwindled radically prior to Ronan's contact with them. Interaction with the Europeans had brought diseases foreign to the Seawomen and their Wampanoag brethren, and many had perished as a result of their contact while showing kindness to the newcomers in their land.

Ronan had decided to become a Keeper in this region after encountering a foreign, all-female pod in lower Narragansett Bay who had massacred and eaten a crew of European merchants. Cross-references in the Archives lead us to believe that these females may have been under the direction of Bestla or Kolga (*See Species Archive #14*). To briefly summarize the account, the females, including Kolga, had eaten the men after killing them.

Shortly after that time, Ronan had decided to explore the areas to the north towards what is now Boston Harbor. It was on this journey that Ronan encountered the Seawomen for the first time. These cousins of ours on the global *Homo aquaticus* tree did not warmly welcome him at first. A cautious, tentative inspection of each other took place over a week's time. Ronan thought their reservations prudent after the devastation already caused by many European land-dwellers in that region.

But in time, the Seawomen decided that Ronan was not a threat and so they held a great celebration for their new cousin at the beach on a warm summer evening. Ronan enjoyed the delicacies of the local waters, including crab, fish, and other unusual creatures with long tails called lobsters. This particular seafood delicacy turns a brilliant shade of red once cooked. Ronan felt a strong bond with these individuals. He recognized that they were much like his own kin in Ireland—agricultural and fishing-based peoples who loved to tell stories.

The women's hair was so black that in full sunlight it appeared green. Ronan was informed that the land-dwelling Wampanoag often made fun of their sea-dwelling cousins, particularly in regards to their oversized eyes, describing them as squares.

A bond formed between Ronan and these fine people, who treated him as a distant relation, including him in important tribal ceremonies and the fall harvest celebrations. In time, Ronan learned the language of the Wampanoag, a skill he then used to serve as a translator, expressing the needs of the First People to several holy men from Europe. These religious pilgrims perceived Ronan to be a traveling explorer.

Ronan sent the following two recordings. The first is a sort of delightful folktale from the Seawomen. The second is a more grim personal account.

Folktale:

A Seawoman named Squant was determined to ride a great finback whale whose skin shone like white sea foam. She followed him daily, and every day the whale denied her that which she desired. She offered him food, but he did not want it. She offered him her love, but he had no need of it. She offered him jewelry she had fashioned from seaweed and shells, but he only laughed at the ridiculous notion of a whale wearing jewelry. Each time the whale denied Squant a ride, the Seawoman desired a ride all the more.

One day, Squant revealed herself to a great whale hunter along the shores of the inner harbor. She told him of the pale finback who had denied her a ride. In her anger, she offered pearls to whoever would kill the willful whale. But the whale hunter had no need of pearls. A new cooking pot in which to cook his dinner, yes, but the whale hunter laughed at the offer of pearls.

The Seawoman frowned at her would-be savior. Where was she to get a cooking pot? Was there nothing she had on her person that the whale hunter desired? The whale hunter knew that if he lay down with Squant, he would never be rid of her, so he thought better of this offer. To make the Seawoman leave him alone, he made a suggestion. He told her to go tell the whale that his life would be spared—as long as he gave Squant a ride.

Delighted with this offer, the Seawoman swam as fast as she

could to find the pale finback. Upon hearing of his pardon from the great hunter, the finback allowed Squant to climb aboard his mighty back. Off they went, around the great arm of the Long Land. The Seawoman was finally happy. She sang a sweet song, her hair blowing in the gentle breeze and her scales glittering in the sunlight. She was so transfixed by the experience she did not notice the whale winking at a passing school of cod fish as if to say, "Watch this." After the strange pair rounded the tip of the Long Land's arm, that tricky whale dove beneath the waves, charging ahead towards the far shore.

Squant held on as tightly as she could, until her grip began to fail her. Feeling her body slipping from his back, the pale whale shot upwards towards the surface and exhaled all his air through his great blowhole. Up, up, up went the water and Squant with it. Her whale ride had turned into an air ride. Over the harbor she flew until she landed in a pond close to the gateway of the Long Land. The story ends with her there, to this very day, sulking in the bottom of the pond. It is said that her beautiful scales can be seen shimmering on a sunny day.

The second tale explains the near-hostile stance the Seawomen and their kin had taken towards Ronan upon their first meeting. The timing herewith is based on approximations made by Ronan and his knowledge of Wampanoag time keeping.

Personal Account:

Around the end of 1624, a European pod of merrow made the Long Land their new home, integrating themselves with the Seawomen. This was the same all-female pod that Ronan witnessed a few years later, in 1636. The water people of the Wampanoag took in these newcomers as they did Ronan much later.

They arrived early in the summer, these hauntingly pale women, as Ronan described them. The Wampanoag counted eight but thought there might be more. One among them did not favor her sisters' bone-white complexion and coloring. She was dark-haired, fair skinned, and had a much slighter bone structure than the others. This one had been the most problematic of all. Ronan recognized the Seawomen's description of this particular merrow, remembering certain females who stood out in his memory of that horrific event. Ronan had called them Big White (whom we believe to be Kolga), Smaller White (a daughter of Kolga), and Dark Hair. (This particular female has come up repeatedly in recent times. We know little about her, but she seems to cause a great deal of trouble for our people.)

Many members of the tribe had nodded vigorously when Ronan had told his own tale of the destructive female merrow. One of the Seawomen, who went by the name of Abbona, became very upset at the telling of these tales. Ronan said that tears had run down her fair face, and she was so distraught, she had to leave the fire. When Ronan inquired about her distress, the elders spoke with hushed voices, telling Ronan that she had loved one of the pale merrow, the one with the scars, and was still mourning the loss of her love. But an incident had occurred that had forced the Seawomen to ban the European merrow from their hunting waters. They would not give all the details, but indicated that the dark-haired one had caused most of the trouble. Once the relationship between the European merrow and the Seawomen of the Wampanoag unraveled, the European pod had moved south.

It was shortly after this that Ronan encountered the females on his own.

Note: Many other incidents regarding the interactions between Ronan and Kolga's pod can be found in more recent recordings.

Ronan has not sent much word regarding the Seawomen in many years, and we have begun to wonder if the disease and pestilence that had plagued their people in the times between 1630 and 1667 may have wiped out these kind and generous individuals.

24

The Elizabeth Islands
June 18, 1625
6:14 AM

Nomia

Nix's head broke the surface of the water first. Her hand, held high above her fair head, firmly grasped the peculiar creature—an overly large, insect-like thing, writhing in a way that made my skin crawl. Dark in color, with a reddish hue, not blue as they sometimes were, these strange creatures had strong claws that could pinch with force, leaving bruised welts that lasted for days.

The one they called Abbona came up beside her. She, too, held one of the two-clawed beasties. Abbona's was much bigger, almost twice the size of Nix's. My pale-haired sister frowned at being outdone. She had won the game of finding dinner first, but she had not won the size competition. The two girls laughed and pointed at each other's prizes, shoving their beasties in each other's faces, threatening to take off the other's nose.

I sat on the shore and laughed along with them. The seas

had been unusually rough the previous few days. A warm, strong wind had brought heavy storms up from the southwest, making the water choppy and tumultuous.

It had been a year and three months since I had jumped from the bow of the *Eendracht* into the icy waters off the coast and stood, for the first time, on the shores of this strange, new land. The journey across the Atlantic had been an adventure, to say the least, and not one I wished to repeat any time soon. I learned much about myself and discovered that my outward appearance could be used for manipulation. It had been necessary. We had also needed to make a decision. A moral decision regarding survival.

Halfway through our journey, my sisters and my mother, exhausted from keeping up with a long-distance sea vessel, had fallen to exhaustion. I had placed ropes along the stern, each night allowing my kin to hold on when they were tired or to climb aboard and rest in the middle of the night when the deck activity had dwindled to nothing and I could easily distract any curious crewmembers. But the favors I needed to perform for my family's safety began to come at a higher and higher price. Before long, my sisters and mother were starving, too tired to fish for themselves and keep up with my shipboard journey. Something needed to be done. And he had it coming.

Hadn't we suffered enough?

Europe had become too dangerous. Hunted everywhere we went, our safety was always a tenuous thing, like a frail branch in a gale. We had grown so tired of running. Tired of hiding. Tired of the ways of men. We needed to find a place where we could live as ourselves without the need to hide our true nature from the common folk who treated us as if we were vermin or a plague, something distasteful that needed eradication. The New World was our answer. Wild, savage, mostly uninhabited, free of laws, free of any real civilization. It sounded too good to be true. I don't remember which of my sisters had first heard the news of the strange, wild land across the sea, but they had brought the information to our mother, Kolga, and she made the decision.

However, my condition, my flawed nature, dictated our need to travel by way of ship. These shortcomings of mine had nearly divided my family. Some of my sisters were in favor of leaving me behind. Nix, however, came to my rescue. She wouldn't hear of abandoning me, and a physical altercation took place between her and two of my other sisters. Kolga had ripped them apart, settling the matter. *We will find a solution for Nomia's crossing. That is the end of it.* Her voice, deep and full of gravel, had boomed over all of us, silencing the squabble.

Nix and I had gone to the harbor. We smiled broadly at all the men who whistled as we strolled about in search of a ship bound for the New World. Despite the cold, we were, as always, barefoot and brazen, heedless of the talk about our presence that spread like wildfire through the harbor town. It did not take long for us to find what we sought. A ship, the great *Eendracht*, whose name meant Unity, was set to sail in four weeks' time, not long after the Christian Christmas season.

Passage came at a high price. We'd had, up until this time, very little use for currency. We had always acquired whatever provisions we needed on our own. What we did not have, we created. But this was different. After learning the cost, Nix and I knew that we could only acquire enough money for one person to travel. There were only so many pockets we could pick in a short amount of time.

It had been decided previously that two of us would travel above the surface of the sea, while the rest trailed alongside. The two of us on board would throw lines for our weary sisters. Now, with the difficulty of acquiring the passage fare for just myself, I would have to be alone on the vessel and carry out this task without the help of my sister. But that seemed the easier task. The more difficult task of swimming alongside a transatlantic vessel is beyond my understanding. I have no idea how they kept up. Their strength remains an enormous mystery to me. I am indebted to their abilities to endure such a hardship on my behalf so that I, too, could travel accompanied by family. Were it not for me and my genetic shortcomings, they would have been able to take a more leisurely journey across the sea, taking a different route and stopping at islands along the way to rest before continuing on.

It was my love for Nix and my gratitude for their commitment to me that drove me to do what needed to be done, to sacrifice my innocence and lay with that wretched man so that I would be able to do all that was necessary for the survival of my family. To commit the awful act of taking a few men's lives so that those closest to me might live. I played a somewhat god-like role, and once the horror of my actions wore off, I have to admit that the power I had experienced was addictive. I cannot deny the need I felt for it, the undeniable craving to take another's life, to watch their existence fade away like a candle extinguished. It was a thrill like no other I had ever experienced.

But when the time came, when the call *Land ho!* rang out across the decks, I felt a great relief wash over me. I did not look back. I plunged myself into the dark, icy depths and rejoined my family. We made land on our own, every single one of us completely exhausted in our own way.

Passage. It changed us all.

I had grown weak. My muscles had atrophied, and my desire to be in the sea had waned. In stark contrast to my frailer state, my sisters and my mother, while utterly spent, had grown stronger than ever. Their bodies seemed leaner, more muscular, their senses more attuned to the ways of the sea. They heard things I could not, saw things I did not, as if the chasm between my physiology and theirs had increased by twenty-fold.

On that first night in the savage new land, we made shelter beneath enormous trees, gathered wood, and built a fire using matches I had taken from the ship. We attempted to keep warm with my few clothes along with a waterproof sealskin, one of my only belongings. We said little to one another. Exhausted from the crossing, we could barely keep our eyes open. Looking back on that first night, I don't even think we had had the foresight to set someone as watch. We had, instead, every single one of us, slept, dreamless, long into the next day.

The subject of what had transpired in the passage, what we had done, what *I* had done for the survival of us all, was not discussed. The eating of a human's flesh was *not* something our people did. But it had been necessary. And besides, with that first one, it was going to be either him or me. I chose me. That filthy sailor had repeatedly put his hands all over me, attempting to overpower me with his strong arms and foul breath. I didn't mourn his passing as I threw him over. And I don't believe my family felt any ill will when they, starving and exhausted, had eaten his flesh. I had done my best to steal provisions from the hold, but I could only take so much and for so long without arousing suspicion. After that disgusting man laid his hands on me the first time, the captain had stepped in, taken me into his cabin, and the rest... Well, the rest played itself out. I had my family to look out for. I understood what needed to be done to ensure survival for us all.

As we sat around the blazing fire in our new homeland, we kept the grueling events of our long journey to ourselves. We did not speak of them. However, I knew if I ever needed to repeat what I had done, I would. *Because I had liked it.*

As the weather grew warmer, we sent out small search parties to travel north along the coast, following the migration of the fish in the warm currents. When the parties returned and reported that they had found an even better location, we all moved. We traveled past rocky beaches and small islands. The water teemed with food, untouched by all the massive numbers of people we had left behind, so far across the ocean. We felt at peace, having seen little to no human activity in the strange, abundant new land. We thought ourselves alone. Then one day, we were not.

We had been swimming in the summer-warmed waters near a string of islands, enjoying the longer days and better weather. My sisters had been teaching me how to stalk and grab a fish with my bare hands. I had been chasing a long, narrow one with blue-toned scales when something large and swift caught my attention. I thought it was seal. We had not seen many since our arrival. I thought little of it and swam to rejoin my sisters, empty-handed. They were gathered together in a huddle, whispering and pointing to a line of rocks jutting out from the beach, beyond where we all treaded water. I followed their gaze and saw *them* for the first time.

So dark, like a perfect negative of my sisters. Their skin, their hair, their enormous eyes—all dark as night. It was clear from the start they were just as curious about us as we were of them. One of them smiled and lifted a webbed hand, tentatively, in greeting. Nix waved back, which caught all of us by surprise. My fierce sister, always cautious, always suspicious, offering a greeting to strangers? We looked at one another, our brows raised in astonishment at both the new arrivals and Nix's gesture.

Like the symbiotic behavior of a shoal of sardines, they moved as one, disappearing into the water. Nix followed. We waited for her return with our breaths held. When she finally *did* return and we were beyond relief and onto anger in regards to her strange, rash actions, she informed us that she had been unable to find them. That night, on one of the islands we had begun to call home, Kolga announced that we should have little to no contact with such peoples. *Only bad things can come of this. I can feel it.* Her warning had been clear to us all. The next morning, Nix disappeared. No one saw her leave. To this day, I still do not understand why she left.

Two long days passed, and my heart felt as though it had been torn into several pieces. I spent all my time pacing the shore, hoping to catch sight of her white hair bobbing along the surface of the water. When Nix finally did return, Kolga was furious. We all sat by the fire after their explosive argument, quiet, sullen, lost in our thoughts about the actions of our *fallen* sister. Nix had directly disobeyed our mother, something none of us had ever done. Why had she disobeyed? Kolga had demanded. But Nix was beyond explaining the *why* of her actions. She had made contact with a new people.

She said they were kind, generous, and welcoming—once they had gotten over their initial fear of her strange appearance. Slowly, over time, we met these new creatures, and they did accept us. They taught us how to live in our new home. They taught us about their food, what they liked to hunt, and how we, too, could hunt it. They taught us how they made shelters, far superior to the flimsy ones we had constructed. We learned about the various plants in the area, the sour red berries that grew in swampy areas but were excellent when stuffed inside a freshly caught fish and cooked over the fire. Nix became our ambassador, picking up their language quickly. When the warm weather turned cool, they taught us about their custom of moving inland to avoid the harshness of winter along the coast.

There were others in the area, they warned us, not like us, not like them. Their land-dwelling cousins had frequent conflicts with other tribes. Attacks were not unknown. We needed to stay alert at all times. But we had a hard time believing it. We seldom saw anyone other than these fellow water people. *How could any harm come to us in such a vast, vacant land?*

We lived well, gathering our strength. Life was good. However, I had to adjust to life without Nix, my sister who had always been by my side but was now no longer my constant companion. She had found someone else—Abbona. Once first contact had been made, the pair had become inseparable. Nix became our conduit to the new peoples, and likewise, Abbona became her own family's go-between. The pair was skilled in languages, and soon, Abbona spoke to us in our own words. Even though she had taken my sister away from me, it was hard for me not to like the kind woman. She had an easy smile, a warm disposition. I felt better when I was around her and sad when she was gone. She made everything into an adventure. There was always something new to explore, something we just had to see. When she was not attached to my sister, she spent time with me, teaching me the language of her people. I, too, realized that the words came easily.

The pair was opposite in every way. Nix pale to Abbona's dark. While Nix stood tall, Abbona was almost childlike in stature, standing only a little taller than Nix's waist. While Nix was surrounded by her many sisters, Abbona had all brothers. And like Nix, Abbona had a brother who stood out from all her siblings. Before the incident, I never spoke more than a few words to him, but on the rare occasion that our paths crossed, we shared a look that said, *Your sibling took mine.*

In time, Abbona showed us how to hunt in the forest. How to find the delicate, brown creatures with long necks and thin legs and their large males with branches on their heads. We had hunted similar animals in Europe, but the meat tasted different here—more wild, like the land. Abbona and her people proved more skilled than we were in making weapons for hunting. We eagerly learned from them all that we could.

Now in the water in front of me, the inseparable pair of Abbona and Nix waved these wild creatures with huge claws at one another. I found it difficult not to smile at their merriment. It was infectious. Abbona promised us that the meat inside these creatures was like nothing we had ever tasted, that the hard shells turned a brilliant shade of red when placed in a large pit dug into the ground and then covered in layers of seaweed, coals, and other shellfish culled from the sea. We were fascinated by this, by the appearance of such a bold color, the color of blood. We had seen it on a bird in the forest. A brilliant red, with a tiny crown on its tiny head and a black mask around its eyes. I had gasped the first time I saw it, not believing my own eyes. *How could something be that red?* But my eyes had not deceived me. There it was, in the trees, a blaze among the branches. Back on the shore, watching Nix and Abbona swim towards the beach, I found it hard to believe that these brown creatures would turn a scarlet crimson.

Nix emerged first, shook out her hair and came running towards me, her arms outstretched before her with that awful, wriggling thing in her hands. I laughed out loud and stood, running in a zigzag to avoid her as she chased me with her clawed beast. Then Nix stopped, her face a mask of stone. I turned and saw Abbona standing, unmoving, on the shore, the beastie no longer in her hands but running towards the sea on its many legs.

Far out in the water, several long boats made from hollowed out tree trunks paddled rapidly towards us. Each boat was filled with men, dark and ruddy-skinned with their heads shaved high on the sides and a thick shock of hair running down the middle of their scalps. Abbona screamed a high-pitched wail towards the sky, and after shooting us a look of raw fear—a look that I had never before seen on her round face—she ran towards the trees behind us. Nix and I followed, my own fear squeezing my heart and my lungs, leaving my fingers cold.

I ran through the trees. Branches tore into my arms, legs, and across my cheeks, but I did not stop. Nix did not stop. Abbona did not stop. Her ebony head could be seen just ahead of us, bobbing along, her long dark braid swinging frantically behind her as she went. She called out again and again what I assumed was a warning cry to her people. Soon many of her kind joined us. We moved as one, a pack of prey running though the scrub brush, an unknown predator behind us. I had no idea where we were headed, but I knew our survival depended on flight. Then we could hear our pursuers in the trees behind us, running. Something narrow rushed close by my ear and struck a tree in front of me. An arrow with a red feather hanging from the end. Anger rose inside me. Hatred bloomed like an ugly flower.

I hated them. Whoever *they* were, whatever they wanted. I knew whatever it was they wanted wasn't good. Goodness does not come from those who chase women through the woods while attempting to shoot arrows through their backs. Something inside of me snapped. I stopped running. I looked for the largest tree and climbed it, allowing Abbona and Nix to continue ahead with the others. Making my way up the branches, I could count those who chased us—fourteen in all. They moved through the forest with a speed and grace that surprised me. These men were nothing like that disgusting, unkempt man who had attacked me on the ship. Just the thought of his eager hands and wretched breath reignited the fire in my gut, making my focus sharper.

I watched as the men passed beneath me, their attention on the women ahead. They never noticed that I lurked above them. As the last man passed beneath my tree, I let go, falling on top of him. The rage within me fueled all that transpired next. I tore him apart. He cried out before the life left him, alerting his kinsman to his fate. Two more returned to the scene, and I knew from their eyes that my appearance was gruesome. *Blood.* It covered my arms, my chest, and my teeth. I screamed at them and dove for the first man. I wasted no time in snapping his neck. I threw his limp body to the forest floor, then felt the strong arms of his companion pulling me away from the dead man.

He bent my right arm back. Something snapped in my hand. I screamed, but the pain didn't slow me down. It did nothing to impede me from what I needed to do. I spun around, taking the man with me, and rolled, bringing us both to the ground. I sat astride his chest, my thighs beside each of his ears, and reached for the nearest, heaviest rock with my good hand. Using the palm of my right, I brought the stone down, again and again, on his weathered face. I stood, my chest heaving up and down, the fingers in my right hand bent back unnaturally, pointing in strange directions. I grabbed them and snapped them back into the correct position. I kept the cry in my throat, hoping to contain the anger within me.

Another man entered the small clearing beneath the tree where his three dead brothers lay on the ground. I bared my teeth and hissed at him. He showed me his own teeth and leaned forward, his arms outstretched. In one hand he held a crude mallet, covered in blood and bits of bone and hair. *Whose hair?*

I screamed and charged him. He swung the mallet at my head, but I was ready. At the last moment I ducked and rushed his chest, throwing him backwards to the ground. I climbed atop his chest and grabbed his wrists, pinning him to the ground. He was strong. The man arched his back and threw me to the side. My own back slammed into the ground with a loud *thud*, forcing some of the air out of my lungs. I gasped and wheezed, begging for the air to return. He was on top of me in seconds, his hands at my throat. The world dimmed as he squeezed my neck, constricting my windpipe and preventing the much-needed breath from entering my lungs. *I would not go down this way.*

I lifted my knees and brought my feet up towards the man's back, slamming them into his spine. He keeled to the side, and the air rushed back into my thirsty lungs. I gulped it in. The blackness receded from the corners of my eyes. I arched my back and kicked, launching my own body to a standing position. I turned around, but the man was gone. My chest heaved in and out as I spun in a circle, searching for the man. I heard a rustling in the brush just beyond the clearing. This man was craftier than the last. I would need a weapon. The man's mallet lay on the ground not far from me. I dashed towards the fallen tool, snatched it up, and dove into the brush with the mallet held high above my head.

I brought it down when I felt my body make contact with something warm and living, hiding in the scrubby plants. I raised it over and over, bringing the weapon down on the person beneath me. I stopped when I heard the screaming. It was not my own. It was not from the man I sought to destroy. He was already dead. The screams came from Abbona. Her shrill, sharp cry filled with sadness as it rang out across the clearing. There are still times when I wake up, my body covered in sweat and that cry echoing in my head. But at that moment, I didn't understand. I had saved her. Saved her from these men with their anger, their weapons, and their thirst for our destruction. I had done what I was born to do—destroy those who sought to do wrong.

But I knew the moment she ran to the man before me. The man I had killed with a weapon that was not mine—and not his either. I knew when she moved the brush away and revealed the smashed and broken form of her brother, lying on the dusty earth, his eyes staring at the heavens forever, the large pupils no longer focusing on anything, and they never would again. He was not the one who had nearly strangled me in the clearing. *Where had that man gone?*

Abbona looked at me and I, to this day, will never shake the feeling of complete loss, complete anguish on her small face. I had killed her brother, her favorite brother. I knew this love. I had Nix, and I feared this same kind loss in my own life. It was what had spurred my rage. I had meant to protect, to defend the one I loved. I had failed. *I had failed them all.*

It had been chaos after that. Several members of Abbona's tribe had been killed by the attacking men who had chased us. We later found out that this incident had been one of many attacks acted upon Abbona and her people over the last few years. With the arrival of the Europeans, violent change had come to their land. Our presence and the presence of European land-dwellers had sparked many rifts in the delicate balance of the indigenous peoples. The events of that fateful day were merely a battle in a great war to come. My heinous crime had marked the end of our good relations with the Seawomen and the Wampanoag people. We left that night. All of us, my sisters and I. That was the beginning of the end for me, for my relationship with Nix. I had burned something that had once connected us. The bond lay in ashes. One end on her side, the other on mine, no longer woven together. Our other sisters were divided. Some saw the mistake. Some saw the crime. All were angry that we had to leave. We traveled southwest, arriving in a bay that reached far inland, teeming with fish and other things to sustain us. We kept to ourselves and avoided those that lived on land. Never again would we throw in with another band. We had one another. That was all we needed.

Except I needed Nix, but she had closed herself off from me.

How long can one hate another?

When you live as long as we do, it can be centuries.

25

Ephron

Ephron James, attorney, grabbed another drink off a passing tray, nodded to a congressman, then threw a smile towards the attractive wife of the silver-haired gentleman. The slinky beauty smiled back, flattered by the attention, but he knew she wasn't interested. Perhaps she had no need of something new, something shiny—such as himself—to amuse her late into the evening or before her tennis match the next morning. Perhaps she had already had a toy of her own.

Tonight the attorney kept to himself, keeping his smile genial, not inquisitive. No need to bait the line or put energy into the subtle game of seduction. Not tonight. He moved through the room like a shark navigating waters teeming with ribbons of blood. A blonde here, a brunette there. A mahogany-skinned beauty as tall as his own six-foot frame with green eyes and a dress that left little to the imagination. All of her wares were on display as she allowed her long, claw-like fingers to linger on the lapel of the man next to her. And not just any man, a dangerous man. A man best left alone. Normally the emerald-eyed beauty would have been the attorney's challenge. The thrill of stealing something valuable from a worthy opponent. But ... not tonight.

The cavernous room soared above him, a masterful arrangement of glass and steel. The northernmost point of Narragansett Bay lay just a stone's throw away, beyond the massive windows. Even now in the darkness, the sparkling surface could be seen shimmering just below the partygoers as the ambient light from Providence graced the water, making it sparkle and glow. The glitter of the arched Providence River Bridge framed the three smokestacks of the Manchester Street Power Station as well as a smattering of Providence's diminutive skyscrapers. Their red lights winked on and off again and again in endless loops, flashing caution beacons for low-flying planes.

The attorney observed the flow of traffic on 195, white lights streaming on one side, red on the other, all traveling one way or the other over the confluence of the Providence and Seekonk Rivers at the northernmost tip of Narragansett Bay. The tiny harbor sheltered a few seafaring vessels, mostly tugs asleep in their moorings, waiting for something larger to bully up or down the Bay.

Ephron threw back his drink, then dropped the empty glass on another passing tray. He moved on from his beverage, anxiously waiting for his time to arrive. His fingers reached into the interior of his custom-tailored suit jacket pocket and felt, not for the first time that evening, the small plastic rectangle tucked within. His passport to the big show. The coveted keycard.

His invitation had arrived three days prior. A courier had delivered it to his penthouse in the city, several stories above the swanky coffee bar he had initiated, and then backed, for his own enjoyment. While in Rome in his younger years, he had discovered the bliss of the perfect espresso, and although the fine establishments of Federal Hill—the Italian section of Providence—had offered a close approximation of the beverage he had experienced in his twenties, he did not find it to his liking. Any other man would have bought a fancy coffee machine, but that was beneath the attorney. Why make it yourself when you can open an establishment that will make it for you whenever you want? Why not have a location where you can take your friends and clients to showcase a delicacy they could not find anywhere else in the city? He could probably thank his business prowess and his perfect demitasse for the invitation to the party this evening.

The attorney and a mysterious man introduced as *The Collector* had shared an interesting conversation over cocktails at the governor's mansion. The meeting had not been accidental. A discreet friend of a friend, who knew about certain unorthodox pleasures Ephron enjoyed, also understood the financial capabilities Ephron might present to The Collector. The meeting at the governor's mansion had been the first of many meetings, all in lavish settings, often with other well-known individuals who ran in the same circles as the attorney. The *Sammlung* had been alluded to, waved under Ephron's nose like a scent he could not refuse, but an invitation for a viewing, and possibly more, had not yet materialized. Then one day, his world changed.

A knock echoed throughout his enormous studio apartment early on a Tuesday morning. Still wearing his robe, the attorney had answered his door and found a black-clad, dreadlocked bike messenger standing politely on his doorstep. The youth had kept his gaze down and offered a clipboard, a request for the attorney's signature. Ephron, not yet fully awake, had taken the pen and scrawled something illegible on the paper, paying little attention to name of the sender. Still saying nothing, he yawned and handed the clipboard back. The young man swung his large satchel, carried across his back, to the front of his body. Reaching inside, he pulled out a shoebox-sized package, then handed it to Ephron. No words were exchanged. The attorney appreciated that. He produced a twenty from his robe pocket and slipped the bill to the unusual, silent youth. The messenger nodded, kept his eyes averted, then headed to the building's stairwell and disappeared.

Ephron stood for a moment with the package, a quizzical look on his unshaved face, before he closed the door. Making his way to his leather couch, he sat down and placed the box on an ornate, hand-carved coffee table. He leaned back, lifted one bare ankle onto the exposed knee of his opposite leg, and lit an imported cigarette found in his other robe pocket. Thoughtfully, he smoked and stared at the package. It was wrapped in brown paper. Ordinary brown paper tied with a black satin ribbon. Reaching forward, he grabbed the box and pulled on the end of the ribbon, which slithered off, whispering as it undraped itself, sliding away from the paper. He carefully removed the brown paper, revealing the contents of the package—a teak box with gold hinges and a strange symbol resembling a birdcage embossed in gold leaf on the lid. He opened the lid, revealing the inner sanctum. Lined in silk the color of blood, the box held a gold plastic card and a single folded piece of paper. With a shaking hand, he extinguished his cigarette and lifted the card to his nose while inhaling deeply. It smelled of the ocean mixed with something else, something exotic that he could not quite place. With a satisfied smile on his face, he read the contents of the creamy white paper:

> *Dear Mr. James,*
>
> *Your generous donation has been received, and your request to visit Sammlung has been approved.*
>
> *Your viewing time is as follows: Saturday, June 20, 9 p.m.*
>
> *If you desire to have a more intimate experience with the exhibits, an additional donation will be required prior to your viewing.*

There was no closing salutation and the note was not signed. Ephron placed the note back in the box, then grabbed his phone. The screen lit up his face in the dim room. It had been set to camera mode the night before, and the attorney found himself staring at his own image. His chin was quivering, and sweat now appeared across his upper lip. He noticed the developing perspiration mingled with the fast-growing stubble spreading across the lower half of his chiseled face. A few of the hairs were white. With a shaking finger, he tapped the phone, making his way to the main menu.

He inhaled and found that he was having trouble swallowing.

"What are you up to, love?"

The woman from last night padded over to him from the bed twenty feet away. She wore nothing, her perfect body unmarked by age, childbearing, or aesthetically challenged genealogy.

"Get out," he mumbled.

"What?"

"Get out," he repeated, his voice louder this time.

The perfect woman crossed her arms over her naked chest and looked down at the attorney for a long, hard moment. Realizing that the situation was not in her favor, she retreated back to the bed and set about recovering her clothes.

While he waited, he stared out the window. When he finally heard the apartment door slam behind her, the attorney reawakened his phone and tapped the box marked *Finances*.

He punched in the right numbers—all of them—then hit *transfer*.

The attorney then lit another cigarette.

His nicotine addiction screamed at him as he scanned the room in search of another drink. He needed something to take off the edge. The thin packet of coke in his jacket pocket seemed to suddenly call his name. *Where was the restroom again?*

"Mr. James?" A large hand was on his shoulder. The owner of the hand stood several inches, maybe even a foot taller than Ephron. He needed to raise his chin to gaze at the one who had addressed him. The man looked like a linebacker, maybe had even been one at some point. The big man's massive bare skull shone in the light, while his complexion glowed a deep reddish brown, reminding Ephron of a woman he had once dated. Her skin had been gorgeous, mesmerizing, and he had to work hard not to stare at the man while he reminisced. Ephron noticed a communication device visible on the man's left ear. When he spoke, the man's deep, throaty voice could be heard over the din of the party, but it didn't carry. A skill, Ephron thought, the man had honed for his profession.

"*Yes?*" Ephron. His squeaky response came out like a child's voice. The attorney cleared his throat and repeated himself, more assured this time. "Yes?"

"It's your time. Follow me, please." The man turned from the attorney and made his way through the throng of well-dressed, upscale clientele.

While clenching and unclenching his palms, feeling the

sweat forming in sticky patches across the center of his hands, Ephron followed.

This is it, he thought. He worked to keep up with his escort. Ephron's legs, toned and strengthened from years of cycling and running, were no match for the large man in his even larger suit. They made their way to the elevators. The same ones the attorney had used to arrive at the party. Beneath them was a restaurant. Beneath the restaurant, several specialty shops, similar to the ones found in high-end casinos, skirted the edge of Narragansett Bay, their large glass doors opening out onto a terraced walkway.

The two men entered the elevator alone. When the door whooshed closed, the two stood side by side and shared a long, uncomfortable moment of silence. Ephron's guide broke it first.

"Do you have your card, Mr. James?"

"Oh," the attorney stuttered and unbuttoned his suit jacket, reaching inside to retrieve the small plastic card.

"Uh, yes," he stammered. "It's right here." He offered the card to the man, who did not move to take it.

He kept his arms folded behind his massive back and tilted his head, ever so slightly, at the security camera in the corner of the elevator and said, "Place it in the slot at the bottom of the elevator keypad, sir."

"Oh," said the attorney. "Right. Sorry about that." The attorney laughed a little as he placed his card into the slot. The mechanism absorbed the card and the elevator hummed to life, whisking the pair down to their destination. Ephron felt the usual suspended stomach lurch as the elevator rapidly approached its stop. The giant box slowed down, shifted up, and then sank back down again. Then nothing. They had reached the end of their journey. With a click, the attorney's card was spit back out of the panel. The man pulled out the card and handed it to Ephron, who slid it back into the confines of his jacket pocket once again. An almost deafening silence followed for another uncomfortably long moment, and then the doors slid open.

Ahead of them, the walls looked as if they had been carved out of bedrock. The imposing building had been built into the side of a massive rock cliff overlooking Providence Harbor.

"Hmm," mused the attorney out loud. "Impressive."

The larger man raised an eyebrow, then indicated with his enormous timber of an arm that they should proceed to the right. The pair stepped out of the elevator, and the doors hushed closed behind them. Looking to his left, Ephron saw only solid bedrock. The elevator whirred, whisking the car away. They were alone now, with nowhere to go—except down the hall to their right.

"Right it is," said the attorney.

His guide said nothing as he moved down the long corridor. Several industrial caged lights intermittently spaced along the path illuminated their way. A blue glow spilled downward from each one, leaving an eerie darkness on the polished cement hallway between them. The hallway went on and on. Ephron thought they would never reach the end and that perhaps he would be doomed to walk forever through the stone world, staring at the back of the immense man in front of him. Not a word had been said to the attorney since they had left the elevator.

"How much farther?" Ephron asked.

No answer. The bare-headed man just kept moving, his giant, meaty arms swinging in time with the click of his shoes on the cold, hard floor.

Ephron heard a steady drip of water. Each drop slipped from its source onto the smooth cement, making a hollow-sounding splat. He looked around and noticed the walls of the hallway had grown damp as they traveled down the hallway. When he passed under another light, the attorney reached out and ran his hand along the rough, gray walls. They were indeed wet. He rubbed his thumb and middle finger together, sliding the moisture on his finger pads back and forth.

"Where are we?" Another question aimed at the back of the shaved head.

Still no answer. The guide had, however, stopped moving. Ephron was examining the moisture on his fingers and nearly ran into the solid human wall.

"Sorry," muttered Ephron, looking down at his feet. The larger man turned and shot a withering look at him, then faced forward again.

"Your card is required once more, sir."

Peering around the man, Ephron saw the most impressive door he had ever laid eyes on. Like something straight out of *20,000 Leagues Under The Sea*, the magnificent hunk of metal expertly resembled a submarine door. The attorney stood there, marveling at the intricacies of the massive portal, at the many polished brass gears, levers, and contraptions intertwined together, all in some way connected to the central wheel. Without thinking, he reached out to touch it, drawn to the golden, shiny surface, but he stopped midway. Mr. Big Head had cleared his throat. The sound echoed off the door, startling Ephron, his hand still outstretched towards the wheel. The smaller man slowly turned his head towards Mr. Big Head.

"You need to place your card here, sir." Mr. Big Head reached towards the left of the door and flipped up a small metal flap similar to the cover on a minuscule mail slot. It revealed a thin card-access panel much like the one the attorney had used in the elevator.

"Oh," Ephron said in a near whisper. He reached into his pocket, removed the card again, and inserted it into the slot. Once more the card disappeared, devoured, it seemed, by something within. He did not see the card ever again. Yet nothing happened. Ephron looked at the other man expectantly, but his companion only shifted his weight, then stared at something nonexistent somewhere above the right side of the door.

Just when the attorney believed that his time had *not* come, that, perhaps, his funds had been stolen and the opportunity of a lifetime had been denied to him, the door sprang to life. Gears whirred, levers shifted, tiny pistons clicked, and then the giant wheel spun. The attorney could hear heavy locks sliding back into their holding positions, releasing the door.

Mr. Big Head stepped back and Ephron, once he understood why, did the same. The massive barrier groaned and swung towards them, coming to rest against the bedrock with a heavy, final thud. A warm blast of humid air, smelling faintly of a stormy day on the coast, flew out through the open doorway and caressed Ephron's face.

"I'll leave you to it, sir."

The attorney looked at Mr. Big Head, but he was already retreating back down the damp hallway, his massive form visible, then disappearing and reappearing as he passed under the many pools of light.

Turning back towards the entryway, the attorney felt giddy. He clenched, then unclenched his palms, now damp with perspiration. Acidic warmth spread across his groin, similar to arousal but more akin to anticipation. It was the same feeling he had experienced as a child when his father had taken him to a seaside amusement park for the first time. He remembered the strange sensation of knowing that *he* had been brought to a location for no other reason than fun, for curiosity fulfillment, for pleasure.

His throat felt dry, and he found swallowing difficult. *Move, Ephron*, he thought. *You've arrived at the threshold, the chance of a lifetime.*

Finding the ability to move his limbs, Ephron took his first step forward, passed through the hatchway, and entered the *Sammlung*.

26

John's Residence
Seaview Avenue
Cranston, Rhode Island
Tuesday, June 16
11:48 PM

Evie

"I am not going to be your lesbian lover, and that's final."

"Ev, it's not going to work if you don't turn on that inner butch we all know you're hiding."

"I do not," I said, frowning, "have an *inner butch.*"

Rachael stared at me with her hands on her hips.

I stared back and said, "What exactly are you saying? I'm *so* not butch."

"All I'm saying is I think you have 'butch potential.' It's not an insult. Butches can be quite hot. True story."

I raised both of my eyebrows at Rachael.

"We need to get into the club as lovers. It's not like you've never kissed a girl. I mean, come on now," said Rachael. She was at the bar pouring another drink.

I sighed heavily and stared at the ceiling. Rachael could be exhausting. We had gotten word from Shep and Hazel. In order to access the club, we needed an invitation from someone on the inside. Our swinging lovebirds from the Parkway had no trouble scoring an invite for Wednesday night, but it had limitations. However, it didn't really matter since we had access codes and knew our way into the secret underground *secret, secret* chamber. Our main problem, however, was that the invitation specified a *man* and a *woman*. Rachael reasoned that if one of us, apparently *me*, went butch, we could argue that there was a misunderstanding with the stereotypical nature of the invite. The whole idea seemed flimsy. Also, Nomia's participation in the heist was an issue we had yet to solve.

Rachael refreshed my drink and placed it next to the computer. On the large monitor, I had multiple maps and schematics open, attempting to find an exit or some sort of a fire escape where we could let Nomia into the building. Our slippery new frenemy had yet to return from the patio. The discovery of her sister's imprisonment and current *on sale* status had probably put her over the edge. Understandable. *Totally* understandable. Earlier, I had stepped outside for a smoke and to see if she was out there. As I slid the door closed, I hadn't seen any sign of her.

John's property sat at the very end of the Point. The evening had cooled down, and the pale pink sky glowed with an atmospheric light. Even though Providence is not, by far, a raging gigantic metropolis, it does give off a fair amount of its own evening luminescence, preventing any major stargazing. But the view of Narragansett Bay soothed my jangled nerves nonetheless. I sat down on an expensive patio chair, the ones that look like sofas but are made out of some crazy-ass water-proof plastic and are way beyond the mere peasant's decorating budget. *Those chairs are comfy, btw.* The waves gently lapped against the enormous breakwater beyond where I sat, and I could hear people laughing—that and the gentle music of lines rattling against metal on the boats in the nearby marina. *Someday, I will get to just appreciate all this wonderfulness that comes with living so close to the water.*

I sighed. That day was not today.

Collecting my thoughts, I considered all the information we had gathered so far. Richard—still missing. Nix—not missing, per se, just incarcerated in some sick, high-end freak show. Me—buddy-buddy with a bitch who had tried to kill me. *And* absent from my life—both my husband and my child. I'm telling you, I couldn't make that shit up.

A plane roared overhead on its descent to T.F. Greene Airport. Lights blinked on and off on either side of its enormous belly. Across the Bay, I could make out the fatheaded outline of the water tower in East Providence. That did it. I started to choke up. When Savannah was a toddler, I told her that water towers were filled with old pants. Every time we passed one, I would point to the big monolith and say, *What's in there, munchkin?* To which she would reply, *Old pants.* As she grew older, she would say it with annoyance, as if I had just asked her for the zillionth time, *What color is the blue sky, honey?* I would smirk, my secret knowledge-bomb deeply embedded in her psyche. I hoped, someday, she would be out with friends, pass a water tower, and say something like, *Huh. I wonder how they get all those pants inside the water towers.* And then her friends would look at her like she was insane and tell her that water towers contain—wait for it—*water.* That's when she would get the joke. *My mom, what a cut-up! Can't wait to call her and tell her that she's an asshole. Ha! That zany mom of mine …*

Tears rolled down my cheeks and I wiped them away with the back of my hand. *I missed her so much.* I missed her sweet little face, her laugh, her giggle, her tiny little hands that fit so neatly into mine. I missed the way her hair smelled when she was fresh from the bath, the way her clothes always end up on the floor, right beside her laundry basket, and the way she talked to her little stuffies as if they were real and whispering back secrets only she could understand.

I pulled out my phone again and dialed. It rang and rang and I almost hung up when,

"What do you want, Evelyn."

Oh that brogue. I missed that brogue.

"Paddy! You answered!"

Silence on the other end. I strained my ears, trying to hear my favorite squeaky little voice, but then I remembered how late it was and I knew she would be, *should be,* in bed. Try as I might, I could not hear any other background noises. Nothing to give away where he might be. Then I heard a man's voice, one I did not recognize. He muttered something low. The tone was not friendly.

"Where are you?" I asked.

"It's best that you not know," he answered.

"Why? Is there something wrong? Paddy, did you get my messages? Nomia is back, but she's okay—I think. But her sister's gone and so is Richard. We're trying to work out a plan to get them back and I don't want to be Rachael's lover—"

"You are unbelievable, woman!" Paddy interrupted. "You've involved *Rachael?* And you are conspiring with the same woman who tried to kill … I don't have anything else to say to you. I never should have answered your call. We are leaving in the morning. That's all you need to know. There was, uh," he paused here, "an incident. Savannah, Catherine, Tony—we're together, but we are moving. You are not helping. You and your …"

He stopped talking and I heard the man again, murmuring to him. It sounded muffled, as if he held his hand over the mic.

"I don't know when I'll speak to you again." He stopped there.

"Paddy!" I said, a pleading tone to my voice. "What does that mean? Who's with you?"

"I don't know. Just don't call me again."

"What?"

There was a long pause. I could hear him breathing heavily and then he said, "*Múchadh is bá ort, mo rún.*" Then the line went dead.

Tears fell from my eyes and I couldn't breathe. I sobbed loudly into the night. *What did that mean?* He said our words— *Smothering and drowning on you, my secret love.* That meant he still loved me, right? But then he told me not to call and *what incident?* and *who was with them?*

I needed answers and I was not getting any. I needed this all to stop. I needed a conclusion to this stupid tale. I needed Paddy. I needed Savannah. Hell, I would even take the judgmental frown from Catherine all day, every day for the rest of my life if I could just get my life back. But the only way to make that happen was to finish things. The plan was the plan. I needed to see this shit through to the end, then I would get my family and move to Vermont—or some other landlocked location far away from these godforsaken fish peoples.

I took a few deep breaths and looked out at the night, composing myself. Then I stood and walked around the patio, lighting another cigarette. Nomia must have gone for a swim to clear her head. I didn't blame her one bit. Something white caught my eye near the edge of the deck. I bent over to pick it up and confirmed what I had suspected. Nomia's white dress. She had gone into the Bay. I looked out across the water, but I didn't see anything—not that my night vision is all that great. I finished my cigarette, then flicked my butt into the water and walked back to the slider. If I was going to get back together with my family, I needed to make shit right.

Back in John's house, Rachael and I continued to argue the finer points of being butch for the next half hour. The sliding door *whooshed* open and the both of us, a little fuzzy from Mr. Bourbon, turned to face the doorway.

"Well," purred Rachael. "Hello there ..."

"You've got to be fucking kidding me," I said.

"Hello, Evelyn," said Ronan. "It's been quite some time."

Ronan, the *Innkeeper*, or whatever the hell he's called in *merspeak*, stood in the doorway, dripping wet and—like always—naked. This man had saved my life three years prior, and shared a branch, a twig, or a root with my husband, somewhere on their odd, nautical family tree. Beside him stood Nomia, her white dress clinging to her slim, damp body, her hair soaked through. I looked at Rachael. Her mouth was on the floor, while her eyes crawled over Ronan like an army of ants that had just discovered a fallen ice cream cone.

"Oh my dear God," I said to her. "Get it together, woman."

I heard a *click* as her teeth snapped shut.

"What *the* ..." I fumbled.

"We need help, Evelyn," said Nomia. "It took convincing, and he needed to see that you were okay, but I think, now," she looked at Ronan and gestured towards me with her hand, "he can see that you are all in one piece."

"Well," I said. "Here I am."

"And there *you* are," said Rachael like a giddy schoolgirl. Then she just about knocked me over as she stumbled towards Ronan, her hand outstretched. "I'm Rachael and I'm an Aquarius."

27

Ephron

At first, the dark chamber revealed nothing. It took Ephron a few moments to allow his eyes to adjust to the almost complete lack of light, and when his pupils found their proper dilation, he realized that he was not anywhere—not just yet. Another dark hallway lay before him, dimly lit at the end, where another door, similar to the first one he had just passed through, gleamed in the distance. The tunnel had a smooth, rounded ceiling and walls. Ephron wondered if he was in a large tube. A walkway of steel grating, similar to the landing on a fire escape, stretched forward along the bottom of the tube, leading towards the second door. He adjusted his stride to the somewhat uneven surface and his dress shoes made a hollow ringing against the landing. Feeling slightly deflated by the delay of access, Ephron frowned and took a step forward.

"Welcome, Mr. James. We've been expecting you." A silky female voice came from everywhere, all at once.

Ephron spun in a circle, his shoes clanging against the metal, startled by the sudden greeting. He could not detect any speakers in the smooth, sterile tunnel. In the dim light, everything appeared gray, seamless. Ephron took a sharp breath as the first feelings of claustrophobia set in.

"Move towards the second door, Mr. James."

With nowhere else to go, Ephron continued forward, his shoes clanging across the walkway as he went. He paused when he heard the whir of the first massive door surging back to life, swinging closed, sealing him inside the tube.

"Hey!" he yelled. His voice sounded muffled in his own ears, which popped as if he had just experienced the rapid ascent of a flight takeoff. The dim light went out without warning, leaving the attorney in complete darkness. Fear and confusion gripped Ephron's heart. He questioned his judgment. *What had he done?* He didn't really know these people. Could he trust them?

"Remain calm, Mr. James. The fish can detect your raised electrical impulses. You don't want to alarm her."

"What? Get me the fuck out of here! Do you hear me?"

"Yes. We hear you, Mr. James. I will repeat, *calm yourself.* This is all part of the experience."

Ephron had just bitten deeply into his fingernail when the tube shook and a circle of blue light appeared around the door in front of him at the end of the tunnel. The circle of light grew larger and larger and seemed to rush towards him. He didn't understand what was happening at first, but then realization flooded his consciousness, easing the fear and abating the confusion. Like a sleeve being slid along an arm, an outer sheathing around the tube in which he stood slid towards the door behind him, revealing brilliant blue light that surrounded the entire chamber. A shadow passed by the attorney on the right, dark, slim, and fast-moving. He caught sight of it out of the corner of his eye, and when he turned to face it, the shadow was gone. *Had he seen something?* It was hard to say. He suddenly felt exhausted, over-stimulated, and yet his curiosity screamed for more. *This was only the beginning.* There was so much more to come. *So much more to see! So much more to do!*

The shadow reappeared. This time he was ready. The attorney turned towards his left, training his eyes on the movement he detected in his peripheral vision. A large fish appeared outside the tube. *He was underwater!* A ridiculously wide grin spread across Ephron's handsome face as he spun around and around, examining his new surroundings.

"Amazing," he whispered to himself, as a school of smaller fish whizzed by like a single-minded being comprised of many bodies, all moving as one. Ephron reached out and touched the thick wall of the tube. It was some sort of glass, the thickness of which was impossible to fathom. The light source was unknown. He could not piece together where he was. Was he in the Bay? Or was this a fabricated environment? The water had the appearance of early evening—not full day, not full night.

With the grin still plastered on his face, he leaned his head back and looked up just in time to see an enormous shape glide above him. The enormous creature's tail swung back and forth, almost serpentine in its movements, gliding the leviathan along at an effortless pace. It moved slowly, because it could. This was something he had only seen in movies and nature programs. It was the pinnacle of the ocean's food chain, the stuff of night-mares—the silhouette of a great white shark.

"My God," he breathed, then touched his fingers to his lips. He wanted to stay in this moment forever, watching the shark glide back and forth. It circled back around, gliding even nearer this time, just beyond the glass. It still moved slowly, and it came close. So close that the attorney could make out specific details. He saw a large, black eye—flat, lifeless, like a doll's soulless eye. Scars, longer than his leg, tore across the snout, zigzagging along the great creature's face. The ragged line where the white underbelly met the dark gray of the shark's topside created a snow-peaked mountain range against a stormy sky. *And the teeth.* They snarled their way along the gash of the maw, seeming to sneer at the attorney who stood, small and helpless, no different from a bank deposit slip lying in a narrow, pneumatic tube at a drive-through bank.

The attorney watched the mammoth beast retreat into the darkness that seemed to go on forever beneath him. Sadness filled him as he realized that he might never see the shark again. He yearned for its return, much like a child yearns to experience something new and exciting, to repeat the sensation over and over. *Again, again, again.*

"Her name is Catherine," came the voice. "You are very fortunate, Mr. James. She doesn't usually appear to our guests.

We hope you enjoyed her."

"I did," said the attorney, wondering where his voice was going.

"There is so much more to see," came the response, followed by a hissing sound and then a *whoosh*. Ephron's ears popped for the second time as the door ahead of him swung open on its own, revealing another dark interior. "Please step through the second door, Mr. James, and enter *The Sammlung*."

28

Richard

The blade changed in color. Slow at first, then quicker. It turned from a dull gray, to red, then to a blinding white. Smoke rose from the handle, wrapped intricately in leather, as the heat crept up the steel. The boy could see the change in the metal from where he lay. His eyes should have been closed, but they were wide open, moving between the flames and the star-filled sky above. Beneath him, the ground, warm from the generous heat of the summer sun, cradled his prone body, and he tried again to relax and allow his consciousness to slip into nothing, to flow with the chantings of his grandfather who sat nearby, rocking, singing, his eyes closed in deep meditation. But the fire would crackle and spit small sparks into the night sky, tiny and elegant like fireflies. The sporadic interruption of the chanting would grab the boy's attention, forcing him back into the present moment.

Somewhere off in the distance, he could hear the summer peep frogs announcing their presence to the nocturnal world. They chimed a pleasant song, and he sent his focus to their high-pitched croaking but found he couldn't hold it there. The anticipation of what was to come proved too great. The boy's muscles tensed. This time the older man noticed. He stopped chanting and opened his own eyes, gazing down at his son's son.

You need to let go, boy.

I know.

Trust in me. We will start again. It would be better if there were more elders. The chants would be stronger. But I am all that is left. You are all that is left. That is why this is so important. If only your father had stayed the course. But he did not. What's done is done. We move on.

The boy closed his eyes and nodded. He tried to let go of the events to come. To let go of his own father's disdain for him, his grandfather, his sister. The boy understood. He knew the importance of this moment. He knew the pain ahead of him would be temporary, a small fleeting moment as he walked the path to bettering himself, to becoming who he was born to be.

He had heard the stories of his ancestors from the time he could hold his head up and his grandfather had held him in his strong arms, carrying him through the woods before he could walk, whispering tales in his ear, lovingly filling him in on all that had come before.

The boy's favorite tales always circled back to the one they called *Ochse*—the German word for ox. This particular ancestor had been enormous, the great hope of his people. *Ochse*. A legend. *A great legend.*

Tell them again, the boy would say to his grandfather, urging him over and over again to tell the hunting tales. Tales of yesteryears, when the rivers and lakes of the motherland had overflowed with the vermin his people had vowed to eradicate. His people. *Wasserschutz. Protectors of the waters.* An extensive line of trackers, hunters, skilled killers. They had existed for as long as time had been called time, striving to drive out the abominations lurking in dark bodies of water. *Nixe, rusalka,* and *vodník*, these names had come from the common folk— interesting, exotic-sounding monikers. The boy simultaneously loved and hated these creatures. The recitation of their names captivated him, made him endlessly hungry for more stories of the filthy water creatures and their inevitable demise at the hands of his forefathers.

The *vodník*, this thick, mouthful of a name, scared the boy the most. Large, ugly half-men who resembled monstrously enormous, hairy frogs. These huge, solitary creatures targeted both men and women, torturing their prey in countless horrific ways until they were bored, and then they destroyed their broken toys. Situating themselves beside mighty rivers, these foul, wretched monsters often worked as millers, grinding wheat with their great wheels, scanning the roadways and water for their next victims.

In comparison, the nixe and the rusalka were lovely to behold. Their feminine beauty had inspired many a song among his people, but their elegant disposition only served as a mask, hiding the true, violent nature of these deceptive wretches. These beings focused primarily on men, making use of their beauty and grace to lure unsuspecting victims to watery graves.

In the beginning, God had bestowed the task of ridding the earth of the water filth upon the Wasserschutz. And so it had been ever since. Travelers by nature, they had lived in caravans, going where they were called, using their skills to track and destroy anything unnatural in their path. Many of the villagers they encountered thought they were gypsies, and sometimes they allowed these rumors to stand. But they were not gypsies. Gypsies were a different breed altogether and best left alone. The gypsies had their own problems.

The boy knew that Ochse, who had lived in the land now called Germany, had been taken from his mother at age six. At age seven, Ochse had registered for the Hesse-Kassel army— as decreed by the Landgrave leader at that time. Ochse then trained as both a Hessian and a Wasserschutz, making him one of the most formidable warriors ever seen by his people.

As he grew, Ochse's height had become of great importance to the Hessian army. It had qualified him for the elite Grenadiers—those who fought on the front line, a brass miter cap atop their heads, increasing their height so that they appeared as juggernauts, as monsters. Foreign opposing forces often told stories of the Hessian giants, several hands taller than the average man, their ferocious mouths housing not one, but two sets of razor-sharp teeth. When the young boy hunted, he felt the spirit of Ochse running beside him, guiding him towards his prey, steadying his hand on his bow. The boy kept Ochse alive in the world, comparing his own path with that of the great man, now long gone from the earth.

And now, like Ochse had done centuries before, the boy had begun his own training. In the previous six years, the boy had mastered the arts of rudimentary weapons construction, creating a shelter, tracking, foraging, and hunting, as well as extensive offensive and self-defense tactics. He knew in his heart that he would never be as tall or as strong as Ochse had been. It did not deter him from trying. He would make up for his lack of size with his cunning. Born with a quick mind, strong logistical thinking skills, and the ability to read people's intentions and actions, he already possessed a cache of skills that he believed surpassed those of his idol.

As he lay beneath the blue-black sky in the forest, the boy opened his eyes and thought of Ochse. That once-great man had lain down, as he now lay, and had awaited his own fate, staring at the same stars that this boy gazed upon now. It gave the boy solace, and he closed his eyes once more.

The old man had waited so long to perform this ritual. Many years past, he had attempted the training with his own son, but the son had refused. He had slammed the door on tradition, on the beliefs of his people. The arguments had been long and brutal, always ending with the father standing on one side of an enormous relational sinkhole, while the son stood far away on the other side. As time passed and the disagreements grew more and more intense, the chasm had widened until, one day, the father could no longer recognize his own son, so far across the void.

When this estranged son had brought his own son into the world, the new father had paid little attention to his own offspring. The old man had swooped in, seeing an opportunity to reignite the light that had been extinguished when his son had turned his back on all that had made him who he was, who he could be. The new father's gross neglect of his own child had opened another door, and the grandfather had walked right in.

Now looking down on the boy, this son of his own son, the older man felt a range of emotions travel across the wrinkled road map of his tired and weathered face—pride, fear, adoration. All the prerequisite emotions of one who cares too much about another human being. The knowledge that he needed to subject this person before him to the dangers of the world crushed his soul. But he knew what needed to be done, and the doing was moments away.

With a sigh, he took up the chants again. A deep, sonorous thrum filled the clearing in the woods around them. In time, the old man let go of his own mental clutter and eased into the rhythm of the ancient words. The syllables rose and fell, rose and fell in a deep baritone, almost a growl. Over and over, he repeated the words, his body giving over to the sound, rocking in time to the rhythm.

The boy on the ground focused all his attention on the low tones flowing over his body. It was then, once he gave over to the music of his grandfather—the music of all the grandfathers before him, stretching back until time began—that his mind let go. His limbs relaxed, his torso sank into the warm earth, and a deep, full breath escaped his lips. His chest rose more and more slowly, easing into the cadence of his grandfather's voice.

The boy let out a deep breath. It flowed from his lips and entered the night sky. The old man heard the release of his grandson's conscious breath and opened his own eyes. The boy had finally let go. Still chanting, the old man rose. His knees popped as he stood, and his ankles creaked like neglected wooden stairs, but he kept the chant steady, not wanting to disturb the fragile state of the younger man.

Moving towards the blazing bonfire they had built together earlier in the day, the old man crouched down, his knees protesting, emitting more sonorous cracks. The popping of his knees echoed the sounds of the fire. Another log exploded from the intense heat, sending glittering sparks into the night. Keeping the music flowing from his throat, he reached for the thick bundle of leather on the warm grass near the roaring flames. The old man carefully wrapped his right hand with the leather, protecting his palm, and reached into the fire. He took hold of the knife. It lay on a large flat stone close to the base of the blaze. Still singing, the man held the knife to his face, examining the blade, now pure white from the heat. Satisfied with the state of the instrument, he turned towards the boy.

The boy's bare chest rose and fell, slowly and steadily, like the ebb and flow of the tides. The breath rolled into his strong, muscular rib cage, then a few moments later, eased out of the strong jaw and full lips, just barely kissed with evidence of facial hair. The beginning of his journey to manhood. After this evening, a boy would no longer occupy this prone body lying beneath the carpet of stars. A man would take this boy's place and inhabit the newly initiated body of a *Wasserschutz* adult.

Bracing himself, the man crouched down next to the boy. His knees screamed, but the boy did not alter his slow and careful breaths, did not react to the loud cracks and pops from the older man's joints. The grandfather nodded in approval, satisfied that the deep unconscious state had held true. Leaning over the unmoving boy, the old man brought the knife towards the boy's chest without hesitation. He made the necessary cuts. Crisscrossing the pectoral muscles, creating an intricate pattern, the older man carved a design of wounds that would swell and soon scar, permanently marking the boy as a man. The grandson never moved. Never bled. Beneath the great moon above, the old man worked the magic of his people, moving across the young, tight skin, the heat of the blade cauterizing the wounds in an instant.

With the work completed, the older man laid down the blade and grew silent. The night wrapped around him, filling his ears with its own music. He sat back and closed his eyes, breathing deeply, and listened. The crickets sang songs to one another, creating their own lullaby. A soft night breeze pushed against the limbs of the trees above them, gently rustling the abundant leaves, and then disappeared as quickly as it had come.

He reached into his pocket and pulled out both his smoking pipe and tobacco pouch. Completely white, the pipe was made of bone—the bone of a beast long gone. The old man had been given this pipe on the day of his *Returning*. He intended to pass the pipe along to his grandson, when the boy returned, *when he returned a man of the Wasserschutz.*

Knocking the base of the pipe on a rock, the old man dumped

the remnants of used tobacco onto the grass. Painstakingly, he packed the bowl anew, then reached for a stray stick, setting the end ablaze. Placing the pale ivory bit into his mouth, he clicked his teeth down on the bone. Using the flame from the stick, he lit the pipe. The old man breathed in deeply and watched the crushed leaves of tobacco ignite. The tiny blaze illuminated his face, temporarily blinding his already failing vision.

When the smoke and the fire of the pipe had died down, he saw that the boy, now almost a man, had awakened and was sitting up to examine the wound on his chest. The young man's eyes were wide now, the pupils large in the dim light. With an open mouth, he looked to his elder.

You're almost there.

The old man stood, a slow and painful process. The young man did the same.

Remember what I've taught you, and you will know what to do.

The older man placed his hands on his grandson's shoulders. The grandfather smiled, then left the firelight, heading back the way they had both come together when the day had been new.

The young man stood alone in the clearing, naked and wounded, watching his grandfather walk away. He kept his gaze on the older man's small, aging back until the darkness swallowed him and his footsteps could no longer be heard.

It was only when he was sure that his grandfather was gone that he allowed the pain to enter his full consciousness. His face contorted and twisted, consumed with the agony that roared across his chest. Reaching up with a shaking hand, he tentatively felt the wounds. The skin blazed hot, as he grazed his calloused fingertips over the swollen, bumpy flesh. He'd had no idea that it would hurt this badly. He had thought it would be minor, like a scrape from a bad fall. He had not prepared himself for the intensity of the blinding, burning pain. But he could not be distracted by such things. He had trained for this. He would not disappoint his grandfather or his forefathers, like Ochse, who had endured the very same trauma and had come home as men, *warriors*.

The blessing of warm weather was a gift denied to his grandfather and many of the Wasserschutz before him who had undergone this ritual before the boy. They had been left, wounded and alone, beneath snow-swollen skies. He shuddered. His situation was not ideal, but it could always be worse. It could be below freezing.

His training kicked in. *Observe your surroundings.*

He glanced around the clearing, taking stock of what he had at his disposal. By the light of the bonfire, he saw a length of leather a yard long, maybe more, a knife, and, of course, the fire. It was enough. He needed to survive the next week with these simple tools and in this condition. He would not fail.

Priority number one—treat the wounds. Without proper light, there was no way to truly assess the extent of the damage to his skin. He knew he would have scars for the rest of his days, the marks of his people.

If he survived the next few days.

Failure was not an option. He shook the temporary self-doubt from his mind and, for a second time, reached up and felt his wounds. Running his right index finger over one of the many swollen cuts across his chest, the young man stopped near his left pectoral muscle and pushed, *hard*. He fought the urge to cry out with every ounce of his will.

He would not yield to this. He would not yield to anyone, ever again.

29

Brown University's Crew Dock
India Point Park, Providence Harbor
Friday, June 19
11:13 PM

Evie

I sat on the edge of the dock and looked down at my feet, which no longer resembled feet, at least not human feet. I had flippers. No, I had not magically transformed into a mermaid. I was wearing a wetsuit, *moron*. I looked like a beached walrus, all shiny, black, and plump. Nomia tread water below me, staring up with an expectant tilt to her strange face. I found it difficult to look at her. I also found it difficult to look *away* from her. Her natural state, if you want to call it that, is alarming, and yet I found myself struggling to both look at her and turn away. There is something achingly beautiful about her, in a way that anything rare in nature can be hauntingly captivating. Tell me you wouldn't gawk, mouth open, at a wolf or a whale or—*I'm just going to say it*—a mermaid.

You know you would.

Sitting on the dock, experiencing this rare specimen, this exotic beauty, knowing that she no longer posed a threat to my personal safety, it occurred to me why someone would throw Nix into a cage. It also made perfect financial sense to charge a redonkulous amount of money to get a glimpse of such a rare, mythical creature. And then—as an added incentive to part money from the über wealthy—to provide an opportunity to have personal relations with said creature. *I needed to stop that line of thinking.* It was making me ill.

Nomia made a strange clicking sound, stirring me from my thoughts.

"What?" I barked down.

She cocked her head to the other side and tipped up her chin, as if to say, *You coming in or what?*

I have scuba dived once in my life. I was young. I met a Rhode Islander named Ed at a conference, an older man, who thought I had a lot of potential in the funerary industry. At the time, Ed had been part of a scuba diving club. One night at the hotel bar, post workshops, I mentioned that I might be interested in seeing the world below the surface of the sea. Ed took me up on my notion. A few weeks later, I was in a boat on Narragansett Bay, with Ed and his wife and two kids. It was dark, like night dark. Around us, there were four other boats with divers aboard, and we were all about to enter the inky-black water. Ed's wife had grown tired of scuba diving and so I was wearing her gear—minus a weight belt. One by one, the experienced scuba people dropped into the depths with their flashlights. They receded into the black water, like headlights fading away on an unlit country road.

"I'll guide you over to those rocks," said Ed before he stuck his regulator into his mouth, then fell backwards into the water. Seconds later, he popped up like one of those red bobber-thingies people fish with, his masked face just above the water level, his tank floating behind his head.

"You need to drop in," said Ed after taking the regulator out for a second.

"Right," I replied.

Taking a deep breath, I had trusted Ed and flipped backwards into the void. But instead of sinking down, I floated like a balloon, round and buoyant. I couldn't right myself. I stared up at the blanket of stars above me, while my weightless body drifted around, aimless.

I faintly heard what I thought was Ed's bubble-filled laugh and the next thing I knew, I was being jerked back towards the boat. Someone had tugged on my balloon string. It was Ed. He had tethered me to the boat. He handed me a flashlight and pointed to my regulator. I hadn't tried to breathe yet, hadn't even noticed that I had been holding my breath with the ridiculous mouthpiece between my lips. I took a deep breath in, heard the *whoosh* of the airflow from my tank into my mouth, and then breathed out. The bubbles flowed upwards and I sunk a little. Ed gave me the thumbs up, then towed me over to a rock jetty, invisible to me until we were on top of it. Then he gave me another thumbs-up and disappeared.

I looked around. Blackness. Pitch blackness, like nothing you've ever experienced unless you happen to be blind, or buried alive, and that's how it felt at first. It felt as if I were completely alone in the absolute absence of light. I remembered my flashlight and flicked it on, shining the beam over the rocks. Tiny bits of sea matter, so small they looked like dust motes, floated in front of my solitary light beam. A lobster scurried up the rock in front of me, then disappeared into a crack between two slimy, underwater boulders.

Then I surprised myself. I did something rash. I turned my light off again. My heart raced, and I felt bubbles rapidly brush past my face. I thought my fear would spontaneously cause my body to explode, but nothing happened, and I started to relax. I turned the flashlight back on, looked around, and had a fantastic time.

But tonight was different. It shouldn't have gone down like this. I'm not really sure how it *should have* gone down, but this wasn't it. No way. Not me entering the water alongside a homicidal mermaid, on our way to rescue a boatload of individuals, namely, my brother, her sister, my best friend, Ronan, and anyone else we felt needed to be liberated from potentially homicidal masterminds. Masterminds who seem to have more money than God and who seem to have a world-class security system in place.

On Wednesday, Rachael and Ronan had entered the club using Shep and Hazel's invitation. I don't know how she pulled it all together so fast, but with preternatural speed, Rachael had gathered clothes for both herself and Ronan and created an impressive plan. I hadn't liked the thought of the two of them entering the dragon's mouth on my account, and neither had

Nomia, but once Ronan had been caught up to speed, he had made a valid point—*Nomia and I were too recognizable.*

"We're just going to scope things out," said Ronan before they left. "We'll leave Rachael's phone in the car in case we get searched. Once we get a sense of the place, we'll leave. We'll call you when we get back to the parking lot. Don't worry. We'll be back before you know it."

Rachael had been all gussied up. I had frowned on her outfit choice, a skintight, red dress with a deep, plunging neckline and stiletto heels that made her the same height as Ronan. Honestly, my memories of Ronan rarely included him in clothing, so this was a first for me. Ronan looked incredibly handsome with his tailored pants and jacket. Somehow, Rachael had convinced him to wear shoes, which he had fought tooth and nail. Since Ronan wasn't known to be verbal, it had been interesting, to say the least, to hear him argue his case against shoes, but Rachael's anonymity argument had rung true. And then she had showed up in that dress. So much for anonymity. They left. We waited.

The call never came. After four o'clock in the morning on Thursday, I had repeatedly called Rachael's phone. It had gone straight to voicemail. By midday Thursday, we used one of John's cars to do a drive-by. The parking lot was empty. No sign of Rachael's car. Either they had never made it, or they had been busted, and Rach's car had been *removed*. The only thing we could do was wait, and wait, and wait. So we waited. The hours passed with the speed of an over-medicated slug and still no word came from either of them.

By Thursday night, when we were certain that Rachael and

Ronan were not coming back, we developed a new plan. We tried our best to pull up any and all schematics of the existing building, trying to see if we could get a lay of the land based on what we had seen on the USB stick and what we could find on the web. We discovered that the building had previously been a nursing home. We also found blueprints on the web from the city of East Providence. That entire section of land, along the coast had been slated for commercial and public use. Shopping, restaurants, green space, all along the water, facing Providence. It had been Nomia who'd finally had the mental breakthrough.

"If they have my sister in a tank," she said. "They would need fresh sea water."

I nodded. "Go on."

"How would they get the water into the building?"

"Maybe they don't," I had said. "Maybe they're using artificial means to create saline in the tank. It's not like all aquariums are on the water. Or are they?"

"I try *not* to go into aquariums," said Nomia.

"Hmm," I said. "I see your logic. Let me do a quick search and see what comes up when I type in *seawater intake system aquariums*."

Plenty of information came up about the Monterey Bay Aquarium's *Open Sea* exhibit. An enormous tank with a ninety-foot-wide viewing area. It was the only aquarium in the world to keep a white shark alive in captivity for more than a few days. It used an impressive pump system to pull water from the surrounding bay into the exhibit, saving thousands of dollars by not using an artificial system.

"Look!" I said, all excited. "There's even a live cam, like your sister's ... never mind."

"I'm going to see how close I can get," said Nomia, pretending to ignore my last asinine statement. She stood and moved towards the slider again. "I'll be back."

She had gone up the Bay to check things out. When she returned an hour later, she had a big grin on her face.

"It's doable," she had said. "There's definitely an intake pump, but I'm going to need your help."

Nomia had headed for the garage, motioning for me to follow. Once inside, she dragged some scuba gear out of a storage cabinet and pointed at it.

"You know how to use this?" she asked.

"Um," I stammered. "Sort of."

For the record, this plan sucked from that moment on.

"How do you even know if this scuba stuff is fully operational?" I asked.

"John used it last week before he left. He always fills the tanks when he finishes a dive. He's efficient like that."

Gee whiz. Thanks, John.

"I'm not doing it," I said with defiance.

"Good thinking," said Nomia. "Why should you? It's not like people you care about are in jeopardy. You should just play it safe and not bother trying. Maybe go get drunk. That seems to be your solution for a lot things that bother you, right?"

I closed my eyes and inhaled deeply through my nose.

"Fine," I said. "What's the worst that could happen?"

"My sister's life is at stake, too," said Nomia. "I won't let anything happen to you."

"Wait a second," I said. "Why do you need me to go? You could go save your sister yourself. I could go save the others by myself. How do I even know you won't use me as bait, or as a decoy, or worse? How do I know this isn't some elaborate plan to kill me and feed me to someone in your immediate family? Speaking of which, where the hell are the rest of your sisters?"

Nomia grew quiet and looked away. "I couldn't find them. I looked, but they're gone. Nix is all I have left. And believe it or not, I love your brother. I'm concerned about his well-being. I'm concerned that *I'm* the reason he's missing. And now Rachael and Ronan are gone, too. Maybe those soulless monsters that took my sister and put her on display like a zoo animal, maybe they had been after *me*. Maybe your brother had been involved with them, and then they followed me. This could all be my fault. I'm the one who should be in that tank, not Nix. We need to rescue them together, Evie," she said. "You *and* me."

And that's how I found myself in a wetsuit, sitting on a dock. I had a weight belt on this time and a diving companion who I hoped to God above would not leave my side.

"You *promise* you're not going to leave me?"

Nomia nodded and waved me into the water.

Just like when I had trusted Ed, I let go and fell backwards into the void. I knew I had to dig down into my soul and believe that somehow, a fuck-up like me could be a hero, if I just trusted in Nomia. *So weird.* I hit the water, and the fear of not being able to breathe on one's own set in. I felt overwhelmed by the darkness, the overwhelming nothingness. I couldn't take it.

I panicked.

The regulator fell out of my mouth and I swatted the water, searching for my only means of breathing underwater. But I couldn't see anything. My flashlight fell out of my hand. Gravity kicked in, and I started a rapid descent towards the bottom. My head felt like it was filled with cotton. I was sure that *this* was it. I was going to drown. But I didn't. Somehow, the regulator found its way back into my mouth. Air filled my lungs. Instantly, I felt calmer, more adapted to my environment.

Evie, calm down.

For the first time, I didn't mind the mental intrusion. It was weird, but Nomia was now my lifeline. Like it or not, my life depended on her existence, her knowledge of life beneath the surface. I felt her strange hand slip into my own. I felt her guiding me along. We crossed the harbor, feeling the thrust of the Seekonk River push us towards the open water of the Bay. We headed towards the monolithic building, far across from the dock from where I had just been sitting. For most of the journey, I heard nothing. No voice in my head, no boats in the water. *Nothing.* Just the steady whooshing noise of the regulator. But as we grew closer, I could hear a thrumming, a *whomp whomp whomp*, as if a giant fan spun lazily in the distance. It had to be the compressor.

This was the plan. Nomia needed to find something to jam into the giant machine. Once she shut it down temporarily, we would wait for a maintenance crewmember to come down through the service hatches. Once they arrived, Nomia would dispose of them. When we got inside, we would divide and conquer. In other words, *we didn't really have a plan for what happened once we got inside.*

I felt her hand on the back of my neck, but I still couldn't see a damn thing. I felt her guide my hands to a grab bar, which I grasped with both my hands. I stayed still, listening.

Wait here.

Like I had a *better* choice. I waited for what felt like an eternity, then heard a high-pitched screech followed by an eerie silence. The compressor had been shut down. *Check task number one off the list.* I continued to wait. My eyes had slowly adjusted, but I could see very little—just shadows, and the glow of faint blue light somewhere in the distance.

I'm here, off to your right. I can see the service hatch. Just stay where you are.

I heard a metallic clang and then a whirring of mechanical gears. A thin line of artificial light grew off to my right as the service hatch swung open, creating a large bright rectangle in the darkness. A flashlight beam bounced out from the opening. I held my breath, not wanting to alert the person with the bubbles from my regulator. But it didn't really matter. Nomia flew at them. I still couldn't see her, as I was blinded by the maintenance guy's light, but I felt her as she flew past my side. The interior light from the hatch behind the man silhouetted Nomia's slim figure as she wrapped herself around him. I heard a gurgle-like shriek, a crack, and then nothing. The light beam drifted down into the darkness below us. I watched its lazy descent. Then I saw Nomia swim down and retrieve the flashlight from its now limp owner. She swam back up towards me and handed the light to me.

I'm going to restore the compressor. Stay here.

Sure, no problem. A few moments later, I heard the familiar thrum of the compressor restarting. Nomia returned and we entered the hatch together. Once inside, Nomia turned around and closed the door behind us, spinning the enormous wheel closed with a loud clunk. While she checked the hatch, I turned the beam of my new flashlight towards the interior of our confines, which were lit but not very well. A long corridor stretched fifteen feet away from where we floated, the diameter appearing to be about six feet across. Another hatch loomed at the other end. This time, however, the hatch access was in the ceiling of the narrow passageway. Between us and the other end, two doors exited across from on another. I moved towards the left and examined the door. It read, *Main Tank Access - Authorization Clearance Required - Proceed with Caution.* I turned to the right, *Sub Tank B - Emergency Access Only.*

A toss of the coin. I looked at Nomia. Her giant eyes glowed in the darkness like on those nature shows with night-vision goggles, where the predators' eyes reflect the light back at the camera. I shrugged my shoulders as if to say, *Now what? Which door?*

She tried *Sub Tank B.* It didn't budge, locked shut. She turned to the *Main Tank Access* door and tugged on the large steel wheel. At first, nothing happened, but she didn't give up. I saw the strain on her face and the tautness of her muscles. The door gave just a bit, so she pulled harder. The wheel slowly creaked to the left, then the door clanked and, with a pop, swung open.

This chamber was shorter, like an antechamber, with another hatch in the ceiling. Instead of being flush, this hatch bulged upward, like the plastic, rounded cup lid on a slush drink. I assumed the hatch door opened up and over. No hinges were visible, just a sign that read, *Interior Hatch Door Must Be Closed Prior to Opening Main Hatch.*

Nomia glanced at me, then entered the small chamber, I followed, pulling the exterior door closed behind me. I struggled beneath the weight of the heavy door. Nomia gently moved me aside and gave the door a quick tug, closing it easily. Then she spun the wheel, sealing us into the antechamber. She wasted no time. Once she let go of one wheel, she grabbed ahold of the one above us and started spinning it to the left. She gave it a good shove, and the door opened.

Blue light streamed down from above. *This was it! It was just like the Live Cam! Nix must be in here!* Nomia flew through the door into the tank. I followed, streaming bubbles behind me. I turned off my flashlight beam immediately. Above us, a giant tube ran across the enormous tank, bisecting the space overhead. I watched my bubbles float upwards, bump into the tube, go around it, then proceed towards the surface, which I could vaguely see, far above me. The bottom had a darkness that the rest of the tank did not share. Something shimmered, like a thousand birds, moving as one. I realized it wasn't birds. I was seeing thousands of tiny fish, sardines or mackerel or some other fish that shares a brain and moves as if they were one creature. They swam past, mesmerizing me, capturing my attention and not letting go. I didn't remember seeing fish around Nix. Maybe they had added them, the way people put stupid tiki heads at the bottom of fish tanks.

My attention broke as something caught my eye, something big, drifting—no, gliding—above the giant tube. I heard metal clank against metal. I turned my head to see that the hatch had swung closed on its own, our exit no longer an exit. Nomia saw it, too. Her head swiveled down to the closed hatch, then back up to the shape above us. Her eyes appeared wider than normal.

Evie, we are in danger!

I looked above and saw nothing. The shadow had disappeared. I had no idea what it could have been, but Nomia seemed to know. She pulled the weight belt off of my waist, then grabbed my arm, tugging me towards the looming tube. Without the added weight, my body rose with little effort as I kicked my fins.

Swim up!

I did what she demanded and kicked as quickly as I could. Something approached us from the left, the same dark shape I had seen above the tube. It moved too fast. Fear flooded my senses, paralyzing me in the water. I kept floating upwards, but I wasn't accelerating anymore. The only thing accelerating was the...*Oh my dear God! That's a shark! A big one!*

Go!

Nomia grabbed my legs and pushed me upwards as the shark, all teeth visible, raced towards me. At the last second, she propelled herself backwards and punched the beast in the snout. It shook its massive maw, and I could see rippling muscles along its body as it recoiled from the blow.

I wasted no time and swam upwards, kicking for my life. I made it to the tube, wondering why a giant tube was even in this tank. When my body slammed into it, I saw what it was—a corridor, a viewing corridor connecting one side of the building to another. Inside the tube, well-dressed people held cocktails and tiny napkins. They all had big stupid grins on their faces, fully enjoying the spectacle of my imminent death.

Well, fuck you, people. Evie will not be part of the food chain. Not tonight!

I didn't look down. I didn't look for Nomia, something I would regret later. I just kept on kicking. The farther I rose, the better I could see the surface. I left the gawking assholes in my wake.

Off to the side, I could see a ladder dipping into the water. I focused all my attention on that ladder and made a beeline for it. In record time, I crossed the distance and scrambled up the rungs, leaving Nomia and the shark below me. I arrived at a metal platform. I spit the regulator out as soon as I was over the lip of the tank and gasped at the cool night air. The platform extended out over the water. As I struggled to get my oxygen tank off my back, I heard splashing beneath me. I scrambled to a standing position to get a better look. The water grew still. *Where was Nomia? Should I jump in? What should I do?*

Before I could ask any more questions, my world went black. Someone had just struck me from behind.

Really, asshole? They were the last words I remembered.

Evie

The screen door slammed shut, and I turned from the sink where I had been washing dishes. Richard dropped five dead rabbits on the kitchen table. They sat there, a pile of blood and fur. Five sets of terrified bunny eyes stared back at me, imploring me to stop their inevitable demise. *Too late, kids. Should have stayed in the den and watched cartoons.* Richard's aim had improved.

"Charming," I muttered and turned back to the dishes. Oma and I had just finished making the best kringel yet. The kitchen smelled amazing. It was hot as hell in there, but the intoxicating smell of pastry made it totally worth it. I wiped the sweat from my upper lip on my arm and dunked a large porcelain bowl into the soapy water.

"Smells like pastry," said Richard. I heard the telling rip of fur.

"You're really going to gut those in here?" I barked.

"You're really going to eat more pastry?"

"What are you saying?" I growled and spun around from the sink. I was ready for him. He had been making a lot of fat jokes recently, and I had had enough.

"I'm not saying anything."

"*Except?*"

"*Except,* you're eating a lot of pastry since we got here."

"*And?*"

"*And* it's starting to show."

I narrowed my eyes at him.

"On your ass."

That was it. I dove over the wooden bench next to the kitchen table and lunged for his throat. I don't know what came over me. I just knew I needed to throttle that fat joke out of his self-righteous face, and if I killed him in the process—so be it.

We fell to the floor, rolling over and over. My soapy, wet hands were firm around his neck, but he wasn't going down easily. His hands found their way to my throat, where they squeezed—hard. The edges of my vision started to dim.

I rolled to the side and brought up my knee, catching him square in the groin. He gasped, and I tightened my own hold on his neck, then rolled right. Like demented hillbilly alligator wrestlers, the two of us, locked in a death roll, kept on going. We smashed into the table leg, and the rabbits fell on top of us. I screamed as I felt the blood and fur hit me. Richard used my momentary lapse in attention as an opportunity to flip me onto my back. His knees pinned down my thighs and his elbows landed on my forearms. With one of his hands on my throat, and the other against my ear, I felt him begin to torque my neck. I screamed again. The tendons stood out on his jaw, and his eyes bulged with a wildness that scared the hell out of me.

"Richard!" I gasped. "It's *me!* Your *sister!*"

Something in his face softened, and he let go. He rocked back onto his feet, balancing in a squatting position, and rubbed his face vigorously with his palms. I didn't know what to do. I just lay there among the dead rabbits, watching the ceiling fan spin above us. Richard stopped rubbing his face and looked down at me. His eyes were back to normal, and the vice grip of fear around my heart loosened just the tiniest bit.

"I'm sorry, Dill." Wow. He hadn't called me *Dill* in a long time. It was his nickname for me when we were really small.

As a preschooler, he had a thing for dill pickles. One day, our mother was on one of her epic phone calls. *Oh, wait,* I need to explain the significance of *the phone call* to any post-cell-phone readers out there. Phones used to have cords. *I know, I know,* hard to believe, but the term *wireless* actually came from something that indicates *wires.* Anyhow, people who owned phones with wires had to go to a certain location in their own homes to make or take phone calls. In fact, there used to be chairs in a lot of houses specifically designed for sitting on while taking a call. Our mother would pour her morning high-ball glass of scotch, grab her ashtray, and cozy up to the phone. I have no idea who the hell she was talking to, but it seemed like she always had someone to bitch at, gossip to, or gossip about.

What you need to know, dear reader, is that we were unsupervised—a lot. Richard thought that pickles were so good they needed to be shared—with me, his younger sister, who had been plopped in a high chair for safekeeping while Mommy took her call/drink/forty-fifth cigarette of the day. I ate so many pickles in such a short amount of time that Richard decided we needed a second jar. He climbed up on the counter, got another jar, somehow opened it, and the two of us shared more pickles. The salt from the brine started to make my tongue swell, and I was sticking it out between bites. He thought this was hilarious and was rolling around on the floor laughing at me. This was when my mother *finally* noticed what was going on. She came into the room, screaming at us, "What the hell is going on in here?"

Richard couldn't answer her. He was gasping and laughing, yelling, "Dill! Dill!" while pointing at me. The name stuck, and from then on, he no longer called me Evie. To Richard, I was *Dill*.

But Richard had stopped calling me Dill when he turned thirteen. In truth, he had stopped addressing me at all around the time he had turned into a real teenager. I'm guessing that was also around the time he realized that I was a huge embarrassment to both him and everyone else in our family.

Now Richard stared down at me among the rabbits and their entrails and held out his hand. I took it tentatively, and he hauled me up to my feet. It was at that moment that I realized how much we had both changed. He had become a man. I could see a thin growth of facial hair on both his chin and cheeks, spreading under his nose. I noticed, for the first time, the pronounced Adam's apple, the sharpness of his cheekbones, and his strong jawline. He was kind of handsome.

Eww.

That pissed me off. I was not *becoming.* I was not *blossoming.* Nothing about me was developing into something feminine and lovely. I was becoming more and more disgusting with each passing day. I had terrible acne and, like some unfortunate teenagers, I smelled bad—a lot. My hair was an unremarkable shade of blonde, somewhere between hay and dishwater, and it sprung like a frizzy mop from my fat head. And my smile? *Forget it.*

I had gone through the trials and tribulations of orthodontics, but it had done very little to improve my smile. I had thin lips and an overly pronounced nose, no chin, and big ears. I had little going for me, but I accepted that. I accepted that I would, most likely, not ever be noticed by someone of the opposite sex, and that was okay with me. But here, before me, was someone achieving perfection in almost every way, except one. His treatment of his sister. He had almost just killed me.

"What the *fuck*, Richard?" I said, helping him put the kitchen back in order before Oma saw the mess. She was out in the garden somewhere, and *Opa*? I had no idea where he was. I almost never saw him. His attention span was only as wide as Richard—and I, as usual, was invisible to Opa. That was just fine with me.

"I said I was sorry," mumbled Richard. He actually did sound sorry.

"Where did you learn how to do that?" I asked.

"Do what?"

"That thing you did. You almost snapped my neck. How did you learn how to break someone's neck?"

He turned away from me and grew silent.

"I don't know what you're talking about," he said under his breath. "I didn't *almost snap your neck.*"

"Yes," I said and grabbed his arm. "You did."

It had been my intent to spin him around and force him to face me, but he had countered my grab, spinning me and bending my arm halfway up my back in a half nelson.

"Richard!" I yelped. My arm hurt like hell, and I was stunned that he had just assaulted me—*again!*

"*Richard! Lass deine Schwester los. Was bildest du dir nur ein?*" The booming voice of my grandfather filled the room, and Richard released my arm.

Richard hung his head to his chest and mumbled. "*Entschuldige, Opa. Ich weiß nicht, warum ich das getan habe.*"

Richard now understood—*and spoke*—German? *And* he was turning into a ninja?

What the fuck was going on?

"Are you all right, Evelyn?" Opa came over to me, lifted up my arm, and inspected the length of it. It was a strange moment. He normally never talked to me, let alone touched me. I froze. Moving only my eyes, I looked at my arm, then at him, then at Richard, then back to my arm.

"I'm fine," I squeaked.

The oven timer went off, and I jumped. Eager to be away from them both, I ran over to the stove and pulled out the pastry.

"Kringel, anyone?" I said, placing the baked sweet treat on the iron grates while hoping they would decline so there would be more for me. I did not turn around. I wanted them both to leave the sanctuary of the kitchen. Reluctantly, I finally turned around. They were gone, and so were the rabbits. I slowly let the air out of my lungs and leaned back against the kitchen counter. Then I walked over to the sink and looked out the window.

Across the yard, near the edge of the woods, I saw my grandfather slap Richard across the face. I was stunned by the act. I had never seen my grandfather treat his favorite grandchild that way. Richard looked down as my grandfather walked away. A moment passed, then Richard followed him.

The two disappeared into the woods, and I burst into tears.

31

Evie

"What the fuck?" I said out loud just to hear myself, just to hear anything. I reached up to the back of my head, and my hand came away feeling sticky. I was definitely bleeding, and a large lump had formed where I had been struck. I blinked my eyes for the bazillionth time to see if they were shut. They were not. The blackened room revealed nothing to me. I could not see, hear, or smell a damn thing, and I had been here for what seemed like days. Or maybe a few hours, I couldn't tell. My head hurt like hell and I was pissed. Pissed and crazy hungry—which meant I had skipped several meals. Nothing made any sense. None of it. Not one shred of it. I mean, *Does shit like this happen all the time and people just don't talk about it? Or is it just me? And why me? Why does this shit always happen to me?*

I screamed at the top of my lungs for the sake of screaming.

Nothing. A long, endless stream of nothing. I hated it. I hated being alone. I hated the thoughts that had started to flood my consciousness. I had managed to keep them at bay all week long, like sitting on a chest filled with evil monsters with long tentacles. If I just kept my weight on the chest lid, nothing would ooze out and attack me. But I had been knocked off the lid. The monsters were out and they were metaphorically, and possibly literally, coming for me.

I could feel their imminent arrival, like vomit rising in the back of my throat. A tidal wave of emotions smashed into my psyche. I broke down. The tears flowed from my eyes, and I sobbed, a wretched string of hiccups and gasps. I could feel the knots forming in the back of my neck, right beneath my head injury. The telltale sign of a migraine crept into the back of my skull. Pinpoints of lights started to dance behind my eyes. They were coming for me. My monsters of loss, of regret, of bad decisions.

Why had I left my little family? What had I done? I missed them so much!

I screamed again. I screamed at the futility of the situation. I screamed because all that had transpired in the past few days had kept me from what I should be doing, what I was supposed to be doing—being Savannah's mom *and* Paddy's wife. I have never been perfect, never claimed to be, but lately, I had been trying, more and more, to be there for them, to be a better person, a better mom, a better wife.

Look at you. The monsters I had kept in hiding for so long now whispered into my ear, wrapping their ugly, slimy arms around my heart. *You're a failure.*

I was in a dark place. For real life, like literally in a dark place. Alone. With the monsters in my head. The irony. I howled in pain. I howled for the irony. More tears soaked my cheeks, more gasps and sobs erupted from my chest. I choked and coughed on all the sadness and frustration. I tried to calm myself, to recall the faces of Savannah and Paddy, to picture my loves somewhere safe, full of life, laughing, and having fun— without me.

Without me. Are they better off without me? Am I truly useless?

Yes, the monsters whispered. *You are useless. You're a terrible mother, just like Nomia. You should just abandon Paddy and Savannah forever. They'll be better off without you.*

No, I countered. *I'm not like Nomia.* I didn't understand how she could create a life with a family and then abandon it. *But really, who am I to judge people?* If I could've given my right arm to see my little girl, I would have. *When was the last time I saw her?*

I sat down on the cold floor. It felt like stone and was damp to the touch. The air around me had a clammy vibe. My skin felt hot and sweaty from my agitation, and the confines of my wetsuit clung to my overheated body. I unzipped the front, then peeled the neoprene back from my arms, letting it hang behind me like a molted skin. The suit reeked of urine. *Great, I peed myself. God, I'm disgusting.* The cool air felt good, soothing, but it wasn't enough. I put my head in my hands and sobbed.

Has it been a week? Two? This had all started when I got that shit email from my godforsaken brother. *That asshole.* He's always been an asshole. *Why the hell did I go out on a limb for him?* Paddy was right. I should have ignored Richard and stayed with the people who love and care for me—my chosen family. I belong with the people who have become my safe harbor.

But no, what did I go and do? I turned my back on the family who loved me in the hopes that my brother, my only living relative from my past, would maybe ... *what? What? What were you hoping for, Evie? He left. He never looked back when he chose to go. He left you. End of story.*

The reality of my desperation, my need to have someone love me, made me sick. My eyes filled again, and I let the tears go. I felt like I was at rock bottom. I sat in the heart of darkness on a stone floor, realizing that I had been pining for something from my past when I already had what I needed. I felt so stupid.

"God. Fucking. Damn it! I have had it! I want to speak to someone!" I screeched at the top of my lungs. "I want to know where my friends are! I want to pee! I want to go *home*! Where the fuck am I? Someone answer me!"

Some things never change ...

Had I just heard a voice? Was I hallucinating?

Your language. Always expletives. Always crass.

I *had* heard a voice.

"Who the fuck are you?" I yelled.

Light flooded the room, blinding me. I couldn't see. Everything radiated white, burning my retinas. My eyes struggled to focus, to adjust, but they couldn't do it fast enough. I suddenly felt like I was in an operating room, but the anesthesia was wearing off. Everything appeared blurry, fuzzy. I could make out a few shapes, maybe a cot or a chair, and something else, off to my left. On the right, I detected a large, tall rectangle, darker than the rest of the walls. Something moved in the rectangle, I snapped my head around to face it.

"You're stronger than I thought you would be," said the moving shape.

That voice.

The shape moved closer. I scooted backwards across the floor away from it. All the instincts in my body screamed at once— *get back!* My backside hit something solid, and I could no longer escape the shape. It was large and it kept moving closer and closer. My breath came out more and more ragged.

"Get away from me," I mumbled and wrapped my arms around myself. I was a rat in a cage with nothing around me to use as a defense weapon. I curled up into a ball.

"Interesting. I thought you might try to attack, but I see you're the same old Evie. The same cowardly, lumpy, useless sack of shit you always were."

I know that voice. Fucking asshole.

I rocked forward onto the balls of my feet, keeping my arms wrapped around my knees. I didn't like this one bit, but I needed to do what I needed to do. I screamed and jumped up, keeping my weight tilted forward, angled towards the approaching person, then I charged. I made contact with a loud *thud*, knocking the intruder onto his back. Astride him, I kept all my weight on his chest, curling my legs beneath me, kneeling on his rib cage. My hands turned into angry fists and I started swinging. I punched his head over and over, as hard as I could while a stream of gibberish and frustration flew out of my mouth.

"You motherfucking *asshole*! I knew you weren't dead. I hate you! I hate *you*! You should have left me the alone, but no, you fucking asshole! *You* ..."

The surprise wore off, and he reacted after my fifth or sixth swing. He arched his back and threw me off, sending me flying across the room. I hit a wall, and all the air blasted out of my lungs. I wheezed and coughed as I slumped down to the floor.

Laughter. That's what I heard, followed by, "Whew! You do have it! I knew it! I wasn't completely sure, but wow! You sure just took me by surprise, Dill. Opa might have smiled at that move. Maybe." This was followed by more laughter.

My breath took its time returning. When I got it back, I said, "Richard, *what the fuck is going on?*"

"Oh, Dill," said Richard. "We have so much to catch up on."

He came over to where I sat, splayed out on the floor. With a little too much force, he grabbed my arm and jerked me up to my feet.

"Let's go catch up in my office, shall we?"

Office?

Like I had a choice. My brother, who was not missing *or in danger*, grabbed hold of my upper arm and walked me out the door. My toes barely touched the stone floor as we passed over the threshold. I turned my head and looked back into the room where I had been held. It was a small, almost empty cell, containing an old army cot and a toilet.

Richard dragged me away from the room. I felt like a common criminal being taken to an interrogation room for questioning. The fight had left me. I had no choice in the matter.

I let my brother haul me like a rag doll. As we moved down a corridor that looked as if it had been carved out of solid bedrock, I realized that was exactly how I felt—like a rag doll or a puppet. My mind started spinning, the cogs turned, pieces of the puzzle flew into place with each turn of events that passed into my consciousness. I reviewed the tapes in my head. The email from the previous week, the photo of Nomia and Richard, the carefully placed USB drive in the toilet tank. He had played me like a fiddle.

Richard, you're still an asshole.

The hallway seemed endless. We walked in silence. I had nothing to say to him. I felt stupid and confused. I mulled over the strong possibility that I had just been masterfully manipulated. Tears rolled down my cheeks, and a lump formed in the back of my throat. These were not angry tears. These were the tears of the defeated.

My back ached from where Richard had thrown me against the wall, but the back of my head, where I had been struck, hurt the most. I reached up my right hand, the one not forcefully held by my douchebag of a brother, and touched the base of my skull. The bump I felt earlier had doubled in size, but I was no longer bleeding. If I had played a doctor on television, I would have recommend a CAT scan. But I was not a doctor. I was just a silly woman being dragged by her insane older brother down a long corridor, somewhere deep beneath Narragansett Bay. All the frustration, anger, and sadness I had felt earlier was replaced with humiliation and a sad apathy. I felt useless, something I had thought I had overcome.

We stopped moving when we got to a recessed door in the bedrock. An elaborate keypad set in stone pulsed red, then green, then back to red. Shaped like a hand, the access panel looked like something out of a spy movie. I cast a sideways glance at my brother. He had aged well. A fact that did not in any way surprise me. He was still incredibly handsome and fit but with the surefire signs of aging in the slight salt and peppering of the sideburns along his chiseled cheekbones. His hair was fair like mine, thick and full—the envy of most men his age—threaded with the occasional white streak. Richard's crystal-blue eyes focused on the keypad. He typed in an access number, then covered the pad with his strong hand. A green light moved up and down the length of his palm, and the recessed metal door slid back to reveal a darkened room. We entered and Richard pulled me in.

"Lights," said Richard.

Hidden somewhere near where the walls met the floor, illumination brightened slowly, a reverse dimming, giving the room a soft glow. I looked around. The room was enormous, the ceiling low, just slightly higher than Richard's six and a half feet. It must have been the length of an Olympic swimming pool, but it held very little. At one end, a large metal desk, slim in nature and modern in design, sat perpendicular to a large window that spanned the entire wall opposite the door through which we had just entered. Two swivel bucket chairs sat before the desk, and another sat behind it.

The other end of the room had two large chocolate-colored leather couches that sat across from one another, both slightly angled so that a person could sit socially across from another individual on the other couch and look at the dark glass wall on the opposite wall.

Richard moved us towards the desk and dumped me into one of the two visitor chairs. He then walked around to his side of the desk and sat down. I rubbed my arm where he had grabbed it. Looking down, I saw four red finger marks on my white skin. Right before my eyes, I watched as they turned from red to a pale shade of purple. I pursed my lips. It had been a long time since he had bruised me. I had not forgotten the incident in New York when I had been twelve and a half and he sixteen.

Spinning away from me in his chair, Richard pushed a button that I had not previously noticed in the gray stone wall behind him. A large panel of rock opened forward, like a closed writing desk flipping down to reveal a surface on which to write. But instead of a writing surface, a small bar appeared with crystal glasses and decanters. A soft blue ambient light glowed behind the bottles. He reached into the back of the chamber and took out two dark-gray round stones. They were smooth, worn down by the sea or a river. Richard placed them into the bottom of each elegantly cut glass. The smooth stones must have been frozen. I watched vapors waft into the air. Richard grabbed a decanter and poured an amber liquid into each glass, then returned the decanter to its proper place. He picked up the two full tumblers, turned, and slid one of them over to my side of the flat, empty desk. He lifted the other to his lips and took a small sip.

I just stared at him.

"Go on," he urged. "It's better than the cheap dregs you normally imbibe to poison yourself."

I didn't move. *Fuck him.*

He shrugged and said, "Suit yourself."

He curled the glass against his chest, right beneath his chin, and then crossed his legs, leaning back in his chair. I sat where I had been placed, like a lump on a log. I could smell the stink of my own urine drifting up to my nose.

Good. I hope it stains his stupid chair.

I felt out of place in this environment. It all felt artificial. Superficial. Above my station in life. We stared at one another. Brother regarding sister, sister regarding brother, probably thinking the same thing, *Do we really carry the same DNA?* His brow screwed up with disgust, then the moment passed, and his face grew smooth, passive, unreadable.

"Do you have questions for me?" he said, breaking the silence. The frozen rock clinked against the side of his glass as he took another sip.

I had a thousand of them, but I didn't know where to start. I continued my silent protest and said nothing.

"I see," he said. "The silent treatment. It's so out of character for you, *don't you think?*" He winked at me. "That's fine. Maybe I'll just show you what you've done for me."

He spun around in his chair and plucked a remote from behind the row of decanters, then turned to the dark glass wall. Pointing the remote at the glass, he pushed a button with his forefinger, then dropped the remote on the desk where it landed with a dull clunk. Richard stood, and with his drink still in hand, strode towards the wall.

A soft humming filled the room as the dark panel behind the glass slid from right to left. As it glided past where I sat, a massive tank revealed itself. The light from the tank filled the room with a brilliant blue glow, different from the electric lights behind the tiny bar in the wall. This blue illuminated the room and silhouetted Richard. As the wall continued its journey to the left, I noticed that we had the view of not one, but three tanks.

No, I thought. *He didn't.*

I stood and walked over to the first tank. Pressing my hands and forehead to the glass, I looked down. The distance between where I stood to the bottom of the tank floor was impossible to tell for sure, but I imagined it to be about twenty feet. I tipped my chin back and looked up. The surface rippled far above my head. The brilliant light from the tank hurt my eyes, so I cupped my hands around my face to narrow the intensity. It helped, and my eyes adjusted. I scanned the large aquarium, and that's when I saw her curled up in the fetal position near a corner at the bottom of the tank—Nix, her blonde hair swirling above her head like seaweed. She appeared lifeless. Then I saw her pale lashes open and slowly close again, confirming that she was alive, though perhaps her soul no longer existed.

"So sad," said Richard. "Isn't she?"

I looked at my brother from the corner of my eye. He had one arm crossed around his chest as he sipped his glass with the other.

"She was feisty when we brought her in, but the spice seems to have left her. Maybe we can cheer her up."

Richard strolled past me and grabbed his remote from the desk, then walked towards the middle of the room. He stopped fifteen feet from where I stood and looked at the glass.

"Ah," he said. "Here she is. My pretty girl."

I looked down at Nix, who hadn't moved, then moved towards my brother and stood beside him. He's so much taller than me, favoring our grandfather and our parents. As for me, I got Oma's genes. Short and squat. I had never liked standing next to Richard when I was younger. I didn't enjoy it now.

Following his gaze, I peered through the glass and realized that this was an entirely different tank. A wall separated Nix's tank from this one, which held ...

"Richard," I whispered. "What have you done?"

In this second tank, I saw the dark-haired beauty who had messed with me at the Village Playground three years prior. Nomia darted from side to side in the aquarium, now her prison. Undulating like a dolphin, she propelled herself back and forth against the sides of her new chamber, testing the strength of the walls. Crimson blood streamed from her head where she had struck it against the hard surface. Relentless in her pursuit of finding a weakness in the walls, Nomia struck over and over again, systematically moving upwards, searching for a way out.

"She'll settle down," said Richard, "just like her sister."

He moved on, and I followed. The last tank to view. I had no idea what or who could be in it. He had both the sisters. *What more did he need? Oh, wait ... he's missing a male.*

My God. What have I done?

"You were perfect, Evie," said Richard as he sauntered along.

He was so smug. I felt the anger rise within my gut. I didn't like where this was going.

"I knew you'd do what an Evie does," he said.

"And what exactly does an Evie do?"

"You fuck things up," he said. "It's your specialty. I've kept tabs on you for years, Dill. You surprised me a few times. Like taking out Kolga," said Richard. Then he shook his head and breathed in through his nose in agitation. "That was impressive. But it should have been *me*, not you. Our forefathers are probably rolling over in their graves. They had their sights set on her head for centuries, and it was you, *a woman*, who came along and took her out. What did you do? Sit on her? Accidentally push her off a cliff because you're so goddamn clumsy? Oh, right. You stabbed her in the eye. How did you reach her? With a *step stool?*"

How did he know about that? I turned and faced him. "What the hell are you talking about?"

"Have you ever experienced nausea around Nomia? Maybe felt as though you were going to be sick in her presence?"

"How do you …"

"I thought so," he said and laughed. "What a cruel joke— you were born with *the* gene. *You.* Oh, the irony of the universe. Opa thought you might have it, too. But just look at you! You're pathetic. So weak, fat, and lazy. And you're a *woman!* You have none of the physical qualities of the Wasserschutz and yet, you took down *Bestla*, The Great Mother, Kolga. *You.* Of all of us, it was *you* who took her down. You struck an incredible victory for our people when you killed that bitch. Do you know how many of our kind she has killed over the centuries? *Hundreds!*

And you come along, a bumbling idiot, and take her down like some lame twist on David and Goliath."

Richard paced the room, anger seething from his jerky movements as he spat the words at me. I backed up and almost fell over one of the sofas.

"I never meant to kill her," I mumbled. "I regret that I did. Killing is wrong. I've seen too much death in my life. I never wanted to be the cause of it."

"*What?*" Richard stormed over to me and pushed me back onto the sofa. "*Let's get something straight.* You are Wasser-schutz—The Water Protectors. The blood of our ancestors runs through your veins. You are part of something bigger than your stupid little existence in Pawtuxet Village. For generations, our people have cleared the earth of the freaks that threaten the lives of humanity. Your nausea is proof that you have the abil-ity—an extreme case of the ability—to track down these crea-tures, and yes, kill them."

I thought back to the summer when Richard wasn't at the farm. I thought of when I puked blueberry pie all over the place after I bumped into whatever was under that tarp. *Oh dear God, what was under that tarp?*

"What are you *saying?* You and Opa *killed* people?"

"They're not *people*, Evie," said Richard inches from my face. "They're vermin."

I pushed him away from me. "You're a monster."

He threw his head back and laughed. "Oh, that's rich," he said while laughing. "*I'm* the monster."

Richard grabbed my arm again and hauled me to my feet.

I cried out as his fingers found the same spot already marked from his large fingers, fingers that had killed how many? *How many innocents?*

I tried to shrug him off, but he was too strong. He dragged me over to the last tank, the third tank.

"This is a monster, Evie," he said and then pointed back at the other two chambers. "Each one of these tanks contains a monster. Three monsters worth a lot of fucking money. But this last one—the one you led right to my doorstep—this is the real moneymaker, and I have you to thank for it."

Ronan swam in a circle in the third chamber. He moved slowly, carefully, examining the walls, occasionally touching them with his long fingers. I had never seen Ronan in this state. He was so different from Nomia and Nix. His tail was a lot longer, and his feathery gill slits were much larger. Tiny hairs along his neck floated in the tank water, swishing as he moved.

Ronan, I'm so sorry.

"You are more useful than I thought you could ever be," said Richard. "And because you are my sister, I'm going to give you some time to consider an offer."

"I want nothing to do with this, Richard."

"You might want to rethink that, Evelyn. My niece might want to go to a nice college, would she not? She might want to grow up to see six, *would she not?*"

"You would never ..." But as I said the words and looked at the tanks, I knew he would. I remembered how ruthless, how *cold*, Opa had been with me. I could see the same frozen heart in Richard.

"Where are Paddy and Savannah, Richard?"

"They're safe. For now," he said with a smirk. "They're on Prudence. My people are keeping a close watch on them."

He had this all wrong. These creatures, these beings that had existed so beautifully, so secretly beside us for so long, these were not the monsters. *We were.* I opened my mouth to argue with him, but he put a finger over my lips.

"Don't say anything you're going to regret, Dill."

Then he walked back to his desk. I stood and moved away from my brother, along the tanks. I stopped at Nomia's.

I don't know how this works, Nomia. But I hope you can hear me.

She stopped her frantic movement and grew still.

I hear you. I think I found a way out. Have you found your brother? Is he safe?

I closed my eyes and placed my forehead and hands against the glass. When I opened them, she was right in front of me. I don't think she could see me, but I knew she could feel my presence on the other side.

With all my concentration skills, I sent this thought her way, *Don't trust Richard. We are Wasserschutz.*

Her eyes widened in front of me, and she pushed off from the glass. I didn't hear anything else from her. She had broken the connection. God only knows what she was thinking. She probably thought I was part of it all, and maybe she was right. *Could I be trusted?* I was the reason she was imprisoned right now. How many other lives had I ruined?

And wait, oh my God ...

I spun around to find Richard. He had opened another panel on the far side of the room, closer to Ronan's tank. He was fiddling with something, his back to me.

"Richard!" I called out. "What have you done with my friend Rachael?"

He turned around slowly. "Who?"

"The woman who came with Ronan," I said angrily, pointing at the last tank.

He scrunched up his eyebrows and thought for a moment. "Oh, her. She wasn't my problem."

I heard the door open behind me and spun around to see a man the size of a refrigerator walk into the room.

"Richard!" I yelled. "What do you mean *she wasn't my problem?* And what about my family, Richard? Don't you dare fuck with my family! I'm warning you!"

That got his attention. He walked closer to me, a smirk on his face. "Oh, you're warning *me?* I don't think so." He motioned to the walking refrigerator, who grabbed me from behind and started to drag me towards the door. His arms were so big I could barely see around them. I did the only thing I could think of. I bit down, hard, on his arm.

He gasped in surprise but did not loosen his grip. My head was well below his, near his chest. I could hear him gnash his teeth at the pain.

"Lady," he said in a deep baritone voice. "Don't do that."

I released my bite and started to cry. "Richard!" I shouted. "What is wrong with you? Don't you dare hurt my family! *And tell me what you did with Rachael!*"

But he wasn't listening. He had pulled out a cell phone and was listening intently, completely ignoring me. He nodded as I watched the color drain from his face. The big man dragging me stopped and stood motionless. I tried to look up at his face, but he had me in such a bear hug, I couldn't turn my head.

"I see," said Richard into the phone. "I'll take care of it."

Then he pulled the phone away from his head and looked at the screen. He pushed a button before pocketing the phone. "We have a big problem with Mr. James."

"Sir?" said the big man, still not letting me go.

"Put her back in her cell, then get right back here. We need to talk."

"Yes, sir."

The giant man continued to drag me out of the room while I howled at my brother, "Richard! I swear to you, if you hurt them, I will kill you! I swear it on Oma's grave! Richard!"

The guy put a chokehold on me, thwarting my ability to yell. Within seconds, we were back at my cell, where a tray of food and a robe had been placed on the floor. I felt the man release his grip. He quickly threw me into the room and slammed the door, locking me inside once again.

When I heard the lock click into place, I started screaming. But no one heard me. And no one came to my rescue.

AUTHOR'S NOTES

To the patrons of WildFlour, Providence, I would like to fully apologize for the complete public meltdown I suffered in your presence. I hit the wall, hard. I could no longer find it within my weary soul to continue writing.

My jaw had been aching for days, and at around 10:52 a.m. on January 16, 2015, I discovered that the pain was intensifying each time I looked at my manuscript. Book 2 was causing me real physical pain.

I think I started shouting. There was definitely intense whining, most of it directed at my laptop. However, my work partner, the lovely Meada, took the brunt of it. She gently suggested that I "just try to accomplish a small goal." To which my brain responded with a loud, distinct *ping!* and I proceeded to storm out of the cafe.

My dear readers, it's good to have friends. Iris, my longtime friend, soulmate, and project manager, talked me off the ledge and gently suggested that I take the month of January off (and maybe even February). Meada is still my friend and forgave my outburst, and I hope you will, too. If you are a fan of Book 1 and were waiting for Book 2, this is why it was late.

Apologies all around.

To those of you who read this from a historical standpoint, I apologize for the following: the Elbe River does not flow west, and the waterwheel I referenced was not invented until the 19th century.

Second draft was completed on October 13, 2015, 12:03 PM after a glorious weekend of mountain biking in Vermont. My dear friend Meada sat across from me in a Starbucks in Cranston. That morning I spoke with my sister from another mother, Iris, and she told me to clean up two things in the book. I did. "Seaweed" by The Fruit Bats played in my headphones.

That sums up my journey for you, my dear readers.

Until next time ...

ACKNOWLEDGEMENTS

I would like to thank the New Bedford Whaling Museum Research Library (http://www.whalingmuseum.org/explore/library) for allowing me to hang out one icy day in January of 2015. I spent the afternoon reading *Journal of the Whaling Vessel, The Bark Leone of Fairhaven, 1865* by Master Moses R. Fish. This ship's log was instrumental in the writing of Chapter 21.

To the good people of the Warwick Historical Society (http://www.whsri.org/), thank you for allowing me to hang out with you on Wednesdays in the fall and winter of 2014-2015. I enjoyed reading through old newspapers and other historical documents so lovingly kept by volunteers and local Rhode Island history buffs such as Felicia Castiglioni Gardella and Patricia Woodard Harmon. Specifically, I would like to thank Robert Geake and Henry AL Brown for spending so much time with a freaky-haired girl like me.

Henry, your Smurf thanks you.

To my editor, Jo. You are an amazing woman. I don't know how you manage to accomplish all that you do with such grace and patience. Thank you for being my friend and my co-worker. We are forever bonded over waterwheels, tides, and Czechoslovakian rivers. Sending you dark chocolate forever, my friend ...

To Amanda, thank you. From the moment you contacted me with corrections and pointed out my imperfections, I knew we were going to be friends. I enjoy our FB chats and the window into your life. Someday, we will sit down and drink wine—together.

Cliff, you are a god among formatters. Thank you for making me look so professional. You will forever have a special place in my typographical heart for the following sentence: *For the in-chapter separator, I like this one because it is subliminally constrictive, which is a quality that I found in Nomia.*

A big thank you to the following supportive indie bookstores: Twice Told Tales, Symposium Books, Wakefield Books, and Curiosities and Mischief in Narragansett.

And, last, but never ever least—Joe Mazzenga, Christine DePetrillo, and Penny Watson. Without the wisdom, kindness, understanding, and hilarity the three of you provide, I would be lost. This journey would be so lonely without you. Thank you for being in my life.

BIOGRAPHY

Writer, artist, and underwater fire-breather Heather Rigney likes to make stuff. Stuff with words, stuff with paint, stuff that's pretty, and stuff that's not. Heather's stories reflect her childhood spent alone in the woods of northern Rhode Island.

Having discovered the works of both Stephen King and Clive Barker at the age of eleven, she started to wonder if she truly was alone in the woods, or perhaps not. The *perhaps* was what kept her up at night. Her imagination cranked out stories and dreams that she kept to herself. She was a strange child and didn't need one more reason for the neighbors to cluck, "That Rigney girl is so odd …" But now that she's comfortable with her oddness, Heather loves sharing her stories with you, dear reader.

The first book in this series, *WAKING THE MERROW*, was adapted from the short story, "Mermaids Are Not Nice," which can be found in the anthology *DIVE: A Quartet of Merfolk Tales*.

Stay up to date with all of Heather Rigney's events, new releases, and fan extras when you sign up for her newsletter: http://eepurl.com/RqfUj

FOR MORE ON HEATHER RIGNEY
www.heatherrigney.com
www.facebook.com/heatherrigneyAuthor
Twitter: @yourFAVmermaid
www.goodreads.com/author/show/6542620.Heather_Rigney